Reaper

J.R. Lightfoot

Angel—North Richland Hills, TX
ISBN: 979-8-2180251-0-6
Library of Congress Control Number: 2022911480
Title: *Reaper*
Author: J.R. Lightfoot
Digital distribution | 2022
Paperback | 2022

This is a work of fiction. The characters, names, incidents, places, and dialogue are products of the author's imagination, and are not to be construed as real.

Dedication

To my wonderful wife who supported and pushed me when times got tough, loved me when I was down and kicked me in the butt when I slacked.

Prologue

A full moon smiles upon the kingdom of Colley as a mother does her children, providing protection and giving light to the darkness. Down below the people of Colley enjoy another night of celebration. The Midnight Festival signifies the ending of another harsh winter and the beginning of the spring season. Nothing ends the drudgery of wet and cold like a week of overindulgence in ale, mead, wine, and carnal desires. The wealthy of Colley look forward to this time of year to envelope themselves in all things carnal. Everyone else looks to drown their sorrows and forget the nightmare that just ended.

It is this night Duke Palo returns to his villa after a wild evening of drink. Palo is dressed in a royal blue pants suit with a waistcoat. His ruffled yellow shirt is highlighted under the coat, decorated with red jewels along the top. Two necklaces hang around his neck, bringing the treasure count high. Sitting beside him in his carriage is his beautiful wife Helena, wearing a matching yellow dress to his shirt. The front of the dress is cut low enough that a full view of her breasts are visible. The bottom half of the dress flares out, giving even more of an extravagant appearance. Her hair is pulled up into a bun, decorated with an array of smaller jewels.

The couple ride along the cool night in their unique carriage. Duke Palo paid handsomely for the plain wood to be dressed up and painted with exquisite patterns of purple and gold along with markings distinguishing his carriage from all others. Oversized wheels are painted gold to match the gold trim accentuating the Eastern style of patterns that adorn the outside of the carriage. The magnificent vehicle is pulled by four large brown horses.

A man of his stature always travels with an entourage. This night finds six fully armed men on horseback with two more on the carriage, one driving with the other riding alongside with a crossbow. The men on horseback are in full armor, complete with plumed helmets and chest-plates with the Palo emblem emblazoned on it in blue. Two men ride in front of the four horse carriage, one on either side with the remaining two bringing up the rear. The group travel at a leisurely pace along the wooded trail back to the summer villa.

Men like Palo own two very different houses. The main house rests inside the city walls for protection. This house traditionally is the larger of the two, the one by which the Duke is measured against. All the amenities are located here with no expense spared. Their second house, or villas, are located on land outside of the city walls. Villas are quaint, cozy places where small parties are thrown, they want to get away, or off the book business occurs. A getaway is the purpose sought out by the couple inside the carriage.

Only one crossbowman. The figure in the trees looks intently on the carriage traveling below. Either the Duke has no clue who is waiting for him or thinks himself too powerful to care. Either way, this night will be rewarding. The warrior continues to survey his surroundings, looking for any indication that other soldiers are about. Satisfied that the eight soldiers below are the only ones around, he slides back into the shadows, preparing for death.

Oh, that barmaid at the Grey Goose. She had a set of juicy jugs on her. If only I had time to taste her wares but no, duty calls. After my duties are complete, I am paying a visit to the Grey Goose. Sexual thoughts invade the mind of the crossbowman on the carriage. The driver has been fighting sleep the entire trip to the villa and constantly doses off. Lucky for him, the horses have traveled this path so many times, they no longer have to be led. The driver contemplates his situation and battle with sleep. Might have something to do with those two meads he slammed down while waiting at the festival. A smile crosses his face. Everyone else was inside and what could it hurt. It was good mead, real good stuff. Cannot wait for this ride to end and get back to that bottle.

The man shifts in his seat, trying to wake himself up. He straightens his legs out to kick start the blood flow through his legs. As much as he tries, the effects of the mead continue to have its effect on him. Exhaustion continues to attack his consciousness, urging him to lean back and take a small nap. Just a couple of seconds could not hurt. What can happen in a couple of seconds?

The driver shifts slightly for comfort before leaning back against the carriage. The bowman does not pay the man any mind but focuses on thoughts of the barmaid. The bowman continues to doze in and out of fantasy world until it happens. His eyes fly open once he feels a sharp pain in his neck. He quickly reaches up to touch metal. Pain continues to flood his brain followed by the man having issues with breathing. He looks at his fingers to find blood coating them. He tries to call for help but his voice is missing, only a gurgling sound is heard.

He reaches to his side to get the attention of the man there. The driver pulls his arm away from the annoying man but his persistence pays off. The driver finally looks over.

"Mother of God!"

The driver's companion is leaking blood all over the uniform. He looks for the source to find a shuriken sticking out of the man's neck. The driver looks over his shoulder to find a dark figure standing on top of the carriage. Before he can sound the alarm, a blade slices across his neck, sending his head flying into the woods. The killer grabs hold of the reins as he kicks the dead bowman and the driver off the carriage. He lets the horses go by slicing the reins.

By this time the six men on horseback have recovered from their initial shock of seeing two men killed without any effort. They pull their horses to a stop as the carriage is stopped by the man dressed in black pulling on the brake lever. The soldiers encircle the carriage and quickly draw their blades. The assassin remains still, watching the soldier escort ready for battle.

"The contract is not for you. Killing you affords me no joy. I give you this chance to leave and I will not hunt you down. If you stay, I will be forced to bloody my weapons on you for God. I don't enjoy killing innocent things."

Two soldiers that rode behind the carriage look at each, contemplating their choices. Either ride off and face desertion charges or face this mad killer and surely die tonight. They might be able to make it out of the land before the king has enough time to gather a posse and hunt them down. But this madman just killed two soldiers without blinking and without breaking a sweat. Horses mirror the thoughts of the two men as they prance around nervously.

"If you two yellow bellied arses even think about running, you won't have to worry about a desertion charge. I will kill you myself!" Bellows the leader

The two men look at each other. One finally has the courage. "You have to kill that monster first!" Pointing at the assassin. "We don't think you can do that. We will take our chances."

Two soldiers on horses flee the scene, happy to ride away with their lives.

"Last chance?"

"Four on one. I like our chances, assassin. You don't even have a sword." The four soldiers surround the carriage waiting for the assassin to move.

If the soldiers could see under the mask, their nerves would freeze looking upon the smile.

The man dressed in black vaults into a back flip off the top of the carriage. The soldier stationed in the side looks in disbelief as realization hits him he is going to be the first victim. He watches in horror as the man lands in front of his horse and springs back high into the air. Before the man can react, a blade extends from the wrist of the assassin and slashes across the neck. Blood pours from the gaping wound as water over a waterfall. The final moments of the soldier's life is falling off the horse, the front of his uniform covered with his blood.

The leader commands for the remaining two soldiers to position themselves in front of the door to the carriage. He pulls his reins to the left, urging his steed to the back where the dead man lies. He looks at the soldier twitching for the last times in life. Instantly scanning the woodline reveals no assassin. Almost satisfied with the assassin gone, the soldier relaxes a bit only to be shocked back into action.

A blood curdling scream brings the soldier out of his stupor. He raises his blade and pulls his horse back around. He finds himself looking at one of the soldiers hanging at the end of a whip. The man kicks wildly trying to escape death. The soldier's eyes open wildly as the whip begins to glow a white light. The white whip begins to tighten more before

POP!

The soldier's head flies into the air as the body drops to the ground. Blood squirts high in the air showering the ground with fresh liquid before settling to a steady river flowing from the body. The lead soldier cannot believe his eyes. The whip disappears leaving the soldier to question if what he saw actually happened.

He snaps back to the situation at hand when his only remaining soldier begins to yell at him.

"Oh shit! What do we do sir!? We are going to die! What are we going to do?" The frantic screams and yells mirror the chaos in the man's soul and the tension in the horse who runs in circles much like a dog having fun.

"Shut up and fight man! Grab your balls, draw your sword and fight like you have never fought before."

The two men pull their horses together to stand guard in front of the carriage. Inside both men know they are dead. There is no way out of this situation. Eyes desperately search into the woods, hoping to find the assassin but hoping not to. A whistling sound interrupts the quiet air.

Both men look at each other in horror. They know one of them is going to die in a second and reluctantly they wish for it to be the other. The lead soldier watches as a throwing knife enters into the side temple of the skull. He cannot pull his eyes away but watches as the man sways back and forth, blood streaming from his temple. A look of surprise is permanently painted on the victim's face, forever haunting his leader's dreams.

"Looks like the only smart soldiers here are the ones that left. How does it feel to lead your soldiers to their slaughter? Their deaths are on your hands." The assassin comes into view. The man is dressed in full black light armor. In each hand the assassin twirls a short sword. The blade moving so fast the soldier cannot make out the blade against the hilt. A pullover mask covers all his head except his eyes. Those black eyes pierce the soul, leaving all others to dread the outcome. Will the look send them to hell or heaven? Those eyes seem to reveal the answer.

"To hell!" With a roar, the last soldier spurs his horse forward into battle. If death is to come today, I will greet it in battle.

The assassin does not move, nor does he stop twirling his blades. He simply watches as the rider fast approaches, bent on trampling the assassin in front of him. The assassin releases his blades at the hard-pressed soldier. The blades impale the soldier lifting him out of his saddle, sending him flying back towards the carriage. He lands hard on the ground, sliding to a halt.

Without its rider, the horse gallops right past the man dressed in black and continues to run down the trail, never stopping.

The man walks over to the soldier lying on the ground. He watches the life force drain from the chest. He reaches down and yanks the twin blades from the man's chest. A soft wheezing is the only response he gets from the soldier. Stabbing the blades into the dirt cleans the blades before sheathing them on his back.

Inside the carriage, Palo and his wife, Helena, listen in complete horror at the screams from outside. Now the couple sit in complete silence, not knowing if his men are victorious or are they about to die. They hear faint footsteps approaching the carriage. Blood rises in their ears, pounding so loud, almost draining the footsteps out. The door opens and to their melancholy, it is the assassin who stands there.

"Good evening ma'am. Unfortunately, I cannot say the same for you Palo. I have been tasked to end your life tonight." The voice behind the mask is steady, without emotion.

"Are you the one they call Reaper?"

"That I am."

"I will give you more gold than you can imagine. Enough for you to live comfortably for generations. I will give you the money and disappear. Just let me live." Palo's voice cracks under the stress. Tears swell up in his eyes, looking for an ounce of compassion but finding none.

Reaper raises his arm, leveling it at the crying man. "May God have mercy on your soul, demon."

Palo looks at his chest to find a blade lodged there. He raises his eyes to look at Reaper. Blood begins to fill the man's mouth to spill out, running down his chin and onto his shirt. He attempts to stand and look once again at his death.

"But I am no demon."

Reaper watches the man fall out of the carriage. Dead. Another contract completed and another demon killed. He watches and waits for the transformation. Demons can only hold their magical disguise while alive. Once killed, they revert back to their true nature, their true form.

x

Reaper watches and watches but no transformation occurs. What the…!

Reaper dives to the side at the precise moment skin across the top of his back is ripped open. A cartwheel turns into a series of four black flips taking the assassin to a safe distance. He turns to find Helena and not yet quite Helena. Standing before him is a female form dressed in the same yellow gown that Helena was wearing. Yet standing in front of him is some kind of new demon. This one has kept its female form. All former demons he has killed were male in form, despite sporting a female persona. Her skin has darkened to a red color. On the ends of her fingers are long, curvy, deep nails that resemble claws. What is most troubling is the large set of wings that have extended out of her back. It is these wings that now lift Helena into the air. She smiles at the man below, licks her lips before licking his blood from her claws. A loud shrill of a laugh sends the female demon off into the night.

"Damn" Reaper looks over his shoulder best he can. Three long gashes run along his left upper back, through his armor. He can feel the poison seeping into his bloodstream and knows he has minutes before it is too late. He stumbles over to a large bush just behind where he landed on the carriage. He reaches into the bush to pull out a satchel and finds the small vial inside. Thumbs pop the cork from the vial. Shaky hand reaches over his shoulder to pour the water onto the gashes.

Holy water is the one thing that combats the poison of the demons. The water blessed by God deters and eliminates all poison from the body,

By now the gashes are black and swollen. The man grits his teeth as the liquid runs over the gashes. Teeth clench harder, eyes close as the pain becomes almost unbearable. Muscles tense as he fights the antidote and poison that runs through his body. Eventually the pain begins to subside. He looks over his shoulder to watch the green poison begin to drip from the open wounds. The serum is working, drawing the poison out of the bloodstream and out of his body. The man removes his mask, revealing a man from the depths of the jungle tribes. His shaved head indicates his position as warrior monk and his clothes reveal that he is indeed an assassin of demons.

The man crawls in a prepared position.

Satisfied he will not be discovered by anyone, the man loses consciousness.

Chapter 1

The war of the Eternals wages on for centuries, since the time of the Casting, where Lucifer and his legions were cast out of the heavens to dwell in the sanctuary known to man as hell, while his brethren continue to sit with the Heavenly Father in the celestial Heaven.

This is known as the Time of Angels.

Soon after the Casting, Lucifer gathered his fellow outcasts, known as the Fallen, to wage war on the heavens. Brethren fought brethren for the power of God. Lucifer wanted to be God's equal, to dictate how the heavens were run. Yet time and time again, the forces of Lucifer failed. His army was thwarted and defeated. His forces retreated to their sanctuary to lick their wounds and plan the next attack. Defeat was not an option in the eyes of Lucifer. His blind ambition drove his brethren ruthlessly. His goal became their only purpose, his desire to live, and his cause of so many deaths.

Then came God's creation, known as man. Lucifer first sought to destroy man as a means of victory but soon found the angelic forces surrounding them in God's protection. After suffering more defeats, Lucifer found another tactic, to taint God's children. Make his greatest creation into his worst failure. Lucifer found many ways to infect the children of God.

Yet again Lucifer found that his sure successes ultimately turned to failure. Instead of destroying, he found God restarting. First came the infection in the Garden. God cast out the infection to become simply man and woman. Before Lucifer's eyes, God's creation grew in number but that did not alter his plan. He infested a civilization to turn their back on God. His plan almost worked save for a single man. God restarted with the floods.

Lucifer infested another civilization to enslave God's chosen people. God used another man's obedience to free his people. Through plagues and poison, this man led his people through the Red Sea and was able to free God's people.

God watched his people flourish for many years. His creation praised him and his miracles. Then Lucifer infected another civilization. This time the poison came in the form of debauchery and hedonism. God cleansed this civilization through fire. Lucifer lost many Fallen in that battle.

And on went the war. Lucifer failed attempt after attempt to infest man into becoming unclean. The number of Fallen Angels are nearly cut in half. He knows he has to change tactics if he is to gain victory with his brethren. He creates foot soldiers, known as demons, to continue the war. No longer will Lucifer lose valuable brethren in the war, just the soldiers that he has created.

Time after time man, through the protection of God and his heavenly host, is able to overcome the infestation and demons to once again gain favor in the eyes of the maker.

Then came the time for man. God made the ultimate sacrifice when he sent his son, Jesus, to earth. This new twist in the war brought many more defeats to Lucifer.

Finally came the fateful words spoken by Jesus while on the cross, "It is done"

The war shifted. God has allowed man to fight in this war. Man, who has longed to be a part of the war, is now on the front lines to battle and die in the name of God. When the time came for the war to be taken up by man, the warrior angel Reaper knew man would need assistance as Lucifer's demons would be a formidable opponent. Reaper sacrificed himself to be that assistance. His essence is used at the end of a monk's training to infuse that monk with angelic power. The receiving monks were known as Reapers.

In times of desperate need, when all seems lost, a Reaper can call on the power of the Angel Reaper to save them. The calling was magnificent but monks would pay a heavy price for this gift. The power to harness and use the angelic power saps power from the monk. As long as there is evil in the area, the monk fights on but the longer he uses the power, the longer his recovery.

It is now in the year 548 of our Lord Jesus Christ. Christianity has flourished through the veins of the Roman Empire to spread throughout the known world. This new Christianity has brought a new warrior to the battle. Priests of God known as Reapers. Men who wander the land to eradicate the demons on earth. Trained by Angels themselves for battle, these Reapers know the fighting arts

2

used by heaven's warrior angels for centuries to battle the minions of Lucifer.

This war continues to wage on.

No longer in the Age of Angels but in the Age of Man

✦

Sunshine. God's gift of light to this earth.

Early rays fall across the sleeping Reaper, arousing him gently. The man rises to his knees to give thanks to God and his holy mission. He ends his morning prayers the same way each morning.

"May your will be done O'Lord and may the blood of your son forgive the blood that I must cause in your name. Amen"

With his morning meditations done, Jaml looks over his shoulder to look at the wounds from the previous night. The poison has been dealt with but the wounds remain. Jaml knows he must seek attention from a healer lest his journey ends with infection.

A scowl comes across his face while contemplating over the fight a few hours ago. A new demon for sure. In all his travels, Jaml has never seen a demon keep its feminine form. The demon has always reverted back to its true male demon form. He must pray and meditate on this. And find someone who knows.

He gathers his supplies and begins his journey to the kingdom of Colley. He drapes a full cape over his shoulders before pulling the hood over his head, concealing a better part of his face. With his sack hanging over his shoulder, the Reaper heads to the castle on the horizon.

Jaml walks for the better part of the day, the image of the kingdom on the horizon coming closer and ever closer until he finds himself standing at the gates. The huge wooden gates are open as people travel in and out at will. The guards stand lazily at each corner, not paying much attention to anyone entering or exiting the gates. Their Roman inspired uniforms shine brightly in the sun. From the highly polished breastplate and armguards, to the knee length battle dress to the calf high metal covered boots, the soldiers of this kingdom hang on to the past glories of the Roman Empire.

Three soldiers wield short swords on their hips and carry a spear. The fourth soldier wields no spear, only sword, and his armor is adorned with a cape. This one must be in charge, so this is where Jaml heads.

"God bless you my brethren." Jaml keeps his tone light, drawing no needed attention to himself.

"God blesses no one here stranger. Less you are of the Royal Family." The sergeant spits the comment out. He follows it with a snarl to show his contempt at the king

"Whereas it may be. I have no money and need shelter. My horse was killed last night in an attack that I barely survived myself." Jaml knows that no money means he will always be directed to the local church. He waits for his fruit to bloom

"The church is through the market and to the left. Ask for Mother Karva and she will take care of you. I feel for your misfortune but count your good luck. Seems like a band of killers are about as one of our very own Dukes was killed along with six good men."

"Oh my. Was his wife ravaged?" Jaml fakes an air of concern.

"Luckily no. The men sacrificed their lives so she could get away on a horse. She returned last night to tell the whole horrific tale." The sergeant shakes his head at the sacrifice they made.

Perfect!

✦

Jaml makes it to the church at dusk. As he approaches the front doors to the church, he watches two nuns bring in another lady. The nuns are dressed in simple brown garbs that hide every aspect of womanhood. Their hair is placed under a hood. Around their neck is a wooden cross on a chain, signifying their obedience to the Almighty God.

The woman they are attending to has signs of violence. One of her eyes is blackened by a strike, blood cakes her hair around a gash on her forehead. Her clothes are half torn from her body. That poor soul has been raped. Jaml says a prayer for her soul.

He approaches the three women. One of the nuns turn to face him, a look of displeasure on her face.

"Stop gawking at this poor creature." She pulls a blanket over the woman's naked shoulder. "What do you want?"

"Please forgive me." He bows. "I only seek refuge and an audience with your Mother Supreme."

4

"Forgive me sir." Her facial features soften. "Times are hard and as you can see, our work is never done." The nun takes a wet cloth and begins to wipe some of the blood from the victim's forehead. "Please go inside and rest. There is a pot of stew near the fire. Help yourself to whatever is left. Once I finish dressing this child's wounds, I will fetch Mother Karva for you."

"You are most kind." Jaml bows again as he takes his leave.

After eating his fill of the stew, Jaml sits in the corner of the room to await Mother Karva. The waiting room is not furnished but the size of most dining halls, therefore every person inside is sitting on the ground away from one another. Most are eating under suspicious eyes, guarding their food as if their life depends on it, which it does. Jaml can see several people contemplating the opportunity to snatch a purse or cut a throat. But none act on it as they know the church is a sanctuary. No one is to be harmed here.

Jaml begins to doze off when a woman's voice brings him back to consciousness

"I don't have much time for strangers."

Jaml looks up to find himself looking at a beautiful woman in her early thirties. She is dressed like the others except for the long cape she wears, presenting her as Mother Nun. He quickly rises to a knee and bows before her.

"Please rise stranger."

Jaml does just that. He notices a young girl dressed in nun clothing standing behind her. He gives the girl a smile before looking into the eyes of Karva. Karva looks at Jaml in a side glance before urging him to follow her. She leads Jaml at a brisk pace through the church and into the back rooms. She shoos the young girl away before leading Jaml into a dark room. She lights three lanterns on the wall which gives the room an eerie presence. Inside the room there is a bed in the far corner and a desk in the center. She urges Jaml to sit.

"My apologies. If I had known you were coming, I would have prepared better." Jaml gently places his hands over hers, stopping her attempts to straighten up the table.

"No, no. It is I that owes you an apology. I am at your service, not the other way around."

"Are you...." Karva has trouble getting the word out of her mouth.

5

"Reaper? Yes I am."

Mother Karva has only heard stories of the famed demon assassins and their extraordinary fighting gifts. She never thought she would ever meet one. Such battles between the Reapers and demons don't happen in small kingdoms like Colley. Nothing happens in Colley save for bandits and the poor. Then worry comes across her face. If a Reaper is here, there must be demons. This means death.

"Yes Mother. The look of concern is warranted. I am here to do my duty and rid this earth of demons. First I would ask that you look at a wound I acquired recently. Then I will explain it all."

✦

The two priests sit in the room for over two hours. Karva studies the wounds and stitches them up as Jaml relates the events in the woods and his mission in this kingdom. He asks several questions about the kingdom and the people here.

"I am telling you, it was a demon that kept her feminine person." Despite speaking what he saw, disbelief continues to hang on his voice.

Jaml sat on the pew bench inside the large church. This house of God is modest compared to others in nearby kingdoms but impressive nevertheless. This house was built to bring in nearly one thousand parishioners which makes up over half of the inhabitants of the kingdom. The royal family has been very generous in providing the best amenities for the church to include a solid wood pulpit to deliver the message as well as a distinct area for the common folk to hear the word without the upper class dealing with the commoners.

"Lucifer has been busy. But these new soldiers are more like spies than soldiers. It had you dead to rights and left you alone." The lady looking at the wounds pauses. "Or they do not know you are a Reaper and expect you to die there."

Jaml pulls his shirt up before responding. "That very well may be. We shall see. But why here? This little kingdom does not hold the population or wealth to be of consequence. The Pope never visits here. Well, the Cardinals never come here either. Mysteries will unravel but until then. Just keep bandaging me up so I can get out there."

6

The two priests laugh, sharing a light moment in the war against evil.

✦

After evening prayer Jaml sits Karva down, this time in the room that is prepared for him.

"I do not know how long it is going to take me to rid this kingdom of its demons."

"You are welcome in this house for as long as you please."

"My thanks to you Mother Nun but I will not hear of it. The work I do often brings death to my door. I will not hear about putting this church in danger. Tomorrow I will purchase a large home to which I will be able to better see our enemies. The thing I ask is I need a wife to carry out this facade." A look of surprise jumps across Karva's face. "No, not like that. Marriage in name only. There will be no ceremony or consummation. Just for appearances sake."

"I" Karva looks down. "Would be honored."

"As would I. But I need your work in the church. Not playing make believe with me." He notices Karva releases her breath. "Do you have someone that is not well known and can be trusted? I give you my word that no harm will come to her."

"Canda."

"Please call her in. I will not put another in danger without them knowing full well the consequence" Jaml bows as Karva leaves the room.

Jaml does not wait long before a soft knock is heard at the door. He opens it to find three females standing there; Karva, the young girl who never leaves her side and the nun Jaml first met at the steps.

"Jaml, this is Canda." Karva motions to the young lady standing behind her.

Canda steps forward and bows. "Father Jaml. I beg your forgiveness for my earlier outburst."

"Please do not ever bow to me or call me Father. I have neither nor will I ever earn those accolades. I am a mere sinner in this world trying to do what is asked of me. With that being said, has Mother Karva informed you what I am about to ask?"

"She has and I accept." Canda's eyes remain on the ground.

"First of all, look up." Canda's eyes are greeted by a gentle smile. "You are Lady Canda. Wife to Duke Jaml, delegate from the dark jungles. I will secure us a home and the proper channels into this kingdom. We will live their lifestyle until my work is done. You will see things unimaginable and most times deadly. I will protect you with my life but you need to know that death might come at any moment. If you accept me terms..."

"Yes of course" The interruption surprises all in the room, including Canda herself who immediately looks down, wondering if she spoke too eagerly.

"Then we are going to have to take this lady shopping." A smile remains on the face of the Reaper.

"Please Jaml, we do not have much money." Karva sounds defeated.

"Worry not Mother Karva. The Lord provides." With that remark, Jaml gives a flamboyant bow to the ladies.

✦

Over the next four months, Jaml establishes his identity in the kingdom. The Royal Family and an array of Dukes have welcomed him and his wife into elite status. Jaml attends socials thrown by the aristocrats, enjoying the social life.

At night Jaml goes out as Reaper, trying to get intelligence on why demons have been spotted in this kingdom. Reaper knows there is something unsettling in this kingdom but cannot put his hand on it. In the meantime, Reaper spends his time helping the less fortunate, protecting the innocent and spreading the gospel through his actions.

One particular evening Reaper is sitting on the church tower, his normal spot. From the church tower, Reaper is able to see out most of the city inside the gates. He can look behind him at the Hills, where the rich reside. The palace is also located there. In front of him, he has a clear view of the marketplace and the Bottoms, the poor side of the kingdom where most of the visible sin is found.

He is watching to the left when a faint scream catches his ear. He attempts to locate the source of the scream. Eyes continue to search, from the houses to the bars and finally to the alleys. That is where he finds his answer. Four men have cornered a woman in the alley, advancing on her with malice in their heart.

Reaper leaps from his perch onto the roof of the next building. He runs at full speed across the roofs, leaping in full stride to the next one. The strength in his legs never waivers but continues to propel him towards his prey.

She screams numerous times but no one heeds the call. None of the guards patrolling the streets have come to her aid. What good are they then? She looks frantically at windows in the alley and knows the shutting of the shutters seals her doom.

She is wearing a cotton top with a skirt. Nothing provocative, just simple clothes for a simple woman. Visiting her mother results in an over extended stay. Her husband is working the merchant wagons which left her walking home alone. And now this.

She first notices one man following her. She turns down several alleys trying to evade him. The predators are the only ones who find success as another man appears, forcing her to go in a different direction. A third man alters her path once again and she soon finds herself in this alley where a fourth man blocks the far exit.

Three of the men have encircled her against a wall, cutting off any avenue of escape. The tall lanky one in the middle is licking his lips while squeezing his crotch, getting ready for a taste. The other two men close in on the sides, comfortable in letting lanky get first taste.

He reaches for her breast and gets a slap on his arm for his actions. All three men laugh at her feisty behavior and knows this is going to be fun. He reaches once again and when she attempts to slap him, he grabs her arm with his other hand. He quickly pulls her close, licking her lips, cheek and neck. His hand roughly grabs her breast, squeezing the soft flesh under the top.

"What the hell!" The words invade lanky's ears.

Lanky turns around, obviously upset at his friends interrupting his fun. He is about to scold them for ruining the mood when he stares at the reason for the comment. Standing a mere two steps away is a man dressed in black. The suit is some type of armor that forms to his figure. His face is inside a hood, thereby giving Lanky no knowledge of who could be there standing in front of them. He turns to face the stranger in black.

"Who are you? You might want to leave before I get mad. You are interrupting my quiet time with my wife." All three men laugh at his comment.

But the strange man did not move, only replies

"You have one chance to let this maiden go. Lest you incur the wrath of God." The voice carries through the alley.

"Oh friend, you are beginning to piss me off." Lanky nods at his companions. "Get him."

His two friends turn to the Reaper who walks directly at them. Both men are dressed in brown pants with a dark brown shirt. The redhead throws the first punch, aiming at the temple of Reaper who moves instinctively, turns and sidekicks the man. The redhead drops to his knee, the other leg unable to carry his weight. The brown hair rushes forward, throwing a wild punch. Reaper turns and kicks out, catching the man in his midsection, doubling him over.

Red gets back to his feet, reaches inside to pull out a knife. A smile comes over his face, the knife drawing the full attention of Reaper. The man stabs and slices, neither connecting. Reaper takes two steps back, one for each attack, then rushes forward. An elbow strike to the temple sends stars in red's eyes. A back elbow breaks his nose. Red takes several steps back, trying to regain his bearings.

A spin kick catches brown hair, ending the sneak attack. His head snaps back, blood fills the air from his mouth. Before he can fully recover, his chest collapses under the barrage of strikes. Blood quickly fills his mouth to spill out the corners. He cannot catch his breath as blood fills his lungs. Brown hair drops to his knees before falling to his side. Dead.

Lanky watches in disbelief as one of his buddies is dead and the other is not doing much better. Red yells his battle cry before charging Reaper. At the last second, Reaper throws an uppercut, catching the man under the chin, standing him up. Force of the blow is so great that Red's head flies back, breaking his neck. He slumps forward, falling on his face.

Lanky cannot believe what he just saw. His two best friends are killed right in front of his eyes. His vision goes red in anger, urging him to take it out on the source of this mess, the woman in his arms. He reaches behind his back to pull out his dagger. He is about to thrust it into the woman's belly when he screams, the pain in his hand is great. He looks down to find a throwing dagger has pierced right through his wrist, causing him to drop his dagger. He grabs the hilt and attempts to pull the blade out but to avail. He looks up to find Reaper standing directly in front of him.

"Will you repent your sins?"

"Screw you!" Hands grab his head and twist violently, breaking Lanky's neck.

✦

In the shadows at the end of the alley, a man slides out and heads down the road. He continuously dips into alleys and double backs on his trail, all for the purpose of making sure he is not followed. Satisfied that he is indeed alone, the man heads to the Boars Pub in the Bottoms.

This tavern is like many others in the Bottoms, cheap ale and women with a good time to be had by all. The man enters this tavern and heads to the back of the tavern to where five large men stand close to each other. The man approaches the men before stopping within striking distance.

Another man walks up behind him. "Welcome Miko."

"We have an issue." Miko's voice does not waver

"We always have an issue. Why is this one any different?"

"It is."

"Tell me." His voice is calm, soothing.

"I will tell Bala." Miko's voice is just as soothing

"Let him pass." A strong woman's voice interrupts.

Five men move aside to reveal a woman lounging on black cushions. A cloak is draped over her shoulders, covering most of her body. But what is revealed is ample breasts. Eyes travel down to reveal jeweled shorts and black battle boots. Despite the scantily clad body, no one dares touching her. The last one who tried had his dick and balls hanging from a lantern in the tavern for all to see. The only part of her body that is not revealed is her face. She wears a skull mask that covers her entire head. Her long black hair hangs from the bottom of the mask.

"What is it Miko? What is our issue?" She waves her arms, and everyone laughs

"Reaper."

"Is he real? I have not seen nor heard from him. It has been months since Duke Palo's death."

"He is real. I just watched him kill Zun and his two goons. They didn't last long enough for me to take a piss. He killed them without breaking a sweat." Miko does not break eye contact with his leader. "Zun was about to have fun with a little lass when this Reaper appeared. He even gave Zun a chance to repent his sins. If this one is going to save Colley from sin, we could be in trouble."

"Point taken." Bala looks off into space while rubbing her hands together. "Continue operations as normal, just double the men at shipments. Tell the guild to lay off going out alone or small groups, at least for a while. We need to get a hold of Mr. Reaper. Find who he is and where he lives."

"Yes Bala." Miko turns to find himself staring at Kreen. "Move slime."

Kreen steps aside allowing Miko to walk out of the tavern.

✦

The palace gardens shine brightly in the night. Torches are arrayed close enough to maximize the light. Entertainers roam the gardens, performing their tricks and wares for the enjoyment of the wealthy. Men on stilts higher than any tree walk around juggling fruit or anything else they can get their hands on. Acrobats tumble and roll their way along the edge of the gardens. Female servants carry tray after tray of decadent morsels of food for all guests to try. The servant girls are dressed in a very short skirt, so short that if they must bend over their female parts are displayed. As it is, their breasts are completely uncovered so a handful of breast occurs as often as a handful of food.

Jaml and Canda are introduced to the party upon arrival. He is dressed in slacks and loose fitting red shirt while she is brought to life in a purple dress that is form fitting up top and falls directly down to the ground from her waist. Her long hair is brought up into a bun and fastened with gold clips that shimmer in the night air. The male servant, dressed in flamboyant colors, calls out their names as the couple walk pass. Two servant girls immediately arrive, giving each one a goblet of wine and their first morsels of food.

"This is a disgrace to the Almighty." Sounds of disgust taint Canda's words.

"Lucifer has been working here with great success, of that I am sure. Choose your words well so we are not discovered." A smile to another couple hides the contents of their conversation.

12

"Do I not?"

"You do. My comment is more for me. You have always been great at wearing this guise of royalty." Jaml gives Canda a wink before escorting her to the first couple of the night. Dressed in a similar suit but a yellow shirt is Duke Zell, a delegate from the western kingdoms. His fiery red hair and pale skin reveal his origins and distaste for the sun. His wife, Lady Blait, shares the same pale skin but her hair is jet black. She hails from the northern kingdoms. Rumor has it Zell's father kidnapped Blait for himself, but he could not handle her lustful appetite, so she was given to Zell. Since Zell cannot produce, their relationship is full of lust and carnal desires. Using their servants for sex toys is their hobby.

"Well, if it is not my good friend Jaml. Glad you can make it. And you bring your lovely wife Canda." Zell clamps both hands on Jaml's shoulders before taking Canda's hand to gently kiss each one.

"Zell, how good it is to see you and your lovely wife Blait." Jaml returns the greeting to include the hand kiss of the other wife.

"The king really knows how to throw a party, eh?! It is said this party is to get our minds off Palo's death." Whispers Zell as if he is telling Jaml something that is secret.

"Didn't his wife, the lovely Lady Helena, make it out alive? Rumors I hear is that Palo and his guards laid down their lives so she could escape."

"That is what the rumor is. She is right over there looking as stunning as always. Especially for someone who just lost their loved one." Jaml and Canda follow the pointing finger of Zell to find Helena standing on the other side of the garden, talking with two Dukes and their wives. She is dressed in the customary black dress of someone who is in mourning. Her demeanor is of someone living life to the fullest.

Jaml feels a small hand grip his forearm, squeezing him.

"Relax. Not now." Canda was informed at the beginning about Helena being a demon. Jaml wanted to make sure she did not put herself in a situation with the demon. Discussions have also been had about what this means. The only conclusion that they could come up with is she is a foot soldier and nothing more. Which means there are more important demons residing in the castle. The fact that she is able to hide her true nature to her deceased husband means any one here could be a demon.

A wink lets Canda know he is in control. She smiles before letting his arm go.

"Complicated to say the least. Yet no one knows for sure what it all means." Jaml realizes that Zell has been talking nonstop. He quickly nods at the man and instantly looks interested. Canda strikes up a conversation with Blait to ease any tensions that might have been seen.

Duke Indi and Lady Tyra soon join the conversation. All three couples openly discuss matters of the crown that they are aware of. Trade becomes a hot topic of discussion as the merchant trade expected to suffer due to the Duke's murder continues to flourish as it always had.

Conversation shifts to the weather with all having to listen to Zell complain how hot it is and how wonderful his country is at this time of year. Jaml tells the group how wonderful and cool this temperature is compared to his homeland. All get a laugh at the contrasting stories.

The conversation continues as the evening progresses on. Jaml keeps an eye on Helena, waiting for her to leave. She is currently talking with some young duke Jaml does not recognize. Zell and his wife are feeling the effects of the wine and their hands have begun feeling on each other. She giggles uncontrollably as he showers her with kisses and squeezes on female parts of her body.

"I need to talk to you."

Jaml almost misses that subtle exchange between Prince Baric and Duke Indi. Indi excuses himself and follows the prince out of ear shot. Jaml's attention is soon taken away as Helena and the young duke walk out of the garden. Jaml excuses himself and quickly leaves, Canda excuses herself to another part of the party.

"The king is most disappointed. You promised you would have the artifact here tonight and yet here we are, you not making good on promises and myself having to be the bad guy." Prince Baric is the older of the king's sons. His chiseled jaw is a favorite with the ladies in Colley but gives a menacing expression when he is not happy. Indi knows that he is not happy.

"Sire. I am fully aware that I have missed the deadline." Bad choice of words. "I am rectifying the situation as we speak. You will have the artifact within the next moon cycle, this I swear."

"Tell me Duke Indi," The title drips from the prince's mouth with contempt. "What will happen if the king does not get his artifact?"

"That is not going to happen so we will not have to worry about it." Indi takes a deep breath knowing he is on thin ice right now and one bad step will cost him his life.

"You have until the rising of the next full moon."

"But that…." Indi's voice cracks as if puberty just hit again

"Exactly." The sneer on Baric's face is all Indi needs to see. He quickly excuses himself and almost runs back to his wife who is standing alone. Zell and his wife have long since gone to more private times.

✦

Reaper sits on top of a rooftop scanning for the missing demon Helena. From this vantage point, he can see her estate a mere two houses away. He waits patiently, not wanting to miss out on this opportunity. His patience pays off. He watches a very drunk man escort Helena home, her hands constantly rubbing on him to let him know of the carnal desires that are about to occur. The man is eagerly accepting of her advances.

Helena opens the door then grabs the man by the front of his shirt, pulling him to her. Their lips crash together as two rams vying for dominance. Their lips stay together longer than any love filled kiss. This is sheer lust. When their lips part, she playfully bites his bottom lips, pain and pleasure mix. He pushes the door open and leads the lady inside. Reaper watches the door close before moving.

He moves quickly. He sprints across the roof before launching himself into the air. Landing at a full sprint enables him to launch himself once again into the air. This time he lands in a forward roll on top of Helena's chateau. He springs to a knee and listens intently to see if anyone noticed the man flying through the air or Helena heard the landing. He gets a negative response from both.

Reaper moves to the edge of the roof before stepping off the edge. Fingertips clasping the edge of the rooftop stops the fall. He hangs there for a second before releasing his grip. He falls and again fingertips stop the plummet, this time on the window ledge.

Without any sound, Reaper pulls himself into the window. He walks silently through the house, towards the sounds of passion. He steps into the doorframe to find himself watching Helena and the young man groping each other on the bed. She frantically pulls at his shirt, trying to rip it off his body. Both his hands cup her breasts, squeezing them through her dress. Reaper has seen enough.

"Hello Helena, remember me."

The couple turn to find the source of the words. No doubt the man was expecting the late Palo to be standing there as his exhalation reveals a bit of relief. Helena's expression is one of annoyance, her playtime with her play thing is over. Her response is quick.

"You!"

Sensing the bad blood between the two, the young duke stands with his sword drawn. A stern look captures the features of his face. Underneath the boyish look is a handsome stern man with great potential for leadership. His eyes demand respect. His shoulders pulled back, his chest puffed out like a peacock looking for his mate.

"I don't know who you are but since milady is obviously upset that you are here, I am going to ask you once to leave. The second time will be with my sword." He swings his sword in an X shape to demonstrate his proficiency with the blade.

"I urge you to put away your blade for it will cost you your life. You do not know what you are fornicating with. I will not repeat myself."

Instead of heeding Reaper's words, the young man confidently strides forward for battle. Reaper shakes his head knowing an innocent man is going to die for a demon. Reaper steps to the side at the first thrust. A back slice follows which Reaper avoids as well. The look on the man's face reveals his astonishment at the Reaper's speed.

More determined than ever, the man puts on a series of strikes and slashes, each meant to kill his opponent. Unfortunately for him, none of the swordplay finds its mark. What did find its mark are Reaper's three punches to his face. Helena's boy toy staggers back, blood running from his nose which is broken and the corner of his mouth. He spits the blood at the ground and lunges forward into the attack.

Reaper turns to watch the sword chop to the ground in front of him. He steps on the blade with his left foot before kicking the young man in the face with his right. His adversary has to let go of his blade as he falls back. He crashes into a table, shattering the flimsy wood. The would-be savior gathers himself and rises once again to his feet. He pulls a dagger from the back holster and drops into a fighting stance.

"You don't have to die tonight. Drop the dagger and I will allow you to leave. You have no business here." Reaper's voice remains calm underneath the mask.

"You have insulted my lady friend. You have insulted me. And you think I will simply walk out? No stranger, tonight you will pay the consequences for your actions." The young man spits out more blood as he readies for the next attack

"So be it."

Reaper catches the direct strike aimed at his chest. He turns over the arm before slamming it from the bottom. Immediately a scream fills the room as the bone is knocked through the skin. This arm will never hold a sword again. The scream is cut short as the outside of Reaper's hand strikes and collapses the man's windpipe. Reaper turns and punches the man directly in the center of his chest. A sudden gulp followed by wheezing is heard from the man. He has trouble breathing before falling to his knees, death coming quickly for him. He looks up at Reaper with eyes asking for forgiveness.

"Only God can forgive your soul. But know young man that I am praying for your soul." Reaper puts his hands together in a moment of silent prayer.

The young man turns his head to steal another look at the beautiful woman he is dying for.

Standing where Helena should be is something else. A thing resembling Helena stands there but her pigmentation is now a bright red. This Helena has fangs and long claws. The stranger is right, he doesn't know or understand what is going on. With the look of confusion plastered on his face, the young suitor dies.

"I should have killed you when I had the chance." Helena licks her lips in anticipation.

"Your issue, not mine." Reaper pulls his two short swords from his back scabbards.

"Don't worry human, I am about to rectify my issue." She unsheathes her falchion, the thick blade seems to have dried blood on it.

She comes at him with an overhead swing, meaning to cleave the human in two. Reaper raises his sword to block the chop, which he does and regrets it. The power Helena generates has enough force leading to Reaper's right arm going dead.

A second deflection allows Reaper to slide to the right buying time for the feeling in his arm to return. Helena senses the issue Reaper is facing and immediately presses the issue. Reaper is forced to defend only, and with his off hand. He can hear her laughter through the clanking of steel and knows she is moving in for the kill.

Unfortunately for Helena, Reaper begins to feel his right arm again. For now, he continues to give ground and defend. The demon presses forward, chopping and stabbing at the man in front of him. Yet respect is gained as Reaper's blood has not been shed. Reaper spins out of a stab, blocks the second strike, reverses his blade and slashes across her stomach, drawing a line of blood. First blood.

Frustration can be heard through Helena's yell as she is yet to draw blood. She increases her pace, moving her blade in and out of routines at a quicker rate only to be thwarted time and time again. She has never seen a human this fast and knows her window of opportunity is about to close.

Reaper spins away from her next attack to face her at a distance. He flexes his fingers in front of her.

"Ahh. About time. Time to die demon." He tosses his blade to his other hand before attacking. She meets his attack with vigor but realizes this is different, he is more in control and much quicker. His attack moves her to her right and before she realizes it, he can pick up his other blade. She finds herself facing a very skilled swordsman with all his weapons. He moves his blades high and low, striking at her weaknesses and exploiting her inability to fine tune her swordplay.

She soon finds that she has a dozen or so cuts on her body. None fatal but the culmination of so many cuts is beginning to wear on her. Her breathing has become labored, her arms have begun to drag just a bit. She is exhausted and needs to recuperate. Her wings unfold and extend open as she readies to escape out of the window. Before she makes it to the window, she screams at the sharp pain in her wing, a blade pierces the leathery wing and pins her to the wall. She reaches for the sword and screams once again. This time her other wing is pinned to the wall by his second blade.

Despite the pain in her wings and the fact that she is pinned to the wall, she begins to laugh.

"Come on little man, come on over. Come retrieve your swords so I can give you a hug. Come here little man." She continues to laugh.

"Oops, forgot about these." Reaper flicks his wrist, activating the wrist blades.

Her face drops as she looks at the eight-inch blades extending from the top of his wrists. He takes three quick steps before launching himself into her. With speed faster than an eye can track, Reaper unleashes a fury of punches into the demon's midsection. Each punch sends at least six inches of steel into her abdomen, sprouting a new fountain of blood each time. He steps back to see his handiwork.

Pinned to the wall is the demon known as Helena. Her wings are outstretched, pinned wide by two blades, one in each wing. Her midsection is a bloody mess as blood flows from at least a dozen stab wounds. The final flow of blood streams from her mouth which happens to be the largest flow. She looks up at the man who has killed her.

"Who are you?" She coughs blood.

"Reaper."

"No really. Allow me to see who has killed me."

"No."

A combination laugh and cough spews a glob of blood from her mouth. "Then know Reaper that you will not be able to stop us. The Fallen has shown us what to do and you will fail. We will rule this kingdom and then the heavens."

"You talk too much." With a sweep of his arm, he opens her throat for the killing blow. Blood flows freely, draining the life force from her.

✦

"It is done."

Karva is startled which is shown by the small scream. She turns from her desk where she had been studying the Book of God. Her room is lit solely by two candles and since she heard no one enter the room, she never expected to hear a voice inside her sanctuary.

"Wish you would knock sometimes. Did you get any information from her?"

Movement in the corner catches Reaper's eyes. Instantly his hand is on the hilt of his sword. He tilts his head slightly, trying to get a better view of the corner.

"Evening Priest Jaml. It is quite late for a man of God to be out and about. Are we doing God's work all the time?" Out of the shadows appears the young girl who has been at Karva's side each and every day. The little girl rarely speaks so for Jaml to hear her voice is unsettling. What is even more unsettling for Jaml is there is something about her that is different yet very familiar.

"God's work must be done all day. Lucifer does not sleep so we must be diligent in our ways so that he will always be defeated. Now little one, isn't it a little late for such a precious member of God's flock be up? Now run along and get to bed." He pats Allie before sending her to bed.

Karva waits for the door to close before addressing Reaper once more.

"Thank you. Now where were we?"

"As I expected, there are more demons at work here. She is not working alone which means there is something afoot here that we don't know of. This also means there is something important here that we are not aware of. That is our first order of business, to find out what is so important. She is not a high enough demon so there has to be more powerful ones around. What scares me is she eluded there is a Fallen involved." Jaml walks over to a table and pours himself a drink of water. "If there is a Fallen involved, we might not be enough to win out. Casualties will occur on both sides." He takes a gulp of water, enjoying the taste and feel of the liquid going down.

"I did not take my vows to back out when things get tough. Death is inevitable which means I get to see our Lord that much faster."

A smile creeps across Jaml's face as he downs the remainder of the water.

Chapter 2

The large room inside the home is considered Indi's personal space and business center. There is a wooden desk situated at the opposite end of the room from the door. Underneath the desk is a bear rug from lands far away from Colley. Lit by a series of torches around the room, a feeling of power is felt once inside the room.

Indi is seated at the desk writing on a scroll when a knock interrupts him. He looks and smiles then leans back in his chair as a lion looking over his territory with pride. A smile comes across his lips as he calls out for entry. The door swings slightly open, a guard peeks inside to catch Indi's eyes. He announces the arrival of Desi over some business venture before stepping aside.

Enter Desi, a robust man with extreme power in the kingdom. Desi has the monopoly for the buying and selling of all goods into the kingdom. He controls the legal and illegal trafficking of goods and services in the kingdom. Merchants are required to pay two tolls when entering the city; one to the king and a larger one to Desi. In most cities, when the black market is exceeding in profits, there is a letdown in the legal sector. In Colley, with one man running both the legal and illegal markets, some question who really runs the kingdom.

Indi stands up to greet his visitor. The two men shake hands across the desk, Indi retaining the power stance between the two while behind the desk. His hand motions for Desi to sit down on the other side in a small wooden chair. Desi finds it hard to get comfortable in a small chair with no cushions but he does what he needs to.

Indi wastes no time with pleasantries. "Where is my artifact? I paid you good money to retrieve and deliver that thing so where is my merchandise?"

"Easy young duke. Your product is here but I acquired some additional costs. Because of this, I am going to have to ask for 5000 more gold pieces."

"Have you lost your mind!?" Indi rises to his feet. "I paid for my product, now hand it over!" Words are coming out as screams.

The response is something Indi did not respect. Instead of a commoner realizing his place and acting accordingly, the merchant Desi simply begins to laugh. It starts as a simple giggle and as Indi's face gets redder with rage, the laughter intensifies until Desi is laughing uncontrollably holding his midsection as if attempting to hold in his innards

"The whelp has some balls." Desi spits out, still trying to control his laughter. "With demands."

"I don't find any humor in this. Now if you wouldn't mind going and retrieving my property, we can close this matter."

Suddenly the smile and laughter are gone from Desi's face. "Listen here you little piece of rat shit. No one and I mean no one demands anything from me. Less you find yourself lost somewhere. Understand?"

"My product."

"My money! Once I get the rest of my money, you get your product." Desi leans back in his chair, satisfied that his point is made. Then he has an additional thought. He sits up and leans forward for effect. "If you ever think about threatening me again, I will not be so nice."

Indi stutters the next words. "I...I..I am sure that..that we can reach a mutual agreement. Expect the money in the next two moon cycles."

"Of course. You are most kind Duke." A slight smug smile creeps over his face. Got to keep these young rich kids in place. Playing Duke, bah! Just another child.

Indi rises from his chair and extends his hand. Desi follows suit and clamps forearms with the Duke.

"This concludes our business. Thank you, Desi, for visiting with me today. Safe travels."

Desi returns the greeting before walking out through the entryway.

✦

Daybreak sunlight is always the worst. A high intense beam of brightness invades a person's dreams and fantasies, making the previous obsolete. Jaml fights a losing battle trying to combat the very invader of dreams. One eye opens. Fragrances and aromas invade his nose mercilessly, forcing his eyes to fully open. The jasmine fragrance lifts an already bright morning even brighter. It reminds Jaml of distant lands that he has not been to in forever. Jasmine brings him back to a time where worries were the issue of studies, not weapons.

Then it hits him. Food. The aroma of cooking flesh seasoned just right. The aroma of biscuits cooking on the stove brings out the severe hunger pains brewing in his midsection. He pulls himself to a seated position to make sure of the aromas in the air. Satisfied he is smelling right, he rises to his feet.

Jaml looks around his room. Despite being the Duke of the house and presenting a consummated marriage with Canda, Jaml sleeps in the guest room next to the master bedroom. He chooses to sleep there instead of sleeping in the same bed with Canda. They have not been married in the eyes of God, Jaml does not want to violate her sanctity in any way. They both adjourn to the bedroom together, allowing the servants to see the marriage. Jaml merely walks through the room to his room. Servants are forbidden to come into the room after sunset, lest they walk into carnal coupling. Their secret is safe.

His room is big enough to fit the bed which he is seated on. There is a small table to the left with scrolls from God's word on it. In the corner is a locked chest which holds his Reaper attire and weapons. On the wall to the right hangs a sword, more decoration than battle tested. All his clothes remain in the main chambers so when servants come to clean, they see his clothes as they should be.

The door opens revealing a beautiful redhead dressed in a simple white gown. The gown falls to her lower calves with shoulder straps made of lace. Her long red locks cascade over her shoulders, giving her an air of innocence. She speaks and reality sits back in

"What are you doing? I didn't work from early dawn to get this meal ready for you to get up and walk out. Now sit back down and eat this. I will hear nothing more on the matter."

23

"But I am getting up to get the food." Pleads Jaml

"Oh. Sit down anyway. Here is your breakfast."

Jaml rises, puts his arms to the sky and stretches. Because he does not wear a shirt to bed, every morning Canda is afforded the opportunity to look at his chiseled physique. There is not an ounce of fat in his well-trained body but what is present is the abundance of scars arrayed on his torso. What catches Canda's eyes each morning is the tattoo of the cross that adorns his entire back. The replica wooden cross that Jesus gave his life on is tattooed on every Reaper's back upon completion of their training. It serves as a reminder to the Reaper of his mission and why he does the things he is tasked to do.

Canda waits for Jaml to finish stretching and sit back on the bed. She prepares two plates of food and places them on the small table and gently sits beside him. The couple say their prayers before eating. Canda watches Jaml eat, frantically shoveling food at a terrible pace into his mouth.

Jaml senses something is wrong. He peeks up to find Canda nibbling on her food. She has a concerned look on her face. Jaml breathes deeply while putting his fork down.

"What is it Canda?" He tries to sound as caring as he can. But he is hungry.

"It's nothing. Enjoy your food." She takes a small bite of her biscuit.

"Pray tell. Don't expect me to beg. I won't." He leans back on the bed.

"What happened last night? I realize we are not really married and I do not have a right to intrude on your calling but I do care. I have feelings and concerns and fear. I worry that one morning I will find Karva in here when I come in so she can tell me to pack up because you were killed. I know you went after a demon last night and the only reference I have with demons is what my mother told me to scare me."

Jaml can see the tears swelling in her eyes. For all his training, Jaml forgets the people he has to intrude on have feelings and sometimes they end up caring what happens to him.

This is one of those moments.

"I am sorry. For all my prowess in fighting, sometimes I forget the ones I impact the most are humans and have emotions. Listen, I will keep you informed from now on. Ok?"

A slight nod is all Jaml looks for. Then he tells her everything he knows about the situation before telling her about the speculations. He does end the soliloquy on the possibility of there being a Fallen around. He finishes only to find Canda short of breath.

"Are you ok?"

"Yes. It is just a lot to take in. So much going on that I had no idea could happen." She accepts the goblet of water from Jaml with a shaking hand.

"You wanted to know." He watches her drink the water.

"No. I know. I mean thank you. I needed to hear that. How can I help?" Her voice stops quivering, a sense of determination comes over her.

"You do understand that the more you get involved, the bigger the chance that you will get hurt if this goes bad. Are you accepting that fact?"

"Yes. How can I help?" Her eyes lock in with his, he responds with a smile.

"You have access to the Duke's wives. I cannot believe every Duke is innocent in this. Can you listen and get me any information about shady dealings around the merchant side. Any rumblings about the Royal family and things of this sort. Can you do that for me?"

"Train me." Her eyes never quiver or stray with those words.

"I was trained by an Angel. I do not have the knowledge or authority to make you a Reaper."

"I know that or better, that is what I have heard." She gets closer to his face, an effort to show how sincere she is about the next words that come from her mouth. "I want you to train me in the techniques. If I am going to do this, and I am going to do it, don't you want me to be able to defend myself? Especially if I am in a situation and you are not present."

Jaml leans back and chuckles which is not the response Canda expects. She is about to take offense to his actions when he says.

"My little flower wants to kill."

"Fight for my life."

"Fight for your life. Ok. Understand it will not be easy and you will suffer some."

25

◆

"Fix it!"

Vair is a small man with many talents. Despite being one of the smallest men in the city, Vair holds a certain power base with both the legitimate and illegitimate clientele. His slick back hair and pointy beard gives off an air of royalty which he plays every step he can. Vair grew up in the shadow of a castle near the vast oceans in the west. Being the son of the groundskeeper afforded Vair the opportunity to see how the wealthy lives. A lesson he has never forgotten. When he reached the age of manhood, he no longer desired to live poor so set out to make a name for himself elsewhere. His travels brought him to Colley where he has reinvented himself as fixer of problems, whether it be by persuasion or violence. Presently his services have been acquired by Duke Indi. Vair set up the deal with Desi for Indi.

"How do you propose I do that sire?" Vair's squeaky voice is very non-threatening but those who have crossed Vair know otherwise.

"You are Vair! It is your job to fix this. The best in the business, earn your reputation." Indi is in constant

"I will talk with…"

"I am tired of talk. I want action!" Indi's enraged voice fills the room and is heard by the soldiers standing guard outside. "My life depends on that artifact reaching the king's hands."

"The most efficient way to get results would be a contract. The only issue there is we don't know where the artifact is. A premature death and the artifact would be lost forever. The second option is if he has something of yours, you get something of his and make an exchange. I know where his family is and a word from would set events in motion."

"An eye for an eye option is gone. Put a contract out on him. I want him dead. As far as the artifact is concerned…"

"That thief either never had it or it was destroyed in the fire."

"Yes. Yes. Make it happen." Color returns to Indi's cheeks.

"As you wish, sire."

Vair bows low as he backs toward the door. Without any instructions yelled out, the door is opened by the guard, allowing Vair the chance to turn around and walk away. Thoughts of who

26

would be best for this assignment already running through his mind. He knows this would be a golden opportunity to eliminate his rival and get complete control of the merchants. This move would see him elevated to royalty or near royalty. All he has to do is to have Desi killed.

A smile creeps across his face. Time to go see an old friend.

✦

The midday sun beats down on the Kingdom of Colley. In the Bottoms, the heat seems to hit the citizens ruthlessly. There is little activity during this time except for the occasional children's scuttle or merchant who has stayed a few minutes afterwards to sell his remaining goods for the day. The yelping of a dog chasing rodents breaks the silence of the streets.

Once the east side of the Bottoms is the row of bars and houses of repute. All are closed during the day to recover from the previous night's celebrations. Prostitutes are rising for the day to begin preparations for another night of work. Barkeeps are stocking more beer and ale for the upcoming evening while others are fixing damaged windows and doors from previous fights. It is in this desolate arena that Vair walks casually welcoming the feel of his childhood past that he left behind so many years ago.

Dressed in a plain brown shirt and pants, a man crouches at the corner of a street. This beggar with the steel cup and ragged clothes is no regular beggar, he is a first line of defense for the Skull Guild, watching and ready to alert his brethren in the case the king's guard decides to clean up the streets or a rival guild gets too happy with expansion. His position as beggar is better than anyone in the alley or rooftops. People look for those hiding in the alley and up on rooftops, but no one expects a beggar to be nothing more than a cripple who cannot function and therefore is harmless.

This particular beggar lifts his head slightly to see Vair walking with purpose towards the Boars Pub, a cheap bar at night and the base of operations for the Skull Guild. The man crouching on the street slowly turns and lifts his head up before making a whistle call. He does not wait for an answer. After completing his watch tower duties, the man lowers his head back down to resume his façade, while keeping guard over his guild.

Vair raises his balled fist ready to bang on the door to the Boars Pub when it opens. A mix of opium and lavender fragrances invades his nostril, the mixture creates an overwhelming stench that is putrid to those not under the influence of the opium. Two men stand at the door to greet Vair, both wear simple brown pants and shirts. Around their waist is a blue sash, the mark of the Skull Guild. Both brandish short swords but Vair knows this is not their only weapon. Thieves carry an array of daggers for any situation that might come up.

Vair raises his hands to show he is not armed nor has any intentions of causing harm, especially to himself. The man on the right grips the hilt of his sword while the other man moves forward. Starting with his neck, the thief checks every inch of Vair's person, right down to the sandals on his feet. The pat down takes several minutes but finally the man is allowed entry into the bar.

With a man in front of him and one behind, Vair is escorted through the bar, which is barely lit, only twenty percent of the torches are being used. Bodies are arrayed in all positions around the bar as thieves and prostitutes attempt to recover from the previous night and prepare for the night to come. Vair finds himself more than once stepping over bodies on the floor.

The trio stop in front of a table where four people are busy counting coins. Three men continue counting the coins as the lone female looks up. Her black hair is swept from her face in one motion with her hand revealing a beautiful woman. She stares intently at the intruder and slightly cocks her head to the side.

"I would like a word with you." His voice does not quiver despite being surrounded by thieves and cutthroats.

"So would a lot of people. What makes you so special?" She mirrors his stare.

"Money."

"Leave us." Her nod of the head sends the three men at the table scurrying away. Once they are relatively alone, Bala returns her gaze at the man in front of her. "Go ahead Vair."

"I have a mess for you to clean up. My employer has paid for merchandise from Desi who is refusing to deliver the goods. I need you to get the merchandise. My employer is willing to pay double your fee."

"Indi went swimming with the sharks and got bit." Bala chuckles. "Now he wants you to clean up his mess."

Vair is not surprised that Bala already knows the situation. That is her job. She runs the largest thieves' guild in the city and nothing gets by without her knowing about it. Every Duke and member of the royal family should know that there are members of her guild working as staff members in their homes.

"Since you are aware of the situation let us bypass formalities." Vair hates having to go to the Bottoms. It reminds him of the life he left and the pain he was subjected to as a child. He also knows that the work he does requires the use of people dwelling in the Bottoms. People like Bala.

"How do you propose we find this artifact?"

"Kill him. Go through his stuff and find my artifact. You are supposed to be the best, can you handle the job?"

The challenge is out there. He has called her reputation into question. Vair leans back in the chair and waits. He does not wait long.

"Nice pressure Vair. It didn't work but the job was already taken. My men are out there piecing together a plan to execute. Double the pay sounds fine." A smile cracks across her face.

Vair rises from his seat ready to leave this place when he is interrupted.

"Vair, are you going to be willing and ready to do what must be done as the new merchant master?"

It is Vair's turn to smile. "Whoever said I was asking for the job?"

Bala breaks out in laughter as Vair exits her bar, a smile proudly displayed on his face.

✦

Vair is not the only one enjoying the afternoon sun. Jaml and Canda took time after lunch to take a stroll through the marketplace. They find themselves amid the noon day market rush as people push their way through the enormous crowds, trying to find the best deals for the goods needed today. Carts covered with tarps are lined along the streets, merchants yelling prices while customers respond with counteroffers. Small children run up and down the streets, grabbing an apple here or a carrot there, all in the fun of the moment.

Their appearance in public is essential to keeping up the facade built so carefully. Jaml stops at a cart to buy a piece of fruit for each of them. He pulls out a copper piece and hands it to the portly man at the carriage. The man's eyes widen and frantically thanks Jaml for his generosity, a copper piece should have brought the entire basket of apples.

Jaml simply nods his head in appreciation before turning from the marketplace towards the temples. Between bites, the two of them talk lightly about what they have seen in the royal court and share stories of how they entered the mission. Locked arm in arm, the couple enjoy the opportunity to just be another person away from the mission.

A flash to the right catches Jaml's attention, his body tenses making Canda aware of a situation. He places his hand on top of hers, squeezing to alert her danger might be near. Their eyes meet, and she immediately knows she must leave for sake. Despite the training she has been going through, she knows she is no match for a demon fight, so she returns the squeeze before releasing him. She quickly turns to the right and heads directly to the church.

He searches the landscape until he sees the flash again, between two houses near the end of the street. Despite not having any weapons on him, Jaml is far from defenseless. He walks diligently towards the third flash, controls his breathing, readying for a battle. He doesn't think about the battle or revealing himself to everyone, the only thing he can think of is destroying whatever demon awaits him.

When he finally gets to the alley between the two buildings, every muscle in his body is tensed for battle. He controls his breathing and therefore the adrenalin that pumps throughout his body. By slowing his walk, Jaml can bring everything into focus. He enters the alley fully prepared.

What he finds is nothing. The alley is empty except for the rodents scurrying out of his way. The stench of moldy food and stale beer floods his nose senses. Jaml cautiously walks up and down the alley, looking for anything resembling the flash he saw moments earlier.

Satisfied that all is safe, Jaml walks casually out of the alley to find Allie standing there. Her dark stringy hair falls over her shoulders. Her plain brown dress hangs loosely on her build, more function than fashion. The simple garb of a nun in training. Simple sandals keep the jagged rocks from cutting her tender feet. Despite this, Jaml's heart warms to the smile that welcomes him.

"Did you find what you are looking for Priest Jaml?"

"No little one, I did not. Now what are you doing way out here alone? It is not safe for little girls to be running around the alleys around here. You might get hurt." Jaml kneels in front of her, ensuring the little girl does not get scared but getting his point across nevertheless.

"Not any more dangerous than a priest of God looking around as if to find demons. Is that what you are looking for?" Her head tilts slightly to the side with the question.

"You got me there little Allie. I guess we both better get back to the light before the darkness overcomes us." He stands up, places a hand on her shoulder, and walks out of the alley with her.

The two of them walk together back to the temple where they find Canda and Karva waiting impatiently for them.

✦

Two men stand outside the entrance to the large villa. Torches located behind the men illuminate the entire area, as close to daylight as one can get. A gentle breeze disturbs an otherwise calm evening. Flames from the torches embrace the breeze, dancing in the moonlight to the wishes of the breeze.

The two men are obviously mercenaries by their dress. Neither is dressed like his partner nor are they brandishing the same type of weapon. The keffiyeh, or head dress, worn on the head of the first man reveals origins stemming from the holy land or close by. His long beard distinguishes him as a man of many battles. And many victories. He wears loose fitting grey pants along with a red vest, closed only with a chain, exposing a jungle size chest covered in black hair. Tucked into his sash at his side is a huge tulwar. The two-handed weapon can easily be handled by the trunk sized arms on the mercenary.

His fellow guard is not as large as this partner, but his weapon reveals a different type of mercenary. Light armor adorns most of his body, able to stop most blunt or spiked weapons. The helmet that sits on top of his head resembles the ones worn by the Roman soldiers' years before, minus the feather plume. A broadsword swings at his waist along with a large dagger on his opposite hip. His face is void of all hair which normally signifies youth but in his case the eyes tell a very different story. Small scars tell of a man seasoned in battle and yet able to tell the tales.

A trio of horses with riders approaches the gate. Both men instantly move their hands to hilts, waiting to see if the horses bear friends or foes. Both men relax when the lead horse comes into view, their present employer Desi. There is no mistaking the robust man sitting on the horse, almost engulfing the entire saddle. The animal beneath him stands tall but one has to question how much pain the horse is actually in.

They pull their horses to a halt right in front of the guards who continue to stand at attention. The smallest of the riders quickly dismounts to grab a stool from behind the bush. He places the stool on the side of Desi's horse before stepping back. The self-proclaimed ruler of trade in Colley slides to the side of the horse. Once his foot touches the top stair, he swings his other leg to join the first. Satisfied that he is presentable, he turns to walk down the stairs.

As flamboyant as he can be, Desi steps down the stairs, his garb flowing behind him. Underneath the long light blue coat is a matching yellow top. He wears a saber on his hip, more for show than actual combat. His boots come all the way up to his knees, essentially hiding his black trousers. His demeanor is one born and bred in royalty but his eyes show a street urchin who grew up establishing himself through questionable means to become one of the most influential men in Colley...

The two men who rode in with him quickly depart with Desi's horse in tow. Desi does not wait for his entourage to leave before walking into his villa. He pulls the handle on the wood doors, giving himself enough move to maneuver his large body inside the door. The weighted pulley system closes the door behind him. Inside the villa, lit torches line the walls, giving off a soft light in the room. A huge bear skin rug lays spread eagled in the center of the room. Along the west wall is an array of pillows for lounging with concubines, his favorite way to spend an evening. It doesn't take much but a simple command and an assortment of women are instantly at his disposal.

Not this night, he has business to attend to. His precious cargo is in his possession and his demands have been made. That duke is going to have to come up off some more gold if he wants this.

Rumor is the king wants this package in the worst way and has put a deadline on Indi. Desi chuckles at the situation Indi has put himself in. Bad for Indi, good for him. Indi can play hardball but if he does not come up with the gold, he will have to answer to the king and then Desi will be in complete control of the situation.

He walks over to the back of the room where his private wine collection is located. Along the way, Desi has the opportunity to shed his overcoat. He opens the door to his cellar, grabs a torch and proceeds inside. His nostrils are filled with the scent of aged wood, the canisters that hold his priced wine. He takes a moment to inhale the sweet smell. He keeps this room dark as he finds the exposure to light lessens the sweetness of the vine.

Tonight is going to be the exception, as there is cause for celebration. He knows he is going to be incredibly rich in a few days. He cannot stop smiling at the riches he will soon have.

"Good evening Desi."

An intruder in his cellar? How dare someone intrude into his villa without his consent? The smile commonplace a moment ago is replaced with a combination of fear and anger. He has long since removed his weapon and now stands exposed in his own house with an intruder who has not revealed his purpose.

"Sit down Desi. If I wanted you dead, your blood would have coated this floor already. Tonight I am but a messenger." The voice is soft and sweet. As if spoken by a female...Bala!

"Ah. How wonderful to see you again. To what do I owe this unannounced meeting?" Putting on a more relaxed face, Desi moves to the cushions to the side. Despite having a long dagger there, he knows he is no match for this killer. If it came down to it, he is a dead man. Nerves have him dreading if he will see the sun rise again but he is Desi. Even in the face of death, no one will ever see his fear.

"Enough!" The command in her voice makes Desi more concerned for his life. "I came here to tell you that there is a price on your head. Yes, I was hired to kill you. As you know, I always take a day to plan. You have a day. The next time I see you, it will be the last time you see the sun."

The thief quickly moves to the nearest window. She places a foot on the opening before turning around once again. "Remember, either you kill the contract, or I kill you. Fare you well Desi."

She disappears out the window and into the night.

A flood of emotions overcome Desi at the precise moment. Fear knowing Bala can get to him without any problem. For once in many years, Desi feels vulnerable. A feeling he has made sure he would never feel again since the last time his father beat him. Desi has always been overweight and as a boy he was ridiculed by everyone, to include his own father. Desi's father was a well-respected merchant who spent most of his time traveling from the holy lands to the new lands selling and buying goods. Desi remembers his father bringing exotic gifts to his mother but never to him. His father was ashamed of Desi's appearance and often beat him in public to show everyone his disapproval of his son.

It was during his sixteenth season that his father beat him for the last time. Desi remembers coming home from the market with a honey pastry in his hand. Desi knew his father hated watching him eat sweets and often beat him for it with his fists. It was not uncommon for Desi to go to the market with bruises after his father came home, especially if Desi was caught eating sweets.

On this occasion, his father was not supposed to be home for another week. Desi remembers the knot in his stomach and the pain it caused when he opened the door to find his father there. His father immediately moved towards him, and Desi knew he was going to die this time. The look in his father's eyes said enough is enough. Desi must die.

It was in that moment that for the first time, Desi reacted violently. He grabbed the spreading knife and his father began to laugh. Not just a chuckle but a full chest bellowing laugh. Then those frightful words.

"It's time you met your God." And his father sprung forward. Desi does not remember much about the next couple of seconds but when he came to his senses, his father lay on top of him, blood pouring from the spring in his neck. Desi pushed his father off him, stands up and looks at the massive amounts of blood that covers his shirt. None of which is his own. He remembers looking down at the dead man who was his father, who died at his own hands. It was at that moment Desi swore he would never feel fear again.

Standing in the room where Bala just left, Desi not only feels fear but anger. With all the money he openly spends on mercenaries, this thief just came in and threatened his life and not one of his highly paid mercenaries is around. Excitement is another emotion. For the first time in years, his blood is flowing. The events of this evening have brought a thrill Desi has been missing for years. Wielding his power has brought a certain measure of complacency. He has never been challenged but now that it has happened, he loves that danger that it has brought. But first the in competencies.

Desi walks fiercely down the hallway to the front gate. He finds the two guards still there with another two about to take their place. He walks confidently to the man from the Middle East. He stands proudly in front of the man.

"Why did I find a thief in my room moments ago? Why was there a person in my room alive?!"

The man immediately glances over to his partner. Seeing no help from the other guard, the guard with the headdress lowers his head to the man who pays him.

"I cannot answer that. I do not know."

Before anyone can move or comprehend what happened, Desi pulls a knife from his waist and plunges the blade into the neck of the man. Blood squirts out as a fountain in the royal gardens. Desi quickly pulls the blade out, allowing the man to bleed out all over the ground. The man drops to his knees, his hand pressed hard against the knife wound but to no avail. Blood pours out between his fingers, his life force literally running through those same fingers. It takes but a couple seconds for the man to fall on his face, dead.

The two new guards quickly grab hold of the dead man's partner. Each one grabbing an arm, holding him as still as they can as the guard attempts desperately to break free. Without a second thought, Desi walks up to the struggling man and shoves his blade upward this time. The blade enters from the underside of his mouth. Desi watches the blade move upward from the guard's open mouth. Once the hilt hits skin, Desi pulls the blade free to open the fountain of life energy. Blood pours out from the opening as the struggles of the guard begin to lessen. Within moments, all life has drained from the man who dies silently.

Desi looks up at the two guards holding the dead man.

"I just saved me some money. Guess I can go get some whores and enjoy the evening. Understand?"

35

Prince Baric strides confidently down the east wing of the castle. This wing houses the king's quarters and nothing else. The long hall is well guarded as soldiers are posted intermediately, providing not only enough manpower to stop an invasion but also give the royal couple enough notice and time to escape through one of the many secret passages inside the castle. Torches provide enough light that assassins would find it impossible to make it down the hallway without being seen.

Baric arrives at the double doors located at the end of the hall. Two guards stand at attention and do not dare move in the presence of the prince. Baric steps to the door and bangs on it three times. He waits patiently for his father's voice. The guards open the door silently when the king yells enter. Baric slides through the opening as the doors quickly shut.

Inside the chamber is nothing short of exquisite. Cushioned chairs are arranged in a semi-circle on the left side of the room. In the center is a rectangle oak table with ten chairs arranged around it. The table rests on a white fur rug from an animal killed in a distant land by the king himself. Off to the right is the entrance to the royal bed chamber. Only the king and queen have ever seen the inside of this room. The walls are decorated with paintings of wars and naked women. At the far end of the room, behind the table, is the largest painting of all, depicting the king himself wading through his enemies in a battle that occurred years ago.

Standing to the right of the prince once he enters the room is King Taras himself. Taras is a giant of a man, towering over anyone in the kingdom save his two sons. Long gold locks drape past the shoulders of the king. His beard also hangs low, giving the effect of a battle worn warrior, not some pampered king. He wears a simple white tunic with a belt at his waist. In his hands are two goblets of wine, one of which he hands his son.

"Come Baric. Sit with me a moment."

Taras leads his son along the length of the table to the other side. Taras takes his seat at the head of the table while Baric takes his place, as the eldest son, at his father's side. Goblets clank together at

Baric's toast before lips taste the sweet beverage provided. Both men drink heartedly while taking in the moment.

"Duke Indi has not delivered my goods." His voice is low as if sharing secrets in a tavern.

"Does he have them?"

"My sources say they are in the city." Taras takes another drink. "No one can say with certainty if Indi has them or if they are still in the possession of Desi. Either way, we have to get them before anyone knows what they have in their possession.

Baric looks his father in the eye. "What exactly are they?"

"They are the tools that will turn this war for good. The Fallen will rise and defeat the angels. What we are talking about my son are the weapons of the Four Horsemen of the Apocalypse. With these weapons, the Four Horsemen will rise and the end of the world as we know it will be upon us. Once we get these weapons, the Fallen will sing our praises and we will be as equals with them. Son, with any one of these weapons, we are invincible to both sides! We can kill and rule if we like!"

Taras takes another gulp, calms himself down, and continues. "Those weapons are the key to our immortality. Once in our possession, everything changes. Now do you see the importance of your mission?"

"Yes father." A smirk steals across Baric's face. "Why not just go and kill both men and just take it? Seems to me that would be so much easier."

Taras laughs, slaps his son on the shoulder and responds. "That's my boy. But without knowing exactly who has the weapons and where they are, we only guarantee our deaths. We have to gain possession before we can kill them all. And trust me Baric, once we have the weapons, I will gladly unleash your wrath upon everyone here. For my pleasure of course."

Both men spend the remainder of the day toasting and planning how they are going to gain possession of the weapons and with them cause excruciating pain on all.

✦

"Yea, though I walk through the valley of the shadow of death, I will fear no evil: for though are with me; thy rod and thy staff they comfort me. Amen."

Karva stands at the door listening to Jaml read from the scriptures and wonders why he has chosen that verse to read aloud at the service. The room holds less than one hundred people at capacity but today that number has been pushed. In the short time Jaml has been part of the noble congregation, greater numbers of the wealthy are attending the noble service. She can only wish Jaml could speak at the commoner service but his station in life prohibits that.

His elegance with scripture brings people out. They are intrigued to hear a dark-skinned man preach the word of God. He recites scripture from memory better than most can read it. With Canda at his side, Jaml openly discusses the word of God without hesitation.

The service breaks up and Jaml is visiting with other members of the aristocracy. Pleasant words are exchanged among friends when he notices her in the doorway. Without being rude to anyone, Jaml makes his way to Karva who waits patiently. When he arrives, they both slide down a dark hallway and into her chambers. He closes the door behind them.

"Excellent verse reading. May I ask why you chose that verse this morning?" Karva turns her head slightly.

"Of course. I have encountered demons here like none I have seen before. There is no reason for their presence in this small quaint kingdom but we both know they are here for a reason. We also know that there are more demons around. I just wait for the moment they become known and God gives me the strength to die in his name for his people." Jaml's humble amen after reveals his sincerity in his mission.

"I may have found out something. Word around is that some powerful artifacts are located in the city."

Jaml looks up. "And what might they be?"

"The weapons of the Horseman." Karva looks puzzled. "Have you heard of these?"

"Yes." A heavy sigh will begin his tale. "Please sit." He waits for her to be seated. "Scripture says that during the time of Angels, one became full of pride and thought himself equal to God."

"Yes Jaml. I, too, know the story of Lucifer and his fall from grace. How he and his followers were cast out of the heavens and became those we call the Fallen." Karva's voice is filled with irritation that he would suggest she did not know about the Fallen.

"I do not question your faith and knowledge on such matters. I only tell you of these things to prepare you for the next part." She nods her acceptance of his apology before he goes on. "Lucifer had four generals that led his forces against God. These generals are known as the Four Horsemen of the Apocalypse. These four Fallen were especially ruthless and created weapons that could kill their brethren, the angels. It is written that these four lost sight of what the struggle was truly about and simply enjoyed the killing."

"Needless to say, when the Heavenly Hosts prevailed, these generals were banished separately from the rest of the Fallen. It is written these four are banished where not even Lucifer himself knows the location or has the means to free them. Their weapons were cast out and buried in different locations, unknown to man or the Fallen."

"Despite the evil that fills his heart, Lucifer still had compassion for his brothers and that is why he created demons to carry out his bidding. One is to find the weapons of the Apocalypse, so he can free his brethren and start the war once again."

Astonishment washes over Karva's face. "Are you telling me these weapons are angel killers? And if we fail in our mission here, the war of the heavens will begin again?"

A determined Reaper looks up at Karva. "I am telling you that God has revealed my mission. I will not fail regardless of the consequences."

"Our mission!" Astonishment turns to resolve. "And if you think I am going to sit here and watch my world be destroyed without me being involved, you have another thing coming."

"Death awaits me. I don't want to drag you into its maw."

"Then let death come." Karva becomes more indignant. "This is my fight as well and you are not going to leave me out of it. Understand?!"

"Then let us prepare." Laughter fills the room.

Chapter 3

"I trust this will take care of any expenses that you might incur."

Words fill Bala's head but every fiber in her body is locked into the small chest in front of her. The chest is filled with an array of precious stones and gold coins. Enough to buy a small kingdom anywhere one seeks. Bala reaches for the chest without thought only to find it gently closed by a slender hand.

"Do we have a deal, my dear?" Bala looks up at the dark-haired woman seated across from her. Her elaborate multi-colored gown flows snuggly against her body. The front of the dress dips deeply to reveal ample amounts of cleavage, an obvious advantage when dealing with men. Her light green eyes twinkle as if entrancing all she talks to. Her fingers are adorned with rings of precious stones of various sizes and colors. The vision of perfection is complete with her lying on white pillows inside the carriage.

"Let me get this straight. You are going to give me all this when I give you the packages in Desi's possession. You are aware that I have already been hired to get those packages?" An air of suspicion looms in her voice.

"Is this not enough?"

"It is plenty." Bala looks at the closed chest in front of her. Dreams form instantly in her head. Thoughts on where she will escape to, how she will live out her life and to what extend she is willing to go to achieve these dreams. No more slums. No more being hungry. No more killing. Her answer is never in question, just a matter of both women hearing the words.

"You will have your artifacts." A gleam of excitement is in her eyes.

"Splendid!" The woman's face lights up, hearing the words spoken by Bala. She reaches beside her to emerge with a leather pouch in her hands. "For your troubles."

Bala snatches the bag out of the air. Without taking her eyes off her benefactor, she opens the pouch and pours a bit into her hand. Eyes light up at the sight of diamonds. She pours the gems back into the pouch, secures the strings and the pouch disappears. The lady smiles at her.

"Then we are finished." The lady bangs on the wall and seconds later the wall flap is pulled back. She enters the dark void left open by the flap and soon disappears inside.

Torches burning brightly along the streets of the city do little to pierce the dark night. With no breeze blowing, the night air sits heavily on the kingdom, a forbearance of the evil that seeps throughout the kingdom. The streets are bare except for the occasional prostitute who struggles to find her next customer. Several torches no longer are lit despite the lack of a breeze. Shadows normally numerous among the alleyways have now lain a blanket over the landscape.

Moving without a care amongst the shadows is the king of the underworld, Desi. On either side of the merchant master is one of his burly oversized muscled guards. The master wears the bright colors he favors. His overcoat is yellow trimmed in purple while pants match the brightness of his coat. Both guards wear dark pants with an open. On their hips rest thick shorts words, ones exclusively used by the Roman Empire.

The trio walk through the streets without care, owning the darkness that envelopes them, knowing the thieves that prey on the weak are employed by Desi himself. The man himself takes in the scene with a smile. He inhales deeply, enjoying the aroma of trash, human waste and death. His hands rub together while walking the streets that he owns without question.

The message had been very clear. Monies will be brought. That little weasel of a duke has finally come to his senses and now must realize Desi runs this city not the king. A chuckle escapes his lips as he nears the designated meeting place. He fears no ambush by the duke, the man does not have the courage or cunning to do it.

To his surprise, there is only one man standing at the end of the road without any packages. Two bodyguards sense the trap as well and pull their swords clear of scabbards, ready to die in the service of Desi the fearless. In unison, both men move away from their

41

master, ready to do battle and provide their benefactor time to get away. By enlarging the defense, the men have created a buffer for the safety of Desi. The pitfall of this technique is it leaves the target open and vulnerable to arrow and crossbow fire. Both men constantly scan the rooftops, ready for the multitude of fighters that will signify the trap.

The lone figure does not signal for the attack but walks confidently towards the three men. The bodyguards close ranks back to Desi and positions themselves as human shields. The lone figure stops his advancement under one of the lit torches so his adversary can look at him.

"Reaper! What are you doing here? This is of no business to you." Desi watches the man's eyes and instantly understands. "You sent the message."

"Hand over the weapon and no blood needs to be shed tonight." The voice is soft but stern, like a father trying to give his wayward son one last chance to apologize before the son gets into real trouble.

"And if I don't?" The cockiness in Desi's voice stems from the size of the two bodyguards. Desi pays good money for the best killers in the land to follow his instructions.

"Desi, hand over the weapon. This does not need to be your final night amongst the living. You do not know nor can fathom what you are actually holding onto. Do not be foolish nor allow your men to attack. They cannot win.

"Alright boys, go earn your keep. Double pay for the one who separates his head from his shoulders."

With weapons in hand, the two men move confidently to the Reaper. They position themselves one in the front and one to his rear. Reaper smiles at the obvious tactics, however useless. He slides his two blades from their back sheaths. He points his weapons downward, waiting for the attack.

He does not wait long for the man behind him to attack. The guard quickly takes two steps forward before ramming his blade where Reaper had been standing. Reaper immediately fell into a crouch, the blade aiming for his back passed harmlessly over his head. The assassin spins on the balls of his feet while bringing his blade to his neck level. He does not have to watch but knows his mark is true. His blade bit deep through armor, clothing and skin. Reaper finishes his spin, the other blade sweeping across the man's neck.

When Reaper finishes his spin, his adversary has dropped his sword and is clutching at the two fresh wounds, both spewing a fountain of blood. A look of surprise and fear sits in the man's eyes as he feels his life force rapidly draining from his neck. The man does not stagger but simply falls to his knees, looks up at his killer and falls on his face, dead.

The death of the first guard springs the second guard into action. His attack is the traditional slash moves common for Roman foot soldiers. Reaper is forced to step back for a second to recognize his foe and seek the weaknesses. The man is relentless in his attack, slashing both horizontal and vertical, aiming to end the life of his partner's killer.

Suddenly Reaper stops and stands his ground. He reverses the grip of his blades before catching the guard's blades in his. The man is astonished at the skill of the Reaper. Not once in his days has he seen any man catch another's blades in the middle of the attack.

The pain in his knee brings the guard back to reality. Reaper's low kick staggers the guard, dropping him to a knee. He attempts to free his blade but cannot. For his troubles the guard's jaw is broken when Reaper's second kick connects with the guard's jaw. The force and the power in the kick causes the guard to drop his blade.

The guard looks up, the lower half of his face completely disfigured, with determination in his eyes. He reaches for his blade, grabbing it as he rises to his feet. He stands for a very brief moment before Reaper's blade slices across his neck, blood flows like wine from the open neck wound. The guard drops dead.

With both guards dead, Reaper turns his attention to Desi. The man who rules the underworld looks around for some help, only to find Reaper the only living person around besides himself. Desperation fills every fiber of his being. How stupid to have only two guards, I have asked for this.

"I will ask only once more. Give me the sword or tonight will be the end for you."

"Wait! Aren't you some kind of monk for God?" Desi moves backwards, slowly trying to put some distance between himself and this killer.

"And?" Reaper's voice drips with sarcasm and irritation.

"You can't do this. It is not the way of the prophet!" The assassin continues to move forward, thwarting Desi's attempt to quickly turn and run.

"You have forsaken that walk of life years ago. In the face of death you want to find my God again? Do not blasphemy his name. You are not a child of God."

Reaper senses something is not right. Out of the corner of his eye, or a strong feeling from God, he sees a throwing knife speeding towards him. Instinctively he leans back in his stance to watch the blade fly by harmlessly. He turns his head to find the source of the knife.

Walking confidently towards the Reaper is a giant of a Northman. His long blonde mane hangs half way down his back, and his trimmed beard shines the same color as his hair. The blonde man grips a huge battle axe in his right hand with a round shield, customary to the north, on his left arm. The man is shirtless, revealing bulging muscles rippling under his sun-drenched skin. His breeches are black and tattooed across his chest is a skull.

Thoughts begin to circulate through Reaper's head. So I am not the only one after the sword. Reaper would never have thought common thieves and killers would be after it unless there is great wealth to be had for such an article. Does the Skulls know what the article is capable of or is just a paycheck? He contends himself with subduing this man pacing at him, and not to kill him unless absolutely needed.

Unfortunately for the Reaper, his adversary has no intention of talking, just killing. He takes two steps back as the axe head swings incredibly close to his midsection. Before he can counter, the wild mane warrior reverses the swing, bringing the blade back towards the masked man. This time Reaper spins against the swing, bringing him closer to his adversary. Reaper brings his short blade across the lower back of the man, sprouting a thin line of red which soon runs with blood.

The blonde giant swings his axe yet again, this time buying himself time to get away from the man. He spins to face the masked man and instantly knows he is outmatched. He looks over the man in front of him with disdain and admiration at the same time. He bellows his war cry before charging into battle once more.

Reaper side steps the downward stroke as he brings his blade across, catching the larger man's midsection. Pain fills the warrior's cry. Reaper follows with a kick to the back of the knees, dropping his adversary.

Just then Reaper realizes Desi is escaping. Fighting his man has given his target a means to escape. A kick to the back of his head sends the warrior into unconsciousness. Satisfied that the blonde is not getting up soon, Reaper darts off in chase of Desi, who has turned into a bar.

Reaper swings the doors open to find himself amongst a throng full of people. There are in excess of one hundred patrons in his particular bar. Finding Desi here is like finding a needle in the haystack. Reaper looks over the top of the crowd for his needle, luck has smiled again. If Desi had blended into the crowd, Reaper would have been lost but human nature takes away common sense and instills fear. Desi does not blend in the crowd but continues to push through to escape. Reaper does not see his target but finds the trail of heads being pushed to the side.

Reaper turns and quickly walks out of the bar, ignoring the wiles of the young beautiful brunette dressed in a simple brown dress who attempts to lure him in with promises of countless pleasures. Reaper considers witnessing to this young lady but has no time. His quarry comes first.

He climbs the outside wall to the building with ease. The natural cracks in the mortar is more than enough space for Reaper to use. Seconds later he is racing across the ceiling to the other side. Right where Desi was pushing his way to. Reaper stops at the edge and waits for the door to open and his quarry to come out. Seconds later, the door bursts open and Desi stumbles his way out. He looks back to see if he can find Reaper in the crowd, which he doesn't. Satisfied that he is safe, Desi brushes off his clothes. Word has gotten out to his men to come quickly. Within minutes he will be safe.

He does not have minutes.

Reaper lands in front of the King of the market, whose face takes on a sheet of utter fear. Before Desi can respond, Reaper grabs hold of his shirt and pulls him in close.

"What does the Skull want with the weapon?" Reaper's eyes penetrate deep into Desi's soul to find nothing more than a spoiled child.

"I will not tell you anything!" Desi follows the bold statement with spit to Reaper's face.

"So be it." Desi screams as a blade slides in through the skin with little resistance. Fat does nothing to stop a blade like muscle does and with years in luxury, there is no question what lies under Desi's skin. Reaper slides three finger width of the blade into the soft belly of his target, whose screams have become cries.

"Stop! I will tell you where the sword is but you must let me go. Do we have a deal?" Tears stream from his eyes and slobber runs almost as freely from his lips.

"Speak before I lose my patience."

Suddenly Desi grabs Reaper's arm and pulls himself further onto his blade. Before Reaper can react, Desi has pulled the entire length of the blade into his midsection.

"May your will be done O'Lord and may the blood of your son forgive the blood that I must cause in your name. Amen" Reaper repeats the verse as he lays the dying man to the ground. He pulls his blade from the man, wipes the blood on the dead man's jacket before sheathing his blade.

Reaper walks out of the alley only to find the blonde warrior standing there. Blood streams from the man's head from where he struck the ground and from the cuts inflicted by Reaper's blades. In the man's hand rests the battle axe. In his eyes is simple rage. The man breathes deeply and slowly in preparation for his war cry.

Just before he gives his final battle cry, a familiar voice stops him. A soothing confident voice that brings the giant to pause.

"Now now Kreen, let's not throw our lives away so quickly."

Out of the far alley strides Miko. The assassin wears the customary black garb, form fitting like a second skin. No mask hides his features on this night, for the mission is one of killing, not assassination. He wields a long sword in his right hand while his left rests out of sight across his lower back. Miko turns to regard his target, Reaper

"You are indeed skilled, Reaper. Unfortunately we cannot have you disrupting our money. Which simply means Desi must live. We don't have an issue with you going around praising God and such. Hell, that sort of thing brings fear to the people which is good for business." A giggle escapes his lips, an evil laugh that carries nothing but contempt with it.

"Let me get this right." Reaper turns to ask Miko the question but is very aware of the position of both men. "If I turn and walk away, leaving Desi alive, you are willing to walk away right now and all is good?"

"That is correct Reaper. All we ask is you just walk away." The smile on Miko's face grows like that of a cat after catching a rat.

A similar smile creeps across Reaper's mouth, underneath the mask. Neither man will ever know. "In that case I am going to have to decline your invitation and take my chances meeting my God." He slides effortlessly into his fighting stance, feet shoulder width apart with his short swords ready at his side.

"Then so be it." Miko slides to his left as Kreen moves into position behind Reaper.

Kreen is eager for the kill, a little too eager. He rushes forward, his anger still fueled by the beating he received a short time earlier. Bringing his axe high overhead, ready to cleave the Reaper in two. His voice is silent but his movements can wake the dead. Reaper turns to face the onslaught. Reaper first side steps the attack by the blonde before striking. A well placed kick to the upper leg staggers the giant man. Reaper spins, his blades ripping open two long gashes across the man's back. The man howls in pain, staggering forward, the pain crippling him for a time.

Reaper moves in, ready to finish the blonde giant off. He thrusts his blades forward, Kreen's back is the target. The blades are a handbreadths away from tasting blood when a sword bats them down. Reaper immediately brings his leg up, snapping a front kick in the direction of the block, more for defensive measures than anything else. The strike does not connect but enables Reaper to confront his newest adversary.

With a longsword in his right hand and a long dagger in his left, Miko stalks forward, measuring the man in front of him. He had watched the earlier encounter between the two and was impressed with Reaper's skills from afar. Now it is time to put those skills to test. Miko follows the block with a step back to avoid Reaper's kick. He wastes no time to attack. He backs God's assassin up with a series of thrusts and slashes. He cannot afford to let Reaper recover enough to attack before Kreen is able to join the fight.

The best plans do not always come to fruition. Reaper recovers enough to mount his own attack. His swords dance, moving at speeds unseen by Miko's eyes. Just as it seems Miko has an understanding of the technique, a blade licks out, producing a new wound on him. The skull's assassin reverses the attack, attacking the legs and midsection of Reaper. But more importantly keeping Reaper's blades low and occupied as Miko continues to buy time.

Reaper sees an opening and moves in for the attack. By keeping Miko's focus on the right blade, he sees an opening to use with his left. With a series of attacks by his right hand, Reaper sets up the killing stroke. He senses something is wrong and immediately barrel rolls to his right. He lands in a crouch position before he feels the pain of the deep cut on his left leg.

Using techniques taught to him long ago, Reaper is able to push the injury and pain to the back of his mind. He looks up to find Kreen once again standing proudly ready for the battle. Miko smiles at his adversary before springing into action.

Reaper finds himself in the battle for his life. He is fast losing blood from the wound on his thigh but more importantly the muscle is struggling to react on demand. There is nothing wrong with his swordplay and it becomes evident to the two men attacking. He thwarts the skilled attack of Miko before beating the brutish clumsy attack of Kreen. Reaper ducks under the axe swing and follows up with a downward stroke, cutting across Kreen's forearm. Another howl from the giant is music to Reaper's ears. This cut renders Kreen's left arm useless, thereby eliminating the huge war axe.

As Kreen tries to find ways to stay in the battle with his axe, Miko quickly finds himself at a disadvantage. Without the big oaf, he must face Reaper alone. Reaper wastes little time in pressing the attack. His short swords move and swirl in techniques never seen by Miko and yet at the end of each movement, Miko seems to end up with another cut.

Miko drops a smoke bomb from his arm pouch. The swirl of smoke distracts Reaper who immediately reverts to defensive measures to ensure his safety. Once the smoke begins to dissipate, Reaper watches Miko scale the wall of a nearby house. He checks to make sure Kreen is still out before giving chase to the other man.

Reaper is at full speed when he reaches the building. He jumps before catapulting off the wall. Fingertips grab a window ledge, pulling him past the ledge. A foot finds a crevice, which is all he needs, and springs him upward. His fingers touch the roof edge lightly, pulling him onto the roof. He reaches behind to unsheathe his swords once more.

Miko stands on the other side of the roof, his weapons ready. Reaper stalks slowly towards the man.

"May your will be done O'Lord and may the blood of your son forgive the blood that I must cause in your name. Amen"

With his prayer said, Reaper closes in to end this battle. Miko simply stands at the edge with his weapons at the ready, not moving to meet the attack.

Reaper spins but not before feeling the bite of a blade sliding into his side. He completes his spin to find the leader of the Skulls standing there. In her hand is the dagger dripping his blood. Reaper wastes no time engaging this new enemy. His blades once again move lightning fast, instantly putting Bala on the defensive. She can all but defend the onslaught from God's assassin. Her blades are no match for the ferocity and speed she is fighting against.

Reaper feels the desperation in her movements, so he presses forward. His attacks move high, keeping her blade high in defense. Satisfied her arms are tired enough, Reaper catches her sword between his blades before retching it from her grasp. She watches as her blade flies from her grasp to imbed itself into a mortar wall.

Reaper moves in for the kill and realizes she stands defiant but more importantly her gaze leaves him for a split second. Reaper spins just in time to block an attack from Miko. He pushes Miko's blade to the right but collects another cut across his chest. He punches Miko with the hilt of his blade, sending the man crumbling to the ground. Reaper turns quickly to turn aside Bala's knife strike. In doing this, he leaves his body open for the kick that follows, sending him over the ledge.

Bala and Miko meet at the ledge of the building. They both look over expecting to see a dead or severely damaged Reaper. Instead there is no sign of the man. They both look at each other full of disbelief and wonderment.

"Shall we go down, find him and finish him off?"

Bala looks at her wounds and Miko's as well before responding.

"Go ahead. Let me know how it goes. We have got to secure the weapon and fortify the compound. This is getting too messy!"

She turns and walks over to pick up her weapons. She sheathes them and waits for Miko so they can help each other off the roof.

In an otherwise quiet night at Jaml's villa, a lone figure silently works his way to the east side of the house. The figure stops outside a window to make sure he has not disturbed anything or anyone. Reaper slides through the window opening. He falls to the fall before picking himself up to a standing position. His room is completely void of any light, causing him to feel his way through. The pain from the fall along with the bleeding cuts make it hard for him to move, each step, each breath is labored. He struggles to keep consciousness and steadies himself regularly against the wall.

A tub of water awaits him in the next room which brings a smile creeping across his pained face. Every night since joining him, Canda has drawn his bath with no question or complaint. He remembers telling her on multiple occasions that this was not necessary but yet she still continues. He shakes his head, partly in disbelief, partly in relief that she continues to ignore him.

The weapons are the first to come off and drop to the ground. Next comes his mask and shirt and within moments Reaper is no more, just a battle-weary Jaml. Once all clothes are removed, Jaml hobbles over to the side table by his bed. He has stopped most of the bleeding on the cut on his thigh but the stab wound still continues to bleed. He grabs hold of the candle with one hand and draws his dagger from the pile on the floor. He heats the blade until it glows red. He grabs a piece of cloth and bites down hard on it. Satisfied that the preparations are completed, Jaml places the red hot blade against the open wound in his side.

Screams emerge as muffled moans as Jaml fights to keep consciousness. The pain is intense but along with his battle weariness, the cauterizing of the wound is almost too much to bear. He is forced to grab the table in order to stay upright.

Moments later Jaml stands erect once again. The wound has been closed and the cloth removed from the mouth. He waits a few minutes for the burnt flesh to cool and seal itself. What he doesn't want is for the bath water, which he longs for and stares at intently, to reopen the wound. He reaches back to find the sealed skin cool to the touch. He stammers over to the tub and literally falls in. The splash is more noise than intended so he listens intently for any movement that might come from an awakened Canda. Satisfied that he did not wake the woman masquerading as his wife, Jaml sinks back into the hot water, letting it wash away the sins of the night.

Morning sunshine creeps through the window opening to find its way to the face of a sleeping Tyra. Slowly an eye responds with a peek from behind dark eyelids. The eyelid closes tighter this time to keep the sun out, the owner ready for more sleep. But sleep is not to come. Ears catch the subtle noises of movement inside the room. Not of a peaceful movement but of someone running around. A sudden crash and yell alerts the ears that this is not a dream.

Tyra opens both eyes while sitting up in her bed. As with every night, she sleeps completely naked so her breasts are completely exposed. The source of the noise is none other than her husband Duke Indi. The man stumbles back to the leather satchel, from hitting his foot against something, to place a stack of clothes inside a brown leather bag. She follows his movements to another large storage cabinet before returning back to his bag, again stuffing clothes into it. Her bewilderment becomes annoyance.

"What are you doing?"

"I'm sorry." Indi does not stop but continues to shove clothes into his traveling bag. "I am so sorry that I have done this to us. But I have no other choice, this is what must be done. My coins have been played and now I have to deal with them. I love you Tyra but to keep you safe, I have to do this."

"Stop!" The yell startles Indi, who comes to a complete stop and stares at her." What are you doing? How is this, this packing and leaving me the best thing to do? What is going on?" Tyra bursts into tears, large sobs fill her chest like water fills a dam, violent and fast with no regard to the surroundings.

The sight of his beloved crying hysterically snaps Indi out of the trance. He quickly takes a seat on the bed and wraps his arms around her sobbing shoulders. Her shoulders continue to rise and fall to her sobs despite her beloved's arms comforting her. He gives her a reassuring squeeze before holding her at arm's length, his eyes locked in with hers.

"I am so sorry my love but the less you know the better it is for your life. I have been collecting things for the king through Desi. Things that are from the heavens. Weapons." He looks over her shoulder to make sure no one is listening. "These very things ended the life of Desi last night. I fear for your safety and that is why I must leave."

Tyra shakes her head violently, trying to dismiss the entire situation as nothing more than a bad dream, a nightmare. "But why you? Can't you just talk to someone like all the times before?"

"Not this time my love." He grabs her shoulders tightly, getting her full attention once again. "I promise you this. Once I am able to re-establish myself I will send for you. We'll be together once again, very soon. I ask that you allow me to do this for our future, our family."

"Ok."

He presses his lips against hers for one last passion filled kiss. A final hug is the last thing they share as Indi completes his packing and hurriedly rushes out of the house, leaving his wife sitting on their bed, crying hysterically.

Chapter 4

The smell of fresh bread invades the silent dreams of Jaml, urging him to swim back to consciousness. An eye opens to inspect the surroundings. The smell is overwhelming, filling the priest's every sense with bread, causing mouth to water in anticipation of the taste. Jaml opens both eyes to find himself in his bed, the early morning sun rays break through the covered windows,

He attempts to sit up only to find the wounds of his dreams are real. His head swims and threatens sickness, nausea from the medicines that run through his veins. He successfully fights back the urge to vomit to find himself naked save for breeches, his wounds dressed and covered, even the burnt wound. A bowl of hot liquids sits beside the bed, the steam from the broth inside rides up into the air as ghosts from the graveyard.

Unsteady feet balance the battle worn man for a moment before walking is attempted which almost fails when nausea returns. He holds himself up on the wall, fighting for control of his body once again. After several moments, Jaml is comfortable with his body enough to walk and go find anyone in the house.

His search ends in the prayer room where he finds both the priestess Karva and his companion Canda. Both ladies look up at the man stumbling in. He uses the door frame for support as he smiles at the two women. Both women react instantly, jumping up from the seats and running to stand beside him. Instantly arms are supporting him on both sides as the women work in unison for the safety of the warrior priest. They gently walk him to his study chair and sit him down gingerly, not wanting to reopen any wounds or cause him any more pain. He settles down in his chair before thanking the ladies for all the work they have done.

"I am eternally grateful for your help. May God shower you with his blessings for helping me in my time of need? None of what you have done here will be forgotten but it will be rewarded." Jaml smiles

"No need to say another word about this." Canda smiles warmly at him before gently kissing him on his forehead. "You have done so much for us and this city, what we did here is no comparison. I just hope your night was successful enough to warrant such injuries." Both ladies wait patiently for his tales from last night.

Jaml recounts the events of last night before continuing. "Desi has the sword but the location he took to his grave. The one thing that keeps ringing in my ears is the color of the sword; black. He goes on to say he does not know the connection the Skull Guild plays in all this but their presence and conviction smells of large sums of money being involved. The source he will have to find.

Karva quickly rises to her feet. "Wait here. Give me a second." She sprints out of the room leaving Canda to care for Jaml's wounds.

The priestess returns soon, carrying a scroll in her hand. She takes a moment to catch her breath, as if she just ran the Olympic run from Rome to Sicily. Jaml and Canda wait patiently for Karva to regain her composure and breath.

After several moments Karva is able to unroll the scroll.

"You say the sword is black?" Her question fills the room with a sense of dread.

"That is what is said." Jaml searches for answers but he knows he is not going to like what he is about to hear.

"As you know Jaml, not all the writings from the Apostles are about their lives and the life of Jesus the Messiah. Some tell of the future. Many of these scrolls are lost but some are still around. Here is one such scroll. When you said a black sword, it ignited my memory. Here it is written about the Four Horsemen of the Apocalypse." Karva is about to read when she is interrupted.

"The four horsemen who will bring down hell on earth. These four will bring about the second coming of our Lord Jesus Christ but not before destroying earth and laying waste to our civilization. Unless I am wrong, there are four weapons, each one belonging to a horseman." The look is stern, determination but behind the look is one of dread for himself and man. "But how did the sword get here? I was told the weapons were scattered and the secrets well hid. How did Desi learn of its existence, and to be able to find it and bring it here?"

"I cannot answer that." Karva continues to read the scrolls. "What I can tell you is the last places these weapons were seen. The Axes of Damnation is supposedly located in a monastery a short ride from here. The Scythe of Death is somewhere in the south mountains while the Dagger of Fire's location is not spoken of."

"Then my path is clear. Since I do not know where this sword is, I must retrieve the axe. We must secure it and hide it from human and inhuman eyes. Lucifer must not be able to wield such weapons. His horsemen are the harbingers of death and I will not let that happen. If the horsemen rise, all is lost." Jaml rises from the seat only to fall victim to nausea. He gently sits back down. "My quest for the axe will start in a week but first I need to get my strength back first"

Both ladies laugh at him.

✦

King Taras moves down his royal hall with great speed and determination. He waved his guards to stay and protect the Queen as he made it quite clear that no one is to disturb him. Thoughts in his head tell of importance that will change the world. Changes that will shift the power in the War of the Heavens in favor of the one that is cast out, Lucifer.

Taras walks into his chambers and immediately places the bar into place. The bar is a piece of wood as long as a man and as thick as a young man's waist. The board is meant for two guards to lift and put in place in times of need or attack. The board rests on steel u shaped attachments.

Satisfied that he will not be disturbed, Taras pulls the rug away from the center of the room to reveal a carving of the five pointed Star of David. He walks over to a cupboard, opens it and pulls out a sheepskin flask. The flask is opened and instantly his nostrils are filled with the scent of blood. A smile creeps over his face while he pours the blood along the star until each line is covered.

Tara strips off his shirt before kneeling in the center of the star which has taken on a green hue color. He begins a series of incantations, each one builds upon the previous in both loudness and intensity. His body rocks back and forth on its own as his body becomes nothing more than an instrument of the spell.

A mist begins to form above the center of the star. A white wisp begins to form, swirling itself into existence. The mist grows, swirling and spinning without smell. Soon the mist has grown larger than the man conjuring it to reveal the face of an angel. The soft skin without blemish with soft white hair. A normal person would not understand who he is looking at until his eyes. The orbs of the eyes are completely black which most would not understand, angels in God's favor have golden globes, the eyes of this angel tell of one that has been cast out.

The face in the mist is one of the Fallen.

King Taras keeps his eyes averted to the ground as he is not worthy to look upon an angel of the heavens. The black globes look upon the kneeling king.

"You honor me with your response." The room is filled with the angel's booming voice.

"Of course milord. I have failed milord. The Blade of Darkness remains out of my hands. A reaper has arrived." His eyes remain averted as he waits for his master's punishment.

"I have seen your failure but know it is written such. Your incompetence has given rise for another opportunity. The Reaper you speak of has learned of another weapon of the Apocalypse."

"Yes milord. Praise be to Lucifer. I know the importance that this Reaper cannot possess both weapons. I will not fail you again." Confidence builds in the king again.

"The Reaper does not have the sword either. But we must make sure he does not get the Axe of Damnation. Send Baric to retrieve the axe and bring it to me."

"Yes milord." The mists dissipate leaving the king alone on his knees. Once he is satisfied the Fallen will not reappear, Taras rises to his feet and strides confidently out of his chambers, after putting everything back in place, especially the rug.

✦

Candlelight casts an illuminating glow over the naked woman dancing in front of Baric. The prince lies on his large cushions, as he is apt to do, surrounded by beautiful women, enjoying the luxuries afforded to him by his station. The room itself is small for one of his stature but that is how he wants it, cozy. At one end of the room is the large bed on which Baric rests with a woman on either side of him. Dark tapestries line the wall, not only darkening the room but allows for the constant array of shadows in the torchlight.

Baric leans his head back, opening his mouth to receive the large grape dangling over him. The lady on his left giggles uncontrollably while the first drops grape after grape into his mouth. He chews on the sweet fruit, letting the juices run down the corners of his mouth, only to be licked off by the woman on the other side.

Hands are in constant motion, rubbing over his bare chest, feeling the manhood that is the prince. The dancer finishes her performance and seductively walks over to the bed to join the triplet located there. She crawls up over him, teasing him with every crawl step along the way. His eyes are locked in on the woman crawling up his body, full of anticipation for the events to come.

The lady crawling up his body is now a hand's breadth from his face. His heart rate picks up, anticipation builds for the orgy about to occur.

BOOM! BOOM!

All three ladies jump at the sudden banging on the door. Instinctively they all cover up their nakedness, not wanting to appear as the sluts they are portraying. To the contrary of their behavior is Baric's. Anger quickly boils over as he is not accustomed to such rude interruptions. His anger is such that he grabs his sword, ready to gut the idiot that walks through the door. Then gut the guards that are supposed to stop such intrusion.

The door bursts open and it is none other than King Taras who walks in dressed in black silk pants and an oversized white shirt unbuttoned to his navel. The stern, almost pissed off, look on his face conveys what must happen next.

Three ladies burst into action, grabbing clothes and scrambling to get off the bed and leave the room. None bother to dress but do remember to bow to the king before they pass him. Taras waits until he hears the door close behind him before he speaks.

"What the hell are you going to do with that stick?"

The sword clangs to the ground.

"Forgive me king. All but you have died by this stick when they interrupt my play time without invitation or permission." Baric rises to his feet and pulls up his pants. He bows his head slightly to the king, acknowledging his station in life.

"Prepare to leave." Without further instruction or comment, Taras turns to leave.

"Milord. Father, why am I leaving and to where?"

"To hunt my dear Baric. Gather what you need. It is time to end this priest, don't you think?"

"Absolutely." Baric's widening smile tells of his approval.

✦

Sunlight creeps over the horizon to spill on Jaml's face. He opens his eyes on the fifth day of his journey and what promises to be the last day. From what the scrolls have written, the monastery is no more than half a day's ride from his present position.

It isn't long before Jaml is rolling up his bed mat. He chews on the jerky prepared by Canda. He kicks dirt onto the embers from his fire that still shine brightly. He is not concerned with hiding his position, especially since he has been followed the entire time. It was the first day of his journey that he noticed the seven riders following him. Initially there was concern for an ambush but after the first night, that notion was gone. He realized whoever was following him was doing so to trail him. On the third night he doubled back to see who it was to find Prince Baric and a half squad of the Red Guard.

Jaml swings himself into the saddle and urges his steed forward. Over the last day the terrain has begun to change. The rolling hills are giving way to steep inclines making it harder for his horse. Tree shade and thick under bush has given way to multiple bushes. Finally, the well-traveled trail of dirt has turned to rocky terrain, thereby slowing the pace but not enough to prevent getting to the monastery this day.

The sun is on the decline when Jaml finally comes upon the monastery. The gray brown building looks nothing more than a large shack. To the right of the building is a pen full of farm animals being raised for consumption. To the left of the building is a cemetery. There are no windows in the monastery and from the looks of it, there is only one door. Hanging to the right of the door is a large bell.

Jaml dismounts his horse and ties it to a nearby tree before walking up to the door. He picks up a small stick hanging from the bell and uses it to ring it twice. Before he has the opportunity to ring the bell again, the door opens.

Stepping into the light is an elderly man dressed in a brown robe with a black sash around his waist. The man walks closer to Jaml before addressing him.

"What do you want, Reaper?" His voice has no inflection, denying Jaml the opportunity to know if this is a hostile situation or not.

"My name is Jaml. How are you called? How do you know I am Reaper?" Jaml does not move, giving the monk in front of him no reason to consider his presence a threat.

"So many questions and yet not the right question. I am called Seve and I am an elder monk here. None come around unless they are ill or want something. And since you look healthy, are you going to tell me what you want." The monk does not move.

"You obviously know why I am here. I only seek to gather what I need and leave without incident." Jaml bows to the monk, showing the utmost respect for the elderly man standing in front of him. The monk slightly bows in response.

"You asking does not make it so. We, at the monastery, will not just hand over such an evil weapon to just anyone. We have to make sure your intentions are not only pure in nature but you have the abilities to protect this evil weapon." Seve regards the man in front of him with serious intent. A warning as well as a sizing. "Come. We have things to discuss."

Seve leads Jaml into the monastery. The minute Jaml clears the door, it closes behind him. Jaml does not acknowledge the closing or the man standing there. In fact, he has seen several men standing at the ready while he and Seve conversed. Now that he is inside, the men no longer stand in the shadows. Warrior monk after warrior monk emerges from everywhere and soon Jaml finds himself moving through crowded halls.

Seve leads Jaml through the halls to a set of large double doors. Encrusted on the doors are dragons and other mystical animals. Standing in front of the door are two monks, both clothed in the customary plain brown robe with a leather rope wrapped around their waist. The younger of the two monks walks up to Jaml, arms folded. The monk does not speak but waits patiently for something. Seve smiles at the monk before turning to Jaml.

"He awaits for your weapons. They are not needed here."

Without question, Jaml unstraps the holsters that hold his short swords. Without hesitation, he hands them over to the young monk. He retracts the knives from his boots and the small of his back before handling them over as well.

The young monk bows slightly, acknowledging Jaml's actions. He turns and walks down the hall, his every movement watched closely by Jaml. Seve interrupts Jaml's observation.

"Do not worry Reaper. Your weapons are in no danger and neither are you." Jaml quickly turns his head to meet the gaze of Seve. Instantly eyes lock but Seve quickly relieves the tension, "Yes, we know who and what you are. As you said before, we know why you are here and yet we still must make sure the decision to hand over the weapon is the right one." A wink flashes at Jaml. "We wouldn't want to hand over the weapon only to see it fall into Lucifer's hands, now would we?"

Jaml finds himself smiling at Seve. He is more informed than Jaml thought.

The lone guard opens one of the doors, allowing Seve to lead Jaml inside.

Jaml does not hear the door close as his eyes are transfixed on what is before him. Jaml expected to be inside the inner sanctum of the monastery, where rows of candles and benches will be. He had expected a library braced against the walls along with tapestries and paintings. His ears expected the humming or prayers but none of that is what he finds himself looking at.

Jaml finds himself looking at a large dirt pit in the center of a huge hall. Inside the pit is white sand. There are walls over two men lengths in height and on top of the walls are row after row of benches which are filling fast with monks. Torches light the room with an eerie yellow light.

"We have to make sure." The words bring Jaml back to his senses. A battle test, of course. They must make sure that I am worthy and capable of protecting the weapon. The fact that I am Reaper is worthy enough but now they must test my fighting skills. He turns to find Seve smiling at him.

"Of course you do." Jaml's tone in his answer is smooth, one that has been battle tested and not afraid to be battle tested again.

"Good. I am glad we have an understanding."

"One thing." Jaml looks Seve in the eyes, searching for any deceit. "To the death?"

"Of course not. We are not barbaric. To submission alone." Seve nods his head.

"Now we have an understanding." Jaml knows that the battle will not be any easier but he will not be forced to end life.

A gong fills the entire room with sound and vibration. The far wall slides open and two figures enter the arena. Both wear the cloak of monks and yet something is different. Jaml recognizes neither wear the rope around the waist and both have their hoods covering their face. They walk in unison, their steps choreographed. Each step is identical and yet they move away from each other. Their hands are tucked inside the sleeves of their robes.

Jaml pulls his shirt over his head before handing it off to Seve who accepts the top and silently moves away. The tattoo of the cross emblazoned on his back reveals to all he is Reaper, a warrior of God. He glides into the arena, ready for the combat test to come.

The two monks step to the edge of the arena. They stand silently for a moment before shedding their cloaks in one motion. The dragon emblazoned on their chests reveals them to be the warrior class of the monastery. And obviously the best of them muses Jaml. The two monks join Jaml in the arena.

Both monks are bald except for a long ponytail emerging from the top of their head. No other hair can be seen on their heads. The one to the left is taller and therefore initially the bigger danger. Both monks stop in front of Jaml, several feet from each other. All three show their respect by bowing before the monks jump into their fighting stance. Jaml remains still.

The shorter of the monks attack first with a series of lightning fast strikes aimed at Jaml's head. Jaml is able to thwart each blow and reverses the attack. A fist strike is soon followed by an elbow as Jaml presses forward. The monk has to retreat under the relentless attack of Reaper. Jaml sees an opening and strikes, a leg kick connects with the monk's thigh, sending sharp pains shooting up the leg.

Jaml moves in, ready to finish this one and get to. The wind is knocked out of his chest. Jaml feels the pain of the kick to his stomach, his natural muscles saving his ribs from cracking. Nevertheless Reaper is forced to stumble backwards, struggling to

61

catch his breath. A second kick to his head is blocked, instinctively by his arm but the force sends him flying into forward rolls.

He lands on his feet and quickly turns to face the two men again. Jaml makes a mental note not to get preoccupied with one monk again, less this test will be a failure. The two monks move into striking distance and get into their battle pose again. Jaml remains still, his arms tenses at his side.

The taller monk strikes first this time with a series of high kicks. Jaml retreats slightly, blocking each kick successfully. He waits for the second attack before jumping. He spins in midair, extends his right leg out and catches the second monk across the cheek. A nice connection but a temple shot would have been better as it would have rendered the monk unconscious.

Jaml lands on his feet and this time does not wait. He leaps forward, back into the fray. The second monk has to dive to the side as Jaml's snap front kick lashes out. He lands in front of the tall monk and immediately launches himself into an attack. The tall monk has to retreat, his arms and legs in constant defensive motion. Jaml keeps his attacks close to body to negate the other man's reach advantage. He mixes his attacks from head to body to legs. All aim to keep the man off balance.

Without warning, Jaml flips backwards. The first strike meant for Jaml instead strikes air, inches from the tall monk's chest. Before he can recover, the monk feels the pain of strikes to his lower back. He has no chance to recover when an elbow hits him at the base of his skull. The world of the shorter monk instantly goes black.

The taller monk takes steps back, watching his fellow warrior fall face first to the pit. A steady rise and fall of the back informs the taller monk his fellow warrior is still among the living, not the conscious. He jumps over this partner, landing in front of Reaper, striking with everything he can. Jaml does not step back, instead holds firm his stance. The two men exchange strikes, each one blocked. Fists turn into elbows followed by leg sweeps and kicks, each trying to gain the advantage and rise as the victor.

Jaml sees an opening and strikes hard only to have his fist strike air. He feels the monk spin to the outside of the strike, pinning his arm. Jaml rolls the other way, freeing his arm. An elbow catches him on his jaw, inches from his temple and defeat. Jaml ignores the pain. Before the monk strikes again, Jaml kicks the man's leg out, throwing him off balance. With their arms still locked, Jaml kicks the other leg, dropping the man to his knees.

Jaml unravels the arms but does not step back. The monk attempts to rise to his feet but his leg is kicked out from underneath him again. Jaml spins but instead of striking the monk with his foot he wraps his leg around the monk's neck. The two men spin to the ground where Jaml is able to lock his legs around the monk's neck, squeezing. The monk squirms for a second before tapping Jaml's legs in surrender.

Jaml immediately rolls to his feet and offers the monk his hand. He hoists the man to his feet and the two of them move to the other monk to make sure he is still alive. Satisfied the fallen monk will only have a huge headache, Jaml moves in front of the tall monk and bows in respect. The bow is reciprocated.

Jaml walks to the edge of the pit where a smiling Seve awaits. He bows to the monk before accepting his shirt back. He pulls his shirt on to find Seve smiling. The man motions for Jaml to follow.

"Come. A meal awaits the victor and then we can conclude our business."

✦

Two figures stand alone on the wall of the monastery. Their walk is of two that have known one another for years and share every secret. But in this instance, the two men who walk along the wall of the monastery have recently met, their lives have crashed together only hours before.

"Your God has chosen well." Seve places a hand on the other man's shoulder.

"I am humble that you would consider me as such. I am but a servant to the Almighty and through me his work is done. I do want to thank you again for your hospitality. The meal was delicious. And thank you again for this." Jaml holds the black cloth covered axe up.

"Of course my son." A small smile crosses Seve's face. "Now what are you to do with the 7 warriors waiting on you? Obvious to end your life and retrieve the axe."

"That you will not have to worry about. Tonight another demon will bleed."

Jaml places his hand on the edge of the wall before launching himself into the night.

A cool breeze flutters across the sleep man, shaking him gently, reviving him to his job. The sentry, a young soldier just above manhood, shakes his head vigorously, trying to revive himself. He checks the position of the moon once again, figuring out how much longer he has until he can crawl in his blanket and sleep the rest of the night away. The ride from the castle has not been too bad, following a man who is not in any hurry. He still does not understand why they have not attacked but content on following him. Jarf now walks around his post. Got to wake up

The man, who resembles Duke Jaml, has traveled for little over a week to come to a monastery and now resides within. Could be his twin if he knew better. But what would a duke be doing way out here? At a monastery? Jarf realizes that he is nothing more than a foot soldier and will never understand the ways of the rich. Instead, he shakes his legs and head, trying to stay awake for the remainder of his shift.

So preoccupied with his contemplations that he does not hear the man land behind him. So oblivious is Jarf to his surroundings that he never senses the danger he is in. The only thing he knows is tremendous pain in his head before he is overcome with darkness.

Reaper pulls the unconscious body to the nearest bush. Once in place, Reaper leaves the body covered in leaves before heading into the camp. He stops short near a tree to watch. Inside the camp area, two soldiers sit by a fire, warming themselves while sharing stories of adventures in the past. On a spike above the fire rests the charred remains of three birds. On the other side of the camp rests four bundles of blankets, the other men.

Reaper knows there is no way of eliminating the two guards quietly before the alarm is raised. He quickly scrambles silently up the tree he is standing by. Once into the branches of the tree, he finds the nearest branch that carries his weight. He soon finds himself standing virtually over his two targets. Reaper pulls his swords from their sheaths. Without warning, Reaper drops down between the two men.

The assassin lands softly on the ground and springs into action. A horizontal swing draws a thin red line across the first man's neck.

The soldier tries to scream but all that comes out is a loud gurgle followed by a steady stream of blood from his mouth and the red line on his neck. The other soldier has a look of astonishment on his face. A blade pierces and drives into his chest, the tip reappearing out the soldier's back, covered in blood.

Before Reaper can silence the soldier, he lets out a huge yell. The four men sleeping are aroused from slumber, reaching for their blades.

Reaper stands tall. "May your will be done O'Lord and may the blood of your son forgive the blood that I must cause in your name. Amen"

Reaper leaps to the men lying down, landing on the ground over the soldier. Reaper stabs down with both blades, pinning the man's head to the ground with his swords. He pulls them free in time to roll to the side, avoiding a downward slash from another soldier. The man's blade chops into the dead carcass, making it fold upward for a moment. Unfortunately the chop generated such force that the blade remains stuck in the dead man's spine.

The man frantically tries to pull his sword free, knowing the assassin is near. He looks to his right to see his killer fast moving. The soldier releases the sword and grabs for his dagger that is stashed in his waistband. His fingers have just enough time to wrap around the hilt when the killer's blade bites deep into his face. With his free hand, the soldier attempts to grab at the sword as it slashes deep into his face. Both hands grab at his wound, vainly trying to keep the inside of his face in place.

By this time, three remaining soldiers have risen from their sleep and grabbed their swords. The first soldier flies into battle, dressed in a loincloth and nothing else. Reaper blocks the clumsy stab with his left blade and slashes diagonally across the torso of the soldier. The mark is true, cutting deeply into his chest, sending the man stumbling back, blood pouring out of his chest like water. The soldier falls to his knees before dying.

The two remaining soldiers are more cautious than their comrade in arms. They stand at a distance, weapons ready, waiting for their leader. They don't have to wait long as the Prince steps between them. The prince stands proudly there, seemingly towering over both soldiers by at least a hand's length in height, something that is not lost on the soldiers.

"If it isn't Reaper. Thank you for dropping in, now we don't have to go looking for you." The corner of his mouth turns up in a sneer. "Now if you don't mind, please hand over the axe and we will get on our way."

"You are a jester. Four of your men lie dead and the other two are scared senseless." Reaper turns to the soldiers. "I have nothing for you. Leave before I have to glorify God by taking your heads."

The two soldiers think about the proposition before Reaper watches their grip tighten around their swords.

"So be it."

The first soldier gives his battle cry and charges the man dressed in black. He slashes wildly causing Reaper to spin. As he spins, he brings his sword in a downward slash, cutting across the back of the soldier. The soldier arches his back in pain. He turns and steps to battle again. Swords clang together, sparks fly as two men engage in battle. The soldier with his longsword is no match for the highly skilled Reaper. It isn't long before the soldier has multiple cuts across his body.

Reaper quickly attacks the second soldier, completely catching him off guard. The man is put on the defense, his long blade no match for the twin swords. He does everything in his swordplay arsenal to stay alive, hoping for someone to interfere.

Sensing no help, the soldier makes a lung forward, his arm outstretched, his blade seeking blood. He watches, in dismay, Reaper side step his blade, stepping forward. Dismay turns to pain. He looks down to watch blood drip from a blade lodged in this stomach. Fear washes over the soldier when large amounts of blood squirt out when Reaper pulls the blade out. He topples over, blackness washes over his eyes.

Reaper turns around. The one remaining soldier looks at the carnage in front of him before looking at the maker of that carnage. He looks at the many cuts that bleed freely on his body. He once again looks at Reaper just before a blade protrudes from his chest. His eyes roll to the back of his head, welcoming death.

The blade slides back into the corpse, allowing it to fall to the ground lifeless. The body hits the ground and Reaper finds himself staring at Prince Baric holding a sword dripping with blood.

"I can't stand cowards." Baric licks the blade, tasting and savoring the blood coating the blade. "What is the chance you are going to play nice and hand over that axe?" Eyes leave the blade to bear into the man before him.

"I do have a question for you, Baric?" A relaxed Reaper stands calmly in front of the prince.

"What is that Reaper?"

"Are you going to die in human form or your natural foul smelling self?" A smile creeps in at the corner of his mouth.

"If you insist." Skin and clothes on the body of Baric begin to tear. Baric speeds the process by ripping at the skin and clothing, exposing a red scaly body. Hands begin to elongate and grow enormous razor sharp nails. He grows three head lengths, towering over the man of God. Two wings emerge from his back to flap, stretching as if being cramped inside the skin for far too long. With one clawed hand still holding the sword, Baric tears at the facial flesh with the other hand. His true identity reveals itself. Prince Baric is just another demon.

"To your liking?"

"Thank you." Reaper has to smile as Baric growls at his response. "Now I don't have to imagine how ugly you are, I can just see it."

Baric waits no longer and attacks. He unloads a barrage of overhand strikes. Reaper side steps the majority of the strikes and for the ones he doesn't, he merely brushes the strokes aside with his blade. Reaper senses Baric's frustration grow as his attacks become more and more erratic.

Reaper sees an opening and takes it. A quick front kick is not meant to do damage, it does not need to. The kick catches the demon right above the knee cap, throwing him off balance. Baric stumbles a bit and Reaper takes advantage. Two fast high strikes brings Baric's blade up to block. Reaper pushes the high blade to the side as he moves forward. The exposed midsection tastes Reaper's blade.

The assassin kicks back, connecting with the same knee in the opposite direction. The demon drops to that knee but the howl of pain that is heard stems from the long gash across his back. Wings instinctively beat the air quickly, lifting Baric to safety.

The demon turns to face his adversary, this time from above. He snarls and dives for his attack. Reaper stands relaxed at the approaching demon. At the last second, Baric reverses his dive, catching himself from crashing into his enemy and the ground. Reaper anticipates this move and quickly launches himself upward.

The sudden attack catches the demon off guard. He is only able to deflect one back with his sword. The second blade slides into his shoulder as a well-oiled blade slides into its sheath.

Reaper's leap takes him chest to chest with Baric. But with one blade in the demon and the other blade in his hand, Reaper has no way to stay that close to the demon. Before Baric is able to recover from the shock, Reaper steps down on Baric's thighs and launches himself off of the demon, performing a perfect back flip to land softly on his feet. Since he does not release the hilt, the impaled blade is ripped out of the demon's shoulder followed by blood and chunks of demon skin.

Baric screams.

The blade must have ripped the shoulder tendons for Baric stumbles back, his shoulder completely useless. Reaper does not waste the opportunity for victory and presses immediately. His twin swords thirst for more demon blood. And demon blood it gets. Reaper's blades are too fast and the demon is focused on his shoulder as well. The demon finds himself with many more reasons to worry, Reaper's blades leave several fresh cuts across the demon's torso.

The demon glares at the man standing before him, a look that conjures up nightmares in children across the land but the man is no child and fears nothing but God. With his left arm completely useless and bleeding from multiple cuts, the demon has little choice but to die in a glorious charge.

And charge he does.

Reaper watches with satisfaction the charge of Baric. The demon flaps its wings, hovering slightly above the ground, streaking directly towards Reaper. The man waits patiently for the distance to close. Baric raises his sword to bring it to bear on his killer. Reaper brushes aside the blade and attacks. Baric is defenseless to the velocity of the attack. Again and again the blades enter and exit his body. Before it is all over, Baric stands there with over eight new holes in his body, each one made by a blade wielded by Reaper.

Reaper looks down at the demon. "May God have mercy on you."

Blood flows from Baric's mouth as a swollen river runs over its banks. "I don't want his mercy or your pity."

"Then you shall have neither." Reaper continues to stare at the demon before him. "Die you abomination to God's creatures"

"Abomination you say? Then what are you?" Baric coughs up even more blood. "You are no better than I. Pawns in a war orchestrated by the heavens. We fight and die for causes we know not of. So Reaper, once again, what are you if not also an abomination?"

"I am saved by God's grace and most of all, I am loved." A final sweep of his blade decapitates the demon.

✦

Pain. A great amount of pain fills his head. He takes a moment to feel if he is dead. Satisfied that death has not come for him, he attempts to open his eyes. The brightness of the morning sun is too much to bear. He closes his eyes.

After several minutes he attempts to open his eyes again, this time very slowly. The sun is no dimmer but he is better prepared. The pain in his head continues to throb greatly. Jarf remembers little from the night before. He struggles for understanding. He remembers being on guard and fighting his sleep. Then an overwhelming pain before darkness.

Panic fills his head. The prince must know by now that he has failed in his duties. He obviously fell asleep while on duty. He picks himself up, brushes off the loose leaves and finds his sword and helmet. He looks to find a dent in his helmet but cannot think of any reason it would be there. He squeezes his head into the dented helmet, straps on his sword and walks slowly back to camp.

Jarf enters the clearing and drops to his knees in shock. Dead bodies are everywhere. A quick count of the bodies indicates all belong to his unit. Then he spots it. A huge demon's body lying on the ground. The body is missing its head, which Jarf finds on the other side of the clearing. Another look and count shows the prince is not here. The prince has been kidnapped, obviously by the demons. Especially since one is lying dead. Multiple stab wounds indicate a massive battle where his unit mortally wounded the beast. The prince must have capitated the beast before being pulled away from the other demons.

Must tell the king. Jarf looks around for the horses. He stops in his tracks.

And proof!

Jarf wraps the head in one of the bedrolls, climbs on a horse and rides off to the castle, trying to think of a story that the king would believe. One that did not include him falling asleep on the job.

Chapter 5

The gates of the city are a welcome site. Jaml pushed his horse as fast as possible, needing to get back to the monastery as soon as possible. With the revelation that Prince Baric is a demon, headless now, every nerve in his body screams that the entire Royal Family belongs to Lucifer. His purpose for this mission has been revealed. Enemies have been unmasked and the battle lines drawn for Jaml has no doubt that the king will soon learn of the prince's failure and when that happens, hell will break loose. Jaml is always ready for a battle but now he must ensure his friends are as well.

The squad of guards allow him entry without much questioning, more concerned with the heat and what it is doing to their uniforms. Jaml flips a copper piece for thanks before telling the men not to spend it all in one bar. The squad leader thanks him.

Jaml dismounts his steed and quickly finds a young man eager to make some money. He hands the copper piece to the boy and gives him instructions to bring the horse to the monastery. With the midday crowd in the market, it would take Jaml most of the day to make it to the monastery, that kind of time he did not have. This way he can move quickly through the crowds to arrive well before any harm can come to his friends. So he hopes.

The door bursts open, surprising everyone inside. Since the rumors of demons in Colley, all the inhabitants of the monastery have expected a demon attack on the church. Numerous prayers have included asking God for safe passage out of Colley or protection from the devil's work. So when the door bursts open, many inside know the end is here, visions of demons feasting on their innards, slurping the entrails in their stomach.

All relieved to see Duke Jaml standing there.

"Where is the priestess Karva?" Jaml does not break stride, feeling guilty if anything were to happen to her. His heart jumps to his mouth when he does not hear any response from the people inside the temple. Anxiety fills every bone in his body. Worry creeps into his mind at finding Karva and Canda dead. It does not dawn on him the fact that the other priestess never raised an alarm or cried out in horror at the death of the priestess. The absence of all would indicate everyone is in good health.

A sword slides from its sheath, ready to taste blood. Jaml can see the door to Karva's down the dimly lit hallway. He makes it to her chamber in a half run, his heart pounding in anticipation for the fight of his life. He can see the door is ajar, the glare from a candle inside spills into the hall. He does not slow but lowers his shoulder and plows through the door.

A scream escapes the mouth of the lady inside. There is a man standing in the doorway, swords in hand. Due to the glare behind her, Karva is unable to make out who her intruder is. She is not a fighter and has no way to fend off an attack. Her only defense is sound that will notify the monastery of her present predicament.

"Sister Karva, are you alright?" Jaml stands in the doorway, weapons drawn. Inside the room Jaml only sees Sister Karva. No demons. The fact that she is screaming because of him makes him feel terrible.

"Alright? How dare you ask me this?" Sister Karva's fright has turned into sheer anger. Her eyes tell of a woman ready to chastise as if he is her own son. "You come barging into my room without notice or announcement after you go after one of the holy relics from the Casting. No word or anything, just you throwing open my door like you are going to kill me. And then you dare ask if I am alright?!"

Jaml sheaths his blades. He does not walk too close for fear of the woman's vexation. He stands motionless, allowing the nun to vent her anger at him. He does not interrupt nor does he take it personally. Her anger is due more to her fear than any hatred she may have.

"And one last thing. Do you know how to knock?"

"Where is Canda?" Jaml looks back into the hall looking for the lady that is playing his wife.

"Did you not hear" Her statement is interrupted by Jaml's question again

"Where is Canda? I need both of you here immediately." The look on his face announces the end of her argument and an urgent need to get Canda now.

✦

"Prince Baric is a demon. Was a demon, now just dead. We are going to have to assume that the entire royal family are demons." Jaml looks at either woman, searching for a response. Anything. But all he is getting are blank stares of disbelief.

Finally Karva speaks. "That would explain why the weapons of the Apocalypse are showing up here. It seems the dark lord is making his move. Also explains why you were sent here." She searches his eyes for a gateway to his soul. "Now what? Do we go after the weapons or the king?"

"I believe we should stay the course." Canda looks sheepishly at the other two, not knowing if she has any right or position to speak her mind. "I believe the weapons are the most important things here. If they get hold of all four weapons, they can start Judgement Day. We cannot allow that to happen."

"She is right." Jaml pauses, deep in thought. "But I must insist you two must stay under my protection. The king is going to hear about his son's death. You two are his obvious choice for retaliation."

A deep sigh fills Karva's lungs. "I appreciate what you are doing Jaml but I am a nun of God, picked to serve his people and spread his word. I can do neither being hidden in the monastery. I will continue to do God's work and if it is his will that I die doing his work, so be it."

"The people of Colley are truly blessed." A smile creeps across his face. "Then it is settled. Continue to do God's work and I will eradicate all the demons in this kingdom. And keep you safe of course."

He bows to the two women, getting his point across. They return his bow in kind.

Later that night, when all the nuns have retired to their rooms, Jaml finishes his prayers for guidance and assistance. He rises from his knees and walks over to the large battle axe wrapped in black cloth. He carefully folds back each layer of cloth until the Axe of Damnation is completely exposed. Jaml runs his fingers along the shaft, sensing the enormous amounts of power radiating from the weapon. He takes in a big gulp of air before starting the arduous task of re-wrapping the cloth over the axe.

The task takes him longer than anticipated but once there, he is satisfied with his work. He scoops the weapon into his hands and walks out of his room. With purpose, Jaml walks to the church where he finds the altar. He pulls back the sheets and pulls on an angel statue found there. Two boards slide back to reveal a hidden compartment. He gently slides the axe into the opening. Satisfied with the position, Jaml pushes the lever back into place, sealing the axe away in its hidden compartment.

✦

"Your Majesty, it was horrific. Reaper dropped in amongst us, slicing and stabbing like a man possessed by the devil himself." Jarf is kneeling in front of King Taras and Queen Sera. He arrived in the kingdom at daybreak and immediately ran to the castle. He instantly wanted to recite his tale but the king was busy so Jarf had to wait. While waiting he was afforded a hot bath and clean clothes, luxuries not often afforded common soldiers. After the bath, he was given a full hot meal of lamb, potatoes and warm ale. Jarf has never tasted seasoned ale so the whole experience was like living a dream.

He is now kneeling before his king and queen, reciting the tale that he knew best. One that left out his culpability in the situation.

"Slow down my good soldier." Taras leans forward, struggling to understand the lad kneeling before him. "Raise your head so that I can hear your words. You talking to the floor does nothing for me." He watches Jarf raise his head but not his eyes. "Good boy. Now once again what happened to my son?"

"My apologies sire. I am nervous." Jarf's innards are twisted all inside. What if they already know it was him who was on guard? And failed? But how would they find out? Everyone is dead. Everyone but Prince Baric. Then there was that demon that was also killed. How did that thing get involved? There was no demon that he knew of. Where is the prince? I would feel so much better if I knew the prince was indeed dead.

"What are you nervous about?" Queen Sera's soothing words calms Jarf down. He takes a sip of the king's wine.

"Your Majesty. I am but a common foot soldier and here I am sitting with the great and all powerful King Taras telling him I don't know what happened to his son. I feel like a failure. And to top it off, I am telling you some crazy story about a demon, dead as I recall. My tale sounds crazy to me and I lived it." The more he speaks the more he finds himself gasping for air. It is only a matter of time for the uncontrollable coughing, and hacking.

A female servant instantly appears standing by the guard at the door. She rushes over to refill his goblet of wine which he eagerly gulps down. The queen calls for the guard to come and assist the lowly soldier.

"Take him to his barracks and make sure nothing befalls him. He has done us a great service by informing us of the treachery of Reaper. Take him please before he loses his meal in my room,"

The guards hoists Jarf to his feet by grabbing his arm and pulling. The young soldier is caught totally by surprise by the man's strength but finds his footing. He looks up at the guard, his face partly hidden by the leather mask which exposes his nose and eyes.

Jarf bows lowly, giving thanks to the Royal Family for their hospitality. The guard gently pulls the soldier, leading him out of the chamber. Once the door closes, the queen is quick with her judgements.

"What a spineless weasel! Did not have the guts to stand and fight. He needs to die a horrible slow death! Maybe we can feast on his innards while he yet lives just like we did the couple those years back. I haven't tasted heart pumping warm blood for a minute."

"Calm yourself Sera. Your anger is directed at the wrong human." Taras gets up and walks over the window. He takes in the beautiful breathtaking view of the city. He inhales the scents of the marketplace. "This Reaper is proving more than an annoyance.

Killing demons in our service is the price of business. We have done this before. But now this Reaper has deprived us of the Axe of Damnation and killed one of our sons. This is who we need to concern ourselves with."

"Of course my king. Your wisdom is supreme." She nods her approval.

"Summon Prince Manda." Cool, calculating.

"And Princess Jala?"

"Of course." Turns back to the window as Sera quickly leaves the room. He continues to watch over the city, deep in thought. Where is that damn sword? Who has it? How am I going to demolish this Reaper? Thought after thought swims through his head, each one captivating a new situation and problem. Yet all intertwined. He shakes his head like a dog after a jump in the lake.

He walks over to the table to pour himself a goblet of wine. If nothing else, humans are good at getting me drunk. A smile appears just before the goblet is turned up and drained. Several gulps later, Taras grabs the pitcher of wine, ready to refill his goblet when a knocking at the door interrupts his goals.

"Come in." Despite the intrusion, Taras downs the second cup.

Queen Sera is the first person to walk into the room. She has changed and wears a simple purple gown that falls just above her feet. A gold sash wraps around her waist with matching sandals. The gown is sleeveless and the deep cut in front leaves little to the imagination concerning her ripe breasts.

Following the queen is Prince Manda. The warrior prince is dressed in light chainmail armor on his torso. Long leather boots protect his feet and shins. Across his back rests his two handed blade. Around his waist is an array of daggers, all within reaching distance. His persona is finished off with a gold cape draped across his shoulders to stop just shy of his calves. His long golden mane is pulled back into a ponytail. His face hosts his beard, neatly trimmed.

Following her brother into the room is Princess Jala. Her long black hair bounces behind her on every step. The yellow dress fits snugly on her womanly figure. High slits on either side of the dress allows for her long athletic strides and exposure of her long legs. A closer look reveals daggers strapped on each leg.

The three walk into the room and bow to King Taras. He acknowledges them before leading them over to the table. On the table are three goblets of rich wine. The king carries his. Each one takes a seat at the table. Manda downs his goblet quickly before refilling it. Both ladies take a drink, savoring the sweet grape nectar before feeling the burn as the alcohol goes down.

Once they have all settled in, Taras speaks.

"Baric is no longer with us. Reaper has prematurely ended his reign with us."

"What human is able to defeat one of us?" Irritation turns to anger for Manda. "Tell me so I can get revenge."

"You are so much like my queen. So full of vigor and passion." Taras raises his goblet to toast Manda. "We need to be prudent with this situation. This particular Reaper is very good and I don't feel like losing any of you. So let's think about this, how can we accomplish this without revealing who we are."

"Sire. Are you saying we need to pull him away from the people? Then Manda can deal with this human" Sera sits back in her chair, sipping on the wine in her hand.

"That is exactly what I am saying." Taras leans towards Sera, realizing his bride has a plan already forming.

"Then let's get him out to my girls at the Isle of Pleasure. Once there, your little Reaper will not stand a chance." Sera licks a bit of wine from the edge of her goblet, satisfied with her plan.

Taras bursts out laughing. "Splendid. Manda, help Sera get it all set up. Make sure you leak it to the proper places so Reaper can get a hold of it. Take that shriveling little soldier with you. He deserves a night at the isle as well." He looks at Sera. "Is tonight too soon?"

A smile creeps across her face. "Splendid"

Sera is the first to leave with Manda and Jala following closely behind. Taras looks out the window, a feeling of satisfaction sweeps over him. Soon this place will once again be what he commands. Humans are nothing more than sheep to be herded. In this case, to hell.

✦

"Are you really doing this by yourself?"

The words ring inside Jaml's head. He turns to find Karva and Canda standing there, concern spread all across their faces. He winks and smiles at the ladies, attempting to soothe their fears.

"I will be fine. Everything we know suggests that there will only be one demon there with a few drunk soldiers. Nothing I cannot handle." He winks at the two women. "When I return, we will need to move all the nuns to another location until this situation is handled. Otherwise you and your fellow nuns will become targets."

"Understood." Karva knows he is speaking the truth. Since he arrived, their lives have been in danger and now he has drawn the battle lines. Demons cannot risk exposure but also cannot have this man going around killing them. Either they must eliminate him or control him through his associates.

Jaml slides his blades into the scabbards strapped on his back. He checks his gauntlets to make sure they are secure. He slides knives into his boots and the small of his back. Black leather covers his chain link coat, legs, and arms. Everything but his head. Satisfied, he turns to leave.

"Wait!"

Reaper turns to find Karva standing there with a full length hooded cape in her hands.

"We made this for you. Hope it helps."

Reaper takes the cape and throws it over his shoulder. He fastens it together before looking in the mirror. The black cape blends in perfectly with his black leather.

"Thank you. You are too kind. I know it will serve me well." Reaper walks over the two women, gently kissing each one on the cheek.

He pulls the hood over his head, concealing his features completely. Seconds later he disappears into the night.

✦

Midnight has come and gone. Reaper continues to sit and observe the guests in the Isle of Pleasure. Manda brought six men with him to mourn the death of Baric. A closer look reveals one of the men is the soldier Reaper spared. The young soldier probably alters his story so he can be a victim and a survivor instead of a guard who did not pay attention.

The Isle of Pleasure is a renowned whore house in the south side of Colley. The red brick and clay building is detached from the neighboring buildings and is surrounded by a large garden. Two fairy shaped waterfalls sit on either side of the building. The garden is filled with flowers of all kinds, emitting a pleasant aroma in the gardens. On the porch of the building is a wooden covering that protects the lounge furniture that welcomes the visitors.

Rich red tapestries cover the windows preventing prying eyes from viewing the beautiful women inside. The tapestries also prevent prying eyes from recognizing anyone already inside the place enjoying the hospitality inside.

Reaper moves silently from his place of concealment. Silently he moves around the building, looking for guards or traps and finding neither. Satisfied of his recon, Reaper finds a side door in which to slide in unnoticed. He reaches over his shoulder to pull one of his short swords free. Silently he enters the establishment.

✦

Karva rises from her knees. With her prayers finished, she sits on her bed and begins to study the scrolls that contain the word of God. She begins to read aloud the words, basking in the word when a loud smash fills her head.

She quickly runs over to the window, looks out to find nothing out of the ordinary. Confused, she turns to go to the door. Standing in her way is Queen Sera herself, appearing out of nowhere. The queen is wearing a gold dress that clings to her every curve. At the waist, the dress flares out to allow movement. In her hand she holds a small mace. The look in her eyes is none that Karva has ever seen. The pupils appear to be red.

"Your Majesty. I did not hear you come in. To what do I owe your visit this night?"

The queen casually strolls to the small table next to the bed. She looks around as if interested in the motif. She looks at the scrolls on the table, giving a disgusted sound at the sight of God's word.

"As you know, we are all in danger. There is a madman running through the kingdom, killing innocent people at will. And what I find surprising is this lunatic has friends inside the kingdom helping him."

"That is horrible." Karva tries to make her way over to the right where she can make a dash through the door.

79

"So answer me this, Sister Karva. Why is the church harboring this fugitive?" The casual behavior immediately turns hard. Eyes bore deep at the nun standing there.

"Your Majesty?" Karva realizes the door is her only escape route and the queen has positioned herself in the way. She contemplates screaming but knows it will do no good. Soldiers will assume the queen is passing out judgment and will look the other way. Karva knows she is alone in this.

"Stop playing coy with me. I grow tired of these games." Words fill the room with sheer hate and disgust, all aimed at Karva.

Who responds before thinking?

"So let's be honest demon. Yes, I know what you are. What would your subjects say if they knew who you really are!"

"Which means we must make sure no one in this hole of a kingdom finds out." A sinister sneer crosses the Queen's face.

✦

Must know where all the soldiers are before I attack. The worst thing that could happen is a soldier unaccounted for who creeps up behind me and kills me. Reaper moves down the main hall undetected. He finds piles of armor and weapons resting on the outside of five doors but no noise inside. As a matter of fact, Reaper cannot hear any sounds in the entire place. Quiet.

Sex with whores is never quiet. Men live out their fantasies through coupling with whores which often means loud sex, plenty of screaming and hollering. Some due to pain but all through pleasure. And yet there is no sound emitting from any of the rooms.

Must find the set of armor along with the prince's weapons. He continues to move along the hall until he comes to a corner. He peeks around the corner to find another hall, this one shorter. As a matter of fact, this hall only has two rooms. The room to the right has the remaining soldier's armor outside the door. Good, all soldiers accounted for. Time to double check the room to the left and ensure the prince is in there. Then it is time to go to work.

Reaper moves up the door on the left and listens. The sounds of a female laughing along with a male. There he is. Good. Then a peculiar sound fills his ears. Slurping. The sounds of slurping are coming from the last soldier's room. Then the stench of blood fills his nostrils. The all too familiar smell of death comes from the room. Reaper cracks open the door and nearly vomits.

Inside is a scene only found in stories meant to scare the kids of a household. The room is well lit through candles arranged in the center of the room around a table. Silk curtains are pulled back to reveal the entire scene.

Stretched out on the table is a soldier. Reaper soon recognizes the soldier as the one he knocked unconscious in the woods. The soldier seems to be alive as a steady stream of tears runs down his face. He lies on the table, does not move.

Two females are seated on the other side of the body, facing Reaper. Their faces are buried in the torso of the soldier. That slurping noise that caught his attention is the whores slurping down the soldier's innards. Moans of pleasure escape the mouths of the whores as they feast on the soldier.

Eyes look up to fix on the man in the doorway. Reaper snaps out of his trance and dives forward but not fast enough. He does a forward roll but not before pain fills his back. A blade would have surely ended his life but for his chainmail. Instead the stab is thwarted and the blade opens up a gash across his lower back.

Reaper rolls to his feet and turns, swords raised, ready for the attack. He finds a brunette woman dressed in nothing but a robe standing in front of the prince. In her hand is a sword, red blood coating the edge. His blood.

"Well, well, if it isn't the righteous Reaper. Glad you accepted my invitation. Welcome to the Queen's Isle of Pleasure. Let me introduce you to her pets." A gleam of pleasure twinkles in Manda's eyes. He notices Reaper glancing over at the man on the table. Opportunity to stab another dagger of revulsion in. "Worried about that young man on the table, are you? Let me help. NO, he cannot move. Yes, he is still alive. Yes, he is feeling each tasty morsel coming out of his body."

At that precise minute, one of the whores takes a big slurp of the intestine. It sends Reaper into a rage. He launches himself through the room only to find the whores revealing their true nature, succubus. Their skin quickly takes on a red hue while fangs extend from their mouths. A tail appears along with growing claws where nails were once located.

Reaper's lunge sends him over the table, his sword slashing out, taking the top half of the succubus' head with it. He lands in front of the second one, kicks out, sending her flying back against the wall. He turns to look down at the man on the table. The young man is neither able to move or talk but his eyes beg for mercy.

"May God have mercy on your soul."

With a quick slash, Reaper opens the man's neck, killing him instantly. He runs forward, plunging both blades into the midsection of the second demon. He frees his blade but not fast enough. He turns his body and takes another cut on his upper arm. He stabs his sword into the face of the demon.

A scream alerts him to the next attack. He drops one of the swords to catch the demon at the neck with the newly freed hand. With the demon in his hand, he fills her chest with steel. He frees his sword but does not see the punch in time. The punch sends him sprawling against the wall. His back hits the wall and he instantly springs to his feet to face Prince Manda. The prince closes the gap with his sword raised, aiming to end the fight before it can begin.

Reaper raises his sword to catch the longsword. He rolls his wrist to slide the blade harmlessly away. He punches the prince in the midsection, staggering the demon. Reaper follows up with a series of punches that connect, staggering the demon even more. In his eagerness, Reaper forgets where he is.

A succubus lands on his back. Reaper screams in pain as fangs sink into his neck. He runs back until he pins her body against the wall. The impact causes her grip to loosen. He spins and stabs the demon in the stomach. He fills the poison entering his bloodstream. Seconds later his left arm goes numb.

Reaper realizes his dire situation. The longer he remains, the likelihood he will end up on the table like that soldier was. He kicks out behind him, catching another fiend in with his foot. He picks up his other blade before making a dash for the window.

Two succubus stand in his way, knives in hand. Reaper stops right in front of them. He avoids the slash on his left side by turning his body. He stuns the other demon by elbowing her across the jaw. He shoves the first demon back before plunging his blade into her face. He pulls his blade out free and turns where the second succubus is still dazed. He slashes across her neck, opening up her throat. She grabs at the blood squirting out, trying to stop the flow of her own life.

Reaper does not wait to see what happens. He lunges out of the window and takes off running. He bleeds from several small cuts but the wound on his neck is flowing freely. The gash in his side is also dripping steadily.

He runs through the woods to where his horse is tethered. He slides his blades back into their scabbards so he can run faster. He dodges tree branches and jumps over stumps in his haste to escape his death. He spots the horse right where he left her. He grabs the reins and hauls his tired beaten body into the saddle. Pulling the reins to steer, Reaper kicks the horse into a gallop.

All of a sudden he pulls the horse to a stop. A statement made by Manda while gloating just hits Reaper. "Glad you accepted my invitation."

A trap. All this was set up as a trap. The pieces begin to fit in place for Reaper. The information was leaked so Reaper would get it. They counted on him to do what Reapers do, hunt and kill demons. They knew all along that he would come after Manda, to finish this. How dumb can I be? To walk into a trap that is not well hidden. Wait till I tell. Wait a moment. If they knew I would hunt them. They also knew I would not bring the axe. Killing me was not the purpose! Pulling me away from the axe was!

Reaper spurns his horse faster.

Despite the moon passing its zenith for the night, there are a number of people still on the streets. This slows Reaper considerably as he is forced to dodge people as he tries to get to the monastery. He finds himself apologizing repeatedly after his horse bumps repeatedly into people. Off in the distance, he can see smoke rising from something near the monastery. At least he hopes it's near the monastery.

He spurns his horse even harder, feeling a sense of guilt for falling for the trick that very may cause the life of Karva and Canda. He gallops through the square to pull off in the direction of the monastery. Grief and guilt plague his mind.

Once the monastery comes into view, Reaper jumps out of the saddle at full speed, drawing his swords as he approaches the monastery. He immediately notices the broken door at the front of the monastery and the lack of anyone anywhere outside the monastery. He cannot hear the multitude of voices that is heard throughout the building.

He lowers his shoulder and bursts through the door, sending wood chops spraying the hall but hitting no one. Still nothing. No sound. Visions of finding a raped dead Karva and Canda fills his thoughts, driving him even harder. He forgoes the traditional walk inside the church, sprinting down the hall swords at the ready.

Karva's door is open. The last time he was in the same situation, it was a false alarm. Somehow this feels different. There is an air of dread hanging like a blanket over the entire chapel. Hands grip the hilts with almost inhuman strength. He turns into the doorway, prepared to battle a host of demons. Almost wishing the king and queen would be present so he can end this now. The bloodlust boils inside his veins, ready to explode into a killing machine.

The room is destroyed. Karva's desk is broken in two with one half propped up against the wall and the other half shattered against the far wall. Her bed is also smashed, straw thrown out all over the room. Reaper looks in every corner of the room and finds no one.

Axe of Damnation.

Reaper sprints back into the hall to find Karva staggering towards him. He quickly slams his swords back into their sheaths, offering his arms for support to the beaten and weary Karva. Their eyes locked and Reaper can see the pain on her face and instantly knows the suffering the lady endured. He holds her close as she breaks down, great sobs soak his shirt. He gently picks her up and carries her to another room to lay her down gently on a bed.

He comforts her, rocking her as she continues to cry. Neither say a word. Karva lets out all the pain and anguish she has endured while Reaper battles the guilt that rages inside him. It is hard to be God fearing when you watch your actions cause others pain.

✦

Jaml drops to his knees. The sight in front of him is almost too much to bear. The altar is completely destroyed, wooden parts shattered beyond repair and the masonry sections blown to small pieces. The two sections in the floor are missing, along with the axe that was hidden inside.

Now only has he failed to protect Karva and Canda but little Allie is missing. If she is dead or harmed, Jaml vows to make each and every demon and demon worshiper pay with their lives. Pay with a slow death. A little girl does not deserve death, not at the hands of a demon. She is innocent in all this.

He failed the monks. They entrusted the axe to his care. The demons have been unable to get their hands on the sword and what does he do? He hand delivers the axe to them. The first part of the Apocalypse is in the hands of Lucifer's worshippers.

Anger quickly fills his body. Pity is not going to get the axe back, nor is it going to find that little girl. And heaven knows pity is not going to make the situation right. Jaml rises to his feet, a sense of determination and resolve begins to fill him. He drops to a knee.

"Our Heavenly Father. Please forgive me for my sins. Forgive my shortcomings and bless all those around me. Shield me from despair and reveal to me your plan, your method and your way. Take this humble sinner and transform me into your weapon. Your angels have forged me into what I am today and I ask you to use my gifts for your purpose. Guide me to your child Allie and watch over the ladies who have opened their homes and heart to me. I ask and pray this in your son's name. Amen"

Jaml turns to leave when the word Amen catches his ear. He quickly turns, a blade flies to the source of the word to thud solidly into a plank of wood.

"Show yourself. The next one will not miss."

A rustling and moving of wood, one of which hosts a particular knife, reveals a human figure. Jaml reaches for another knife when the figure looks up. Jaml finds himself looking at Indi, dirty, weathered, and hungry but yet alive!

Both men sit at the wooden long table in the kitchen area. Jaml is able to scrounge up some bread, venison and wine to wash it down. The man sitting across from him has gone through a lot by the stories he tells. Stories that have meaning for Reaper but not for Jaml.

"This is good!" Indi tears another piece of meat off into his mouth. "Anyway, I was the middle man between King Taras and Desi. The scum merchant was supposed to deliver a package to me for the king. Desi did not know the buyer was the king just that I was to get the goods and deliver it to the king."

"You never knew what the package was?" Curiosity perks up.

"No, no. That is not the way it works. Follow me closely. People in your country are so different." Indi shakes his head before continuing. "Lots of the products sold by Desi are not exactly achieved through legal means. So when there is a buyer, he uses a middle man to conduct the purchase. This way no one knows who the buyer is if something goes wrong. The middle man gets a commission for running the risk of the transactions. Got it?"

"Yeah."

"Good. The package came in and the Reaper fellow showed up as well. Anyway, once Desi found out Reaper was looking for the package as well, he upped the price, nearly doubled it. When the king refused to pay the upcharge, the package disappeared. Then Desi dies and all hell breaks loose. The king wants my head for the loss of the package and he takes control over the docks. Rumor has it he is still trying to find the sword but has little luck on it."

"I am sorry my friend for all the trouble I have caused you." A bewildered look crosses Indi's face. "I am also known as the warrior priest Reaper. I did not know my actions would put you in mortal danger."

Indi stands there with his mouth open, his mind desperately trying to wrap itself around the words in his head. He continues to stand there, unable to move, staring at the man in front of him.

"Now I must retrieve the Axe of Damnation before the other artifacts are gathered up and hell is unleashed upon the world. But first, we must move you all to safer places. Then I must retrieve your beloved Lady Tyra. I will put you under my protection. I want you to help Canda with the arrangements to move Karva. In the meantime, I will go get your wife and bring her to safety."

Both men nod, rise from the table and move out, their missions are clear and failure is not an example. Jaml turns to leave, his itinerary clear. He takes one step and collapses, the weight of the world pressing down on his wounded body is just too much. Indi reaches out, catching his friend right before he hits the ground.

Indi lowers Jaml the rest of the way to the ground. As he pulls his hand from underneath his friend, he notices the wet feeling on his hand. He looks to find blood. For the first time since talking with Jaml, Indi notices the wounds suffered by his friend. Fear captivates his next response. To scream for help.

Chapter 6

Sunlight. No. Candlelight. The soft light brings focus back to his eyes. He looks around. Where am I? Am I dead? He rolls his head to the side, still struggling for focus. He realizes that he is in a simple room, the walls blank of any decoration. The table on the far end of the room has a pitcher and cup, nothing more. One thing he can rule out is death. This is too simple to be heaven and too pretty to be hell.

He rolls his head to the other side. His swords rest against the wall and a large bundle sits in front of them. He attempts to sit up and is met with a sharp pain in his back, enough to bring tears to his eyes. He chooses to lie back down but his throat is parched. Thoughts of yelling for assistance wander into his mind but he refuses to lean on anyone. That leaves one option which he chooses. Go back to sleep and wait.

✦

Words invade his rest. Words being spoken but not spoken to him. He struggles to swim through his consciousness to those words. Sleep and rest is what he needs and they have felt so good. But those words, those words draw him from the comfort of sleep, beckoning him to wake up, join the living, and finish his mission.

Eyes crack open, searching for the source of the words. He smiles at the sight of Canda standing over him talking to Indi. Canda seems to be cautioning Indi about something.

"Not a good idea. We need to wait till Jaml wakes. He will know what to do."

"But" The word from Indi is frantic, full of fear.

"That is the end of this. I have to get back to Karva."

"What is wrong with Karva?" Canda and Indi quickly turn their heads to find a very awake Jaml looking at them. "Well, please tell me what is wrong with Karva?"

Canda rushes over to Jaml's bedside. "She obtained some injuries. Nowhere near the ones you suffered but she is resting peacefully. It is good to have you back."

"Can I have some water?" Jaml licks his lips, "Please"

Canda quickly runs over to the table and pours water into a goblet. She quickly returns and gives him the drink. He drains the goblet in seconds. Canda grabs the pitcher and refills the cup.

After four cups of water, Jaml takes a deep breath and relaxes. Indi quickly approaches the man in the bed, disregarding the attempts by Canda to wait.

"Before you passed out, you said." His voice quivers, almost pleading.

"How long have I been out?"

"Two days."

"Man. What is the matter with you?" Jaml's attention turns to Indi.

"I will tell you in a second. What happened?" Despite his problems, Indi shows compassion to his friend.

"Got jumped and beat up for a few coins that is all."

"That is all? That's a lot."

"Ok. Now tell me about your problems." Jaml's interest has peaked and he wants to know what kind of trouble Indi has gotten himself into.

"King Taras offered me an enormous amount of gold for four artifacts. I have acquired two of them through my contact who recently was killed. The king wants his goods. I know I am next on the chopping block! I don't know what to do." Indi's voice borders on hysterical. "I need to keep my wife safe. What should I do?!"

"We move you all tonight and you will be reunited. That I swear." Jaml watches the man break out in tears. "Now please leave me, I need to rest."

The lady in the room moves slowly. She frequently winces at the pain in her body. She has been beaten recently by a demon and now understands the cruelty they are capable of. She limps over to the table and pours herself a goblet of water. She gingerly moves back to the bed, sits down and attempts to enjoy the water. A soft knock is heard at the door.

The door cracks open slightly.

"Sister Karva?"

The response begins with a smile.

"Come on in Jaml."

The door opens and Jaml walks in slowly, partly from his injuries but partly due to guilt for putting this lady in harm's way. She does not need to carry the burden. Jaml feels like a fool to rush off like that only to find it was a trap. Her death would have been on his hands and he has a hard time accepting it.

Jaml enters the room and closes the door. The two spend a couple of hours talking about the events of the past days. He describes the night at the brothel. How the entire thing was a set-up orchestrated by the prince. Her expression changed when he told her about the women there being succubus. She flinched when he described the man on the table being eaten alive. Despite the happiness in her eyes, Jaml cannot shake the feeling that he is responsible for her injuries. They prayed and fellowshipped, reveling in each other's company.

That afternoon, Jaml sends word to his house. The reply is five servants entering into the church. Under Canda's supervision, the servants move Karva and Indi to Jaml's house and under his protection. He accompanies them, makes sure they are settled before returning to the church.

Later that evening, Jaml once again dons on Reaper's garb. Once again becoming God's warrior. Black leather fits over the repaired chainmail, twin swords strapped on his back, daggers fitted in his boots and his cape, the newest part of his uniform, flows from his shoulders.

Under cover of night, Reaper once again goes out into the night to do God's work.

This night is not for vengeance or death. This night is all about protection and love.

Reaper moves through the shadows of the city without detection, taking notes on evil situations in the city that he will have to address later. His movements bring him quickly to the mansion of Indi.

He sits in the alley across from the mansion, not willing to make the same mistake twice. He watches the front of the mansion. The front gate is closed, not uncommon, but the presence of two guards is new. Not the traditional soldiers used by the Dukes in the kingdom. These are no regular soldiers but mercenaries, paid killers who know no allegiance except to money. Both mercenaries carry long tulwars in their sashes. A quick look on the roof shows two more guards, these armed with crossbows. These two are walking along the top of the house, eyes continuously surveying the alleys and streets connecting to the house. Looking for something to shoot at and kill. Reaper studies their movements and soon learns their patterns. Important since he does not want to take lives tonight.

The guards on top of the house move in their predesigned movements, allowing Reaper to slide over the wall without detection. He gently lands behind a bush and waits to see if anyone raises an alarm. While waiting he looks around his surroundings. Much has changed since he last walked through here. The disappearance of the duke plays a huge role in that. Gardens are still in place and taken care of but things have been moved. For security purposes.

A guard house has been erected to the other side of the mansion. Barracks have grown in size to accommodate more men. There are two more guards standing at the front door as well as patrols walking around, three to be precise.

Satisfied he is undetected, Reaper uses the shadows to move up to the main house. He waits patiently for the patrols to walk by before sliding into the kitchen area. Servants still sleep, their duties for the day coming closer. He pulls his cloak over his head, masking his face.

He moves silently down the hall. The extensive training from his childhood as a monk is being used now. Years of learning about God's writings along with extensive physical training and weapons training has forged Jaml into the perfect weapon. God's writings have given him purpose and a sense to kill only when absolutely necessary, otherwise use non deadly force. He takes no joy in killing unless it is demons, even then it is only necessary.

He silently makes his way down the hall. His footsteps make no noise while the shadows hide all his movements. The ability to hide in shadows serves him well as there is a guard standing in front of his destination. The man has been there a long time as his eyes begin to flutter, his body sways, and the constant shaking of his head tells of a man losing his battle with sleep.

Reaper wraps his arm around the guard's neck and covers his mouth so he cannot raise an alarm. He wraps his other arm under the soldier's arm and squeezes, cutting the air off. The soldier struggles for a few seconds before his body goes limp, losing the battle of consciousness. Reaper slowly lowers the man to the ground.

Reaper snuffs out the torch across the hall from the door to make sure no residual light invades the room and wakes Lady Tyra. He slides inside the room silently, pulling the guard inside. He quickly secures the legs and arms of the guard as well as tying cloth through his mouth. Satisfied the guard poses no more threat of raising the alarm, he moves to the sleeping chambers.

He looks inside. The large bed rests on the near wall, opposite the window, making any shot near impossible with an arrow or crossbow. On the right is her clothing bureau furnished with a mirror. To the left is a huge porcelain tub. A quick look around shows no traps or alarms inside the room.

He silently walks up to the bed to find Lady Tyra sleeping on her back. He gently, at first, places his hand over her mouth. Fingers tighten on her jaw. Her eyes pop open and instantly she screams but finds the noise muffled by his hand. He places his second hand on her chest, pinning her to the bed. Her legs kick wildly as she attempts to get free. It doesn't work. Despite all her efforts, she soon realizes she is pinned to the bed at this monster's will.

Her body stiffens and the movements cease. Reaper keeps her mouth covered but slowly removes his hand from her chest. Her eyes go wide but she does not attempt to free herself. Instead her eyes are glued on the dagger at his side and the two swords strapped on his back. Her life is truly in his hands. She realizes he can take it at will. There must be a reason for the monster to keep her alive instead of killing her in her sleep. Her eyes grow big again as thoughts of rape enters her mind.

The man reaches up and throws his hood back, revealing the handsome face of Jaml.

"Shhh. I need you to be quiet please. Can you do that?"

She nods her head slightly, unable to do more since his hand prohibits such movements. He slowly removes his hand from her mouth, ready to place it back if she attempts to scream. She does not.

"I am here to get you and take you to your husband." He watches her eyes gleam in joy.

"He lives? Why are you dressed like that? Are you armed? How? Where is he? Is he harmed?"

Jaml quickly hushes her, not wanting to alert any guards that might be about.

"Listen. I am here to get you out but I need you to listen and follow directions."

"I don't understand why we must leave in secret. Why can't we leave out the front door? I am the Lady of the house."

Jaml smiles. He has to remember that she does not have any knowledge of the recent events.

"It must look like an abduction, else you and your husband's lives will be forfeit."

"If you think that's best. I don't understand but my guess is; this is not the best time for such a conversation."

"You are a woman wise beyond her years." In the back of his mind he knows if she begins to compromise them, he will have to render her unconscious, and he hoped dearly not to have to do that.

Fortunately Tyra is able to follow. With the guard still passed out and bound, there is no one to watch them leave. Tyra does as she is told, following Jaml's instructions to the letter and nothing goes wrong.

Until.

The duo stands behind a tree out of sight. Jaml looks around the garden, waiting to see the familiar patrol of the guards but no guards walk by. Jaml looks up at the ceiling and sees no guards on duty. He looks towards the front gate and once again there are no guards.

"Where are my guards? They get paid well."

An uneasiness comes over him.

Jaml places a finger over Tyra's lips, telling her to stop talking. Again he looks over the ramparts where soldiers were once walking. He knows there is something wrong but cannot put a finger on it.

Then a shadow flies across his face. He looks up to spy the source of the shadow. Overhead there are two figures flying, both appear to have two arms and two legs and a set of wings. Demons!

"We got to move."

"What are they?"

"NOW!"

He grabs a hold of her hand and takes off, almost causing Tyra to fall down. He weaves across the garden, staying in the shadows as much as he can, desperately trying to avoid the attention of the humanoids above.

The two make it to the wall and immediately Jaml realizes his problem, getting Tyra over the wall without the demons seeing. He contemplates for a second before settling on a solution.

He moves the two of them along the wall towards the front gate. If the guards inside the compound are gone, surely the ones at the gate are also dispatched. If they can make it out of the compound and into the populace before the demons see them, they will be safe.

The demons have not been too keen on people knowing they are there. And that is what Jaml is banking on. He moves the Lady and himself through the shadows and foliage till they reach the front gate. He reaches for the handle when all of a sudden the gate opens.

Standing at the gate, in their way, is a demon dressed in soldier's armor. He stands a full head higher than Jaml. His skin has an ashy gray tone to it, as if considerably burned or already dead. His hands are enlarged, knife-like nails extending from his fingers. On the top of each hand is a long knife attached to a gauntlet. The demon has discarded the bulk of the armor and is dressed in breeches, a chest plate which is covered by a manteaux. With one movement of his hand, he pulls the cape off his shoulders revealing heavily muscled arms.

"For God's sake." Mutters Jaml.

"God has nothing to do with this Reaper." The deep bellow of a voice booms from his chest. "Milord figured it would be only a matter of time before you came for the whore. Milord is always right."

A soft boom is heard behind him, turning Jaml's head around to see one of the demons in the sky, a succubus.

"Look at what we have here. Morsels for milord." The woman stands a little taller than Jaml with a distinct red glare to her skin. She is completely naked save for the tulwar blade in her hand.

A shaky voice comes to his ear. "Where is the second flying demon?"

Without taking his eyes off the demon. "Gone to get reinforcements. Luckily these two are going to want to finish this before they get here."

"Why?"

"The more it takes to kill us, the more hands to split the reward. If nothing else, these creatures are greedy."

"That's reassuring."

"When it starts, get out the door and run to my villa. You will be safe there."

"What about you?"

"Either I will beat you there or you and the rest of the group will be leaving immediately."

Reaper slides forward while gently pushing Tyra to the side. Neither demon nor succubus makes a move towards her. Good, I am the target. He slowly slides his twin swords from their scabbards, holding them out to the side, tips to the ground.

"You better hurry, your help is fast coming and that means less gold for you."

The words carry like a battle cry, sending the demon into action. He charges Reaper with wanton abandon, attempting to end the fight before it starts. He swipes his blade downward, aiming to cleave the man in two. Reaper sidesteps the slash, bringing his blade forward to stab the creature. With inhuman speed, the demon is able to leap back to safety.

Almost on cue, Reaper spins to a knee, bringing his blades to a cross over his head. The clang of blades is the only thing saving him. He kicks out, catching the succubus at her knees. She howls in pain. Her wings lift her into the air, away from danger.

Reaper runs to attack the demon, his swords moving faster than the eye can see. The demon is forced to retreat, his blade and demonic speed no match for the heavenly skilled warrior attacking. The demon moves his blades frantically trying to block every blow from Reaper.

But he cannot.

It isn't long before his blade tastes demon blood, a slash across his left arm. Reaper feints a stab with his left, drawing a cross block from the demon. His right slices deeply into his upper arm, rendering it useless. Blood flows from the deep gash in the demon's arm, tendons have been severed. The demon howls in pain as he backs away, attempting to get away from the fury known as Reaper.

The succubus lands behind Reaper, aiming to plunge her sword between his shoulders. She lunges forward, glee spreading across her face. Her expression changes. Reaper spins to her right, the blade disappearing inside his cloak. He continues to spin which causes her arm to get pulled violently with it. She tries to fly away but her arm is completely entrapped in his cloak. He jerks his cloak violently, pulling her off balance but to him. Her mouth flies open wide as she feels a sword slide into her stomach. She looks at the man who has killed her, his expression without emotions. Her features soften as her life blood gushes quickly from the mortal wound in her midsection.

"I would pray for your soul but you are nothing more than Lucifer's work."

"And what does that make you Reaper? Nothing more than a weapon yourself."

"You don't have a soul. Bid your master hello in the underworld." He watches her eyes begin to flutter, death fast approaching. "What that makes me is a child of God, saved by his blood and grace."

Those are the last things the succubus hears on earth.

Reaper shoves the body off his blade before he turns to face the demon. The demon stands steady, his left arm dangles useless. He growls at the man before attacking.

Reaper blocks a thrust with one sword, cutting a slender line across the demon's midsection with the other. The demon screams but rushes forward, hoping to kill his prey before he dies. Reaper spins out of the downward chop, spinning into a kick at the demon's knee. The creature falls to his knees, Reaper crosses his blades behind the demon's neck and with one violent stroke the demon's head rolls away from the body.

Reaper watches the body topple to the ground, blood pouring out of the neck like wine from an open flask.

Reaper looks up to find Tyra standing against the wall, her face a mixture of horror and bewilderment. Her hands rest near her mouth.

"Thought I told you to run once this got started."

"I tried. My feet were like concrete. I had to see a Reaper in action. I am glad I did, otherwise I would never have believed it."

"And if I had died?"

"I am glad you didn't."

Reaper chuckles at her comment. He extends his hand, which she takes and he leads her out of the compound to never return. She steals a quick glance at what was her life but no more. She is wanted by demons and knows they will never let her live now.

She shudders.

♦

When Jaml emerges from his room the next morning, the mansion is in full operation. Servants move around, cleaning and performing their duties. Many greet Jaml as he walks by, which he returns in kind. Part of his training under the angels is how to handle people from other walks of life. Treating your fellow man with kindness and sincerity always rewards with loyalty and a desire to make the person proud.

He walks down the hall dressed in black pants with an oversized white shirt. Since his escapades the previous night, Jaml was too tired to rise for breakfast and now he is paying for that decision. His stomach is growling like a cornered bear ready to strike.

He enters the kitchen to find a plate of roasted duck, sweet bread and rich wine waiting for him. Standing at the basin next to the table is a middle aged lady, gray streaks run through otherwise black hair. Her plump body is hidden well underneath her oversized dress. Years earlier, this woman was extremely beautiful but a hard life, death of her husband, and responsibilities of the housekeeper has begun to take its toll. Nevertheless, her warm smile greets Jaml as he sits down to eat.

"Well look who the cat has drugged in. I am so glad to see the master of the house be able to rise with the midday meal." Her sarcasm is not well hidden beneath her smile.

Jaml smiles and shakes his head. This woman was hired as the housekeeper shortly after his arrival, less than a year after the death of her husband. She was unable to have children so Jaml has become her adopted son. He does not mind her sarcasm, it brightens his day and keeps a smile on his face. Her motives are pure at heart.

"Well it is good to see you as well Anna. I hope my absence did not cause you too much trouble." Jaml tears off a piece of bread, shoving it into his mouth and enjoying the taste.

Anna walks over and playfully smacks Jaml on his head.

"Don't you get smart with me. Just because you are the lord of this house does not mean I will not lay you over my lap and give you a whoopin'"

Jaml looks over his shoulder, ready to spout another remark when he notices Anna's eyes begin to water. Instead of the remark, he takes a deep breath.

"What's the matter?"

"You of course. Just running around all night long, doing God knows what. You have a wife here and responsibilities." Tears begin to run down her cheek.

"Sit"

"Milord, I will not be lectured about my place..."

"Sit. Please." Anna, like everyone else under his roof, does not know who he truly is and his mission. They only know him as Duke Jaml of Erdine, coming to the kingdom of Colley to open trade for his country.

Anna sits down across from Jaml. She takes her apron which is marked with grease and filth and wipes the tears from her eyes.

"I was hoping you would sit next to me." A smile cracks across his face.

"Don't push me milord." She returns the smile. "I know this is none of my business but you are like my son. And it was not so long ago that I lost my Ail to a sword. He was going drinking with his friends when three cutpurses attacked them. Ail and all his friends died that night, all for nine copper pieces."

"You have never shared that with me." Jaml reaches over the table to gently grab her hands, a moment of comfort to provide comfort as she opens up.

"I know milord. And now I see you going out all night, obviously with your Duke friends and I worry. I worry milord that you will not come back to us. And then Mary comes to me the other day and shows me your sheets. And do you know what I saw? Blood milord. It is not my place to tell you what to do milord but with that Reaper man running around killing folks. Oh milord, you must be careful!"

Jaml has to fight back the urge to smile. Now is not the time.

"Anna, I need you to listen. Not everything is what it seems and I owe it to you to tell you everything. As of last night, your lives are in danger and you need to know why. My name is Jaml and I was trained by the heavenly host themselves. I am Reaper. God sent me here to eradicate Lucifer's minions. To make a long story short, there are demons in the kingdom. Lady Helena was one of them. These demons are after certain artifacts and my calling is to stop them. After last night I am afraid that they know who I am. I am worried that I have put your lives in danger."

Anna sits open mouthed at the story, uncertain whether to laugh at the joke or scream in horror. She decides to wait.

"And Duke Indi and his wife?"

"Their lives have been threatened. They are also under my protection."

"And who is going to protect you? This is a heavy burden you carry milord. Who is going to have your back?

"God. Anna. God always has my back."

✦

The room is dark, lit only by two candles that sit on a table in the center of the room. The sweet smell of Jasmin incense fills the room, soothing the nerves of anyone who enters. The floor is bare as are the walls. The table at the center has six chairs around it.

The den of Skulls is a foreboding room where evil is planned and executed. Some say the room stays dark so no one can see the amount of dried blood that covers the wall. Others say it stays dark because Bala consorts sexually with demons and Lucifer himself. And still others have speculated Bala is a dark witch who performs devilish sacrifices inside the room. Regardless of whose story one believes, the room emits an aura of death in it.

The leader of the Skulls, Bala, is a ruthless leader whose actions lead to rumors of her involvement with demons and such. Her willingness to slice open a throat instead of hearing excuses has catapulted her status from petty thief to the ultimate assassin and thief.

Bala is the only one sitting at the table, her eyes constantly taking in her surroundings. A person does not attain her status without making a few enemies along the way. In her case, she has killed people just to show she can. No reason, no remorse. A paranoid person she is not. She knows there are very few, she cannot think of any people who can best her in a fight. At any point in time there are four to six assassins watching her back. Her constant surveillance is more habit than worry.

The door in front of her opens to admit two men. The two men are absolute opposites in who they are. The man on the right towers over most men. He is a blond giant from the harsh tribes of the north. She has cultivated his desire for power and violence to become her second in command. He does not have the brains to ever lead the Skulls but his muscle is well placed as second. His hair hangs in a ponytail below his shoulders. He wears chain link mail under leather, his gauntlets the only visible metal on his body. A great two handed battle axe rests across his back.

The man on the left is shorter than Bala herself. His face is clean shaven, unlike the burly beard of the northern giant, which includes his head. He wears nothing but leather armor, his speed and agility essential for his business. A long sword is strapped across his back along with bands of knives around his right leg. Daggers are also strapped around his waist. His walk is light, like a nimble cat on the prowl. His eyes dart back and forth, always aware of violence. Always craving the violence.

The two men walk up to the table and give the Skull hand signal, the signal of the cross followed by a thumb across the neck. Bala is pleased.

"Sit."

Both men sit across from her. When she holds the leader meetings, these two men flank her on either side. This sends a clear message. To cross Bala is to cross all three. Certain death. She waits patiently as both men get comfortable. Satisfied that she has their undivided attention, she looks at each man before speaking.

"As you know Desi is dead." Neither man reacts to this news. "Unfortunately we have lost the package and what a package it is. Whereas we assumed it was some royal trinket and will fetch a pretty price on the market. What we are dealing with is a relic of heavenly power. No longer a small trinket but a game changer. The power it has will make us more powerful than the king himself. Or we choose to sell it and become the richest people in all the kingdoms. It will be our choice"

She rises to her feet, leaning forward on her hands which are placed upon the table.

"Reaper is after the relic too. And that would ordinarily cause a problem."

A smirk creeps over her face. Each man knows that look, it is a look of death. Someone is going to die soon, very soon.

99

"I recently found the solution. You see, Reaper is none other than Duke Jaml. Yes that dark skinned duke is none other than the thorn in our side. And the only man capable of robbing us of our destiny. I have also found out that he has a soft spot for Sister Karva. Reaper has recently returned from somewhere and is held up in his house. I need someone to get Intel for me so we can obtain some leverage for our dear guardian. I need to know where Karva is. I want to know how fortified his house is, how many guards and how heavily armed. I want to know the names of every servant in that house. Including the housekeeper. When we strike, they all die. Every single one of them. No one is to survive and that is why I need everything. Everyone but dear ole Karva, she is to remain alive but brought to me. After so many deaths, this Jaml will see the light in my argument. If not, he will know he is responsible for every single cut I will put on Karva. Then we will deliver the body to his doorstep."

"Why don't we just torture and kill him." Kreen nods his agreement to Miko's statement. "Less mess for anyone to question. As much as I enjoy this killing, it is bound to bring a lot of attention to us. No other guild has the balls to carry this out. Authorities will look only at us."

"Because my clever Miko, I want to keep both of you alive. We can lure Reaper out and attack but after what I saw the last time, only I and maybe one of you two make it out alive. I don't like those odds."

"Point taken." Miko hunches his shoulders. She is right.

"Kreen. Since you are my second, you do the scouting on the monastery. No killing yet. Just information. Miko, you run scout on the mansion. Each takes five men and gets it done. I want answers by dawn."

The real mission is the mansion. She needs to know the layout of the mansion, guards, and who is staying there. Miko will provide her with the necessary information. How many guards are on duty during the night and what is their walking pattern. More importantly, who is seeking refuge inside his mansion? If she is to deal with Reaper, she needs every advantage possible. She may need hostages in order to make an exit.

One of the reasons she is sending Kreen to the monastery is she knows everyone has abandoned the church. Earlier reports already confirms this. Kreen would have put up a verbal fight if Miko is sent out on an important mission and he isn't. That verbal argument could quickly have the two men go to swords. Losing a leader at this point is not an option. Her goal is too close and she needs both men to accomplish it. Second reason is that Kreen kills first and asks questions later. She cannot afford to have the real mission thwarted by an overeager killing machine.

"And if we find the opportunity to search for the blade?" Miko questions.

"Information only at this point. Killing and finding the sword at another time." Her response is calm, calculated.

A look of disappointment is on Kreen's face. Information only, no killing. Kreen looks forward to the killing. He has killed a whole party when his instructions were to kidnap a particular male. The man in question did not survive the trip back and Bala lost any chance for the ransom.

She knows Kreen is needing permission from her to kill.

"Yes Bala. Will of the Skulls are without question." Both men recite the creed. They bow slightly then exit, leaving Bala to herself.

"Yes, without question. That sword will be mine and with it, I will rule this kingdom. Once a petty thief, soon to be queen. All by my own hand."

She breathes in the incense, reveling in the sweet smell. She gets up from the table and walks upstairs to her chambers, the lone room on the top floor. Once the Skulls obtained the bar from the previous owner, Chall, Bala immediately sealed all rooms on the third floor, save one. She loosened up many boards on the staircase and the floor above so if anyone was to walk on one of the boards, it would collapse along with the entire staircase. All windows on the third floor are boarded up, no entry at all. Crossbow traps flood each room on the second floor save hers. Death to anyone who does not belong there. Many men, to include some of her own, have tried to eliminate the competition only to find their bodies riddled with crossbow shafts.

Bala knows the sequence by heart, since she put them in, and does not trigger any traps. Safely to her room, she closes the door to enjoy quiet time.

A lone figure atop the monastery welcomes the night. Keen eyes search the night for something to kill. Pain drives those eyes that have seen countless deaths at the hands of evil. It is this same evil that he hunts tonight. People that he considers friends have been hurt, all for the purpose of getting him. He will not have this. People will not suffer on his watch because of the good he is trying to do. Now those same people that have hurt his friends must bleed. And bleed a lot.

He awaits the inevitable attack from the king. He has just killed one of the king's sons and prevented the king from obtaining the Sword of Darkness and bringing about the Apocalypse. And the fact that the king is a demon makes the attack all too predictable.

Allie.

Through all the battles and heartache, he almost forgot about the poor little girl. He frantically goes through the events of the past week and tries to remember if he saw her body. He has not. Now tonight has more than death attached to it. He has to find the poor little girl with the wonderful smile and innocence.

He moves out of the shadows and movement catches his eye, so he slides effortlessly back into shadow. He watches intently until he sees it. A figure also moves in the shadows. He tries to discern who it is but cannot. He watches for a few moments and there, another figure. A smile comes across his face. He finally counts six total figures moving amongst the shadows. He admires their skill as they are almost undetectable.

Soldiers have never been that good to move like those are. And in all his years of fighting has he ever seen a demon, let alone six, capable of moving in the shadows. Would the king hire assassins to do his job? Possibly. He is going to have to find out.

Reaper silently moves across the rooftops, gaining on the patrol of men ahead of him. Thoughts of who would attack a house of God enters his mind but quickly leaves. These are thieves and assassins, they have no scruples and if the price is right, they would kill their own mother.

Reaper knows if these assassins were worth their price, one would stay on the rooftops and another would patrol near the entrance. That gives him an opportunity to eliminate one third of the force without raising an alarm. An opportunity to gather information might arise as well.

True to form, one of the assassins stops at one of the rooftops overlooking the entrance to the church. Reaper has three minutes tops before the second one is in position, then killing one without the other raising the alarm would be impossible. His best bet is to kill the first one and let the second one wonder where his partner is.

Reaper hits the ground running, needing to get to the building in question before anyone notices him. He stops on the south side of the house, his back flat against the wall. He waits for a moment to make sure no one saw his approach.

Satisfied he remains under the cover of night, Reaper slides the hand grips on before scaling the wall. On each grip are four hooked spikes. With a little effort, the spikes can be pushed into the hard clay walls and support the weight of a man. A second set is placed around the knees giving the impression of a large cat scrambling up the wall.

Moments later Reaper slides himself over the edge of the rooftop, close to the ground lest the guard has time to warn his group. He quickly scrambles along the flat rooftop, the hooked spikes further assisting his endeavor. Using the spikes the same way as he did climbing up the wall, he glides across the roof.

He coils himself right behind the guard, much like a predator before springing on his prey. Reaper strikes, his hand closes around the guard's mouth, pinning the guard's upper torso to him, a dagger appearing in his hand.

"May your will be done O'Lord and may the blood of your son forgive the blood that I must shed in your name. Amen"

With those words uttered, the dagger slides across the man's neck, opening up the windpipe like butter. Reaper holds him still, waiting for the thrashing about to stop. It only takes a moment before the guard's strength pours out of his neck, flowing onto the ground without any resistance. He quietly lowers the dead man to the ground, closes the eyes and leaves the dead man to meet God.

The second guard peels off from the main group to remain at the front door. He quickly surveys the area, looking for anything or anyone out of place. Outside the three beggars squatting on the other side of the road, he cannot see anything. There is nothing strange about the three men crouched across the street. All are clad in dirty brown tunics, obviously clothes thrown away and later recovered. Nowhere to carry a weapon. No threat.

He searches along the rooftops for his counterpart. The mission is very clear. Once in position, he will signal with three wide arm sweeps with the response of four arm sweeps. He moves several steps from the door so the other man can readily see him. The night torches located away from the opening casts a dark shadow right in front of the door but away from the door, the moon illuminates the streets well.

Three sweeps and wait. The soldier counts to thirty and tries once more. Where is the buffoon? He signals once again and waits. No answer. By this time he is getting agitated. Kreen is going to have someone's' rear and it is not going to be mine. The man signals one last time and waits. As before, there is no response. He turns to signal inside to let them know what happened. Five arm thrusts and he will have covered his rear from Kreen and more importantly Bala.

A shadow moves and the man turns to see what disturbs the air. He is no less a full turn when a blade flashes, slicing through his windpipe like butter on a hot day. The man feels a hand placed on his chest right before he is shoved against the wall. He scrambles to scream. Even in death he will assist his brethren. He opens his mouth wide and a soft gurgle escapes, not the loud boom of a voice that he usually carries.

The man suddenly feels tired. The steady flow of blood is fast weakening the man before him. He allows himself to be braced against the wall. The man feebly twitches before coming to a complete stop.

"May your will be done O'Lord and may the blood of your son forgive the blood that I must shed in your name. Amen"

Reaper lowers the man to the ground. He looks up at the two beggars on the other side of the street. He gives the two men a quick nod and in return the men shake the copper pieces in appreciation.

God's assassin slides into the monastery and quickly disappears into the shadows again. He listens intently, trying to locate the men inside. From the crashing and throwing, they are not too afraid of being discovered. And all the easier to pinpoint where they are.

He continues to move through the shadows, unseen or unheard by all inside. To his calculations, there are only the four remaining from the initial group that are in the monastery. He quickly moves around the monastery, ensuring there are no other potential hostages inside. Satisfied that they are alone, it is time for him to take action.

Reaper stands in the main church sanctuary beside the main entrances, watching the four men inside ransack the pulpit. Three men turn over benches and search along the walls, searching for something. The fourth man watches with intensity.

Realization suddenly hits Reaper. The fourth man is Kreen which means Bala is obviously going after the sword. But why? Reaper can only speculate Bala must have a buyer or why else is she searching so hard through a church.

Despite the mask and the darkness of the church, Reaper can sense the frustration building in Kreen. His body movements tell a man who is on the verge of losing it and going on a killing spree. He begins to pace the floor like a wild animal caged. Searching becomes destruction, pieces of furniture and artifacts are thrown and shattered against walls. Kreen finally shoves his way past the men and heads out into the halls of the church. Probably to search rooms for the sword.

Reaper crawls up the rafters until he is directly over the three remaining men. He watches the men for a second before letting go of the rafters. As he falls from the ceiling, Reaper grabs his swords.

Reaper lands in a crouch, his cape billows outward, adding confusion among the three assassins. Reaper's blade swipes across the first man's throat, opening it up like a ripe grapefruit. The assassin grabs at his throat, attempting to hold the sudden rush of blood in. He drops to his knees as the river of blood flows from his neck down the front of his once black tunic. He falls to the side dead.

The second assassin tries to grab for his longsword strapped to his back. He grabs the hilt and that is all he has time for. Reaper slams both swords into the assassin's chest. His eyes grow wide feeling his life flow from the two blades. He has no time to yell or defend himself before his life is snuffed out. Reaper kicks the body off his blades,

Third assassin has time to pull his knives from his waist and instantly attacks Reaper without sounding any alarm. What a prize it would be to hand Bala his head. And what rewards he will receive when he delivers the head. No one will interfere in his kill, not even Kreen.

The assassin is surprised when Reaper sweeps his blades away with a sweep of his short swords. Assassin follows it with a double stab to the midsection. Reaper steps back from the extension of the arms and spins with his counterattack. Reaper's foot extends over the outreach arms to connect with the assassin's jaw. His head snaps back and leads the way for the rest of the body.

The body crashes into a broken pew, shattering what pieces that were left. The man rises to his feet to watch Reaper stalk him. He realizes Reaper is speaking as he closes the gap.

"...forgive the blood that I must shed in your name. Amen"

The assassin has no time to figure out what Reaper is saying or the meaning. Short swords appear as blurs in the hands of Reaper. The assassin finds himself retreating, his knife skill no match for Reaper's blades. Each thrust is followed by a stab or slice, blinding the opponent with his speed. In a matter of seconds, the assassin feels a blade slice across his chest. His leather armor is no match for the steel which bites clean through the armor and skin underneath.

Before the assassin can respond, Reaper is upon him once more. The assassin feels another cut, this time across his upper left arm. Reaper quickly attacks to his right, forcing the assassin to defend with his injured arm. Within seconds the blade tastes blood once again, this time slicing through the injured wrist, the hand still holding the knife hits the ground. The assassin is about to scream when his vocal cords are severed, dropping him first to his knees then to his face. Dead.

✦

How dare she treat me like a groveling dog? I am supposed to be her second and she has me gathering information from a church. I am one of the greatest killers in all the kingdoms and my talents wasted on this search. If I was Skull leader that damn sword would be in my possession and this castle would be at my knees. And Bala would be my bitch.

Kreen paces like a caged animal, waiting to pounce on his prey. He continues to fume about his situation when the sounds of smashing wood invade his ears. Then silence. It is the silence that disturbs Kreen. If they were smashing wood then the sounds would continue but instead he is hearing nothing. Something is wrong.

The giant man pulls off his mask and draws his battle axe from his back. Anticipation of battle brings a glee to his face and a trot to his step. His trot becomes a gait and evolves into a full run, bloodlust has invaded his soul. He cannot see anything but the blood that is being spilled. He only hopes his assassins have saved him a little bit to kill.

He bursts into the main sanctuary to find three dead assassins. Not the picture he imagined. Hoping to kill a little, instead seeing his men dead. Someone will pay. He looks around the sanctuary to stop at the lone figure crouching on top of a case. The figure looks familiar but he cannot see underneath the hood. The cape encircles the entire squatting body.

"Stranger, you do this?"

"Yes. I will kill anyone who desecrates the church, a holy place." Reaper's head is down, Kreen still does not know.

"Do you know who I am? And who you have killed?" Anger creeps into his words, Kreen is beyond irritation.

"Yes. May your will be done O'Lord and may the blood of your son......"

"What are you doing?" Kreen begins to chuckle at the man crouched before him. "Giving me my last rites?"

"Yes." Reaper removes his hood, giving Kreen his first look.

"You!" Kreen tightens his grip on his axe. In a small corner of his mind, Kreen knows he cannot beat Reaper in a fair fight but his ego will not acknowledge that fact and pushes it further into his subconscious. The only thing on his mind is to see this fool's blood soak the floor. He will have his head or else die trying. Adrenaline fills every part of him and dying is not an option.

"It is done, Kreen. This is the part that I give you a chance to drop your weapon and repent your sins. Your soul is dark with sin as you sit here and destroy a church. My Jesus demands that I offer you redemption through his blood."

"Oh I forgot. You worship that Jew they nailed to the cross." Kreen bellows in laughter.

"That Jew is the only thing keeping you alive right now. Repent so that I can show you your salvation."

"Screw you!"

Reaper smiles.

107

Reaper unfolds his body in a leap, his cape flows behind him. Kreen raises his axe to block the twin swords of Reaper. The left blade clangs down onto the shaft of the axe as expected. The second sword smacks the axe upward. Reaper lands and slides underneath the raised shaft. His left sword slides across the midsection of Kreen, slicing through the leather and chain link armor to create a red line. As he finishes his slide, Reaper spins to a standing position, cutting Kreen across his back.

The thief screams in pain and lunges forward, away from the attacks. He rolls to a standing position before turning to face Reaper. The flow of blood is steady from both wounds.

Both men run to close the gap. Kreen brings his heave axe downward, trying to cleave his adversary in two. Reaper moves to the right, the axe blade slamming into the ground where he once stood. Reaper kicks out, catching Kreen's leg at the knee. Kreen screams from the strain of ligaments at the knee. He tears his axe free from the wood and swings backwards.

And slices nothing but air.

Kreen spins around in a complete circle, searching for Reaper. His search ends when Reaper drops down in front of him. Kreen looks over Reaper searching for an opening, someplace where he can get an advantage. Reaper stands in front of him, swords pointing down, and blood dripping off of both of them. Kreen's blood. The battle rage once again fills his body and Kreen lunges forward.

Reaper reverses his grip on his swords, bringing them to waist level. Kreen swings his axe, aiming to cleave the man in two at the waist, instead his swing is once again blocked at the shaft. Reaper steps forward, head butts the man and watches as Kreen stumbles and falls.

Kreen scrambles to his feet, stars dancing in front of his eyes, blood finds another outlet, his broken nose forcing him to breathe out of his mouth. Kreen stares at the other man through dancing lights, trying to push out the pain and refocus his efforts. He raises his axe in a defensive stance but no attack comes.

The thief shakes his head clear and Reaper moves forward.

"Why is Bala looking so hard for the sword?"

A look of surprise crosses Kreen's face before he bellows out in laughter.

"Tonight is not about the sword, it's about you buffoon! You are going to die but not before every one you love is bled dry!"

Canda! Karva! Indi! The realization hits Reaper hard. The guild is going after him and all he cares about. He looks at the wounded man in front of him, not with mercy but a message must be sent.

Reaper launches himself at his adversary. Kreen is too tired and too drained from the wounds he has suffered to stop him. Reaper stabs forward, sending his blade into Kreen's neck. The blade does not stop until the hilt touches skin. Kreen's eyes grow wide with astonishment at the speed and the pain he knows will soon end. The thief attempts to talk but only gurgling sounds can be heard.

Reaper pulls his blade free and swings it hard. Kreen's head flies from his body to thump and roll across the church floor. The headless body simply crumbles to the ground, wood soaking up the massive amounts of blood that flows from the neck.

"Reaper?"

The soft voice reaches his ear. He spins expecting to find more thieves standing there with his friends in tow, instead he finds himself looking at the one person he wants to see, Allie. Huge weight of guilt washes from his shoulder. He stands fully erect, a smile creeps across his face. Reaper quickly sheaths his swords and runs over to the little girl. His arms embrace the little girl, lifting her up in his hug. They stand for what seems like an eternity embraced in love.

Finally he pulls her to arms' length and looks at the little girl in the face. "Are there others?"

"No. I am the only one."

"How? It does not matter. You are safe and I need to get you to safety."

"Are you going to kill someone else?"

"That is not my intention, little one. The Lord's work is not to kill but to prevent death. I must talk with someone and hopefully the killing will stop. I don't enjoy killing."

"Do what you must, just do it with the right heart."

"God knows I try."

A disturbance. There is a disturbance in the air and Bala senses it. She has not achieved all that she has without being somewhat paranoid. Her gut feeling screams danger. Bala slowly and silently moves from her cushions where she was sleeping. Her fingers wrap around the slender dagger that is always near her hand. She slips to her feet, watching for any movement that occurs. Something is different, out of place, or maybe even extra and there is something that is not quite right in her room.

"You seem worried."

The voice booms loudly inside the otherwise silent room. She quickly spins, dagger raised to strike, to find a hooded figure sitting in the corner, hooded pulled over the features that identify a person.

"If I came to kill you, death would have already claimed you."

She relaxes a bit. The person makes a valid point. There would be no sense to wake her to kill her unless he was crazy or had some sadistic call for vengeance. She hunches her shoulders.

"Then why are you here? You invade my quarters and sit there to watch me sleep? You don't seem the type to fantasize like that. That being the case, you know who I am but I don't know anything about my intruder. Care to share?"

"My identity is not an issue." The figure pulls back his hood and reveals himself.

"Reaper. Of course." She grips her dagger, knuckles turning white against the strain.

"This is a simple warning."

A large sack appears in the air flying towards her. Bala watches him instead of the sack, waiting for an explosion of movements, his attack. It never comes. Instead the sack hits the floor with a loud thud before rolling to her feet. Her eyes never leave him.

"Go ahead." Reaper appears relaxed, as if he was lounging at home.

Bala reaches down to untie the sack, her eyes fixated on the man in front of her. She is successful in untying the sack and reaches in. She feels hair. Fingers entwine into the hair and she pulls the object out of the sack. Her eyes betray her astonishment as she finds herself looking at Kreen. His mouth hangs in open, locked forever giving his final battle cry. His eyes stare blankly into space. The only movement is the drip drip of blood onto the floor.

"Kreen has looked better." Her face remains unemotional, stern, unforgiving. "What are you saying? All you give me is a dead man."

Reaper steps down from the perch and walks to the window.

"Stay away. The church, my house and everyone associated with them are off limits. Do not come or you will find nothing but your death. Do not send and I will not have to come back. Do you understand?"

"You invade my home and kill my people. Then you stand smugly to tell me what I can and cannot do? How dare you!"

"I have killed only the ones that desecrated the church and none other. No one in your home has died by my hand. No one in your home knows I am here. If you do not leave my people alone, you will live the remainder of your days looking over your shoulder. You see Bala, there is no place in the world that can save you from my wrath. You can have all the security known and as I have done here, I will get to you. And I will kill you." Reaper steps onto the shelf. "One more thing. Stay out of my way."

"And if I don't? Are you going to come and hunt me down then as well?"

"No but your men will die."

Reaper launches himself into the night sky.

Bala stands motionless, the dead head of her second in her hand. She lets go of the scalp to hear the soft thud on the floor. She takes several deep breaths, formulating a plan, looking for the next step in achieving her goal. She will have to reevaluate her position and what can be done.

Minutes later her door swings open. A confident Bala strides out of her room and over to the banister. The room is filled with her people. Thieves come and go, dropping off their latest take of goods to give to the Skrull way. Several men sit at benches, taking in the goods and counting the money. To the left are her assassins, waiting patiently for their neck call to duty. The next opportunity to slit a throat or cause an accident. In the meantime, they sit and play cards, sharpening weapons or preparing themselves for a mission already assigned.

She tosses the head of Kreen over the rail. The thud it makes when it lands on a table catches everyone's attention. Every eye is on their leader Bala who simply says.

"Get Miko here now!"

The room erupts as men fly out of the door in search of Miko.

Chapter 7

Princess Jala strides confidently down the castle halls, her hair flowing behind her. Her black dress reflects that mourning of her brother's death, yet the design is distinctively hers. The front of the dress is cut to a point right above the navel, revealing the inner slopes of her breasts. The slits along the side of the dress come up nearly as high as the front comes down. Her sandals match the color of the dress, accentuating her long beautiful muscular legs.

Many guards along the way have been caught staring at her. Their stares are met with her scowl and immediately the soldiers snap back to attention. She knows the women of the realm do not approve of her dress and often refer to her as unladylike which does not bother since this body is nothing but a shell for her true form. She wears the skin as she wears the clothes, for effect and nothing more.

She walks right by the two soldiers stationed outside the counsel room, despite the objections of the soldiers. She opens the double doors and confidently walks in, one of the guards trailing after her. Inside is a large square table at the center of the room with twelve chairs around it. Normally the chairs belong to the area dukes but since Taras took the throne they have not been used. The table top is a clay representation of the kingdom with neighboring kingdoms as well. Along the walls are huge tapestries, each depicting a major battle of the kingdom. On the west wall are no tapestries as not too long ago hung tapestries of Jesus Christ.

In front of the blank wall are two thrones. The one on the left is larger and encrusted with sapphire and topaz gems along the backrest and armrests. The seat part is red velvet with a matching footstool in front. The throne on the right is slightly smaller. The headrest and armrests are encrusted with pearls, matching the color of the seat. Resting in the chair is Queen Sera. King Taras is standing in front of the tapestry depicting Lucifer's casting out of heaven.

He turns to face his daughter, the soldier leaving and closing the door with him. Satisfied that they are alone, the king walks over to the war table, looking over the region. Dressed in chain-mail with a broadsword at his side, the king looks as if he is going into battle. The long red cape is the only piece out of place on him. On his head rests the small gold crown, the one that is worn into battle.

"Jala."

"Father."

"We have suffered. The death of your brother. The loss of the sword. Hell, we are losing." Tara pauses and takes a deep breath. "Master is not happy."

"Then why does he play these games?" Jala's volume begins to rise, her frustration evident. "Why not just attack and smash the church, find and kill everyone inside to include Reaper and be done with it?"

"This is why you are my most trusted." He gestures his approval to his wife, arms outspread to show his approval.

"Because these humans are fickle. Yes they sin willingly and enjoy it. No they do not attend church services but if we move openly against the church, you best believe these humans will find religion once more." Sera rises from the throne and walks over to stand next to her king. She wears a much more modest traditional mourning dress. One that reveals nothing while clinging to every curve on her body. Black lace around the neck and wrists brings the outfit to the proper occasion.

"Fine." Jala folds her arms in a show of anger. "So now what? Reaper has to pay for this. He has to bleed for killing Manda."

King Taras chuckles in his amusement.

"Do not worry Jala, Reaper will bleed and die a slow death. We have another matter at hand. Master has told us that the Scythe of Death is located here." He points to a small mountain range south of the castle. "I need you to go get it, alone."

"WHAT?!"

"Calm down Jala." Taras continues to chuckle as he speaks. "How is it going to look to the humans if they see a platoon of soldiers leave with the princess riding at the helm instead of Baric?"

"Like the princess is going out to meet some prince."

"And when you return? And the men tell of your exploits and what you brought back?"

"I like that a whole lot better than the princess is dead while off on a trip. I kind of like this life, it suits me."

"Stop, you're killing me." King Taras continues to laugh. "You will be well protected. Your entourage will meet you here." He points to a clearing next to the river. "From there you will proceed south and retrieve the scythe."

"And who is my protector?"

"Dwan."

"Nice. I guess I need to pack."

A smile crosses Jala's face. She turns and strides out of the room, confident in her mission and ready to guarantee the success. Especially with Dwan watching her back.

✦

"Where are you going?"

Canda stands in the doorway to the bedroom she shares with Jaml. With her hand on her hip she looks as menacing as she possibly can. Her simple white sundress hides her womanly figure well with just a trace outline. The front extends all the way up to her neck. Her hair drapes over her shoulders

Inside the room is Jaml, shoving supplies into his back. Black trousers and a white top is the customary travel attire for a duke, fitting the profile perfectly.

"You know I have to do this. They have the axe and the sword is still up in the air. I cannot afford for them to get a second weapon of the apocalypse and expect to win. Who knows when that sword shows up? That could very well mean at any point in time they will have three of the four weapons."

"How do you know where to go?"

"The monks also gave me the location of the other weapons."

"So you are going after both of them now? That could take up to one year at best. What about us? You yourself say the demons are out to get us. What do you think will happen to us when you leave and they realize you are gone?" The annoyance in her voice begins to increase the volume.

"I promise that I will only retrieve one at this point. Since the scythe is closer, that is where I will go. That one is south and will only take a couple of weeks. I will be back before you know it." He gently holds her at her shoulders before embracing her in a hug. He holds her at arm's length to make sure she is ok.

"I am going with you." The response catches him off guard. He stands dumbfounded at her statement. He struggles to comprehend and struggles to hide his annoyance.

"What? Are you crazy? I very well can be killed doing this. And if things get desperate, I may not be able to defend you. I will not have your death on my hands because I want company for the trip." Jaml walks away from her, reaching for his bags.

"I am going, husband and that is the end of it. I will not stand idly by and wait for your carcass to be dumped on my lap. I would not be able to bear it."

"I am touched Canda, but our marriage is not real. We have never officially been married. I'm sorry but no."

Jaml turns to leave the room with his satchels but finds Canda remains in the doorway with no intention of moving. Jaml sighs heavily and wonders what it will take to end this conversation. Then she hits him with another statement. One that smacks him in the face just as hard as the first one.

"Either I travel with you Jaml or I follow you. Your choice. Either way, I am going."

Jaml drops his head to his chest and leans back against the wall. He calms his breathing and says a prayer asking God to help him. After ending with an Amen, he looks up at the lady who masquerades as his wife.

"Well are you going to pack or is that the only thing you are wearing?"

A smile flies across her face. She turns and runs from the room to go fetch another satchel and supplies for the trip.

Meanwhile Jaml stands there watching her, a simple nod shows his approval.

The evening of the third day finds two horses emerging over the top of a hill. The terrain in this part of the kingdom is predominantly plains and rolling hills. The cloudy skies have not produced any rain during the journey but the brisk northern wind keeps overcoats pulled tight over shoulders. The mornings are the worst as frost greets everyone at daybreak.

At the bottom of the hill is a small town, no more than five hundred people. This town is no different than any of the other multiple towns that sprinkle the countryside. There is no wall of protection or castle in the center. Along the outskirts of the town are pens for farming animals. To the north of the town are fields where crops are grown. Women can be seen tilling the soil and harvesting crops.

These towns are ruled by a magistrate, usually provided by the ruling king or prince, who is tasked with collecting taxes for the king as well as providing legal solutions for the townspeople. For many of them, the magistrate is the closest thing to a king that they will ever see in their lifetime.

Within an hour, the couple ride into town. A few people look up and take notice but no one talks or challenges them. Jaml realizes these are simple folk, far from the intrigue of the castles. These are the people that Jaml is ultimately fighting for. The ones who live day to day, worship God and do the best they can.

Two young boys appear out of nowhere asking permission to take care of the horses. He looks up at Canda who smiles at him, her way of giving permission. They dismount their horses and get directions to the Boar head where they will be able to get a bite to eat and a soft palate to sleep for the night.

The two tired travelers walk across the street towards one of the largest buildings in the town. There was no second floor but the back end of the building extended the length of another building. Over the door is a large wooden sign, a painting of a boars head on it. They enter to find themselves looking over a large open bar area. To the left is the actual bar with a bartender running back and forth, filling orders. He is a thin wiry man with greasy black hair and a thin long mustache. His long apron is covered in grease stains from the many plates of meat served.

Across the rest of the room are tables and benches for the patrons. Only a few tables are occupied but it is early yet. Many workers have not wrapped up their work for the day. Walking around the room are two young ladies, both look to be in their early twenties. Both wear the simple brown dress with a stained apron. Both ladies move throughout the room with ease, checking on customers to ensure their needs are met.

Jaml leads Canda over to the bar.

"Excuse me."

The bartender looks over with a wide smile.

"Nice to see fresh faces in my establishment. What can I do for you?"

"How about dinner for two and a place to lay our weary heads?"

"Then you have come to the right place. Heck, it's the only place." The man seems to enjoy his little joke and laughs. Jaml follows suit. "My name is Luk. If you need anything, please let me know. I will have one of my barmaids take you to a table while the other one takes your things to a room. Please enjoy the hospitality of the Boars head!"

It isn't long before Canda leans back from the table, her hunger completely sated. She takes another drink from the strong ale of the Boars head and wipes her mouth with the napkin. Across from her, Jaml continues to eat the chicken and potato stew in front of him. She smiles at the man, wondering what things go through his mind.

Three men walk over to the table. The man in front is a portly man, dressed in an emerald green suit. His hair is completely gray and thin on top. No facial hair can be seen. The red sash draped over his shoulder reveals him to be the local magistrate. The tall man on his right has a full beard and hair that drapes from his ponytail to the middle of his back. The sword draped at his side, the only one Jaml has seen, reveals his stature as the local law enforcement. The last man stands nearly as tall as the second man. His head is clean of all hair, as is his face. The long brown robe and stance reveals him to be one of God's priests. One of Jaml's brothers in Christ.

It is the short man who speaks first. "Welcome to our small town. My name is Moe and I am the local magistrate. This is Cur and he is our sheriff. And lastly is Lar and he is our priest. As you can see, we are a small God fearing community and rarely do we see visitors. May I ask who you are?"

"Of course. My name is Jaml and this is Canda, my wife. I am the emissary from Erdine, a small kingdom beyond the great desert. We are just passing through on our way to Rome where we hope to speak with the Pope. I want to thank you for your hospitality. We will be rising at sun break and will be on our way."

"I did not know God's word extended beyond the great desert." Lar looks astonished at the prospect. "God has truly blessed us then."

117

"Indeed we are." Moe extends his arm to Jaml as a token of friendship. Jaml immediately stands up and grasps his arm. "Welcome once again and let us know if there is anything we can do for you."

With no further discussion, the three men walk away, Moe constantly greeting people he passes. Soon all three men have exited through the door, leaving everyone to their drinks.

"That went well." Canda's smile expresses her sentiment.

"That it did. Almost too well." Jaml sits back, rewinding the entire situation in his head.

"Oh Jaml." Canda giggles while shaking her head.

Jaml eats another spoonful of stew into his mouth. Hot food is always good but whoever cooked this stew knows their way around the kitchen. Yet his mind continues to replay the conversation that just happened. The magistrate seemed almost too friendly and eager while the priest seemed scared. The law enforcer was almost disinterested or maybe not completely there.

✦

The only light in the room radiates from the lone candle in the center of the room. Kneeling in front of the candle is a lone man, features masked by the darkness. The figure places his forehead on the ground, motionless.

Wind from an unknown source begins to swirl inside the room. Peculiar since there are no windows in the room. The kneeling figure does not move, makes no motion despite the unknown wind. The wind begins to concentrate over the candle, yet the fire does not quiver. The wind swirls in a circle as a mini tornado.

A shadow begins to form over the whirlwind. Starting as an unfocused blur, the shadow begins to take shape. Colors can be discerned until the shape of King Tara comes into focus. The kneeling figure does not pick up his head but speaks nonetheless.

"Milord. What is your bidding?"

"Two figures are coming your way. A black man accompanied by a white female."

"They are here master,"

"Good. They are very dangerous to our cause. They are after a relic that my daughter is also searching for. If they are to find this relic, we all are in danger. Our way of life will cease to exist. Understand?" The image of the king speaks in a whisper, meant only for the figure to hear, yet the words are important, lifesaving.

"Of course milord. Shall we end their lives tonight?"

"No Dwan, do not reveal yourselves to the people of the village just yet. Allow them to leave and then hunt them down. And devour them entirely!"

"Yes milord. It will be done."

The shadow fades away as the cone of wind dissipates into nothing. All is gone except the candle in the middle of the room, never quivers, never disturbed.

Elsewhere in the town, Jaml walks into the church for his evening prayers. He places his palms together in the symbol for prayer before breaking the threshold of the church. Inside is a bowl of holy water. He walks to the bowl, gently dabs a finger into the water before drawing the cross on his forehead. He places his hands back together and quietly walks in.

He makes his way to the front of the church before kneeling before the cross. He lowers his head to begin his prayers when another presence kneels beside him. He does not look up.

"Father."

"My station tells me to answer my son but I feel it is I who should be confessing to you. Father."

"How did you know?" Jaml does not look over at Lar. There is no need to.

"Call it intuition. A priest should always be able to recognize another man of the cloth."

"Good." Jaml's voice becomes hard. "What is going on here?"

"What do you mean?"

"Don't play with me. There is evil in this town. What is it and why have you not stopped it?" Jaml finally looks at Lar, steel dark brown eyes glare deep into Lar's soul. He winces under the scrutiny.

"What am I to do? People have come up missing. No remains to be found. I know there is evil here but I do not know who or what it is. I first thought it was demons but they leave evidence. It is as if the people either left without telling anyone or were eaten. I cannot tell which. I have asked for help many times. I have sent word to the king but I have not received any answer, let alone help."

"That is because he is a demon."

"How do you know?"

"I killed his son who had taken its true form."

"Then you are Reaper?"

"Yes."

"Then I urge you to watch yourself. Leave while you can. Whatever is here is evil and probably coming for you. All people come up missing in the morning. Watch yourself tonight Reaper and I will pray you make it out of here safely."

"Thank you Father."

Jaml smiles. He knows what is here. He will have to come back this way to deal with the evil but tonight he will finish his prayers and rouse Canda. They leave tonight.

"Lycans?" Canda sits on top of her horse watching as Jaml loads up a pack horse with supplies.

"Most know them as werewolves." Jaml jumps into his saddle and pulls his horse around by the reins. "We have got to get out of here, fast. I don't know how many there are. Don't want to have to fight our way out of a town full of them. Might not work."

"Aren't werewolves just a fairy tale to scare children?"

"No, just not many people have met one and lived. Kind of like demons. They don't just come by and say hi. Now let's ride."

With the reins of the packhorse in one hand, he kicks his horse into action. Both horses erupt into a gallop, followed by another horse, this one carrying Canda. The duo explodes out the south side of the town as if being chased by a pack of scavengers. Their horses reach the trail in seconds and soon are galloping through the woods.

Suddenly the sounds of howling dogs reach their ears. Jaml looks back to see a terrified Canda right behind him. Tears begin to stream from her eyes as the sounds of wolves appear to come closer. Jaml knows if the werewolves attack, she is not going to be of any use in battle. He knows he will be torn apart trying to rescue her. The decision is clear.

"Whoa!"

Jaml pulls the reins on his horse, pulling both horses to a stop. Canda follows suit, confusion and terror are the two main emotions spread across her face.

"What are you doing? We have to keep moving. Are you not hearing those wolves?"

"Canda." His voice calms her down a bit. "Take the pack horse and ride. Ride hard until you clear the woods. Once you get to the southern plains, you will see mountains. Go to the middle mountain and wait two days. If I am not there by then, ride back to Colley and Indi will know what to do."

"What are you going...? You don't mean to stand and fight, do you? Please tell me no. I cannot be out here all alone."

Jaml grabs her by the shoulders and pulls her close. Once their eyes lock, she calms down, breathing becomes normal as she gets her wits about her.

"There you go." Jaml gives her a quick hug. "Now go and wait for me there. I will be along shortly." He winks at her. "Trust me."

Jaml watches Canda and the packhorse ride off down the trail. Satisfied that she is not going to do something stupid like turn around to help, Jaml pulls his swords free from their scabbards and turns, ready for the lycans.

He senses he is being watched and slowly looks over his shoulder. He spots the silhouette in the tree. He turns to the other side and spots the other lycan lurking at the bush. The third lycan walks out in front of him.

"Impressive Reaper. I would not have thought you had the brain power to know your end is near." The lycan standing in front of Jaml is a full two heads taller than Jaml. Its shoulders are wider. The head resembles a dog with long fangs ready to tear into soft flesh. Muscled arms dangle at the side, each ending in a four finger paw, each sporting claws the length of daggers. The lycan stands on his bent rear legs, ones use to running and pushing but not standing. The entire beast is covered in fur.

"I will give you one chance to kneel before your master." Jaml turns to the left to face the lycan there. Words come out as growls where most syllables are found. "Accept his forgiveness and a quick death will be yours. If you refuse, I will have the pleasure of tearing you limb from limb."

"Take them. If you can." Is the lycan's response.

The lycan launches itself at the man in the clearing. Claws reach out, reaching for soft flesh to sink into. Jaml ducks under the lunge and immediately follows the lycan. He spins and leaps after the creature, landing on its back. Jaml reverses the grip on his swords and plunges the blades into the creature's back. The tips of both blades peek through the creature's chest, erupting from the skin like red pimples.

Jaml places his feet against the lycan and shoves the creature forward, off his blades. The lycan tumbles forward crashing into a bush. Jaml somersaults back to his feet waiting for the next attack. Astonished that neither lycan moved, he looks at the dead one, the one that now rises back to its feet and turns once again to face Jaml.

"Quicker than I thought. Not going to make that mistake again." The lycan stalks Reaper, aware of the speed of the man and precision he has with his swords.

Reaper moves to a fighting stance, awaiting the battle to commence. The lycan stops just out of striking range and glares at the man standing in front of him, contempt for what the man stands for. He lets out a growl, one that fills the woods like a lion after a kill.

Reaper does not wait. He closes the gap, swords coming to life in his hands. The first slash catches the lycan across his midsection and the second across his chest. The creature howls in pain but presses forward. Claws fly through, aiming to rip the face off the man's skull. Reaper spins with the slash while dropping to a crouch. He finishes the move by cutting the tendons in the creature's knee.

Another howl escapes as the creature falls to his knees. Reaper does not let up on the attack but moves in behind the lycan. A swift motion by the man and blood pours out from the slit across the Lycian's throat. The creature grabs his throat with both hands. He gurgles his disapproval before falling face first to the ground.

Reaper immediately attacks another of the creatures, gaining the element of surprise on his two remaining enemies and does not mean to lose it. He jumps in front of the first lycan, his swords again moving faster than the eye can comprehend. He slices both knees with his swords, cutting through half of the knee. Both legs collapse with a loud roar from the beast.

The third lycan seems dazed. He neither moves nor makes a sound at the battle before him. More importantly he does not move to attack Reaper. The monk stares at the lycan only for a second before realizing this Lycans is not going to attack.

Reaper turns and runs into the forest. He makes it through the initial brush before spotting a horse tethered on a branch. He grabs the horse and swings himself into the saddle while spurring the creature into a full run.

He knows the other two are healing and the chase will be on. He cannot figure out why his blades did not work. Is this a stronger demon that Lucifer has unleashed? Seems as his blades are useless against these new enemies. Reaper will have to deal with these questions later but right now he has to put as much distance between him and those lycans as possible.

Canda looks over her shoulder with worry. She drives her horse forward, trying to stay alive. Jaml told her to ride like the wind through the plains until she made it to the mountains. Ahead of her are the mountains, at least a full day ride out. Behind her is a cloud of dust riding towards her.

The cloud has gotten larger as the sun drives into the sky. From the distance, she cannot discern whether the cloud belongs to Jaml or the creatures hunting them. If it is Jaml, shouldn't she stop and wait? But doing that means sitting like a grape on the vine for the Lycans, if it is truly them. So Canda rides on, driving her horse to full gallop, wishing to see another dusk.

She thinks about letting the supply horse go, no need to hang on to the horse if it will only cause her to die. After much thinking and contemplating, she releases the supply horse, leaving all her concentration on staying alive. She looks back over her shoulder and the cloud is incredibly close. She kicks the flanks of her steed harder, hoping to go faster.

A short time later Canda looks over her shoulder once again, expecting to find the saliva filled jaws of the lycans bearing down on her. Instead she finds herself looking at a lone rider. A bald dark man approaches. Glee fills her eyes as she recognizes Jaml, with the pack animal in tow.

She pulls her horse up and jumps down, ready to meet her husband and protector. He also dismounts and catches Canda as she flies through the air towards him. They hug in relief. They just looked at death and both have come out unscathed.

"How is my husband doing? Are you hurt?"

Canda refers to Jaml as her husband but that phrase is only in word since there has not been an official ceremony conducted. Their arrangement came into fruition to his credibility as a duke from a faraway land. With a legitimate back story, no one is likely to ask what his real purpose is.

"Jaml! I am so glad to see it is you. I knew you would come back. Did you kill those Lycans?"

His smile slowly turns into a scowl.

"We must hasten as we are being hunted. My blades seem to be ineffective in killing the beasts. For what reason, I do not know. As long as we move fast enough, they will not be able to follow. Besides, getting to the southern mountains first to retrieve the scythe is much more important."

Jaml helps Canda back into her saddle before climbing into his. He grabs the reins of the horse and the two head to the mountains in the distance. Their sights are on retrieving the scythe but inside each wonders if they will see Colley again. Jaml has never found failure in his blades. For the first time as Reaper, his weapons are useless against a minion of Lucifer. Doubt creeps in his mind, how can I rid this world of evil if my tools are ineffective against them. I must pray on this and look for God's answer.

◆

The horse pulls to a halt outside the entrance to a cave. The figure sitting on top of the steed is dressed in a long red cape covering recently shined chain mail. A closer look would reveal the figure to be of a woman, her slender body encrusted in form fitting armor not like the bulky armor favored by the male soldiers.

She dismounts from her horse, dropping the reins to the ground. She pulls back her hood to reveal long jet black hair cascading over her shoulders. On her hip rests a longsword with two daggers sitting on her opposite hip. She pats the horse on the neck as she surveys her surroundings. Satisfied she is alone, Jala takes in the mountain air.

"It's good to be here."

Jala reaches inside the pouch on the horse to pull out a flint and a torch. A couple strokes later and the flint catches, providing Jala light. She throws the satchel over her shoulder and proceeds into the cave, confident when she again sees sunlight, the Scythe of Death will be in her hand.

The entrance to the cave opens into a large cavern. Stagalites hang throughout the cavern, threatening to fall and spear any intruder into this sacred place. The cavern itself could fit ten houses from Colley with plenty of room to spare. The only light inside comes from the torch in Jala's hand. She tries to scan the area with little success. The cavern is entirely too big.

As she walks towards the middle, the center stone catches her eye. What is simply another boulder begins to take shape as she nears it. Distance has altered the true shape of the stone but as she gets closer, the stone begins to look like an altar. The top is smooth, too smooth to be from natural wear, unless a large animal sat on top of it for hundreds of years. In front of the altar are remnants of ashes, obviously from whatever sacrifices were made here hundreds of years ago.

She reaches the altar and runs her torch over the top of it. Red stains splatter across the altar. Blood sacrifices. Teachings tell of human sacrifices from the Fallen to Lucifer. A way for the Fallen Leader to send a message to the Almighty that his creation is weak and God's love should have been reserved for the angels, not for man. Of course this infuriated the Almighty who decided to scatter the Fallen all over the world as punishment for their treachery.

Jala finds herself standing in one of the original Fallen communities before they were scattered. Suddenly she feels like she has betrayed her masters being in human form. She utters the words that transform her back to her true form, one of a succubus demon. With the transformation, her skin takes on a dark red hue as her fingers and toes elongate to form claws. Her hair grows until it rests just above her butt. Her armor falls to the ground allowing her wings to stretch to a full head breadth longer than she stands. Fangs extend from her mouth accompanied by rows of razor sharp teeth.

She laughs at the freedom from the human spell. And soon Lucifer will sit atop the heavens. She walks confidently to the altar, examining the stone for any clue. The top of the altar is smooth to the touch. She runs her hands over rough sides, not knowing what to look for but looking for any signs. On the far side of the altar Jala notices a smooth patch about the size of a baby's palm. A smile creeps across her face. She pushes the smooth patch inward.

A green light extends from somewhere on the far wall of the cavern. The light points at her forehead as if to bore into her head. Jala stands proud. Either her death or vindication is at hand. Either way she is confident that accepts her fate.

The light expands and scans her entire body, the beam moving up and down her entire figure. As quickly as it appears, the beam disappears, leaving Jala standing alone once again. She waits patiently for something, not knowing what, but something. She looks around, searching for the next step in obtaining her goal. Yet nothing happens.

Jala spits her disgust. All this travel along with the exposure to the Christ lovers and for what? Nothing. She turns away from the altar and stops. A smile once again gleams on her face. In front of her is an opening, one that was not there earlier. A glow emits from the opening, the same green glow from before.

She walks cautiously over to the opening, her senses raised for an attack. She peers around the opening and breaks out in laughter. Inside is a small room. In the center of the room is a green globe of light and inside the light is the Scythe of Death. Jala proceeds to almost skip over to the globe, happiness overflowing. She stops at the globe, takes a deep breath and slowly reaches into the globe. A warm glow fills her body.

Fingers wrap around the shaft of the weapon. Once she has a firm grip of the shaft, she pulls the weapon from the globe. The scythe is lighter than she thought, the weight evenly distributed over the length. She stares at the black blade, the inert energy she feels inside is soothing yet deadly. She instantly knows the weapon in her hand is powerful, more powerful than anything that she has felt before. Powerful enough to restart the Great War of Hosts and this time the outcome would be different.

She quickly lays out a red cloth on the ground. She smooths out the wrinkles before placing the scythe on it. She quickly wraps the cloth around the weapon before hoisting it over her shoulder. After taking a quick look around the cavern to make sure she did not forget anything, Jala heads to the entrance of the cavern. As she walks, the spell of human restores itself.

Jala walks out of the cave looking as beautiful a woman as there is on the earth.

All the joy of completing her task drains from her face as she walks out of the cave. Green eyes narrow to slits, glaring at the two people on horses there. To the right is a blond woman dressed in brown slacks with a matching vest over a white shirt. Canda. Next to her is the murderer of her brother, Reaper.

"I want to thank you for retrieving that for us." Despite the sarcasm, Reaper's features stay iron solid. "Please do not have me come get it. Not pleasant for you."

"Who do you think you are?" The words spit from Jala's mouth full of contempt. "A mere mortal who has taken up the cause for the Almighty? Is that your calling? Well, let me inform you, little man, the time is nearing where your God will fall to my Master and when that happens. I will rejoice over the cup of your blood that I will sip."

"Are you finished?" Reaper drops to the ground and immediately draws his two swords, stalking his prey.

"Do not be in such haste." The corners of her mouth rise in amusement. "My friends would like to have a word with you."

Reaper's eyes follow her gesture to the two lycans standing behind him.

"You humiliated one of their brethren and they would like to speak to you about this. Have fun." Her laughter echoes from the cave as she gets into the saddle and rides off with the weapon.

Both lycans stare intently at the man in front of him. Reaper knows his blades are useless against the lycans with his best bet being to injure them and race to safety. But first, he has to get Canda to safety.

"Ride Canda and don't look back. Get back to Colley." She can sense the desperation in his voice. The finality of his pleas. She knows this might be the last time she will ever see Jaml.

She wheels her horse around and rides out at full gallop.

The two lycans stand in front of Reaper. The brown fur is slightly shorter than the black fur one but both are easily head and shoulders taller than him. Their face is a dog, complete with canine jaws. Each paw, as it were, extends four claws like nails for killing.

With a loud roar, the lycans attack.

The brown fur reaches Reaper first, his paw swings wildly, aiming to rip the flesh from Reaper's chest. The man ducks low to allow the swing to pass harmlessly before moving past the lycan, his blades biting deep into the creature's stomach. In a normal fight, Reaper would be watching the lycan attempt to hold his intestines in place. Instead, the creature turns to face Reaper, the deep gash healing itself almost instantly. Even the fur grows back.

Reaper moves past the first lycan to attack the second one. The creature uses its dangerous claws as a sword, parrying and dodging the strikes of Reaper who relentlessly moves forward, striking and cutting at the creature in front of him. Reaper stabs forward only to have his blade knocked aside, which is what he wanted. The second blade follows the first, cutting across the chest of the creature. He brings his first blade back to cut a line across the creature's neck.

Reaper watches as the lycan grabs its neck, holding in the raging river of blood that is trying to escape. Satisfied the lycan is down, Reaper turns to face the brown lycan once again. The creature stares at the man, every ounce of energy focused on killing the man in front of him.

The creature swings with abandon, each one meant to cripple or kill the man in front of him. Reaper ducks each blow while delivering a cut of his own. Reaper's blades move through the defenses without slowing and each time he gets close, the lycan feels the bite of the blades. Soon the momentum switches and the lycan finds itself defending against the onslaught of the Reaper who is determined to end its life.

The lycan roars once more, this time to the sword sliding into its ribcage. Reaper knows it will not last long but he just needs to have a brief moment in which he can escape. A roar catches his attention. The creature in front of him is dying so Reaper knows it cannot be him.

Too late.

The pain of knives ripping across his back gives Reaper his answer. He screams, his back arched, as he tumbles forward, his back on fire from the pain. Blindly he spins, half hoping he dealt a death blow. But his slash finds nothing. He quickly backs up to feel the upward slash he knows is coming. His blades are in motion, giving him a few seconds to get his senses back. The lycan moves forward, this time he is the hunter.

Each swipe is met with a defensive move from Reaper, from parrying the claws with his sword to simply moving out of the way. With each attack Reaper finds himself moving backward. But more importantly, with each passing moment, Reaper is losing blood and he knows his energy will fail him. When that happens, he will be ripped apart by these creatures.

He ducks another lycan strike only to be caught by the second. The hand connects with Reaper's jaws sending the man flying through the air. He crashes into a large bush.

The man emerges from the bush, blood streaming from dozens of cuts. The only thing saving his jaw is he rolled with the strike, taking the brunt of the force with his roll. Nevertheless, his mouth is swollen, blood dripping from the corner of his mouth. His eye is shutting closed due to the enormous amount of swelling. Ever the defiant, Reaper spits blood at the brown fur lycan before launching himself at the beast.

Reaper plunges both swords deep into the shoulders of the lycan. The creature howls in pain, the blades sinking all the way into his body until the hilt hits the skin. The creature's scream is soon followed by a human scream.

Four dagger length claws imbed itself into Reaper's side. Reaper looks over his shoulder to stare at the black fur, contempt and rage bear into the creature's soul. Reaper rips the blade out of the shoulder, tearing a long messy hole in the shoulder of the creature. He turns and plunges the blade into the head of the creature. Reaper falls to the ground, unable to bear any more pain.

Reaper struggles to raise his head, the pain in his back and side is excruciating. Bright lights begin to bounce across his vision. He knows he is dying, the blood loss nearing fatal. He struggles to get to his elbows and knees. He turns his head to stare at the beast that will send him to heaven. Behind the two creatures is another figure. One that is lost in the lights of his eyes. The figure wears a full-length brown cloak with their hood up. He cannot tell if the figure is male or female and more importantly which side of this war does the fighter belong to. In the fighter's hand is a staff.

Then all goes black.

The two lycans watch the demon killer collapse in front of them. A slight rise and fall of his back reveal that he is still living, albeit just.

"Good. I'm not a hyena. I like the kill and the taste of fresh blood. This is going to be good." Brown fur licks his lips in anticipation.

"We need to take his head to prove our victory. Then we shall feast." The black lycan begins to look around, searching for an axe to complete the deed.

"You will do no such thing." The tone of the voice reveals it to be a female and the inflection reveals the anger.

Both lycans turn to look at the woman standing there. She throws back her hood, revealing a very beautiful woman. Her dark brown hair falls just below her shoulders, her blue eyes like steel. Under the cloak, the lady wears brown pants and a matching top. Resting on the ground behind her is a satchel.

"Fun time. You should not have interfered in business that is not your own. Now we shall have a little fun after our meal." Brown fur turns to face the woman, a mixture of lust and cruelty in his eyes.

"I think not beast. Now begone!"

She lifts her staff to the skies and instantly a bright light bursts from the top of the staff. The light is so bright that both lycans have to turn their heads and cover their eyes to protect them from the light. She lowers the staff to point it at the brown fur. A ball of light emits from the staff and brown fur erupts into a ball of flame. His screaming is heard miles away. His body is transfixed in one place. He cannot move, just stand there and burn to death.

Black fur opens his eyes at the sound of his partner's scream. Eyes grow big at the sight of the lycan burning alive yet making no actions to put the fire out. The sight is too much for the other lycan resulting in black fur dropping to all fours to escape as soon as possible.

The mysterious beautiful woman turns her staff towards black fur and watches as he erupts into flames, just like brown fur.

Satisfied that neither creature will be a threat, the lady quickly drops to her knees beside Reaper. She looks at the cuts across his back and quickly retrieves a container from her satchel.

She dares not move the torn chain-link armor for fear of causing more damage. She reaches inside the satchel to pull out a small container. Fingers pop the lid off. Fingers reach in to pull out a green paste like substance. She carefully but generously rubs the green glob along each cut. Satisfied that she has stopped the bleeding, she rolls Reaper onto his side. She globs up the four holes in his side where claws had punctured him not too long ago. Once again satisfied that she is successful in stopping the blood, she leaves him on the ground while retrieving the horses.

Draping an arm around her shoulder, she is able to lift Reaper to his feet. Since the salve has dried over the wounds, Reaper has swum in and out of consciousness. She walks him to a horse and steadies him as he swings his torn body into the saddle. She wraps a strap around his waist, keeping him in the saddle.

She climbs on her horse and takes his reins in her hands. She begins to turn the horses to the east when the wounded Reaper's words catch her attention.

"Colley. Please take me to Colley. As for Sister Karva."

"Then Colley it is." She pulls the reins again, this time heading north. To Colley.

"Thank you. You saved my life." His head droops with those words as if the words have taken all of his energy out of his body.

"Don't thank me yet."

She pushes the horses to a trot, knowing time is of the essence. She wonders if this Sister Karva is going to be able to do anything. He is so close to death.

Chapter 8

"**I**s he going to live?"

Jaml lies sideways on the bed, naked from the waist up, bandages wrapped around his midsection, covering the four holes in the front and the four gashes on his back. His breathing is shallow, fever rocks his body. He has not gained consciousness in the past two days. Not a good sign for someone fighting for their life.

Karva pulls a rag out of a basin of water and places it on Jaml's head. She has worked tirelessly over the past day to break his fever and work on his wounds. But her strength is waning and his condition has not gotten any better.

"It does not look good. His fever remains high and I cannot get him to wake up. I know he is fighting but unless we are able to break the fever I do not think he will make another sunrise."

Karva sits down in the chair beside the bed, exhaustion threatens to overtake her. She grabs a cup of water and drains the liquid in two gulps. She grabs another rag from the basin to wipe the sweat, dirt, and blood from her brow. Despite all she has done, she knows there is little else she can do. It is entirely in God's hands. And his own.

She wearily looks up at the lady standing there. Her clothing reminds Karva of monks, the ones that roam the countryside and live amongst the peasants, many are known as friars. But somehow this lady does not exert the soft gentle demeanor of a friar but rather the hard callous posture of a warrior. In light of everything she has seen, she has suspicions.

"Tell me again what happened." Her voice is much harsher than she intended.

"Regardless of how many times I tell you, it will never change." The response is just as hard.

"You must understand, this Reaper came to us almost a year ago. Since then I have seen evil only imaginable in tales to scare children in the night. I am a sister of the church and hold that title dear to my heart but until this man came to us, I had no idea what true evil really looks like and the war that is going on. So excuse me if I am suspicious but his life, my life and everyone in this household's life depend on me right now and frankly you don't look like a friar. Your clothes say friar but your demeanor says otherwise. So please tell me once again what happened."

"Fine." The lady waits for Karva to take another drink before beginning her tale. "My name is Kem and I have been tracking two men who take the form of lycans at will."

"And a lycan is a wolf?"

"Of sorts. Yes. They resemble large wolves but stand on hind legs. They retain their humanity but their actions become primal. They kill for fun. I have been tracking them since I encountered those two days before. I saw Reaper confront a lady with long black hair with an axe. She calls the two lycans and they attack him."

"I'm sorry but was there another woman with him?" Concern grows for Canda, her friend.

"There was another person but I did not meet her. When I got there, the other person was riding away, fast." Kem takes a drink of water before continuing. "He fought well but his weapons were useless against the lycans. Nevertheless, he held his own and inflicted damage."

"I thought you said his weapons were useless?" Suspicion fills Karva's heart.

"Permanent damage. You see, lycans are able to heal themselves at will. When he cuts or stabs one, the wound instantly begins to heal itself. The way he was fighting I knew he was waiting for an opportunity to escape. But a lycan got his back and stabbed him. That is when I intervened. My staff has the power of God's light, which kills all creatures of the night. I was successful. The last thing he said was to bring him here. So I did." Kem finishes her tale.

"Then I owe you thanks and gratitude. I apologize for my anger but this man has kept us alive in this dark time. And to hear that Canda was not successful in her escape is all the more troubling." Tears swell in her eyes as she fights to be strong.

"Do not fear, Reaper is strong."

Both ladies immediately look up, searching for the source of those words. To their amazement and bewilderment, the only person standing in the doorway is little Allie. The small girl is dressed in a simple brown dress that falls to her knees. Despite her dirty face, her smile lights the room up. Karla answers the child.

"We all hope Duke Jaml will be ok. He is a tough fighter who never gives up and this is no exception. I am with you, Jaml will be ok." Though her mouth said the words, Karva's heart tells her to say her goodbyes to this valiant warrior. She has done all that she knows how and without divine intervention, Jaml is not going to live out the night.

Suddenly Allie appears to grow. Not only grow but glow as well. Karva shakes her head and wipes at her eyes as she questions in her heart what she is seeing. Instantly fear overcomes her as thoughts of the Fallen enter her mind. Has she housed one of the Fallen all this time? Only to see him kill the one man who has brought light to a grim situation?

The glow becomes so bright that Karva and Kem must cover their eyes. Both ladies back away, Kem holding her staff, ready to fend off the next attack. Without seeing, both ladies move in front of the injured Jaml. Then the glare is gone.

"Open your eyes children of God." The voice is much older but soothing.

Both ladies open their eyes to find a ball of light floating where little Allie was standing. The ball of light is about the size of a man and floats just off the ground. Radiating from the light is a warm glow, too bright to look directly at forcing Kem and Karva to look away.

Kem, realizing what the glow is, drops to a knee. Karva follows suit.

"You are of the Heavenly Host. Praise God."

The sphere of light moves in front of the two kneeling women.

"God is pleased with your faith Kem and Karva. You have been faithful servants of God, ministering to the people and bringing God's sheep to the fold. I thank you for that. I am indeed an angel of God, sent to earth to watch over God's creatures and make sure all goes according to God's plan. Karva, your love for this man is genuine. He has touched you as you have touched him. Do not worry, his time among us is not yet over."

The light shines greater as the angel continues.

"Know Kem that you are to be his guide in this world. Both of you will be tested by the forces of Lucifer. You and Jaml must keep each other focused. Know that Jaml will come under great temptation soon and without you, he will fall to the forces of evil. Be vigilant child, for God has spoken."

The light moves over the body of Jaml, gently touching the man on the bed. The body arches upward before collapsing back onto the bed.

"Dark times are coming, my children. Stay vigilant and the Lord will protect you. Now let him rest and be ready for Lucifer's minions."

The light diminishes smaller and smaller. The lights also dim until all that is left standing there is the little orphan, Allie. She smiles at the two women kneeling before turning to leave.

"I am starving. I will be in the kitchen." With that Allie disappears from the room.

Both ladies remain kneeling, trying to figure out what just happened. Karva's thoughts center on the little girl who has shadowed her for the past months and is really an angel. While Karva struggles to wrap her thoughts around that, Kem tries to decipher what the angel meant about dark days coming and temptation being great for Jaml. Both women remain kneeling for several minutes, lost in their own thoughts.

Finally, Kem gets to her feet and takes a deep breath. She decides that she has much to prepare for. The angel said temptation is coming so she must prepare herself, mind, body, and soul. Meditation and fasting are essential. First, she must get out her readings and delve into his Word. Then through fasting and prayer, she will be able to combat the evil that is to come. Without saying another word she walks out of the room, her focus is narrow. She must be ready.

Karva moves over to the bed where Jaml lies. She can see his chest rise and fall, his breathing coming more regular.

As a nun of the church, Karva would never sacrifice her vows. The relationship between her and Jaml is one of respect and love. Not the love between a couple but God's love. One not based on sex or marriage but of two people communing together. Since they met, they have been through so much pain and suffering and yet she cannot think of anyone who she would rather go through it with. Or be able to make it through with. She smiles, looking at the man who has changed her life for the better.

She quietly blows out the candles and leaves the room, closing the door behind her.

✦

King Taras kneels inside the inner chamber, looking for solitude. The inside of the chamber is not distinguishable due to the utter darkness in the room. When establishing this castle, King Taras remodeled this room to block any light from penetrating the room. Every inch is painted a black, thick enough to protect any flaking, so thickly coated that even during the light of the brightest day nothing shines inside this room.

It is inside this darkness that King Taras now kneels, his concentration focused solely on the necessary incantations. Words and sounds never heard by human ears are uttered from the demon's lips. His eyes are downcast for fear of angering his master.

In the center of the room a slight swirl appears. The swirl quickly forms a cone of wind, spinning in a controlled chaos. The cone grows in size, threatening to engulf the entire room. King Taras struggles to remain still, wind beats against his body mercilessly, whipping across his face and disrupting the serenity of the room. Inside the windstorm a light appears. Shining dimly at first, the light grows in intensity becoming a ball inside the storm.

"Taras. Tell of your accomplishments. Reveal to me the glory you bring to my name." The voice is soft, almost soothing and yet Taras knows the cruelty there. He has felt the pain associated with failure from that voice. Pain he has no desire to feel again.

"Master, let there be glory in your name as well as Lucifer's. I am your humble servant and live to only serve. Please accept my report. At this time, we have the Scythe of Death and the Axe of Damnation. We are close master to fulfilling your destiny."

"And the sword?"

"Still unknown. Surely the sword is gone from this place. I will personally send my best scouts to find the blade."

"Fool!" No sooner than the word is spoken, Taras is engulfed in a deep blue flame. Screams of pain spew from his lips as water from a fountain. His body is contorted in a twisted shape, further exemplifying the intense pain Taras is enduring.

Then as quickly as it appeared, the flame vanishes leaving a smoking body huddled on the floor. A closer look reveals the smoke emitting from Taras' skin as no clothing is damaged. Blue flame, or demon flame, only harms and destroys living tissue leaving all else unharmed.

Taras raises his head slightly. "Forgive me master."

The voice inside the cone of wind answers in a calm voice. "Never question my motives, Taras. You are a worthy enough servant but as with all my servants, your existence and rewards are based on your service. Never forget that."

"Yes master." The voice cracks almost to a whimper.

"Good. The blade is still within your kingdom, I can sense its power. Find it! By whatever means necessary."

"Yes master. With the death of the Reaper, nothing stands in our way." A hint of the old confident Taras returns. Thoughts of triumph fills his head as thoughts of failure and pain are pushed out.

"Ah, and yet you do not know. Did she bring his body back? Did you witness the death? Of course not, for if you had you would not have made such a ridiculous comment. The Reaper yet lives." The voice pauses to allow the news of failure to once again sink in. This time there is no demon flame, no pain, and no agony. Just knowledge. Taras is somewhat grateful for this mercy. "He is back in your kingdom. He would be deceased if it was not for an angel who healed his many wounds."

"An angel?! How am I to combat one of the heavenly host?" Fear tinges at the corners of his words. Fighting and killing a human is one thing but I am not equipped to face one of the hosts. Panic fills his mind.

"Fear not." If Taras could look at his master at this moment, would he find himself looking at a laughing demon? Probably. "The angel will not directly interfere. The Almighty forbids it. This is the time of man."

"Why is that Master?" Taras listens as a student listens to their favorite teacher.

"After Lucifer's failure in the desert. Our hands were forced. The events of the Rapture unfolded and man received his salvation. With the resurrection of Jesus from the dead, we suffered a great blow. We realized we would have to attack another way. Man was just too fickle of a creature to rely on. We give the creature all they desire and still they crawl like cockroaches back to the Almighty. To truly win, we must force another restart. To redo the earth like the time of Noah. We must convince him to destroy all that is here and create a universe where we can challenge for rule. Now our best chance for victory rests in the Apocalypse. With the power of the Apocalypse feeding our war, the heavens will fall, man will die and we will restore our place for all eternity."

"All glory to Lucifer."

"With that being said, you only have to deal with the Reaper and his companions, nothing more. Listen my servant and learn. You have confronted this Reaper and lost. And yet you continue to confront him on his terms and you will continue to lose. The weakness of humans is emotions. They have to belong. They have to care. That is what makes them better than the creatures on four legs. That is what puts them above all other creatures and that is also their greatest weakness. Exploit that. You pick the time and place to battle. He has friends, ones he cares for and about. Use this and bring me his head. Otherwise he will be bringing me yours!"

The cone of mist begins to dissipate, mist unraveling quickly, filling the room with smoke. Taras keeps his head lowered, just in case the smoke is a test, one that will cost him his life. He waits patiently for the smoke to clear the room before lifting his head. When he finally looks around the room, his eyes are greeted with a dozen new minions to throw into the fray. A slight smile creeps across his face, the tide is turning and Taras is on his way to becoming a major demon. And on his way, the head of the Reaper will only serve as his coronation.

Sunlight bursts through the crack in the door. Jaml has been resting for three days and it is time for him to check on the people in the kingdom. No one has seen the Angel Allie since the healing, which does not sit well with him. She or he, not quite sure if angels have males and females, put herself in grave danger by exposing herself as an angel. Allie has become a bigger target than he is, one that he swears to protect with his life.

Eyes squint to almost shut as he attempts to adjust his eyes to the bright rays of the sun. Despite the wounds being healed, the muscles feel weak, nausea, legs wobbly, and arms fickle. He braces himself against the wall while adjusting to the sunshine. Once the urge to throw up the soup disappears, Jaml brings himself upright. He takes a deep breath and quickly regrets it. He doubles back over immediately, every ounce of his breakfast soup spews from his mouth, splattering on the stone in front of him. A couple of heaves later and another gush of stomach contents erupts from his mouth.

"You going to make it?" A familiar voice fills his head, the cleric he now knows as Kem. The woman who risked her life to save his. He is in her depth. She has refused to acknowledge it but Jaml will lay his life on the line to protect the woman. He turns to look at Kem, her long brown hair cascades over her shoulders, her brown robe fits snugly, not as a traditional cleric but one born to do battle.

In these trying times, as man's destiny has been put in man's hands, both the priest order and clerical order have undergone some changes. Both have split themselves into two different factions, each able to support its mission. A select few priests have formed Reapers, elite fighters whose mission is to eradicate the demons of the world while the other priests devote themselves to reaching and teaching the masses about Jesus Christ the Son of God. Both parts of priesthood study the Word of God continuously.

The clerical servants have followed the same route. Most study the Word of God while learning about the healing properties of his creations such as plants. A few have taken up the battle and fight side by side with the Reapers. Because Clerics do not use sharp objects in their work, they refuse to use sharp objects in battle as well. Many are experts in the use of the staff or the wooden sticks. These clerics endure grueling training, honing their skills as fighters for the maximum results. Many have been broken and failed in the training leaving the ones that complete the training as finely honed fighting machines for God.

"I'm going to make it. Been down too long. Must check on the people in this kingdom." His words stammer as much as he struggles to walk. The touch of his free arm being lifted in the air to support him brings a warm smile to his face. He looks over to watch Kem hold his arm steady while he fights for balance. She looks back at him. "Thank you." Is all he can muster.

It takes another thirty minutes before Jaml is able to walk without assistance. With Kem at his side, the two of them walk through the Hills. Jaml is dressed in a loose fit white blouse with dark blue trousers with leather boots, the customary garb of a duke. Draped on

139

his left hip is a longsword and on his right hip is a long dagger. Kem walks confidently at his side, shunning the customs of most areas which calls for a wife to walk slightly behind her husband. With no need to covet physical things, Kem wears her simple clerical robe, a simple brown robe that falls to just above her knees. Underneath she wears brown trousers. She walks with her staff, a six foot slender piece of wood designed for combat but used for walking as well. Her hair is tied in the back with a piece of leather.

The couple catches more than one double take as Duke Jaml is walking with another woman, not his beloved wife Canda. Many will talk about the new woman, wonder if his culture allows for multiple wives. Many will speculate on the health of Canda and whether or not she is dead. None have seen her and now this Duke is walking with another woman. Speculation will avail and his motives will come into question.

None of that bothers the duke right now. His concern is the people who have accepted him into the community and he feels he owes a debt to. He strides with conviction and purpose, only looking away from his goal to give a curt nod to a passerby. The smile on his face is forced, put there to appease the population and keep up the facade.

The duo reach the south end of the Hill. Three streets to the left rests at their destination, the villa of Duke Indi. Bigger than Jaml's villa, the gate, for some unknown reason, is heavily guarded. Five soldiers stand at the entryway, fully armed in chainmail armor with an assortment of weapons. On top of the war sit four archers, their bows notched with an arrow.

The Captain of the Guard, a wiry man of middle age, steps forward to greet Jaml and Kem. "Greetings Duke Jaml. We live in troubled times."

Jaml reads between the lines, knowing entry is not going to be as easy as normal. He is going to have to explain himself in order to gain entry. "Indeed we do, my friend. Your loyalty to my friend is greatly appreciated. I would like to introduce my friend Kem. She is a cleric who has traveled many miles to help drive away our demons. We are here to check on an old friend of mine who has welcomed me into his house. I feel obligated to check with him."

"My orders, I cannot let you in. But I know you and for no reason you would do my employer wrong. Do not prove me a fool, Duke Jaml."

"Never." Jaml bows slightly in appreciation and is reciprocated by the man in front of him. The captain moves to the side to allow Jaml entry. Without further word, Jaml walks towards the gate, wondering if any of the soldiers felt differently towards him or their orders. To his relief, the men step aside to allow Jaml to walk in.

The duo walks through the gate and is greeted immediately by Duke Indi. The two men embrace, the weight of worry is lifted from Jaml's shoulders. Standing at arm's length, Jaml looks at the worry on his friend's face

"It is good to see you Jaml. I have been overcome with grief and worry. Things have changed around here. People whisper of demons roaming the land and our king sleeping with them." Indi dares not raise his voice, lest those selfsame demons he speaks of come and get him.

"And your lovely wife Tyra, how does she fare?"

"Only the sheer numbers of guards keep her from insanity. Especially since Lady Blait was called upon and has not been heard from since."

"What?! When did this happen? You must tell me!" Irritation grows inside Jaml. Only the hand of Kem on his shoulder keeps Jaml from physically grabbing the man and shaking him vigorously.

"Come in friend so I can tell you what has transpired and together we can work on a plan." Indi does not appear to take offense to Jaml's aggressive behavior. Maybe because he has gone through the same emotions over the past several days and knows the source of the anger. And it is not him.

Indi turns and walks back into villa followed by Jaml and Kem. The captain nods at each one of them as they pass through the gates. Once all three are inside, the captain nods to two guards in front of him. The two men grab a lever in front of them and push. Slowly the men are able to walk the gate to the villa closed. Once closed, a large oak beam is placed in the steel holders, securing the gate as best as they can.

Three hours later Jaml and Kem emerge from the villa of Duke Indi. They shared a meal together as they talked about recent events and how their lives have been affected. Jaml learns Lady Blait was summoned to the castle by Princess Jala two nights ago, no one has heard from her since. Her husband barricades himself inside his castle, waiting for the day his love returns. He accepts no visitors and some say anyone near his gates will be attacked without warning. Tomorrow night the Royal Family is holding a celebration and everyone has been invited, the rich and commoners alike. The gates will be open, cooks are preparing a grand feast, and decorations are already being placed around the city.

"They are going to execute her, you know that." Kem's words are soft so no one else may hear and she is not sure how he will react to the comment.

"I know." Jaml does not break stride nor does he look her way. His mind is racing on what actions he must take. "I have to get to God's house and pray for guidance. My thoughts are clouded with acts of evil and impulse. I must gain direction."

The two walk in silence for a time more, searching emotions for the task at hand. Kem's eyes keep a vigilant look out for attacks, protecting Jaml as he struggles with the situation. Death is inevitable but one is never really ready for it.

Kem is startled when Jaml suddenly speaks. "You are not safe. Thank you for saving my life and bringing me back but you must now leave me. My path is wrought with nothing but death."

As much as she is surprised by his words, he is equally taken aback by her response.

"That is my choice Reaper." She has called him by his name countless times but to refer to him by his position now rings true that he must heed her words. "If I choose to die in battle with you, I will choose to battle. You cannot protect me and nor will I allow it. Be concerned with the others, I will choose my path, not you."

"Look at you." Jaml's comment brings a smile they share at her remarks. "Then let us go protect the others and choose the manner in which we choose to do battle."

Karva rises to her feet. Kneeling in front of the altar always hurts her knees but the feeling of being close to God is well worth it. Her prayers center on the Reaper and his safety. He has saved her life and her church at least twice and she cannot help but feel indebted to him. She knows he will not accept money so she simply prays for him.

She brushes off the front of her robe and turns to go about her chores. Standing in her way is Allie, which gives her a start. She cannot help but stare at the little brown haired girl who looks to have

142

not seen more than ten seasons. This little girl recently revealed herself to be an angel. A member of the heavenly host sent down to monitor the affairs of man. She recently witnessed this little girl heal mortal wounds on the Reaper.

She drops to her knees, lowers her head in prayer.

"Please stand up, my child stand. I am not worthy of such actions." The voice is young but the words are wise beyond her years. The face has a look of concern on it which alarms Karva.

"What is wrong?"

"The man you call Jaml arrives. The news he brings is grave. He is going to perform a task that may cost him his life. We cannot let that happen. His death could alter the balance of this war. You must listen and find a way to convince him his plan is foolish. Another way must be found."

"Can you not convince him?"

"Unfortunately that is not my purpose here. I am but an observer sent to make sure my brother does not interfere." Her expression does not change.

"But you saved Jaml once!"

"And I have paid a toll for that"

Karva takes a step back. She looks Allie up and down and cannot find anything wrong with her. When she looks at the girl's eyes, she notices the eyes, tired and worn. The eyes have a look of recent pain. A toll.

"I am sorry. I did not know." Karva lowers her eyes in respect.

"I did not share. No apologies necessary. What is important is you prepare for Jaml and his plans. Know that he is willing to sacrifice himself for his friends. This cannot happen."

"Then are we, his friends, just to be sacrificed? To die?" Her face is mortified.

"Of course not. Life is too important to our Lord. We must find another way that is all." After a few silent seconds, "He is here."

Karva looks towards the entryway before turning to look once again at the angel. Only to find herself looking at nothing, Allie is gone. A heavy sigh escapes from her lips. How many times has she just disappeared and I assumed she ran off. A smile creeps over her face.

She hurries off to meet Jaml and Kem and convince them not to do whatever they are planning.

"There is no other way."

The conversation is heated, Jaml is intent on rescuing his "wife" and his friend, while the others try to convince him the situation is a trap that will only get him killed. Canda being taken from his grasp as he tried to retrieve the Scythe and Blait being summoned by the princess drives an emotional Jaml to go through with the rescue attempt.

In the room is a table in the center. The walls are bare except for a large cross hanging on the wall across from the door. Seated at the table are Karva and Indi. The cleric Kem leans against the wall while Jaml stands across from Kem. Candles on the table keep the room lit as the conversation becomes hotter than the candle flame could ever get.

"We are not saying they are not important..." Karva's sentence is cut off.

"Then what are you saying? We need to sacrifice their lives so we might live? What kind of servant of God are you?" The intent is for the words to bite deep. Success.

"How dare you question my faith? Who the hell do you think you are? Just because you are angel trained doesn't give you the authority to say your faith is greater than mine."

"I am not saying your faith is..." This time it is his words that are cut off.

"That is exactly what you said. If you are so self-righteous, how about you go rescue them your damn self!"

A presence in the doorway pauses the conversation as all eyes turn to find Allie standing there, dressed in a simple brown dress. Despite the little girl complexion on her face, everyone in the room knows her eyes hold an eternity's worth of knowledge. No one but Karva has seen her since she revealed herself to be an angel.

"Everyone needs to take a step back." Allie's soft voice fills the room with a firmness not seen in a child. Then again, she is not just a child. Her words bring a closure to the heated conversation in the room. Jaml takes a heavy breath as Karva runs her fingers through her hair. Kem uncrosses her arms while bowing her head.

She continues. "You are both correct. We cannot leave those people to die. This cannot happen." Jaml stands a little more erect.

"And yet Karva is correct in her assumption. This is a trap to isolate you and kill you."

Karva shakes her head. "So what do we do?"

"Come up with a plan. We need to make contingency plans in case of a change in circumstances. Please sit Jaml as we prepare for what is definitely going to be a great and wonderful night."

✦

The following night sees the celebration kick off. The streets are filled with the citizens of Colley and surrounding kingdoms. The streets are lined with tables of food, wine and ale. Slab after slab of warm beef, pork, and deer are brought out and placed on the decorated tables that stand in a line. Beside the thousands of pounds of cooked flesh are placed plate after plate of fresh fruit and vegetables. Warm ale, wine and cold beer are poured by tavern girls walking up and down the various streets, bringing merry to everyone willing.

Minstrels are located on most street corners, playing their bards of chivalry and adventure for all to hear. Some even wander the streets to play to bigger crowds. Their windblown instruments blare through the streets, women frolicking beside them, their dresses pulled up to allow more movement. The celebration brings out people in all walks of life for one night of joyous partying and an escape from the story of demons and devils that has Colley strangled at the neck.

On her balcony in the royal castle, Princess Jala looks down at the festive time had by all. A gentle breeze ruffles her long green gown, the soft silk material moving against her soft pale flesh. Her right thigh is exposed to the elements, a slit in her dress that ends at her hip is carried away from her skin. Her long black hair cascades over her shoulders, stopping just above her buttocks. The whole scene drips of sex, raw rough sex.

The princess turns from the crowd and heads back inside her luxurious room. Large furs lie across the floor in such a pattern that her feet will never touch the hard cold stone that lies beneath. On her walls are paintings of tapestries of naked women, each depicted in a provocative pose. In the center of the room is a bed covered in white fur and satin sheets. To the right of the bed sits a large vanity. The wood polished to a near mirror shine. On the opposite side to the

145

vanity is a bureau, full of the latest fashions from across the continent.

At the present time, she is only interested in the lump on her bed. She casually approaches the lump, which does not move. She leans over and pulls back the sheet, revealing a very drug induced woman asleep. No one is around to notice the smile that comes across the face of the princess. Nor does anyone bear witness to her hand gestures made in the air. The white fur and silk sheets slide away from the sleeping figure on the bed.

Lying on the bed is Blait, completely naked and completely unaware of her exposure. Jala makes additional gestures. The result is a stirring from the lady on the bed. Jala waits patiently as slowly Blait regains her senses. She looks up at woman dressed in the green gown, and slowly her memories return and terror fills her eyes.

"Hello. I see your memories are not lost. Good." She gestures with her hands again resulting in Blait rising to her feet, arms locked at her side.

Blait is fully aware of her nakedness but cannot move her arms to grab for covering. She struggles against her invisible bonds, trying to find some way to break free. No success. She attempts to scream but finds her voice locked up as much as her arms. Panic flashes over her face as realization hits her that she is utterly helpless in her situation. She has no power and is a prisoner in invisible bonds. She gives up, her shoulders slump forward.

"Glad to see you have come to realize the futility of the situation. You are completely in my power, you can neither move or talk without my consent. Now come along Lady Blait, your sacrifice will bring great reward and an ending to Reaper."

Jala turns towards the vanity. She snaps her fingers, Blait lurches forward in a clumsy walk, struggling to place one foot in front of the other. A simple kiss on the cheek by Jala smooths Blait and her walking problems out. Blait succumbs fully to the spell, falling into a deep trance like state. She follows Jala without further incident.

The two ladies approach the vanity when Jala waves her hand. A rectangle section of stone wall next to the vanity slides back before disappearing to the side. The princess does not break stride leading a helpless naked Blait through the opening. Once the spell bound woman is inside the door slides back over and fits right back into place.

Inside, a simple spell ignites a series of torches hanging on walls in a small hallway. So bright are the candles that seem to glow as brightly as the sun itself. If one didn't know better, one would think it was in the brightest part of the day with the sun on high. More surprising is the opening at the other end of the hall. As bright at the hallway is, the chamber at the far end dives back into darkness.

The two ladies walk through the opening at the far of the hall into another chamber. No torches illuminate this room yet the room is lit. There are no windows of any kind. Blait can only assume the light in this room stems from magic. She cannot remember the king having a court mage, her mind races to find an explanation.

This chamber does not look as well kept and lavishly furnished. The stone walls are exposed, not covered in beautiful paintings of naked women. The floor is dirt, which seems odd to Blait as she recalls the royal family live on the upper floors, not the ground floor where dirt is usually found.

The only furniture in the room is a stone table in the center but there are no chairs. As Blait walks against her will, she notices chains on the floor. Being only able to move her eyes, she struggles to get a better understanding why chains are lying on the floor. She notices red coloring caked into the dirt. It made sense. She recalls her temple teachings where monks talked about God's people making sacrifices to God for his blessing. She recalls the men would sacrifice and spill the blood of lambs to glorify God's name. She is to be the lamb.

"Ah, I see you have gotten a grasp of what is to come. Your sacrifice to my master will bring me favor." Jala waves her fingers across Blait's mouth. "You may scream now. But no one will hear you."

"God has never rewarded human sacrifices. You are nothing but a murderer using God's name as justification. You, you, monster!" Blait screams

Jala giggles. "God? You think this is for the glory of God? I serve Lucifer and the Fallen. When my master is able to ascend once again, I will be at his side." Horror flashes across Blait's face. "Now get on the table and secure your chains."

Blait cannot fight the commands and finds herself climbing onto the altar, for that is exactly what it is, a human altar. Tears stream down her face as she shackles her ankles, securing them to the table.

147

She leans to the left, clasping the shackle to her left hand. She finds herself lying on her back awaiting further instructions.

"Good, good girl. My master will be pleased with your blood. So

"She is cut off.

"Lucifer will be disappointed tonight." The voice is definitely male, and distinct.

Jala smiles.

"Welcome Reaper. You couldn't do it, could you? You couldn't sacrifice one human for the greater good. That is why you have failed tonight."

Reaper emerges from the shadows, dressed in all black. Even his face is covered by a black hood that extends to a cape. Reaper walks from the shadows to stand within striking distance of Jala, who simply smiles.

"I see you have been busy already." Her eyes are locked on his twin short swords, both dripping with blood.

"Unfortunately they do not know what they follow and are blinded by your disguise. Tonight you will die and I will show you no mercy. Forfeit your life without further bloodshed and I will pray God will have mercy on your soul. Continue with this and you will die a horrible death today and for all eternity. Your demon family is not here to help you."

"Such bravado Reaper. And impressive." Jala claps her hands. "You are right Reaper, my family is not here and you have killed my human guards but did you expect this."

She opens her arms wide. As she does, the room becomes fully illuminated. Walking out of the stone, an illusion spell, is a large bullish red demon. The demon stands nearly seven feet tall, legs the size of oak trees and arms bulging in muscles. It appears to have no clothing but its skin is adorned with small horns all over. The creature's head spouts two large horns at the top. Its mouth is oversized and filled with razor sharp teeth. In its hands, the creature is holding a large two handed battle axe.

Fear would grasp the heart and soul of any other man but Reaper has seen and killed this sort of demon before. He simply turns to face the creature and readies himself for the clumsy lunge that will come.

"No words Reaper? I hope my warrior will bring some screams from your otherwise troublesome mouth."

The creature lunges forward, its axe held high over its head. Reaper does not move, simply tenses every muscle in his legs. At the moment the demon brings his axe down, with every intention of cutting Reaper in two, Reaper steps inside and to the left.

He feels the hot air of the axe swish by his body and the ground shake when the blade buries itself into the dirt but he is already moving. His right blade cuts across the midsection of the demon causing blood to spurt out. He spins to bury his left blade into the demon's back. He pulls the blade free by kicking the demon forward.

A howl of pain is heard in the room as the demon falls forward into a roll. It ends on its feet and spins to face Reaper once again. This time the demon stalks forward, not rushing in as before. This human has skills. The demon walks by its axe, pulling it free from the ground.

Reaper simply spins on the balls of his feet watching the warrior demon, keeping it in front of him at all times but also not forgetting about Jala. The demon twirls the axe in his hands like a court jester spins a baton. It feints an attack and steps back, laughing at Reaper's reaction of tensing his muscles.

"But I am not the one bleeding." Reaper remarks

The demon immediately responds by swinging his axe in the next attack. Reaper hops back slightly, enough so the axe flies by, inches from his midsection. Close enough to launch another attack. His blades move in a blur, two dancing sticks of death hungry to taste blood.

The demon moves to the side while bringing his axe back around. The blades clash numerous times as the demon is on the defensive, trying to keep the blades at bay. It continues to retreat as Reaper presses forward, his blades tasting demon flesh on several occasions. Reaper becomes relentless, his blades moving in unison and yet attacking at different angles.

Reaper spins low, bringing his blades to the knees of the demon who responds by slamming his blade into the ground. Reaper's blade hits the axe hilt, allowing Reaper to use the momentum to reverse the spin. He brings his blade higher, cutting into the demon's midsection. He follows it up with a spin kick to the demon's side, sending the creature sprawling to the ground.

The demon launches his axe at Reaper who simply steps aside. The blade twirls by to imbed itself into the wall. The creature uses the throw as a distraction and launches himself back into battle. Daggers appear in his hands just as the attack begins.

The ferocity of the attack sends Reaper into a defensive mode. He takes several steps back, moving his blades in a defensive pattern, blocking the attacks by the demon. The sheer force behind each cut is enough to dislocate a shoulder if not careful. But Reaper has outlived all his adversaries by skill, not care. He tilts his blades slightly in such a manner that the attacks are more deflected than stopped by him.

He brings his left blade across his body to block a dagger. The demon is losing control, his attacks more brute force than skill. His attacks resemble chopping meat in a butcher stand rather than skilled knife play. Reaper uses this to his advantage, staying light on his feet allows him to use the momentum of the motion to spin him completely around, his foot catching the demon at the knee, dropping him to that knee. Reaper reverses his grip on his blades before plunging both blades into the demon's neck, to the hilts.

"May your will be done O'Lord and may the blood of your son forgive the blood that I must shed cause in your name. Amen"

Reaper pulls the blades free; blood erupts from the wounds spraying into the air. The horror of death is frozen on the demon's face, blood trickling from its mouth. Reaper watches as the corpse falls to the ground, dead.

Reaper senses something is wrong and dives to his right. But not fast enough. Pain fills his left shoulder, interrupting his dive, causing his dive to turn into a tumble. He continues his tumble an extra few rolls to bring him out of danger. Stopping into a crouch, Reaper quickly scans the room until he finds the newest danger, Jala.

Jala squats in the far corner, claws on her right hand dripping blood, his blood. She slowly straightens to full height, nearly six and a half feet tall. Her body has transformed into something demonic. Her skin becomes even redder than before. Facial features become distorted; fangs extend from her mouth, ears elongate to double size along with eyes that have turned completely red. Her nails have turned into claws, each razor sharp.

She sniffs at the blood on her fingertips. "Good stock Reaper, just as I thought." A forked tongue slides out of her mouth to taste the fresh blood. "Delicious. I look forward to feasting on the rest of your flesh."

Reaper feels the poison enter his blood stream, heading down his arm. He knows he will lose the use of his arm unless he can get an antidote. Unfortunately reaching into his side pouch would expose himself to attack. He has to kill the demon first which will prove challenging since with each passing moment allows the poison to course through his body. He takes a deep breath and launches his attack.

Jala readies herself for the onslaught, knowing the longer she survives, the better chance she has for victory. Once the poison runs its way down his arm, he will battle with one hand which will give her the revenge she desires. She swings her claws with precision, years of training for battle has honed her skills. Yet she has to use every ounce of her training to keep alive now. She has only heard of his skills but seeing him first hand is not only impressive but deadly.

She is so preoccupied with his blades that she is unable to react to a new attack. Sharp pain strikes her thigh, a snap kick. A side kick to her midsection follows, taking the breath out of her. She doubles over for a second before a front kick sends her sprawling to the ground. She lands on her back and immediately rolls to the side to prevent further damage. She rolls to her knees and finds her enemy standing still. She can still feel the pain in her leg and taste the blood that trickles from her mouth. She spits a mouthful of blood to the ground, never losing sight of where he is. He begins to walk casually towards her.

"You should have never gone after my friends. For this you are going to die tonight. Your sins have caught up with you and tonight you will atone for them. May your will be done O'Lord and may the blood of your son forgive the blood that I must shed cause in your name. Amen"

"Save your self-righteous prayer, I don't need it. Oh but you will. How is that shoulder?" Jala breaks out into a shrieking laugh.

Reaper launches himself into battle once again. His blades move in a whirlwind of movement that human eyes cannot follow. Jala takes a step back, trying to find the pattern of the movements before the battle is to start again. She runs out of time, moves into a defensive position and engages.

The two battle at a tempo unseen in many years. His blades move in such a fashion that the demon can do nothing but defend. His attack veers towards her left side as he begins to lose feeling in his left arm, the poison beginning to take effect. She continues to retreat, keeping herself alive and gaining precious moments to allow the poison to work.

Running out of time causes Reaper to press the battle further, faster, harder. He is losing precious moments, knowing he will soon lose the use of his left arm and the tide of battle will turn. As he presses forward, he can feel the poison draining the energy and function from his left arm. Then he will die and all this will be for naught.

"Oh Lord. Give me strength."

At that moment, all remaining feeling drains from his left arm. Jala watches as the arm goes completely limp at his side. She smiles in victory and attacks his left side. Reaper turns his body to protect his dead side. Jala over eager attack over extends her thrust meant to impale Reaper. He sees his chance. He brings his right hand down with all his might and watches as the blade slices through her wrist with little resistance. Both watch as her hand falls to the ground, severed from the stump that is her arm.

Her howl in pain breaks the awkward silence and trance as both stared at the loose hand. In desperation, Jala swings her good arm, casting a wind spell. Caught off guard, the spell flings Reaper across the room. He crashes into the wall, knocking the breath from his lungs. He looks up, ready to defend, to find Jala running up a set of spiral stone stairs near her bed. He hadn't noticed those stairs before.

He looks around and cannot find Blait. She plans on carrying this sacrifice out. The demon assassin shakes his head clear before rising to his feet. His left arm is limp at his side. He walks over to the nearest corner, pulls back the curtain to find a satchel. He quickly rumbles through the satchel until he finds a small vial of holy water. He bites down on the cork the pulls the cork free. He pours the clear liquid over the holes on his back. Despite wanting to wait for the antidote takes full effect, he knows Blait does not have that kind of time. He grabs his blade from the ground and runs up the stairs, ready for anything hell is going to send at him.

He finds the stairs leading to the outer balcony at the top of the tower. Sprinting up the spiral stairs, he cannot help but dread that he is too late. The feeling in his left arm begins to come back, the poison antidote working. Once he gets to the top of the stairs he takes a moment to control his emotions, take in the situation and ready himself for action once again.

The second staircase, a mere ten stairs, leads to the balcony. In two leaps, Reaper finds himself at the top of the stairs, facing the door. He does not hesitate to kick the door open, a cool rush of wind hits him in the face.

✦

King Taras and Queen Sera lounge in their personal chambers. Both are sprawled out on top of their bed. He wears nothing but a simple white loincloth which does little to hide his sexual arousal. He holds a goblet of wine sipping on it continuously. Lying next to him is the Queen. Lounging in a white see through silk robe, open for all to see. She, too, has a goblet in her hand. Standing behind them is a naked servant girl who refills their drinks on a regular basis. Next to her is a table with several pitchers of wine.

The couple is watching two very naked women dance erotically. Their bodies move and gyrate to imaginary music. In the midst of their dancing, they run their hands over each other's body as well as their own. Fingers gently pull at nipples, arousing them.

The royal couple kiss each other then take another sip of wine, their bodies are sexually heightened. Their eyes are locked on the two women dancing in front of them.

A soldier dressed in full battle gear quietly walks to the bed from behind, not wanting to disturb the couple even more than he knows he will. Besides, he wants a full view of the festivities as well. He finds himself captivated by the two women dancing in front of him, completely oblivious to his presence. He quietly leans down and whispers in the king's ear.

"Damn!"

The king sits up, his attention broken from the scene in front of him. He begins to move to the edge of the bed when Sera grabs his arm.

"You leave so soon my king. Surely you don't want to miss what comes next."

"Jala is doing battle in the tower for all to see."

"She can handle herself. You have trained her well. Now why don't you come back to bed so I can show you what I can do."

"In her true form."

"Shit! Go. Lest all our plans are undone"

Taras slides off the bed. He makes for the door even as he pulls on his trousers and shirt. The soldier follows him, carrying the king's sword and battle axe. The duo exits through the door and turns left, heading towards the princess room ready for battle.

Back inside the room, Sera rises to her feet, fuming over the interruption that just occurred. She sheds the robe, standing completely naked in front of the two equally naked dancers.

"Get out!"

The two dancers quickly run out the door, not wanting to receive any of the anger they see in the Queen's eyes. They pull the door closed and disappear.

Sera walks over to her wardrobe and grabs a red dress. She slips into her dress, grabs her staff before walking out the room. Standing in the hall is her personal escort, two full armed soldiers armed with shields and swords. She turns right, heading towards the street, needing to destroy her own daughter if need be. She has worked too long and too hard to get this kingdom right to have some careless little bitch undo everything over revenge.

"Grab those torches and make sure they don't burn out."

Both soldiers grab a torch before jogging to catch back up with the Queen.

Careful not to let the flames go out.

✦

The balcony is a small twenty by twenty foot platform that oversees the south part of the kingdom. Steel railings offer some protection for anyone standing out there. Across from the door is Jala, in full demon form, standing over a scared crumpled woman lying on the platform in a ball. The demon has her hands raised in the air, wings outstretched to full wingspan. The demon has no clothing draped over her body save for a loincloth over her hips. Her skin glistens in the red hue of the demon race. The woman is completely naked and from what Reaper can see, she is crying hysterically.

"Beast, you have forgotten something." Reaper's voice booms over the sound of the whipping wind.

Jala turns her head, the expression on her face is one of disbelief. She is certain the poison in her talons killed Reaper but she hears his voice loud and clear. Her wings fold up behind her, allowing her to face him without bumping into anything. There he is, standing in front of her, sword in hand.

"Guess I will have the pleasure of tasting your fresh blood human." A certain gleeful smile comes across her face, as a female tiger after a fresh kill.

It does not escape her that Reaper is carrying only one blade, the arm that tasted her poison being coddled against his body. Her attack begins there. Her claws narrowly miss ripping his shoulder open again. He leans back just far enough out of reach for his safety. He immediately steps inside, plunging his blade into her midsection. Her howls of pain vibrate inside his head, causing it to hurt.

Her backhand sends the human flying. His back hits the railing, bending him backwards. Before he can recover, she jumps at the opportunity. Her fingers close around his neck, cutting off the little air that remained in his lungs from the impact against the railings.

The hit is unexpected, his grip around the hilt of the blade was not the tightest. Now Reaper finds himself without a weapon, at the mercy of a demon who wants him dead in the worst way. Spots appear in his vision, he knows he has very little time before death accepts him.

With his right hand he grabs hold of her wrist. She looks him in his eyes, mocking him at his feeble attempt at removing her arm. She almost bursts out laughing. To her surprise, Reaper is also smiling, his demeanor relaxed save for the tight grip on her wrist.

"What are you smiling at?" Words drip from her mouth in disdain. "You don't have the strength to pull away. Look at you now, about to leave this world in a bloody mess. I promised you I would feast on your innards while you watched. Now it's time for me to keep my word."

The demon smiles, drool drips like a stream from the long fangs in her mouth. Wanting to enjoy every minute, she slowly lowers her head towards his neck. Reaper quickly places both legs on her thighs even as he swings his other hand with all his might.

A loud thud is heard when the palm of his hand connects with the soft joint of her elbow. She screams at the intense pain she feels in her elbow. Jala looks down to see the damage. Her arm is flipped inside out at the elbow. She looks up as Reaper interlocks his fingers to form a club. He slams his club downward, across her elbow. A second thud is heard when the connection is made.

She screams as every tendon in her elbow is completely destroyed. Her grip fails, dropping Reaper from her grasp. He lands nimbly on his feet and wastes no time in continuing the attack. Two swift hard kicks to her knee shatters the knee cap. She buckles, unable to hold up her weight any longer.

She attempts to rise to her feet and quickly falls back down to one knee, anger and a knowing feeling of defeat seeps from every pore on her body. She bares her teeth in hatred and contempt. Snarls rumble in her throat, threats that can no longer be carried out.

Her wings unfold from her back, an escape from certain death. Jala knows it is forbidden to show her true form around the humans but she is willing to take the punishment to save her life. Wings move back and forth garnishing enough force to lift Jala into the air. Reaper moves with speed too fast to follow. Instantly he grabs her ankle and yanks down hard. The demon is unprepared for such force and finds herself crashing into the wall.

Her breath escapes her lungs, the force of the impact that great. The spots in her eyes blind her from seeing the advancing Reaper who wastes no time in propping her against the wall. Punch after punch connects to her face and midsection, pummeling her into defeat. She collapses to her butt. Her face is grotesquely altered into a bloody mess.

Reaper continues his assault.

Blow after blow strikes the demon who is now fighting to stay alive as opposed to her previous threats of slowly killing Reaper. The beating only stops after Reaper is satisfied Jala is beaten mind, body and soul. He cups her head in his hands, hoisting her to her feet. With one last glare he proclaims.

"May God have mercy on your soul."

Using every ounce he can muster, Reaper heaves the demon Jala from the landing in the castle. The fall is silent as Jala has no more energy to fight. She welcomes death moments before her body smacks onto the ground. Blood squirts all over the ground from several different spots on her body that bursts open upon contact.

With the death of Jala, the spell over Blait is broken. She looks at Reaper with a blank stare as if wondering what all has transpired. Realizing that she is naked, Blait attempts to cover her body with her hands. Reaper pulls off his cape and wraps it around her shoulders. She gives a quick thank you smile.

"Come Blait, we have to go and find Canda. Do you know where she is?"

"I'm sorry. No I do not. I would imagine she is in the dungeons down below." Her voice shakes uncontrollably as she tries to gain her composure

"Then let's not waste another moment." Conviction rings in his voice.

The two leave Jala's chamber alive. And that is what matters.

Chapter 9

Desperation begins to creep into his mind. He is running out of time, not only for himself but for the two women charged in his care. Lady Blait, freshly saved from being a sacrifice, runs slightly behind him. Loose trousers threaten to fall from her small waist. Large boots on her feet slow them down. The only thing comfortable on her body is the large white shirt. All donated from the unconscious soldier at the entrance to the dungeon.

The other woman is locked somewhere in the dungeon, his "wife" Canda, captured in his attempt to retrieve the scythe. He has risked his life for this woman, who has stood by his side since the beginning of this mission. Now her safety is in jeopardy and Reaper will not rest until she is once again safe.

"If you need to rest, can I go ahead by myself and come back to get you afterwards?" The care in his voice is evident. He worries for her so soon after being under a spell. She struggles to keep up, breathing is labored and her effort.

"Please don't leave me. My mind is foggy and I don't remember anything. You tell me it has been two days since I came here and yet those two days are foreign to me. I am afraid of what that demon did to me. What if I am pregnant with a creature of Satan? How will my husband love me when I give birth to a spawn of hell? Oh my God! My life is ruined!"

Her anxiety rises to a fever pitch as all her fears are manifested into words. She clamps her arms around her body, struggling to comprehend her present situation. Blait's body shakes uncontrollably, tears stream down her cheeks as waterfalls open up over a cliff. Reaper knows he is losing time.

"Hey there. Nothing like that happened to you. And besides, I want you at my side all the time. I am just worried that my pace is too fast for you. I would never leave you if that is your wish."

"Then I beg you Reaper in all God's glory, don't leave me behind."

"No need to beg. It is done. As for your fears, squash them. Jala was a female."

"How can you be sure?"

"All was exposed on her way down."

Blait giggles slightly, relief struggling to overcome her fears. But she is better.

The two continue to search the cells, frantically looking for Canda. Reaper wants to release every prisoner inside, to undo everything King Taras has done. Deep inside, Reaper knows that some of these sinners belong here for crimes against God that are completely heinous in nature. Since he cannot discern just from unjust imprisonment, he chooses not to release any of the prisoners. As hard as it is for him to fight the urge.

It isn't until they enter the last wing of the dungeons that they find Canda. They find her huddled in the corner of the cell, arms wrapped around her legs, face buried in her knees. The cell is completely dark save for the light emitting from the torches in the hall. She is dressed in a simple brown dress that very well could be a grain sack.

Reaper opens the door to watch Canda cringe even more. He slowly approaches the huddled figure, not knowing how much mental anguish and damage she has had to endure over the last couple of days. Thoughts that she would blame him creep inside, his heart rate increases tenfold as she approaches. What if she doesn't want anything to do with him? Hates him? He pushes those thoughts aside as he finds himself a few feet away from her.

"Canda. It's me Jaml." His voice is soft, hoping to comfort the scared woman.

Swollen eyes look up at him. He can see pain and hurt in those eyes. She attempts to crack a smile.

"You came for me."

"Of course I did." Those words are all he needs to hear. He covers the ground in a few steps and embraces her in his arms. He gently lifts her to her feet, carrying all her weight in case she cannot. It takes a few seconds before he feels her legs begin to support her weight.

"Easy Canda." Guilt rips through his words. Even though he knows he could not have done anything to alter the events of the past couple of weeks, he cannot quit thinking that he failed these ladies and because of his failure, these ladies almost died. Now he can

159

rectify his mistakes somewhat by leading these ladies to safety. And exact his revenge on those responsible.

Satisfied she has enough strength in her legs, he slowly lets go of her arm, watching for any sign of collapse. None exist. She is strong enough, her balance fully restored. Reaper wants to hear every second of her capture and incarceration. He wants to gather the fuel necessary to exact his revenge.

✦

"She is dead! That son of a bitch killed her! What are you going to do about this?"

Prince Manda stands in front of his father, King Taras. Instead of the decorum of the kingdom, the prince is standing nose to nose with his father screaming at the top of his lungs. Anger fills every word, pain embraces the anger. Even the minions of the fallen angel Lucifer are not immune to the lonely kiss of death. Taras does not stop nor chastise his son, for in the past 2 months, the youngest member of the royal family has seen his brother killed and now his sister. All by the same man. And now the young prince wants answers.

"Calm down son. Be still your words lest I have to deal with them." The words are soft but the threat is very real and understood. "Know and understand that Lucifer has not forsaken us and we move together for the benefit of his rule. Your mother and I knew this time would come when we would be pressed into battle. Long have we lived amongst these humans without detection by man nor God? Casualties do not mean all is lost, simply that we must keep our minds and find the best avenue towards success."

"Yes father." Manda hangs his head, trying to compose himself and his feelings. He cannot help but think of the soldiers in the room. How they must see him as a fool, an incompetent child throwing another temper tantrum. He immediately regrets his actions. He is now the next heir to the throne and no more than ever he must act as such. His father is correct, they knew this day would come when one or more were going to die. But he is not ready for death to begin. In the back of his mind, he always knew not everyone was going to survive this. He never thought he would have to face the finality of the situation. Now that the time is here, he has been acting like a brat wanting a piece of candy. He must do better, he has to do better. He will be king.

✦

Reaper leads the group back down the maze of the dungeons. In the back of his mind, he knows time is running out. A change of guards will be passing any moment now and when the replacements arrive, their lives will be forfeit, their sacrifices lost. Everything he has sacrificed for would be lost.

"Come. Let us not tarry."

The trio move quickly and quietly down a hall, all alert for any voices or clanks of metal. All familiar sounds of soldiers and danger. Reaper leads the way, his swords held at waist high ready for death at a moment's notice. Standing behind him is Canda, a torch in one hand with a dagger in the other. Blait brings up the rear, torch in hand. Both ladies struggle to keep up, Blait shaking off the spell she recently was liberated from while Canda fights to find her strength, so long in the dungeon with no exercise or movement.

Suddenly Reaper stops the group with a raised fist. He peers into the darkness at a lump on the floor. Canda raises her torch higher, illuminating the hall a little more. Reaper immediately grips the hilts of his weapons that much harder. The group finds their eyes locked on a dead soldier but not one that Reaper had dispatched. Using his hands to signal for the women to stay in place, Reaper hands one of the blades to Canda.

Reaper silently turns to the corner to find three more soldiers lying on the ground not moving. He surveys the hall and finds nothing, no one. Looking closer at the lying men reveals much. Firstly, the men's uniforms are clean, indicating the new shift, the very men he was concerned about. Secondly, the doors are left open, indicating whoever the benefactor is, wanted to help him escape. Lastly, there is no blood, no stab wounds, no arrows, just broken bones, bruises, and contorted limbs. The work of a blunt object such as a staff.

Under his mask and hood a smile creeps across the face of Reaper. He is going to have to thank Kem when they return. He realizes he has much to learn from the monk and vows to do so immediately. He turns around to head back down the hall to his companions who await his return.

"Come, we go. Our path has been cleared for us by our guardian angel. Come, it will not be long now."

Both women join Reaper as he leads them from the tower. He leads them through the shadows, eager to get them to safety and under the protection of his house.

✦

Already a crowd grows outside the castle when Queen Sera arrives with a company of soldiers behind her. According to some of the men, many had witnessed the battle between the demon and a human figure on top of the castle. None could describe the man nor had they seen any transformation but many describe the battle and killing of the demon.

The queen has already created an explanation and put it into motion. Immediately the dancers in her room and the two guards at her door were removed and placed in the dungeons. Their deaths would be explained through the course of the battle. All loose ends must be tied away. Any soldiers still alive in the princess area were also rounded up and stored away. Their deaths will be explained by the attack. Any doubt about her story must be eliminated before it begins.

The royal guard erupts from the castle entrance, vigorously separating the townsfolk into two groups, creating a walkway for the queen. She walks proud with purpose and mission, striding from the castle with a look of fierceness on her face. If anyone could look into her eyes, they would see a sense of dread in her eyes. This would mark the death of her second offspring. Two thirds of her offspring have gone back to Lucifer in death. Doubt about the mission creeps into her mind. The weapons of the Apocalypse have cost no one but her family.

She stops abruptly. Lying on the ground in a crumbled mess is Princess Jala. Blood spatter sprays some twenty feet from the corpse, a direct result from the splat when she hit the ground. Massive amounts of blood pour from the underside of the corpse, staining the cobblestones for years to come. Sera looks at the death mask of Jala, foreign to all standing there save her. She has been thankful that Jala's features do not resemble the mask she wore as a human, lest all their true identities would be exposed.

the dark hole and pulls out an unlit torch. Moments later, he has the torch lit and the three head into the darkness.

Reaper leads the group, his torch providing light in the dark tunnel. The trio walks for several minutes before they reach the end of the tunnel. In front of them is a wooden door with a wooden bar set in the metal clasps. Reaper hands his torch to Canda before pulling the thick piece of wood from the cradle. He places the board on the floor and pushes the door open. The group finds themselves staring at the bed chamber of Jaml, Duke of Erndine. Reaper leads them into the room before closing the door and placing the pillows back in front, hiding the door from casual eyes.

Blait looks around the room, then turns to Reaper. "You know Jaml?"

Reaper pulls back his robe, revealing his face to the distraught woman. "You can say that."

Blait throws her arms around Jaml's neck, squeezing him tightly. He feels tears run against his skin so he hugs her back. She laughs/cries at his embrace and squeezes even more.

After a few silent moments, Blait quickly pushes Jaml to arm's length. She looks over at Canda, a look of astonishment on her face.

"I am so sorry Canda. Can you please forgive me? I lost my place."

"No worries Blait. He is a special person and I understand. I am just thankful that I am married to such a man." She wraps her arms around both necks and the trio share a moment now that everyone is once again safe. Blait breaks the moment to look at Jaml.

"Zell?"

A smile comes across Jaml's face. "This way."

Jaml opens the door to the main living area where Karva is kneeling on pillows, hands clasped in prayer. Kneeling next to her is Zell, also in prayer. The group waits for the prayer to end before saying hello. Karva and Zell jump to their feet and rush over to embrace their family and friends. Zell immediately goes to kissing Blait all over her face, telling her how much he loves her and will never leave her side again.

Karva hugs both Jaml and Canda, welcoming them home and seeing if they need anything. After more hugs, Karva brings back a tray with a pitcher and 5 mugs. Each person grabs a mug, allowing

Karva to pour water into each. The five give thanks in prayer before drinking the water.

They all sit down and Jaml goes about telling the horrific story of the events of the night. He tells of Blait's situation and how brave she was in the rescue. He gives her special thanks for her role in the death of Jala. Zell gives his wife another hug and kiss. Jaml continues his tale in the dungeons and how they were able to find Canda. As he nears the end of his tale, he looks at Karva.

"Where is Kem? Without her help we would still be in there fighting our way out. I owe her my life."

Just the next note in a symphony, the door opens and standing proudly is Kem, her long robe waving slightly in the breeze. In her hand is her staff held at arm's length.

"I heard my name."

The room erupts in laughter as all six people find themselves hugging and enjoying each other. That is until Kem looks at Canda, who instantly recognizes her as well. Kem brings her staff to bear as Canda pulls a dagger from the table. Kem moves towards Canda, ready to do battle once again. Jaml places an arm in front of Kem, impeding her progress. At the same time he stares at his "bride". It is Kem who speaks up.

"Tell him who you are, go ahead. Tell him how I know you. I am giving you this opportunity before I have to retell the horrors that you have brought on the people of this land."

Jaml and the rest of the group look upon Canda in surprise and bewilderment. None more than Jaml. He searches for something he can cling to that says what Kem is saying is false. A lie. Something besides those ugly tales Kem is hinting at. What meets his gaze is a look of pride. Jaml knows the woman he has shared secrets with works for Lucifer. Now this same woman stands in front of him, brandishing a blade. The urge to rush forward to plunge his blade nearly overcomes him but this woman has done so much for him. But he cannot figure out if the help was for him or just part of the mastermind for his downfall.

"Jaml, she has betrayed you and would have led you to your death. We cannot allow her to live. She knows too much and will lead the demons to our doorstep!" Kem's words bite deep with the pain of the truth. This woman has lived this charade in his household. But is it any different or worse than the charade he lives

166

out as well. How much of a hypocrite is he? He turns to look at Kem.

"No."

The words are soft but powerful. Kem instantly relaxes. Does she understand? Or is she backing down out of respect for him. He will have to ask this question later. He steps in front of Kem and looks at Canda standing there with a blade in her hand. She has to know that her life is forfeit. She cannot beat the skill of Reaper or Kem, let alone both. Yet she stands with her knife at arm's length, ready to die here and now.

"Put your knife away."

She hears the words from his mouth. She saw the lips form the words and yet she cannot believe what is happening. He is telling her to put her knife away as softly and comfortingly as possible. She is torn. Is this some way for her to lower her guard so they can kill her? Yet she knows that killing her would not be a problem for these two. She swallows hard, readying herself for the killing rush. It never comes.

"Put it away."

This time she drops the knife. The clang of the blade on the stone floor resonates through the otherwise silent room. So much that Canda jumps. She looks into the eyes of Jaml and does not see hatred and contempt. Emotions she understands especially based on what she did. Instead she finds compassion in those eyes. And love? Not the lust filled love but love for her as a person, almost family love.

Everyone in the room awaits to see what is going to happen next. Silence sits heavy in the room as death awaits patiently for the outcome. Jaml takes a heavy breath before speaking.

"I cannot lie to you Canda, every bone in my body aches right now to kill you. But I cannot. You have endured much pain at my expense and have saved my life. I cannot forget these things. For this and this alone you are granted free passage tonight. Go and live your life Canda. I pray that you change your life and do not go back to the ways of Lucifer. But God has given us a choice and I hope you choose life. I will tell you this, if I ever encounter you in the presence of Lucifer or his minions, I will not hesitate to take your life. I pray you never put me in that situation but if you do, you will

167

die. Now go Canda with no fear of us hunting you down nor killing you. You have earned your life tonight. Now go."

The words trail off as sorrow begins to overtake Jaml. There have been many nights that he has contemplated making the marriage real and taking her as his wife, living his life out as a missionary, and raising a family. Now guilt and shame fills him. He feels his eyes begin to water when a familiar voice fills the room.

"Is it done then?" The angel Allie stands in the doorway in her human little girl form. She cracks a smile towards Jaml who looks up at the sweet face. "You have done well Jaml. Angels sing our praises. What you have done today is a comment on mankind and how faith keeps us on the narrow path."

"What have I done besides being a fool?" He pleads, wanting answers.

"My brother in Christ Jaml. You have taken large strides in your devotion in Christ. I could feel the hatred and contempt in your heart towards Canda. I can understand the hurt you must have felt. You were falling in love with her and then to find out she has betrayed you all along."

"I know! And you also knew, didn't you? Why didn't you tell me what she was?!" Tears pour like rivers of pain from his eyes.

"Yes I knew. What did you say God gave man? Choice. And you were given a situation where many men would have failed in the choice. But you didn't, you chose with love not hate. And that is why the heavenly host rejoices tonight. I know it is not much right now. You are hurting in your heart. Take care Jaml, you are fragile but your faith will keep you with God. Rest, and we will talk further tomorrow."

Jaml feels an arm wrap around his waist and both his arms raised slightly. He looks to find Kem and Karva taking some of the weight from his wobbly legs. He gives each woman a smile and gladly accepts the help... They lead him out of the room to a guest room down the hall. He didn't need to sleep in the bed where he spent many a night next to the traitor Canda.

Chapter 10

Five days have passed since the betrayal of Canda, the woman who paraded around the kingdom masquerading as his wife. Since that night Jaml has been reluctant to conversate with anyone, inside or outside his villa. He immerses himself in prayer, reading of the Bible and training. From sunrise to sunset, Jaml is in constant movement, pushing his body and strengthening his mind.

On the sixth day, Jaml enters the common dining area where he finds Karva and Kem enjoying a breakfast meal. Their conversation and giggling are interrupted by his entrance. Both ladies look up at the man entering the room, wondering if he is going to be social or has he just come in to grab some food and disappear once again.

To their surprise, Jaml takes a seat beside Kem. The table is round but has enough seats for six people so when he sits next to Kem, he is literally across from Karva. He breaks a piece of bread from the loaf in the center of the table. He pours himself a cup of milk, takes a sip before biting off a hefty chunk of bread. He looks up at the women sitting at the same table as him.

"You two look as if you have seen a ghost."

"Have we?" Kem's remark is harsh and to the point. His sarcastic meaning does not go unnoticed.

"Look, I'm sorry. I know I have left you two to fend for yourselves. But trust me when I say if anything had gone wrong, I would have been there for both of you. I just needed some time to rectify the situation with Canda. I have never had a close member betray me like that."

"I know you would have been here if we needed it. How are you feeling?" Karva's words are soothing, reassuring Jaml that he is among friends.

"Are you done whining?" Kem's words bring him back to reality. "We have a sword to find before the demon family does. They have the Scythe of Death and the Axe of Damnation. If they get their hands on the sword, the war is all but on and we are going to lose earth."

"Pretty dramatic there, eh?!" For the first time in days, Jaml smiles.

"Glad to see you back in form there. Got any ideas?"

The three go over all the information they have gathered and couple that with all known associates that may know where the sword is, frustration begins to grow. Midday meal has come and gone. The sun has reached its zenith and began its slow decline into the earth. And yet the group remains at the table, where morning milk has turned into midday wine. The group is no closer than they were at the beginning of the day.

Kem rubs her face, washing away hours of stalemate. Karva takes another sip of wine, her head begins to hurt. Jaml sits silently, his chin resting on his fist when all of a sudden he sits erect, a smile comes across his face and he looks at his two companions.

"It's been in front of my face all along. With all that selling and trading that went on, who is the one person responsible for most of it? The one person who has since laid low."

A smile appears on Karva's face. "Bala."

"What is a Bala?"

Karva and Jaml burst out laughing. They continue to laugh until Karva sees the irritation on Kem's face.

"Bala is the leader of the most powerful thieves' guild in Colley, the Skull Guild. When all this started, it was Bala who was handling the sale of the sword. I don't think she knew the buyer was the king. But anyway, the whole deal went sour thanks to your friendly Reaper here. People died and the sword disappeared, as did Bala. Makes you wonder if she knows where the sword is, eh?"

Jaml is able to stop laughing. "Sounds like it's time to pay a visit to my good friend Bala."

"Yes" Karva pumps a fist. "When do we do this?"

The two warriors look at each other. Each wondering who is going to break the news to her that she is not going.

"I can be a second lookout. You two are not going to have all the fun. I deserve some action after all."

"You are right." Jaml nods his approval then looks over at Kem. "She can watch the bar and let us know if reinforcements are coming. Kem, you have my back in the lair, especially if it gets busy. Now let's figure out the details so we can get this done tomorrow night."

The trio spent the next day gathering Intel on the Skull Guild. From what time people rise and leave to recording when thieves check in. They take special notice when Bala and Miko leave and return. Jaml left the group to follow these two, seeing where they go and how long they remain away from the lair. He also takes notice of the hidden entourage that trails her.

That night the three sit in the back room in Jaml's villa, just in case the betrayer Canda chooses this time to launch an attack. Unfortunately his men will die in the attack but it would give them enough time to escape through the back. They had thought about using the tunnel but quickly dismissed the idea since Canda knew about it and would likely wait in ambush for them to escape.

They use only one candle for low light and now bring too much attention to the back room. They had left most of the torches in the front rooms lit to draw any spy or attack to the front end. The back room had a long table with six chairs. In one corner is a small desk that is all the furniture in the room. Sprawled out on the table are countless pieces of paper, all with written notes in three distinct handwritings.

They have been going over their papers and discussing options for well over two hours. This is something new for Jaml as he is used to working alone and making plans without taking others into consideration. What he had originally planned was scrapped as it would have put Karva in immense danger. The pursuant plans all had variations on the first one, just slight differences to take into account all three parties and their roles. After a long period of time, Jaml finally leans back in his chair.

"Finished."

The two women also lean back in their chairs finally looking relaxed but satisfied.

"Are there any questions about how this is going to work? It has to move like clockwork lest we get eliminated." A nod from both women indicates him to move forward. "The three of us will take up space at the Boar's Pub. When Bala leaves for the night, Kem and I will leave shortly after she does. We will take the prescribed route, avoiding the lookouts and entourage along the way. Karva will leave shortly after we do and take up her spot. She will continue to watch

171

the Boar's Pub and if there is a mass exodus, she will light an arrow and shoot it up in the air. Then you will go directly to the church. If you fire the arrow, under no circumstance do you return here." Karva nods

"Kem, you will settle at this point. If you get the arrow, you will throw the clay pot and leave. Go directly to the meet point outside the city walls. Wait one day before collecting Karva and the both of you leave Colley, never to return. I will handle anything that happens inside the room." Both women nod.

✦

After their reunion, Zell had insisted he and his wife go home. They wanted to rest and relax in their own bed despite the objections of Jaml who continues to say they are in grave danger. Blait pointed out that with Jala dead, there is no reason for the king to come after them. They were no longer pawns in the battle.

Blait took a long hot bath, one that had two refills of hot water poured in, and was sitting in the front room with a glass of wine in her hands. She is dressed in a simple white gown and soft shoes. She waits for her husband to finish his bath and join her on the pillows.

Zell emerges from the bathing room dressed in loose green pants, a matching top and a gold robe draped over his shoulders. He strolls over to take a seat on the cushions next to his wife, they share a passionate kiss. Their lips part leaving the couple staring into each other's eyes.

She leans over to kiss her husband once again one of their hired guards interrupts with a clearing of the voice.

"Welcome back Lady Blait." He performs the appropriate curtsy. "The duke has not been the same with you gone. Sorry to interrupt but Duke Dain and Lady Xana await an audience."

"Of course." Zell kisses his wife one more time on the lips. "Please show them into the living area. Get them whatever they want and need and we will be out there shortly."

The guard gives another slight bow before walking backwards out of the room. He closes the door as he leaves

Zell notices the Blait's heavy breathing. He smiles at her breathing and his erection. He smiles while shrugging his shoulders.

"Sorry my dear but everyone wants to see the lady who faced down a demon and lived."

"Shut up" The couple bursts into laughter, even as they prepare themselves.

Dain and Xana do not have to wait long for their hosts. Zell emerges from the room dressed in black trousers and an oversized orange top complete with frills. Draped over his shoulders is an emerald green cape that extends to his waist. His thigh high boots complete his extravagant look. At his side is his wife Blait. She is dressed in a flowing gold yellow dress complete with matching shoes. On top of her head is a gold colored hair piece that seems to radiate royalty.

The hosts stop a few feet from their guests, showing and posing their outfits, letting everyone who can see Blait is back and beautiful as ever.

"Duke Dain, welcome to my humble villa and you bring your most beautiful wife. We are honored." Zell puts on an elaborate courtesy for all in the room to see.

"You are too much." Dain's beaming smile and playful words break any barriers that might have existed. "It is good to see you brother. We have been worried about you since Blait's ordeal with the demon."

Jaml had forewarn Blait and Zell from telling anyone what really happened. None needed to know about who the demon was and their intentions, Jaml had warned. Not everyone in this town is who they say they are. Dangers lurk in every corner for these are dangerous times. Keep to yourself and don't share information with others that were not there. Only those who were there and know what is going on, warned Jaml.

But these were friends, just as much as Jaml is, the truth be told. Zell and Dain shared some wild times together as squires. And Xana was one of Blait's bridesmaids in her wedding. They were practically family. With this rational Blait spoke.

"You cannot tell another soul. Swear!"

"We swear." Xana giggles as she gives her oath. "Now spill it."

Blait grabs her husband's hand before speaking. "That demon was Princess Jala. It was her that kidnapped me and had me trapped in the tower. She was going to sacrifice me to Lucifer that night. If it wasn't for Reaper, I would be dead and some horrible demon would have my soul."

Xana takes a big grasp at the news. She covers her mouth in astonishment of the revelation. She and Blait's eyes locked in disbelief. Blait had told her story and felt like a burden had been lifted from her shoulders. Born in the upper echelon of society, she had been privileged to many court decisions. Her status has always elevated her to knowing more than most. She has been fighting her life code over this period of time on whether to be relevant and share or keep a secret as Jaml instructed.

The next instant showed her folly.

The disbelief in Xana's eyes quickly turned to disgust and hatred. Before her mind was able to register it in, the unthinkable happened. She remembers seeing a flash of metal. She turns her head to find the flash of metal only to find the result. Dain brings his arm sweeping across his body, sword in hand. His swing opens up the neck of Zell, her husband. An instant in time changes her whole life. Her eyes struggle at the sight of her husband falling to his knees, both hands clamped around his neck, unable to stop the steady flow of blood pouring from his neck.

"Now kill her Dain, kill the blasphemer!"

Those words bite deep, especially spoken from who is supposed to be one of her best friends. She had only done what is expected of a woman in her stature. She had not broken any laws and yet she had witnessed her husband be executed right by her. She wants to cry, to mourn the death of her husband. She wants to hold him in her arms one more time. She wants him to come back. Instead she has seen her husband be murdered.

"Kill her!"

Xana's scream wakes Blait from her stupor. They are going to kill her next unless she is able to get out of the house. She turns to run for the far window but knows she is not going to make it. Dain is bigger and stronger than her and will cover the distance between them far faster than she will have to get to the window. The traitor couple stands between her and the door, no escape. She knows her death is imminent but flee she tries. She bolts to the window with everything she has. She knows this is the only chance she has for survival. She can almost feel his breath on her neck as he bears down on her.

She hears a loud thud right before she reaches the window. She grabs hold of the edge before looking back. Her husband, with his last bit of strength, grabs hold of Dain's boot, tripping him. Dain tumbles to the ground. This is all the time Blait needs. She flings herself through the window, into a forward roll and back to her feet. She wastes no time in sprinting down the alley and into the crowd.

Inside, Dain scrambles to his feet while grabbing his sword. He takes a step towards the window when Xana grabs his arm.

"Let her go. When we arrived, there was a huge fight. Blait was hysterical with madness in her eyes. In a fit of rage, she grabs a knife and slits open Zell's throat. I tried to talk to her but she threw the knife at me and fled. I am distraught and will pray for her sanity every day. Now we must make sure no one is alive to refute what happened here today."

Dain turns back to the figure on the ground. Zell continues to fight for breath while grasping his hands around his neck. Dain casually walks over to the man on the ground and rolls him over with his boot. He places his boot in the chest of Zell, who instantly grabs hold of his ankle. Zell struggles to move the boot from his chest, all the while choking on his own blood. Dain keeps his boot in place until Zell lies still dead, drowned in his own blood.

"Come my darling Xana. Let us go tell our queen the horrible fate of Duke Zell and Lady Brait."

Dain sheaths his sword and holds his wife's hand, who smiles sheepishly at her husband's dealing.

✦

Blait runs through the alleys, working her way to Jaml's villa. Her mind raises at what she just witnessed. One of her closest friends just betrayed her. These women grew up together, ran together, and studied together. She was one of the people she trusted with her life. That trust almost got her killed. Hell, her husband lies drowned in his own blood from a slit throat.

Blait rubs the tears from her eyes. This is not the time for one of her weeping poor me fests. She has to survive and tell the others. Their lives could be in jeopardy, and if she cannot keep it together she will be responsible for their deaths as well. She looks around the corner and is about to run when something stops her.

For the second time, someone has tried to kill her. Yet here she is, running alive. Why? Is she touched by Allie as well? The Lord has definitely had her back in all this. She glances up at the heavens and gives a silent thank you.

Blait crouches in the alley thinking, what would Reaper do? She knows she does not have the skill with weapons so she thinks hard. Going to the villa now would mean meeting up with soldiers which would put Jaml in a situation, sacrifice her or fight their way out. She has no question that Jaml would fight for her. Then again she thought the same about Xana. Maybe I need to go to the church. Surely Karva would give her asylum, she is a nun. But if there are soldiers there, she and Karva might be cut down where they stood.

She needs to think. She also realizes that nightfall is the only time for her to be about. Anything other than that would mean her death. So she finds a female beggar in an alley and trades clothes with the toothless hag. Blait may have just signed the beggar's death warrant but she has to take that chance. She huddles down in an alleyway and waits for darkness. In the meantime, she remains vigilant in her disguise and whereabouts of any soldiers.

✦

Things have gotten crazy! Bala strides with purpose down the center of the road in the market's square, something she never does for fear of assassination. Her fear is well deserved as it was the means she acquired her current position. It was on a day like this, hot and sunny, with the market teeming at the brim with activity. People were hustling for the latest deals and bargains while merchants looked for the next sucker. Drag, the leader of the Skull Guild, walked casually down the market square.

He walked with no care in the world as his guild had just squashed the Knife Guild, the second largest guild and next most powerful. Drag's forces had completely overtaken the knife's fighters, the floor of the tavern ran red as crimson. He had lost a couple of men but that was to be expected in such a battle. In the end, Drag walked out of the inn with the head of his rival and all the power in the city.

The one thing that Drag did not have is the ambition of his second in command, his executioner. The raven haired beauty was rumored to be Lucifer himself. Her drive for the kill and love of the hunt brought fear and loathing from all. None opposed Drag as they would have to deal with the killer herself. Bala wanted nothing more than to hear her prey whimper and beg before screaming wildly for mercy.

"You did well last night." The words were spoken but there was no eye contact. Drag was above that.

"Thank you master. What are we going to do with the remaining guilds?"

"Crush them of course."

"Master, what if I took command of the ones who pledge their allegiance and use them to command the docks. For you of course." Bala nods slightly.

"You dare question me? You little whore!" Drag swings his hand catching Bala across the cheek. The woman simply turns her head, accepting the blow. Drag bellows in laughter, bringing attention to her humiliation.

Without thinking, Bala pulls her wrist dagger and plunges the entire four inches into his neck. The shock on Drag's face reveals his disbelief. He holds his hands out as if to catch every drop of blood that was spurting from the wound in his neck with little avail. He drops to his knees. No one raises a hand to help the dying Drag, even as they watch in horror at his murder. Bala places a boot on his chest and rips the blade out through the front of his neck. Blood and gore explode from his neck, showering the ground in red bloody pieces of flesh.

Bala shakes her head of the memory and quickly becomes more aware of her surroundings. A good reason for Bala to walk the streets alone, which she has always done. She finds her personal guard amongst the crowd while others keep pace on the rooftops. She relaxes a bit. Her eyes dart back and forth amongst the ground, trying to find any person stupid enough to attempt an assassination attempt. The other guilds have been quiet and compliant recently and the king's soldiers have been supportive since they profit from the arrangement. No one really wants a city war so given an excuse, people are apt to accept the terms as long as their fingers touch some coin.

Her walk amongst the people to cool her head culminates at the Boars Pub, used as the command center for the Skull's Guild. She smiles at the two beggars in front of the pub. Both men are sitting on the ground next to the entrance. Most of their features are covered by the large blankets draped over their head and body. They have no shoes on, their feet covered in filth, just as the brown trousers and shirt are. Skinny dirty beggars to most but for the ones who know, the beggars are some of the most skilled fighters in the guild. Multiple knives are hidden underneath the blanket, ready to slit throats and end the lives of anyone threatening the pub.

She does not acknowledge them as she enters the pub. Like pubs, this is outfitted with bench seating. Long tables stretch out along the open space. To the left of the entryway is the bar, a long wooden top with kegs of beer and ale lined behind it. The bar is so big that it takes three bartenders to adequately man it. There are no decorations along the walls, the torches that light the main area. It is a three story building but unlike most buildings, the third story is underneath the ground, put in immediately following Bala's ascension to leadership.

Bala walks quickly to the bar area. Despite it being the middle of the day, Boars Pub is near capacity. There are very few empty seats at the tables which is the norm for the pub. Since the guild took up permanent residence downstairs, the pub has experienced a tremendous growth in popularity due to the price of beer and ale being cheaper here by almost half. A man can afford to drink all day at the Boar cheaper than he could drink at any other pub for an evening.

Along with outstanding drink prices, the pub boasts the greatest number of barmaids in the city, all ready to make your evening so much more satisfying. Out the back door to the pub is a smaller building furnished with beds if you desired some additional alone time with a barmaid. The man near the back door ensured only two barmaids were gone at any particular time and they returned in a timely manner.

The leader of the Skull Guild walks to the back of the bar area, where three huge men stand guard, to the small door located there. One of the men opens the door for Bala, who strides confidently through. The lower level of the pub is only one third the size of the upstairs. One torch sits at the far end of the room. One long table is located near the torch with chairs around. To the left of the entryway is where Bala walks towards. A bed sits in this particular corner.

She notices a figure slumped at the table. No doubt drunk and needing to sleep it off. She considers ignoring the thief but it would set a poor precedent, allowing her minions to sleep their drink off down here. Besides, she would probably have to kill someone when they mistake her sleeping form for a barmaid.

Bala walks over to the slumping man. "Hey, who do you think you are sleeping down here? If you don't get your filthy rat ridden."

She pulls on his tunic. He falls to the side, a thin red line across his neck, the front of his tunic soaked in blood. She quickly reaches for the dagger at her side when she feels the tip of a sword pressed to the back of her neck. Pressed so hard that she feels a drop of blood running down her neck.

"Move and the Lord will judge you tonight." The voice is steady, no emotion.

She smiles. "Ah, I was wondering when you would be by. What took you so long? That's right, you have been too busy saving women and fighting demons."

"Then you know why I am here. So let's just get through the formalities and tell me what I need to know"

"And if I don't?"

"Then you are no longer of any use to me."

She feels the tip dig a bit deeper, letting her know how serious his words are.

"Catacombs under the city." Her voice does not crack, no fear

"How?"

"Easy. We needed to put it in a safe place and we were made an offer that made us the most powerful guild and also the richest." A smile comes across her face, hidden from him

"If not the king, then who?"

"Lycans." She couldn't help but snicker somewhat. The irony of the Lycans hiding the sword from their masters. The irony does not evade Reaper either.

"So the dog hides the bone from their masters. No matter. For your honesty, you will live today. The next time we meet, I cannot guarantee your safety."

"Reaper, I cannot guarantee your safety today."

The sound of steel sliding out of a leather scabbard.

"What's the matter Reaper? Did you not think I would have a backup?"

Bala feels the blade leave her neck. She takes the opportunity to turn and face her adversary. The smile on her face leaves as she senses the smile behind the mask as if it is his trap.

"Glad you could join us Miko. This would not be complete without you." Reaper steps back so he can see both of him. "We have some unfinished business to attend to."

Reaper stands facing both people, one to this left and the other to his right. In actuality, Reaper had not expected Miko to show up. His hope was to get the information and leave without killing anyone. Unfortunately God had other plans and Reaper went with the flow. He has taken the element of surprise away from them with his comments and successfully placed doubt in their plan.

Miko flicks his wrist. Reaper leans back but still feels the wind rush by as the throwing dagger impedes into the far wall. Reaper recognizes the strategy and turns to face the charging foe. Reaper turns his body while bringing his blade up, diverting the sword thrust harmlessly to the side. A side kick catches the assassin across the face, sending him across the floor.

With no time, Reaper turns to thwart the knife stab to his throat. He kicks her knee, dropping her to the other one. He brings his swords to bear but a side glance by Bala alerts him otherwise. He dives to the side, avoiding another thrust from the assassin. Miko presses forward, slashing and stabbing, keeping Reaper on the defensive.

Soon Reaper feels the hard wood pressed against his back. He allows the sword slash to skim across his chest, creating a slight line of red. The slash allows Reaper to quickly move forward, catching Miko with a series of punches to the face. With his body over extended, Miko has no way of protecting his face from the barrage of fists. Before he knows what happens, four solid punches have connected with the assassin's face, each blow precise in its delivery, causing the maximum damage possible. The assassin moves back to recover, he feels his left eye swelling fast, his jaw aches and blood flows from his nose. Reaper presses forward with a front kick that catches Miko square in the chest and sends him flying backwards to crash onto the floor. He looks up at Reaper before turning his head and spitting out a mouthful of blood.

By this time, Bala has recovered and retrieved her long knives, her preferred weapon. She quickly jumps into the fray, slashing with her knives feverishly, aiming to skewer Reaper like a slab of fresh meat over the pit. Reaper retreats from her attack, careful to move away from the assassin who finds his way back to his feet. Bala continues to press forward with every intention of killing this man herself. What she did not expect is the complete spin by Reaper causing her to overextend.

As she leans too far forward, she knows she is dead. Her back is completely exposed with no defenses available to her. She closes her eyes, ready to feel cold steel slide into her back. The only thing she feels is her awkwardness as she stumbles all the way to the ground. She looks up to find Reaper engaged in swordplay with Miko. So he decides Miko is a bigger threat than me. For that he will pay with his life.

She quietly rises to her feet, stalking her prey. She knows her second in command cannot hold out much longer. His eye is almost completely swollen shut, blood flows from his nose in a constant flow and the right side of his face is swollen around the jaw area. If he can hold out just a little more, she will be able to end this in a moment's breath.

With his back exposed to her, she launches forward. Her blades raised high over her head ready to plunge each blade into the back of Reaper. What irony. He sneaks into her chamber for information, a move that she has done countless times. The hunter becomes the prey. But this prey has reversed and has once again become the hunter.

With no time left, Reaper suddenly turns to the side, Bala's blades flying by. She notices no weapons in his hands and in that instant she realizes all is lost. He pushes her forward, altering her trajectory slightly. She cannot stop herself as her new victim stands there helpless. Both blades find their mark in Miko's chest. The blades do not stop until the hand guards are resting against his chest.

The two crash into the table behind him, shattering the flimsy wood. Bala finds her face mere inches from Miko's, a look of astonishment in his eyes. She slowly rises from the wreckage to find her worst fears recognized. Miko lies on his back, blade hilts protruding from his chest.

"Miko?"

"Our ride has been great, hasn't it?" His breaths come in short grasps, his lungs quickly filling with blood.

"It has, my dear friend. I will miss you. May the gates of Hell welcome you with open arms."

"Aye." He coughs. Blood erupts from his mouth to run down the sides of his face. "Rebuild and retool. The Skulls Guild must remain strong."

"Stronger than ever."

Miko closes his eyes and dies.

Bala turns to face Reaper, hate fills her eyes as she glares at the man.

"Do not waste your life." Reaper knows that look on her face. She struggles within herself to launch one more attack. They both know she would not live.

"Leave Reaper. You have your information. You have cost me my top two men Reaper. Watch your back."

"Do not threaten me, woman," Eyes narrowed into slits above his mask. "Lest I forget who I am and open your throat as well. You killed the assassin, not me."

Reaper leaves the room, leaving an enraged Bala standing with thoughts of revenge filling her head.

✦

Blait remains hidden in an alley across from the church. She continues to watch as Reaper, Kem and Karva return to the church under the dead of the night. She was about to emerge from her hiding spot when she watches Reaper leave once again. She slings back into the shadows, expecting a horde of soldiers or demons to descend on the church. She knows the women inside would not stand a chance, so she is not going until she is comfortable in her safety.

For what seems like an eternity, Blait waits for the attack that does not come. Tired, hungry, scared, and dirty leads Blait to one conclusion, she has to get up and get over to the church. With this renewed determination, she quietly walks out of the shadows. Still scared beyond her wits, she makes her way across the dirt street. Her eyes continue to scan across the alleys and rooftops. She clutches the dirty dress on her body close to her bosom.

She sees the light from a burning candle inside the church. A warmth washes over her body at the sight. Safety is within her grasp.

She wants to throw away her cover and sprint the rest of the way. She controls her urge and continues to walk.

Safety in the church has arrived.

✦

The catacombs are a series of tunnels built beneath the massive graveyard a half mile outside the northern gate. These tunnels were built for safety from disease. When leprosy hit this kingdom generations back, the afflicted were thrown from the city. Most settled north of the city in refugee camps. People dug the tunnels so they could get food and supplies to loved ones without exposing themselves to leprosy filled air and become one of the damned.

Once the disease was contained, the entire camp was burned. The soldiers used the catacombs to make their way to the camp and kill anyone still alive. They were ordered to burn every corpse as a precaution against the disease. As the soldiers finished killing the people, they followed orders by piling up the corpses and setting the pyre of bodies on fire. Then the killers became the prey when they were killed by the archers still in the catacombs. The dead soldiers fell amongst the dead and burned.

The pyre burned for over a week, the black smoke billowing into the air believed to be God cleansing the air of the poison. Since that event, the catacombs have never been used. Most have forgotten the whereabouts to the entrance and even more have forgotten its existence. The good people of Colley view the catacombs as one of many monster stories parents use to scare their kids and preachers use as a warning from God to obey his words lest they be reopened.

The exact entrance to the catacombs was found in one of the church books. While searching for the location, the group came across some old writings. According to the writings, lycans can only be harmed or killed with silver or a holy or unholy weapon. Lycans are a creation of Lucifer as he wanted warriors to use against the angels. His new soldiers were ferocious and vicious but lacked the cunning needed to lead. This was perfect for Lucifer. What he didn't count on was their blind rage. Early in the War of Angels, lycans succumbed to their bloodlust and killed the angels and the fallen together. Lucifer abandoned these creatures and left them to hunt the humans, thinking they would just die out. The lycans were able to adapt and move forward by infecting humans with their blood.

The blessed weapon must be dipped in holy water and prayed over by an untainted priest or angel of God. Reaper found Allie and the ritual of the blessed was cast over Reaper's twin blades.

He stands in front of the entrance wondering what he will find inside. Since the king does not know the whereabouts of the sword, it is safe to assume neither does Lucifer. The question is why are the Lycans holding onto the sword and not turning it over? Reaper is interested but the acquiring of the sword is foremost on his mind. Reasons may or may not be found out tonight.

Reaper pulls aside the branches to a large thorny bush. He is thankful for the gloves on his hands for the protection they provide. He finds what he is looking for, a rusty steel circle handle. A smile appears under his mask. He quickly pulls the bush out of the way to reveal a wooden door built into the ground. Satisfied he has moved enough of the bush away, he pulls on the lever. After several attempts and clearing away more bush, the door responds and opens up.

His nostrils are invaded by a putrid scent of sweat and death. The smell is so overpowering that tears flow from his eyes and his body wretches as if to lose his lunch. It takes a moment for his nose to get accustomed to the stench.

After wiping his eyes, Reaper lights his torch and ventures into the catacombs. The actual hallway is inches above his head. The width is nothing above twice his wingspan. Not much room to maneuver in a fight, for either side. Close quarters combat is his preferred style so he feels a bit more comfortable. Rats run freely in the catacombs. No chance for stealth and a surprise attack. Everyone's hands will be on the table.

He walks for what seems like a mile when he comes to bend in the tunnel. According to the map, the bend signifies the other opening close by. He sees three sets of green eyes. The eyes of a wolf. He does not draw his blades, information comes first.

"Who dares come to our lair?" The voice is deep and harsh, the words mumbled due to the shape of the muzzle and the enormous amount of teeth inside. Yet the accent is unmistakable, definitely local.

184

"Reaper. Warrior for our God and Christ Jesus." The words are loud and clear.

"Why have you come, Reaper? This is our domain and not to be disturbed. You are disturbing us "warrior of God"."

"Answer my question and I will be on my way."

"I doubt that. Ask."

"How did the original warriors of Lucifer come into possession of the Sword of Darkness and yet your Master nor his new puppets know of it? Has the prodigal son not seen a path into good graces? Surely Lucifer would welcome you back if you would hand over the sword."

"And maybe our kind realizes we are nothing but pawns in a battle. Much like yourself. Maybe we have come to realize we hold true power and when the time comes, we will barter to once again be Lucifer's favorite. Now that we have answered your questions, we have a decision to make. Are we going to allow you to live with this information to bring angels and fallen down upon us? To destroy our leverage? Give us reason to let you live, Reaper?"

"My life is not in your hands, lycans. I beg to say it is the other way around. Why should I let you live? You see, I am walking out of the catacombs with the sword. If you hand it over, I will let you live your miserable life. Otherwise I will be forced to send you to meet Lucifer. Your human side will be forgiven but your lycan side will burn in hell."

The three lycans break out in laughter. Behind them Reaper can see a sword resting on a pedestal. The prize. Reaper knows he is going to have to fight and kill to get out of here. But the information he gained is invaluable. Dissension in the Fallen's ranks. Nice to know.

"Surely you know you cannot kill us. The sweet taste of your blood will be all worth it."

"No, brother, let's turn him. How wonderful will that be? To have a Reaper, with all his training, battle with us. How ironic to God if one of his own highly trained assassins fought alongside us."

"Yes." All three lycans laugh out loud. The fact they never call each other by their human name suggests these lycans do not shape shift. Either they have forgotten how or these are three of the original lycans.

185

"Do you not have a name beast? Can you not call each other by name?" Agitation. An agitated lycan is more likely to give in to his blood lust. If these are human soldiers, blood lust will eradicate all formal fight training. Easier to fight and kill.

"Enough human! I was going to simply turn you. Now my brothers and I will eat you while you yet live. I want you to feel every bite and chew we take out of you. Before you take your last breath Reaper, we will have devoured most of your body. On this I swear!"

The lycan talking nods his head at the one to his left, who bolts towards Reaper. The warrior draws his swords. I hope the scrolls were right or this will be a very short and bloody fight.

The lycan swings with his right arm, claws eager to rip open human flesh. Reaper sidesteps the arm before plunging his blade to the hilt into the creature's side, just below the armpit. The beast howls wildly, his second swing connects, sending Reaper flying backwards. Reaper hits the ground and completes a back roll to his feet. He looks up to see the lycan charging on all three. The arm on the side of the blade hangs useless. As a human hit in the same spot.

Reaper smiles as he readies himself for the attack. It works. The lycan lunges at him, teeth bared, ready for the taste of blood. Reaper answers with a lunge of his own. The man's lunge surprises the lycan who has no time to alter or prepare for him. Their bodies meet in midair, a clash of muscle and will. Reaper is well within the lycan's body, preventing any damage from the creature's long razor-sharp claws.

Reaper lowers his shoulder in anticipation of the contact. This also allows the impact to be a stalemate. Upon contact, Reaper immediately plunges the second blade into the thick hide of the creature. A tremendous noise emits from the creature, part roar, part scream.

The combatants land on their feet, inches from each other. Reaper strikes quick and true, repeatedly plunging his blade into the lycan. Blood squirts from a multitude of wounds, staining the fur coat of the creature. In the frenzy, Reaper grabs hold of the other blade, jerking it free from the lycan. When he senses the lycan claw about to grab hold of him, Reaper leaps high into the air. At the apex of the jump, Reaper sweeps his blades across the neck of the lycan in opposite directions, opening one rather large gaping hole in the lycan's throat.

The man lands on his feet while the larger lycan falls like an oak tree, stiff and loud. Reaper looks up at the other two lycans with unforgiving eyes, ones that foretell of death. He walks over the dead carcass of the creature, stalking the remaining lycans. His eyes never leave them, sizing them up while making sure he knows where they are. He calmly stops within striking distance from the creatures.

"You have seen your brethren fall to my swords. You know I have the ability to kill both of you. Do not force my hand in this. I come for the sword and sword alone not your lives but if you insist, I will send you to the gates of hell."

The lycans stare at him, sizing the likelihood of success. They steal a glance at each other, seeing if either one really wants to go through with this. This human is really good with the swords and since neither one of them have any formal weapon or war training, it would be more of a carnage than a battle. Realization hits both creatures. They have betrayed Lucifer and to go before him in defeat and lose the sword. They both shudder.

The one who spoke earlier speaks once again. "And if we give you the sword?"

"I'll take it." He looks hard at the creatures. "Swear you will never hunt humans again and you will live out your lives in peace. Hunt animals to feed upon, which is all I ask."

The lycans continue to watch the man with caution. The look tells Reaper all he needs to know, they are contemplating their choices. Can they give up the sword and still keep hidden from Lucifer? Reaper continues to watch with interest. The looks tell his option is winning out. His grip on his swords relaxes a bit.

Suddenly one of the creatures grabs hold of his head, howling like a dog in pain. It shakes its head from side to side, trying to get the invader out. His partner watches in curiosity while his partner thrashes his head about. Then the creature stops and glares at Reaper. Saliva drips from the fangs in his mouth.

"The man must die! It is our penance to Lucifer. He has spoken."

The second lycan turns to face Reaper. Whatever reasoning in his head is gone, bloodlust is all that remains. Both lycans stalk forward, razor sharp claws at the ready, fangs anticipating the taste of human blood. Thoughts of tearing flesh from bone gets the lycan in a frenzy, a blood frenzy. They move towards their prey.

Reaper grips his blades once again. It is time to kill. Again. He appreciates the fact that the tunnel is narrow enough to prevent the lycans from flanking him. It keeps the creatures in front of him.

The first lycan charges, galloping towards his prey as fast as he can. Guttural noises, almost like growls, can be heard as the beast approaches Reaper who readies himself for another rush. Right before the man answers the rush with his own, the lycan leaps high. Reaper quickly ducks while slashing down with one of his blades. The lycan flies over to crash against the ground before rising to its back paws. The slash left the creature with a wound leaking with blood.

The leap also left Reaper surrounded.

Reaper immediately charges towards the second lycan. The element of surprise is his best chance for survival. He may be able to battle on two fronts and still be able to defeat them. The charge catches the beasts by surprise and before they can react, Reaper has lunged at the beast before him. The beast is better prepared than his predecessor, backing away and swiping with his claws.

Reaper has to pull up on his jump and impede himself on the claws. He lands to find himself engaged in combat. He brings a blade up to block the claws aimed at his chest. The blade is brought down, taking the claw with it. The opposite blade flashes forward and is caught between claws. Reaper leans back, creating the space needed to kick out. The lycan stumbles back four steps before crashing onto the floor.

Reaper immediately turns around and runs full speed at the other lycan. The creature stands firm, not willing to give up his position. Reaper picks up speed, the lycan readies himself for the lunge. The lycan cannot believe the stupidity of the human to try the same move that got him into the predicament the human is in.

At the last moment the lycan raises his blades to catch the man as he attempts to jump overhead. Instead, the man slides on his knees. He comes to a stop in front of the lycan before slashing away at the creature's knees. Blood pours from the five wounds that appear. The lycan takes two steps back before falling to his knees. The wounded legs are no longer able to support his weight.

A swipe from Reaper's sword as he gets up opens the fatal neck wound.

Reaper turns to face the last remaining lycan as the other one falls to the ground, dead. He begins the walk towards the last lycan, blood dripping from his twin blades. The look of fury in his eyes.

The lycan recognizes he is beaten. The only thing that will come out of this battle will be his death. This human is much more skilled than he is at war. With his blessed blades, the Reaper is invincible. The lycan sees that now. He drops to his knees, bowing his head. Exposing his neck.

"I yield." The rumble of the lycan voice almost drowns out the words.

"Do you really?"

"What else can I do? You are by far the more skilled fighter. To stand against you would only bring me death. As it has my two brothers. No Reaper, I am finished. The sword is yours."

Reaper walks by the kneeling lycan, sheathing his swords. His eyes look forward to gaze upon the Sword of Darkness, one of the weapons to the Horsemen of the Apocalypse. The end of the word by the Revelations. It is written that any human wielder will go mad. The power and darkness of the weapons is too much for any human to withstand.

Reaper takes one more step before launching himself into a high backflip. On the ascension up, he watches the lycan who moments earlier pleaded for his life, now lunging forward to kill him. Blades are pulled out as Reaper flies over the creature. Reaper stops his descent by plunging both blades into the lycan's neck. Once gravity stops the descent, a shove sends both blades plunging deeper until the hilts of the blades stop against the fur and skin. The lycan screams in pain and agony but cannot do anything about his imminent death.

Reaper remains on the creature's back, guiding the dying lycan to the ground. The creature settles on its stomach with his killer standing above him. A steady stream of blood and spit pours from the dying muzzle. To Reaper's surprise, the creature does not fight but lies still welcoming death.

Once the soft rise and fall of the chest ceases, Reaper pulls his blades from the creature's neck. He walks towards the prize as he sheathes his swords. He stops just short of the blade to take a breath.

The great sword is an onyx black from blade to hilt. The blade itself is four feet long with another two feet for the hilt. The hilt is wrapped in a black material unknown to Reaper.

Then it is him

He can hear, no, feel what appears to be voices. Soft voices that he can barely hear. He concentrates, focusing only on the voices. Filtering out all other sounds, just the voices.

"Pick us up warrior of God. Pick us up and feel what true power is. Pick us up warrior and know what Godlike power is. Pick us up......"

Reaper snaps his eyes open, half expecting to find dark evil figures standing there but sees nothing but three Lycans carcasses and the black sword. His eyes narrow on the sword. Natural instincts bring his hands to the hilts of his swords.

"Why grab steel when you can have the power of the heavens? Take us up warrior of God. We will make all your dreams come true. No one would dare stand against you with us in your fist. Take us up warrior...."

Reaper shakes his head for several seconds, trying to get the voices out of his head. Minutes ago he yearned to hear what they said but now wants nothing to do with their evil message. He looks around and finds a large piece of cloth the same color as the sword. He drapes the cloth over the sword before wrapping it up. Satisfied none of his hand would touch the unholy weapon, Reaper carefully picks the package up.

Giving God the glory through prayer, Reaper quietly leaves the room.

◆

What should have been a triumphant return to his villa was anything but. Jaml returned just before sunrise, sword still wrapped in its protective cloth. Before entering the city, he had the opportunity to change into more suitable garb for his station in society. Dressed in a dark blue top with black riding pants, he passed through the gates without question. He leisurely made his way through the marketplace and to his own villa.

His retainers snap to attention at his arrival, though more than one surprised at seeing him ride in. Especially since no one saw him ride out and it was not announced that he was leaving. Jaml dismounts from the horse allowing a young stable boy to get the reins. He tucks the bundle of cloth underneath his arm and walks into the villa.

What strikes him immediately is the quiet. Granted his home is usually quiet but not like this. Almost eerie, too quiet. If it wasn't for the fact that the guards were not alarmed, Jaml would have gone Reaper immediately. Neither Kem, Karva nor Allie have come out. Something is wrong but he cannot put his finger on the problem.

He makes his way towards the sleeping areas, one hand on the hilt of his longsword. As he nears the entrance to his sleeping area, the main one, Karva walks out. The two stand motionless for a second, both relieved to find the other safe. Then Karva rushes forward, throwing her arms around his neck, pulling him in tight. He stands motionless, his ear is filled with cries of joy while his neck is moistened with her tears. He slowly wraps his free arm around her waist, bringing her in tight. The two stand in their embrace for several seconds.

"Where have you been?" The first words from her lips, unexpected.

"I went to retrieve the sword. You know that."

"You took too long. We needed you here." Her voice is filled with concern.

"What happened? Is everyone safe?"

"Come."

Karva leads Jaml into the sleeping area. Inside is dark, only three candles give any type of light for the room. It takes Jaml a second for his eyes to get accustomed. In the meantime, he gently leans the cloth covered sword against the wall. The sight in front of him takes him aback. He watches Karva walk over to the bed to embrace a sobbing woman. Against the far wall stands Kem, her facial expressions lights tremendously when she sees Jaml.

Kem quickly walks over to Jaml and gives him a quick hug, emotions that Jaml did not know Kem possessed. Whatever happened, it has both women shaken.

"What happened?" He whispers the question as he leads Kem out of the room and into the hall.

"You took too long. We were unsure if you had survived."

"I don't understand."

"Do you recognize the lady on the bed?" Her voice grows stern.

191

"No."

"It is Blait."

"What?!"

"Soon after you left, Zell and Blait were paid a visit by Duke Dain and his wife Xana. According to Blait, Dain and Xana are agents of the king. Zell died. We were afraid that the king was making his move and killed Zell. Maybe he sent a unit to dispose of you and frankly we were waiting for a unit to attack here."

"Is she harmed?"

"Physically? No. But just think about it. She has been captured and tortured by a demon who she thought was he princess. She finds out the royal family are devil spawns. Now she has watched her husband butchered by a woman who she trusts and grew up with. Her world has collapsed. It does not surprise me she is losing her sanity. I have prayed and will continue to pray."

"I am sorry."

"For what? You have not caused this woman any anguish. Now what about you, has your night been more successful?"

"I have the Sword of Darkness. Where is Allie?"

"Why?"

"The sword speaks evil to the wielder. Promising great things and greater glory. The temptation is overpowering and I fear I will not be able to withstand the calling much more."

"I don't know but I am sure she will appear soon. She always does. We have to keep the sword safe until we can hand it over to Allie."

✦

"I ask for your divine guidance. Your word, your blessings, your protection. I am your servant. I live to do your bidding."

The room is dark, one candle provides the only light in the room. A thick rug covers the window, providing not only protection from a surprise attack but also blocking the sun.

Jaml kneels in the middle of the room, naked from the waist up, the black pants the only clothing he wears. His knees tucked underneath his legs, humbly lowering his head in prayer. He has been deep in his prayers and meditations, fighting the voices of the sword that once invaded his head. He knows he is vulnerable if the sword is able to talk to him. He needs guidance and direction. He needs the angel.

"Jaml. He has heard your prayers." The words no louder than a whisper, hard to hear in a silent room.

"In Jesus' name. Amen." He lifts his head slowly, turning to find the face of the little girl. He is quite surprised to find himself looking at a light, bright and yet dim to the eyes. It covers the far wall yet does not light the room any further. Jaml knows he is in the presence of Allie's true angelic form.

"Come, we have some work to do."

"Allie." He lowers his head again. "You must take the sword. The evil that is the blade speaks of killing and godlike powers. I am not prepared to wield such a god-like weapon. I cannot be around the blade less it calls for me to action."

"Do you believe in God the Father, God the Son, and God the Holy Spirit?"

"Yes"

"Then you know that God will not task you with something unless he knows you can handle the responsibility. The sword is not evil but it is heavily enchanted. Like all the weapons of the Apocalypse, it was forged to bring mass destruction. The weapon is not evil. What it will do is transform the wielder into the ultimate killing machine. Incapable of reasoning right from wrong. Enhancing the wielder's power a thousand fold in strength, ability and resolve. Yes, the weapon can kill the Fallen as well as the Heavenly Host. The responsibility and burden is great. That is why God tasked you to retrieve it"

"I am honored that the Lord has seen fit that I retrieve the blade. The blade is retrieved. What now? Where can I hide it so Lucifer's host will not get to it? What monastery am I to travel to in order to safely hide this weapon?"

"No monastery." The spoken words are firm.

"Then where?" Confusion runs across his face.

"The Lord is not going to hide the blade. You are to wield it as your own. The end of days cannot rest in the hands of humans who do not know its power and capabilities. It must be wielded by a child of God who is capable to wield it and not succumb to it."

"I am honored. If that is God's will, then I will follow his path." He looks over at the cloth covered sword. Not his favorite weapon but he will follow God's will. He slowly gets to his feet and looks over at the angel. "What about the voices? Am I ready to handle them as well?"

Jaml feels a very warm feeling on his chest. He quickly looks down, ready to put out a fire if need be. Instead he finds a black pendant hanging from his neck. He reaches for it to look but his fingers instantly burn as if close to bursting in flames. He quickly looks up at the angel.

"You cannot remove the pendant Jaml. Only an angel or fallen is capable of removing it. As long as it rests against your chest, you will be able to control the sword's voices most of the time."

"Most of the time?" An eyebrow is raised. Jaml does not like the sound of that statement, as if there is still a possibility for him to go evil.

"You must keep your bloodlust down. If the sword senses your enjoyment or willingness to kill, it will use this evil to try and corrupt you."

"So I cannot kill again?" Jaml is bewildered by the statement.

"Of course not Jaml." Humor is heard in those words. "There is a large difference between the necessity to kill and eagerness or choice to kill. The Lord has chosen you because of this. You do not look to kill but will kill when necessary. Continue to do God's bidding the way you are and this conversation will be irrelevant. Make sure to keep your emotions in check at all times and you will be fine."

But I hate the longsword. The thought of giving up his prized blades for a weapon that could corrupt him and kill him is one thing but Jaml does not like the longsword. He has to remind himself that it is the Lord's will.

"He knows."

Jaml looks up in amazement. Did the words? No, those are my thoughts. Has she been reading his mind since day one? Are there no secrets from this angel?

"Secrets I cannot read but when the difference between your thoughts and words are your lips speaking, it is as if you are screaming. Those I can hear."

A smile appears on Jaml's face. He walks over to the black blanket that holds his new weapon. After taking a deep breath, he reaches to grab it. The bundle immediately crumbles to the ground. With a bewildered look on his face, Jaml grabs hold of the blanket on the ground and pulls. The blanket quickly unravels and two black short swords spill onto the floor.

"The Sword of Darkness?"

"Is now two swords of darkness. Remember that these weapons are godlike weapons and are formed that way. Man has put the limitations on the weapons and their appearance, not God nor the fallen. The weapons are living weapons and as such can transform into what is needed or wanted. Obviously this one knows you prefer two short swords so it has given you your wish."

Jaml grabs the two hilts and lifts the sword into the air. The balance is perfect on both blades and so is the weight. Perfect weapons. The blades look to be razor sharp. The hilts are also perfect for his hand.

Jaml drops to his knees for guidance as the angel known as Allie slowly disappears.

Chapter 11

“Tell me Taras, are you not the king?” The voice is booming in an otherwise silent room. There are no candles lit inside the room, just the sheer darkness with no distracting noises. “And you! So called queen, what do you have to say about all this?!” The tone is unpleasant, rash, and demeaning.

“I have nothing master.” Sera’s head remains bowed, just like her husband’s. For fear of death, neither dare lift it. The master might be in another land but he is still Fallen. His powers are still immense. Neither wish to know how immense.

“Of course you don’t, you worthless cur! And now this Reaper has the sword in his possession. The sword that has been sitting under your noses all this time. Is that what you are telling me?”

“Yes master.” The words come out together.

“I want you two to go get that sword. I don’t care how you do this but I have left you an inspiration. Do you understand?”

“Yes master.”

“We are so close to our goal.” The anger is gone. The voice speaks to his children, coaxing them to do his bidding. “Stay vigilant. Our time will come when we will rule this world and the heavens. Now go and do my bidding.”

Taras and Sera stay kneeling, waiting for any follow up instructions from the master. Satisfied he is gone, they both quickly rise and turn around before walking straight ahead. As if the room was bright with light, Taras reaches forward to grab hold of the latch and open the door.

The bright light from the windows hits the royal couple in the eyes so much they both have to cover their eyes with their arms. After a few seconds, their eyes grow accustomed to the light and they are once again able to see with clarity.

They walk back to their chambers.

On the way, the king informs a guard to retrieve General Wyr and to meet them in the conference room. The soldier salutes his king and queen before hurrying off to do their bidding. Once out of sight, the couple turn towards their chamber, eager to get to safety.

"Where was the sword? And how did he find out about it?" The questions are intense, the queen very pointed

"I do not know. But rest assured, we will have answers. I don't care how many people die. These humans will pay for hiding the sword from me."

With that, King Taras throws open the door to his chambers to find the inspiration the master was referring to. Propped up at attention at the top of the bed are three heads. Not human heads but those of Lycans. Taras immediately knows the inspiration. These three Lycans were the ones in possession of the sword and now their heads sit there soaking his bed in their blood. Not much of an inspiration, just a sheer open threat.

"Oh!" Despite being a demon, the sight of three Lycans heads still surprises Sera. "Nice inspiration."

"I'll say. Very clear."

Sera walks over the bed. She holds her arms out, aiming at the three heads on the bed. Her fingers begin to move intricately as she begins to recite in a language of hell. Her body begins to sway slightly while her eyes roll back into her head. Taras has to fight the urge to step towards her, ready to catch her when she collapses. He intently watches instead.

Black smoke begins to billow out from her fingers. Wave after wave of black smoke appears covering the bed completely. Once the bed is completely covered, a hole opens in the center of the smoke. Suddenly the smoke and everything the smoke touches is violently sucked into the hole. When the smoke clears, the couple are looking at a bare floor, devoid of all furniture. Taras looks at his wife and smiles.

The heads have disappeared.

✦

In the courtyard, sunrise is the best time of day. With the first rays of the sun cresting over the far wall giving the whole area the feel of warmth, many a day is spent eating breakfast and enjoying God's creation. This sunrise sees a young stable boy brushing four stallions. The horses are relaxed and accommodating to the boy. The lad of no more than ten year is very soothing with the animals, relaxing them for the ride ahead.

Two horses have saddles on their back while the other two horses are burdened with supplies for what seems like a long trek. Cups full of oats are strapped to their mouths, giving them one last comfortable meal.

Inside the villa, Jaml and Kem are enjoying their last comfortable meal with Karva. The three munch on fruit and bread. In the middle of the table is a slab of hot goat. Jaml has been the only one to munch on the savory meat. As they enjoy breakfast, they go over plans.

"Where specifically do you go?" The tone of concern in Karva's voice is evident. She has not been a fan of the idea, Jaml and Kem going after the Dagger of Fire especially after Zell's death. "You know they are going to have the hounds out searching for you. Don't you think it would be a better idea for you to wait until this settles down?"

"Karva, we all know that it will not calm down. Battle lines have been drawn and they will attack us either way. With us out on the road, it takes the danger away from you. If we stay we give up any advantage we might have. Sorry Karva but this is the best option." Jaml attempts to sound caring but thinks it comes off as condescending.

"What the big oaf is trying to say is we all have a better chance of living if we leave. Otherwise we are nothing more than sitting ducks. With us out of the way, they dare not attack you openly for fear of isolating themselves from the Christians. They cannot afford to do that." Kem shoots a look at Jaml before shaking her head mockingly.

"I understand. Take care of one another. What scares me also is neither one of you knows exactly where to find the dagger."

"God's will be done. Have faith. God will show us the way." Kem responds

The trio welcomes Blait and they all enjoy a good breakfast. The conversation is light as Blait is still fragile from the last couple weeks that saw her be kidnapped by a demon, almost sacrificed by said demon, and watched her husband murdered by the woman she called a very close friend.

After breakfast the four friends walk to the courtyard where the stable boy is finishing up horse preparations. The four exchange hugs and well wishes before Jaml and Kem swing up into the saddles. They each grab the reins of a pack horse before out of the gate and south.

✦

King Taras sits at the head of the conference table dressed in dark pants with a red loose blouse. Upon his head sits the crown of Colley. Beside him is his wife Queen Sera dressed in a matching red gown, cut low in the front exposing the inner slopes of her breasts. Like her husband, the crown of Colley rests upon her head as well.

They grow impatient waiting for General Wyr who was summoned some time ago and has yet to appear. Fresh in their minds are the headless lycans that were found in their bed. What is unnerving is the warning from the master right before. The couple are functioning on borrowed time and cannot afford to fail again. As if on cue, Taras rubs his neck which does not go unnoticed by his wife. She soon follows his lead, checking her neck as well. Just when Sera is about to make a comment the door at the other end cracks open.

The man that walks in is the newly promoted General Wyr, formerly captain of the king's elite guard until most recently. The previous general suddenly disappeared one day after questioning the queen about some of her guests. Something about treason and getting stripped of rank and stature but no trial was ever held. No charges formerly brought up. Mainly because the general disappeared the night before. No one dares to ask so speculation has run rapid.

General Wyr is a man who has seen his fair share of war campaigns. His hair is a solid gray that extends by his ponytail through the middle of his back. His face is covered in gray hair, one of the most discerning features is his nose, obviously broken multiple times as it now sits crooked on his face. He wears the armor of a general, complete with a red cape. On his hip is a broadsword.

Wyr walks confidently through the room before stopping at the end of the table. He bows his head and waits for a command.

"Sit general. We have pressing issues that need to be discussed." Taras speaks in even tones, careful not to show the panic that rages inside him.

199

Wyr takes a seat at the opposite end of the table.

"Milord."

"This Reaper must be dealt with. I want him arrested. Now would be good." Taras keeps his voice under control.

"That is going to be an issue."

Rage swells up in the king. He feels the soft hand of the queen on his forearm and realizes how tense his body has become.

"Why is there a problem general?" His voice has a distinct bite to the words.

"Milord, the one called Reaper and his companion the monk left at the break of dawn. The sun is at the highest peak which means they have a great head start. I am sorry milord." Another head bow

Taras takes a deep breath. "You have done well my general. Which direction did they travel?"

"South milord." Wyr's head stay bowed.

Both members of the royal couple instantly tense. Rumors have put the Dagger of Fire beyond the kingdoms of the south. Taras instantly begins to form plans in his head. A visit to Bala is in order. Her thugs should be able to handle the situation.

"What is your wish milord?"

"None my general. Keep things as normal. Continue to keep the people in check. I am afraid things are going to get busy around here and I am going to lean on your expertise on people control."

A smile creeps across Wyr's face. "Yes milord. Of course."

"Good. That is all for now. I will call you again when it is time to enact our control."

The general rises to his feet, the smile still on his face. He salutes the royal couple one more time before turning around and leaving.

Once the door closes behind the general, the royal couple immediately leaves the conference room and heads towards their chamber. They do not acknowledge any soldier salutes as their focus is on more important things. They must tell the master before he gets wind of it through other means. The thing that has bothered the couple is how the master is able to stay ahead of them, always knowing what is going on before they have a chance to tell him. They have long assumed they had a mole in the kingdom. And long assumed it was Prince Baric as he wanted to be king. Baric is dead and so they will find out if their suspicions are correct.

The two once again cover all light leaving the room pitch black dark. They kneel in front of the far wall, the same place they always kneel. Both bow their heads and begin their chant, calling for the master to come. They know not where he comes from but that is not their concern.

A voice calls out from everywhere and yet nowhere. The voice is calm, yet very loud.

"My spawn. I know Reaper has left with the sword. Obviously going after the dagger."

"Yes master. We believe he heads south. Rumors place the dagger there. Should we send a garrison or hire common thieves? What is your bidding?"

"You have done well to bring this to me. Reaper is not your concern any longer. I will have my minions take care of them. I need you to put these humans back in their place. I need you to cause fear in every aspect of their lives. When both the dagger and sword are returned to me, we will start the Apocalypse and God himself will be powerless to stop Lucifer."

"Yes milord." The words come out in unison.

"Do what you do best my spawn. Inject fear."

Moments later the king cracks open the door to get the attention of the guard standing there.

"My boy, bring me General Wyr again."

The soldier leaves quickly, not noticing the fingers holding the door are red with long daggers at the ends of his fingers

✦

The duo had been traveling nonstop for the entire morning. The plan is to get as far away from Colley before slowing the pace under the assumption that once the king finds out, he is going to send someone or something after them. Since they got confirmation that the royal family are actual demons, Jaml has been very aware of their movements.

With the race on to the Dagger of Fire, any false movements could very well end up in their death. Their southern direction would reveal the plan to the king. Hence the quickness to put as much distance from Colley as possible. The assumption must be that they are being chased, the question is by what. Would the king make up a false story and then send soldiers after two priests. The other option is to send demons or Lycans to do their dirty work. If they sent the creatures of hell, would he be brazen enough to risk discovery of their true demon nature to catch up with him?

That is a question he hoped he would never find out. In the meantime, Jaml pushes his steed forward. He and Kem had not spoken thus far into the ride, thoughts on their fate preoccupying their head. Jaml rides in black pants with a white shirt. The sword of darkness has split itself into two short swords, the preferred weapon of Reaper. Each blade rests on opposite sides of his waist. Next to him rides Kem, dressed in the monk's traditional robe. Strapped across her back is her battle staff, five feet of tempered wood fashioned into a tool capable of crushing a man's skull.

Jaml raises his hand, signaling a stop. All hour horses are reeled into a halt. Jaml looks at the hilly horizon before speaking.

"They are out there. I can sense it. It ain't humans either."

"Figured. Are you going to be ok with the blades?" Concerned radiates in her voice.

"Pray so. We can go around and avoid them." More wishful thinking than anything else.

"Shut up."

"Just asking." They both smile before urging their horses forward.

The terrain changes from rolling hills and plains to scarce trees and finally a forest. Along with the forest trees comes forest animals. Both sit on the edge of their saddles as their ears are barraged with the squeals and howls of the forest animals. Jaml keeps a hand on his sword hilt, ready to spring into action at a moment's notice. He knows there are demons but can only wait for the attack.

A sudden flight of birds brings their attention to the right. The birds gawk wildly before disappearing into the sky, bringing in tension and anticipation for both travelers. Coming into view from over the hill is a small band of travelers. Jaml stares hard into the sunlight to count five travelers.

"Well?" The word interrupts his thoughts, bringing him back to reality.

"Don't know. We go as planned but be aware of everything..." Jaml urges his horse forward.

The two spurs their steeds forward into a walk. The road is wide enough for four horses. Kem readies herself to drop her horse behind

Jaml's, no need to get into a fight over a road. Suddenly the opposing group pulls all their horses abreast, claiming the entire road as theirs. They bring their horses to a stop. All five are dressed into oversized garments and face coverings, obscuring any hint to their identity. None of them carry any visible weapons.

Lycans.

The figure in the middle is the first one to pull back the cloth covering the face. The pullback reveals a beautiful woman. Hair cascades down her back as a black river. Her lips are full and her nose perfect against her face. But the eyes, the eyes, red.

Normally it is almost impossible to discern a lycan in human form from a human. During the Great War of Hosts, Lucifer was able to create a grotesque version of life, known as lycans. In their natural form, lycans stand head and shoulders above the average man, even female lycans. Hair covers every inch of their bodies, their nose extends to a snout, resembling a wolf. Fangs extend from their mouths, capable of snapping a small log in half. Claws extend from fingers, capable of shattering a wooden shield.

Once Lucifer began to realize his followers were losing, he sent in the lycans to carry on the fight. In their primal form, they know no pain or terror. The perfect fighting machines. He went one step further. He created an elite fighting force of lycans. These lycans were trained in the art of war and combat. Their abilities are enhanced, even over the normal lycans. So fierce were these lycans that many called them angel killers. As the war moved to the age of man, the monks took up the fight against the lycans. With their training and faith, the monks were very successful. Legions of lycans fell under the might of the monks. That is when Lucifer began releasing the angel killers to do his special bidding. This led to the birth of the Reapers.

"Angel killers." The words are low, meant only for Jaml

"Yes. This could get messy." Jaml turns and winks at his partner.

"Shut up" Smiles are shared, prayers are spoken and Jaml takes the lead.

He waits until the two parties are close before speaking. His voice carries in the most polite manner.

"Milady, why have you blocked the road? We are mere travelers who want to make it to the next town by nightfall. Now if you would be so kind as to move aside so my companion and I can move along."

The raven haired beauty lets out a laugh as she turns to look at her group. They all share in the laughter before she turns back around to address Jaml.

"You do know who we are?" She gestures to indicate all of them.

"Of course. You are angel killers. I recognize the red eyes." His tone remains light

"I am going to assume you know we are here to kill you. Right?!" She tries not to laugh.

"I know. I just wanted to give you a chance to repent and leave us be. I really don't want to have to kill today and I was hoping you didn't want to die today." He shrugs his shoulders. "Guess I was wrong."

"You had to antagonize them, didn't you?" Kem's voice fills his ears.

The two riders on the left dismount. No sooner than their feet touch the ground than the transformation begins. Both men throw off their overcoats to reveal brown shirts underneath. The stitches in the shirts begin to strain under the enlarging of the person inside. The stitches cannot hold out any longer and begin to rip, exposing fur on the body. Fingers grow double in length capped off with claws, long razor sharp claws. Their faces grow in length, from facial features to features that of a wolf. Fangs extend from the front corners of their mouth.

Throughout their transformation, their eyes remain red.

Both lycans immediately launch into a full run at the two opponents. Jaml pulls out his blades, black as night, and holds them in a reverse grip. He slides off the horse, he needs them alive. He slides away from the horses to give himself a little more room to maneuver.

The lycans reach behind them to pull out scimitars, the blades shining bright in the sun. Time has run out. The two lycans are upon Jaml in seconds, launching themselves through the air at the prey... The first lycan flies over Jaml, bringing his blade slashing down to open the man's back. Jaml reaches over his shoulder, bringing his blade down his back. The scimitar clangs harmlessly against Jaml's blade.

The second lycan runs by Jaml while holding his blade out. With one arm over his shoulder, Jaml brings the other blade close to his body. The impact is harder than Jaml would have liked. He finds himself flying through the air to land on his back. The only saving grace is he is able to pull his other arm from behind and did not land on it. The warrior lands with a thud but uses the momentum to roll over his shoulder and back to a standing position.

He casually turns to face the lycan who are turning for another pass. Jaml holds his new ebony blades loosely in his hands and waits patiently. The lycan start at full speed, gaining momentum for the clash. This time both lycans stay on the ground, their weapons held out to the side, each capable of cutting the human in two. Jaml continues to wait much to everyone's surprise.

At the last possible moment, Jaml leaps into the air, reverses the grip on his blade and slams one of the blades down.

The blade slides into the warrior hide as a hot knife through butter. Jaml holds tight as the lycan does not slow. The sudden jerk back causes immense pain in Jaml's shoulder, tearing the arm out of the socket in a lesser man. Jaml grits his teeth hard against the pain as he is pulled through the air. The lycan begins to slow, the pain of the knife begins to have an effect on the beast. Jaml takes advantage to plunge his other blade into the neck of the lycan. The creature immediately stops, rears back, blood squirting all over the grass.

Jaml places his feet in the small of the creature's back and pushes, sending himself flying into a somersault to land on his feet. The lycan rears back at the pain of having two blades ripped violently out of his back. Blood and small chunks of flesh pepper the ground between the two. The creature is locked in that agonizing pose for only a second before falling to his knees. His red eyes show the confusion on his face. A moment later the lycan topples over dead.

Three lycans in their saddles shift uneasily. The leader squints her eyes to get a better look at the blades. She cannot sense any heavenly blessings on them. The one thing she does notice is the blades are jet black. She holds the other two in their saddle. She wants to watch.

The second lycan turns to look at its leader, possibly for help but definitely for direction. The response is subtle but predictable, a mere head nod from the lady. The lycan continues to look at her for direction but receives none. Slowly the creature realizes he is on his own, without help from his companions. The creature will have to kill this Reaper or die trying, no excuses, no help.

The lycan approaches the Reaper, knife drawn. The two eye each other for a second before the blades come to life. The lycan presses the attack, slashes and cuts are furious but unfortunately not connecting. Either the attacks are knocked away or they never find their mark, courtesy of the speed of Jaml.

The lycan presses hard enough to push Jaml back in order to retrieve his comrade's blade. The lycan makes one last push, roaring at the top of his lungs while slashing violently with one blade. He quickly picks up the other blade. Looking up, he finds Jaml standing at ease, waiting for the blade to be picked up.

"You got it? Ready?" Sarcasm oozes all over the words from Jaml's mouth.

Jaml launches himself into battle. His blades whirl, slash and stab in a whirlwind of motion, forcing the lycan to retreat. The lycan attention is locked on the sword attacks as he attempts to stay alive. Suddenly his left knee buckles as he feels sharp pain. His knee hits the ground hard, sharp pain again fills his knee, this time in the front. The lycan gingerly rises to his feet only to have his right knee buckle from one of Jaml's kicks. Again the second sharp pain from his knee hitting the ground.

The lycan rises on unsure legs, both filled with pain. He twirls both blades in giant arcs as a child swings a shirt. He roars his defiance of defeat and lunges forward. Jaml sidesteps the overhand chop. The blade lodges itself into the ground where it remains pursuant to Jaml slicing down with an ebony blade, shearing off the paw at the wrist.

The lycan raises his arm, eyes locked on the gushing blood spewing from the handless wrist. The creature looks up in time to see Jaml rear his arm back over his shoulder and follow through. The lycan head flies off the shoulders to roll harmlessly into a nearby bush.

Jaml reaches down to clean his blades on the tunic of the headless lycan. He does not sheath his blades but merely walks closer to the remaining three. He stops just in front of the leader on her horse.

"You do not have to die here today. As much as I long to wipe all evil from the face of the earth, that is not my calling. I do not wish to kill you. Go now. Leave and maybe you will get another chance at a later time. Go before I change my mind."

The remaining two riders look at each other, wanting to make the argument live is too important but choosing not to open their mouths seems like a more prudent choice. Instead, the two men, Lycans, stare at their leader for guidance.

"You expect us to surrender our cause and allow you to go free? Disobey our master for what? No, my simple human, one party is going to die today. Pray to your God and ask forgiveness. For we will not."

Jaml walks back to where Kem and the four horses are kept. He gives a wink to the warrior monk as he stops in front of her. A wink and a smile let's Kem know all she needs to.

"So this is it? Ride or die?" Her fierceness bubbles over.

"I like riding more, if you don't mind. Which one do you want?"

"How come I only get one? I want the two lackeys. You get queen momma."

"I hear you. Let's have some fun."

Kem dismounts and walks beside Jaml. The two approach the three remaining lycans, Kem holding her quarter staff while Jaml holds his two ebony blades. As they approach, the leader and her two companions dismount from their horses. One of the lycans holds a battle axe in his hands while the other one holds the customary Arabian cutlass in his grip.

The battle axe has oversized double edged blades, too big for most humans but Jaml knows once he transforms, the axe will be the perfect size for the lycan. The cutlass is known for the oversized blade tip, great for chopping as well as skewing. This blade is the size of the English two handed sword, a four foot blade on a two foot shaft, perfect size for a lycan. The leader pulls out a three headed battle mace. The handle of such a weapon is two feet long. Connected to the end are three chains, each about four feet long. Dangling from each chain is a mace ball the size of an infant. The ball is covered by multiple steel spikes ranging from half a foot to a foot in length.

The two humans begin to drift apart, putting some space between them for battle. As they part, Kem's eyes are locked on the female leader, which does not go unnoticed by the leader.

"You want me?" The lady turns her head to stare Kem head on.

"I am not looking because I think you are cute." Kem's staff whirls in her hand with little effort.

"Then your wish is granted." She turns to the other two. "Don't overestimate him, just kill him and bring me his head so I can suck his brains out."

The two men begin their transformation into lycans. They stalk forward as their limbs snap and pop into their lycan shape. Both tear off their shirts, revealing their huge fur covered torso, muscles ripple underneath. Despite their hands elongating into semi claws, they are still able to grasp their weapons. Before the transformation is complete, the two have grown taller in height, fur completely covers their body, and their human faces now resemble short snout wolves.

The cutlass wielding lycan attacks first, twirling the large blade as if twirling a twig. Jaml has no time to admire the skill as the twirls turn into an attack. He sidesteps the first slash before turning his body and lifting his swords to stop the backslash. Jaml slides his blades downward, bringing the cutlass with it. The downward movement turns into an up slash that the lycan is able to lean back to avoid.

Jaml knows something is not right so he leaps to the side, barely in time as the axe blade just misses its target. The warrior completes a shoulder roll to end up on his feet. He quickly turns to both lycans and quickly closes the gap for the next attack.

Jaml leans back to avoid the axe slice to follow with a jump back before being cut in half. Unfortunately the jump was not far enough. Jaml looks at the red line of blood across his midsection.

Not twenty feet from that battle is another one. The leader of the lycans is pressing forward with her attack on Kem. Kem's expert use of the staff repeatedly saves her as the lycan attacks from different angles with expert speed. The lycan presses forward, probing Kem's defenses, looking for the one opening to end the fight.

The lycan continues her attack, attacking the head area of Kem. The twirling staff deflects each blow before resetting her defense. Kem can see the frustration grow in the lycan's face, the desperation from a soldier who has never been thwarted so many times in an attack. The attacks become wilder, more unfocused on the task and more on the desire to slash the monk in half. The lycan side is taking over.

Not far from this battle, a front kick stops the axe's swing. With his foot still against the blade, Jaml rotates his body, barely avoiding the slash of the cutlass. He places both feet on the ground before jumping straight into the air, kicking straight forward. The double footed kick catches the cutlass wielder in the chest. The lycan stumbles backward before hitting the ground.

Jaml crosses his blades to block the downward slash of the axe, catching the hilt between his blades. He pulls to the side violently, overextending the lycan standing over him. He rolls back towards his adversary, plunging his blade into the chest of the lycan. The blade sinks to the hilt and the lycan releases a loud scream/howl into the sky. Jaml wastes no time to roll to his knee and sink the second blade into the lycan's abdomen.

Jaml's eyes lock in on the other lycan. In one move, Jaml rips his blades free from the creature. Blood and chunks of skin fly through the air at the other lycan who simply stands there with a grin on his face.

The tide of the other battle involving Kem and the leader has shifted. Kem has begun to regain the ground she lost earlier. The defensive techniques have paid off. The lycan has become frustrated in the battle, resorting to animalistic tendencies of chopping and overpowering its prey. When this occurred, Kem was able to reverse the tide and now is on the attack.

The lycan is having issues separating the attacks from the movements resulting in numerous bruises across her head and shoulders. All high attacks. The lycan blocks an overhead chop with her sword. She immediately brings her sword downward, hoping to slash this woman open. Instead, Kem spins in a complete circle, catching the lycan on the upper shoulder with a strike.

The lycan howls in pain at the sharp pain of her clavicle breaking. She is unable to catch the falling blade with her other hand, raising the good hand to shield her face. The blow never comes.

"I am bound to give you an opportunity to repent your evil ways. If you repent, I will allow you to live and let you go." She looks at the Lycans kneeling in front of her with a curiosity. "Do you repent?"

"I would rather die before I repent to your God!" Spits her answer to the question.

"Good."

The lycan cannot believe the words. Before she is able to think about her response, her eyes grow wide at the sight of Kem bringing her staff back over her shoulder. She watches the staff descend to her temple. Then she knows nothing.

Kem wipes away the brain matter from her staff using the dead lycan's fur.

Running alongside Kem's battle, Jaml has dispatched one beast as the second lycan stares intently at the man before him, licking the chunks of flesh from his muzzle.

"Nice and delicious. But I have feasted on lycan's blood for too long. It is now time for my palates to savor human blood."

The cutlass rips through the air aiming to end the life of Jaml who merely steps to the side, allowing the blade to rip through nothing but air. Thus starts the battle. Jaml jumps on the attack immediately, his twin blades weaving through the air in coordinated attacks, causing his opponent to retreat to stay alive.

A chop to the thigh area brings the cutlass down to block. The lycan realizes his folly when the second blade whistles towards his neck. He understands the predicament he is in but has no choice. He ducks to avoid the slash aimed at his neck but in doing so he cannot avoid the knee fast approaching. A roar is heard when the knee connects to the lycan's muzzle. The beast lurches back while turning his head. He felt the bone crunch and his vision temporarily went away due to the bright flashes. Out of desperation, the lycan spins while swinging his cutlass to keep the man from advancing.

Reaper waited for the backswing. A predictable move to keep an opponent at bay. When the swing occurs, he waits for the precise moment to swing down, slicing through the wrist with no resistance. Another howl. The lycan stumbles back, fights back the pain, and stares at the stump that was his right hand. More importantly, that hand hitting the ground is the hand that grasps his weapon.

With his one remaining hand, he grabs at his stump and squeezes, attempting to stop the free rush of blood squirting into the sky. He looks at his killer and then at the sword laying on the ground. With one final rush, the lycan lunges at Reaper with his mouth wide open, his razor sharp teeth in full view.

The attack is sudden but not surprising. Reaper waits for the lunge, waits for the feel of the creature's hot breath. Without warning, Reaper extends both arms out, an ebony blade in each hand. The move was so sudden and unpredictable, the Lycans could not respond any other way than to welcome the blades into the roof of his mouth. The momentum of the lunge is all Reaper needs. He watches as both blades disappear into the lycan's mouth.

The dying creature attempts to bite down, to inflict any and all the damage he can but Reaper twists his arms which jerks the lycan to the side. The blades rip the mouth open, causing more damage inside the mouth. Reaper makes one final shove to see the tips of his blades poke through the top of the lycan's head.

Kem watches Reaper pull his blades from the lycan's mouth and clean the blood off using the creature's fur. He slides his blades back into place on his hips before turning to look at his partner.

"Was all that necessary? Could you not have just stabbed the thing and be done with it. But no. You had to go and twist, rip and tear all that apart." Despite the word choice, the tone is very light, playful.

"Oh and I take all that crushed skull over there because she fell?"

"Exactly."

The two of them collect their supplies and horses. They replenish anything they run short on with the Lycans supplies. Satisfied they have all they can carry, the two adventurers swing into their saddles and resume their journey to find the Dagger of Fire.

They ride two more days south of the kingdom of Colley when they see on the horizon a large kingdom. Jaml informs Kem that they are looking at the Kingdom of Sagin. Word travels that King Minz recently was carried off by demons in the night leaving the kingdom to his lovely young bride, Queen Lanea. Lanea has not married but has become obsessed in finding all and killing all demons. Unfortunately her people have suffered for her rage.

Jaml pulls his horse to a stop, signaling Kem to do the same. He signals her to go into the underbrush. Jaml dismounts and guides his mounts to a nearby tree where he ties them up. Kem does the same. She follows him through the woods, climbing a small hill in the process. Jaml stops at the top and lies flat on his stomach, peering through the grass. Kem follows his lead and lies beside him. A slight smile creeps across her face, for in the wooded area just ahead is an ambush of demons. No doubt a welcoming party for them. On their side of the road lies three demons with swords. On the other side lies two more demons with swords. The demons are in natural form, obviously not wanting to go through the transformation when they spring the trap.

"Stay here. When I give the signal, take care of these three." He speaks softly, just above a whisper.

She nods her understanding and listens to Jaml leaving, her eyes fixed on her three targets ahead. One sits in a tree while the other two hide in bushes. They have obviously been watching them as they are prepared for the attack.

Kem moves herself into position for the attack. She discerns the one in the tree is the most dangerous since it has the high ground. That one has to go first. The other two lie low, ready to spring. She knows she will have very little time before the demons take to the skies and her advantage will be lost. She knows two must fall before the third is able to react and take to the skies.

Suddenly the two demons in the bush both stand up while the one in the tree points across the path. The signal. Kem stands and steps into her throw. She watches her staff sail through the air to hit her target with pinpoint accuracy. The top of the staff hits the demon at the base of the skull. Silently the demon stands straight up, his arms raised in alarm before tumbling out of the tree.

Kem did not wait for the result. After releasing the staff, she is in full sprint out of the bush. By the time the demon hits the ground, raising the alarm to his comrades, Kem is in their midst. She launches a flying kick, connecting with the chest of the first demon. She falls and springs to her feet, inches from her staff. She snatches the weapon up just in time to block a stabbing lunge from the second demon.

She counters by twirling her staff, connecting with the jaw of the demon, sending him flying to the ground. She turns to advance on the first demon who is recovering. The demon grabs his sword off the ground seconds before she attacks. He keeps his sword high, blocking the constant barrage of blows. Suddenly Kem twirls low, sweeping the demon off his feet. She takes a step back to jam her staff into the throat of the demon. The sickening crunch ends the demon's life.

Kem wastes no time as the second demon attempts to fly off. Again Kem launches her staff, this time on a moving target but with the same result. The end of the staff strikes the demon in the chest. The impact jolts the demon so he plummets back to the earth. She

212

quickly covers the ground to the demon. She finds the demon dying, impaling himself fully on the limb of a fallen tree. Blood flows from his mouth, the demon coughs and sputters, blood filling his lungs as well. She watches as the demon hisses at her one last time before the body goes limp.

Kem finds Reaper waiting for her on the road, placing his blades back into his sheaths. He looks up and gives her a warm smile.

"Everything good?" The question is sincere but the delivery is light

"Absolutely." She matches his light demeanor

"Hurt?" Inquisitive.

"From who? Them? Really?" They both begin to giggle which turns into a laugh.

The two dispatch of the carcasses before continuing on their journey

It is only a half day ride to the kingdom of Sagin. An hour's ride outside the city, the duo see fields of grain and other foods, tended to by what appears to be hundreds of farmers. Not one pays them any mind so they do not interfere with their work. They also notice patrols of armed guards patrolling the perimeters of the fields. No doubt hired hands to protect the crops from scavengers or looters. Or has the hordes of demons openly wages war on the kingdom. Maybe the rumors are correct.

Right before dusk, Kem and Jaml make it to the gates of the city. They both notice the weapons on the parapet, a series of eight crossbows connected to a single wooden bar. In the middle of the bar is a single trigger. Jaml makes a comment about the weapons being ingenious but Kem points out that all the crossbows weapons are pointing towards the sky, as if this kingdom's greatest foes come from the skies.

A soldier dressed in full armor peers over the parapet at the two riders below.

"State your business." The words rang loud and clear. Jaml feels multiple eyes locked on his position, no doubt with crossbows at the ready.

"We wish an audience with Queen Lanea and passage to the south. That is all."

213

The man disappears behind the parapet for several minutes before reappearing.

"State your name and titles." The command is clear. Jaml considers using his noble title but immediately dismisses the thought. No need for the facade here, they are battling demons as well.

"I am Jaml. A Reaper. My companion is Kem, a high monk of the Order of Crucifix. We mean your queen nor you any harm."

Again the soldier disappears. Moments pass when the main gates begin to open. Jaml can hear the oiled gears spin, twirling and pulling to open up the gates. A tall sinewy soldier emerges. Dressed in full battle gear with a longsword draped on his hip. He casually approaches the two visitors without alarm. Jaml knows the man has nothing to fear with all the crossbows pointed at him and Kem. The red cape draped over his shoulder reveals himself as a captain or higher in the army.

"Evening Reaper and monk, my name is Captain Reeves. This is my watch tonight and thereby my responsibility for the kingdom's safety."

"I am sure the queen sleeps well. Tell me Captain Reeves, are the attacks that bad?"

"Let us get back inside the doors where we can talk safely. I will take you to the barracks where you can freshen up before seeing the queen. Come."

Captain Reeves leads the visitors through the gates and into the city. A look of astonishment comes across both their faces at the sight inside along with the sound of the gates closing. Inside the city is a tent city. Hundreds of makeshift tents have been erected all throughout the square. Kids run around the portable city, playing tag and other games while the adults huddle close, daggers in hand. Yet the people do not seem poor. On the contrary, most are dressed in clothes reserved for merchants and upper society. They do not seem hungry either, just misplaced.

Jaml looks over at his companion and sees the bewildered look on her face. He decides not to say anything until they can get somewhere they can talk and ask questions.

Captain Reeves leads them through the makeshift town followed by the business section of the city. Row after row of stores and bars line these streets. Between the stores are dark alleys, rats scurrying through the trash, creating meals from anything they can find. Patrons stumble out of the bars, falling into the alleys, throwing up any food that is in their stomach to create additional food for the rats.

All the while, Captain Reeves continues to walk towards the palace, a huge building located in the center of the city. The building sits on six parapets, a sphere on top of each one. The wall around the castle is not nearly as high as the outer wall but guarded just as much. To the right of the wall is a series of small buildings, soldier living quarters. It is here that Captain Reeves leads them.

Once inside Captain Reeves takes a heavy sigh, pours himself a tankard of ale and offers the visitors a drink. Both decline while sitting down in two chairs. The captain pulls over a third chair to the group before sitting down.

"Sorry about all that. The queen has forbidden us to talk about the situation in front of the people. They are scared enough as is. It is for the best. I have sent word ahead about your arrival and await the queen to send word when she will see you."

"If you don't mind, captain." Jaml chooses his next words very carefully. "Can you help us understand the situation here? The makeshift town in the middle of the square, the choice of weapons on the parapet, it all is troubling for me. Hard for me to comprehend. If you could please?"

"I can't. Understand, only the queen has the authority to discuss matters of the throne to non-citizens. Please" The captain begins his bow.

"No, please." Kem places a hand on the captain's shoulder, guiding him back to sit erect. "No need to apologize. We are just thankful that you have allowed us into your city. We do not want to place you in any unpleasant situations."

The captain looks up at Kem's soothing expression and then over at Jaml who simply nods his approval. He sits up and takes another drink from his tankard.

"Times are weird, that much I can say."

Kem and Jaml watch the captain empty two more tankards of ale before a knock is heard at the door. All three stand up instantly, the captain to address the knock while the visitors place hands on weapons. Despite the hospitality, there is indeed a strangeness here that neither understands. Better to be ready to do battle than to be caught unawares.

"Yes." The boom from the captain's voice catches both by surprise. They have just watched this man down three tankards, moan about how strange the kingdom is, and whisper since they arrived. To hear the boom of his voice startles both, causing them to look at each other and simply shrug their shoulders.

The door opens and in comes a soldier. The fact this soldier did not have a cape nor a sword, just a spear, indicates a lower ranking foot soldier. The boy, not more than sixteen summers, marches into the room, stops in front of the captain and raises his spear in salute.

"Sir, the queen wishes to see the visitors now." The soldier does not look in the eyes of the captain but seems to stare just above his head.

"Very good. You are dismissed."

The soldier spins on his heels in a half circle, stops, clicks his heels together before walking out of the room, not another word spoken. Once the door closes, the captain turns to his two visitors.

"I guess the time has come. My queen wishes to see you."

The walk is not long but the view is breathtaking. The steps up to the castle end at large wooden doors, greater than three men in height. Each door is a man's length wide. Standing on either side of the door are three guards in full battle dress. Overhead on one of the parapets are two of the strange crossbow shooters pointing directly at them. A man grabs hold of the brass ring attached to the wood and pulls. Slowly the doors open enough for entry. Just as soon as all three slip inside the opening, the doors are quickly pushed closed.

Jaml cannot help but wonder if all this is a trap they cannot escape from or is the threat to the kingdom that real. Only time will tell but in the meantime Jaml keeps his hand near the hilt of his sword.

The great hall is indeed a sight to behold. Along the walls are majestic paintings of battles past. Above the paintings are stained glass windows, many depicting religious figures of God's teachings. Along every peer in the hall stands a soldier at attention, their eyes following every movement Kem and Jaml make. Nothing is missed.

At the other end of the hall is a long wooden table. Around the table is one chair at each end with four chairs on each side. One side of the table three of the four chairs are filled with men. From what Jaml can see, one is a priest and the other two stately men. Jaml hears a fourth set of steps and looks over his shoulder to find a huge soldier dressed in full battle gear. Jaml figures up close, he would be looking at the man's neck. The soldier's shoulders are wider than Jaml's, arms like tree trunks and legs resembling an elephant's legs. The soldier has a full white beard and long hair tied into a braid that dangles between his shoulders.

Jaml second guesses his decision to come here.

Chapter 12

At the far end of the great hall sits a huge wooden table with ten chairs around it. Each chair has a high back with the emblem of the Sagin crest. All along the walls of the hall stand soldiers ready for a battle, eyes fixed on the table where there are two strangers amongst them.

Seated at the table are six men and one woman, who happens to be one of the strangers. Her simple brown robe is the garb of the monk. Her brown hair is pulled back into a ponytail. Resting against the nearest pillar is a long staff, the chosen weapon of the Monks of the Crucifix. On her right is a bald black man dressed in trousers and boots. He wears a yellow blouse. Next to the staff lies his weapons, two short swords. These swords are special, forged by angels as one of the weapons of the Apocalypse. The two swords were once the Sword of Darkness but transformed itself into a weapon of its wielder.

Next to Jaml, the black man, sits Captain Reeves who has served as their guide to this point. Dressed in full body armor, sweat begins to bead up on his head. Whether it's from the heat of the alcohol is anyone's guess. The man is easily on his seventh tankard of ale but shows no thoughts of slowing down.

Across from these three are three men. Directly in front of the captain is a portly bald man dressed in similar clothes to Kem. His robe does not have a hood attached as Kem's and the cloth is much heavier. The captain introduces him as Father Nom. Next to the monk sits a wiry man with short black hair. His simple blouse and trousers of the same gray color is a mark of nobility. The captain introduced him as Wayv. Wayv's eyes continue to dart around the hall, half expecting an attack at any moment. Casually sitting next to Wavy as if sitting in a garden is the man introduced as Kark, another of Queen Lanea's inner council. His blonde hair is neatly parted on the right side. His white blouse and black trousers are such a sharp contrast to his partner Wayv.

Sitting at the end of the table is the monster of a man, General Fen. The only conversation that is going on is a religious one, more specifically between Father Nom and the two visitors. They talk about the travels of God's son Jesus who recently walked the earth, died and rose from his grave.

The soldiers snap to full attention, their eyes locked into the soldier across the hall. Their spears are held in both hands at attention. All the occupants at the table rise to their feet, awaiting the queen's entrance.

The door behind the empty chair at the end of the table opens. A beautiful woman with light brown skin emerges, dressed in a long flowing black dress. Despite her beauty, her eyes tell a very different story of fatigue and worry, of loneliness and hatred. All these emotions are easily read by the two visitors. She stops at her seat. General Fen has already moved to her seat and hastily moves her chair out for his queen. He waits patiently until she can take her place at the head of the table. Once she has taken her seat, the general goes back to his chair.

Queen Lanea sits at the head of the table, across from the general. The queen leads the table in a prayer of thanks to the almighty God. After the prayer is finished, she gives a slight nod to her guests at the table to take their seats. The other seven sit and immediately serving girls enter the room, carrying food and beverage.

When a serving girl approaches Kem with a cup and some wine, she refuses. A sharp kick under the table causes her to turn. The glare on the face of Jaml explains the kick and all she needs to know about courtesy. She quickly stops the girl and takes the cup.

Tray after tray of delicacies are offered to all seated. Out of courtesy, Jaml tastes each morsel, a sign of respect for the host. Kem attempts to follow suit but is not successful, much to the delight of the monk on the other side.

After the snack foods, large trays are brought in. One has a cooked pig with an apple in the mouth. A second tray is an array of bite sized potatoes. Another tray has an assortment of vegetables on it. Another tray has bread while yet another tray is filled with fruit.

A huge burly man walks into the room carrying a large knife. He walks over to the pig and begins to slice into the tender meat effortlessly. The sliced meat falls to the tray where the girls retrieve it and serve it to the guests at the table. Other girls serve the contents of the other trays to the guests. Within minutes every guest has a plate full of food.

Jaml follows the lead of the queen and begins to eat. He savors the taste of the tender pork, seasoned admirably and enjoyed by everyone there. While chewing his food, he takes a quick look around the table. The men on the other side are enjoying the meal, shoveling the delicious food into their mouths. The general is slowly eating, never taking his eyes from the two visitors.

Most telling is the queen, who has not taken a bite. Jaml watches as she takes a sip from her goblet and catches his eyes.

"Is there something wrong Sir Jaml? Is the food not to your liking?"

"The food is delicious and you have been a most generous host. Please forgive me but." His words are cut short.

"I have not eaten. It is I who should ask forgiveness. No need to worry, the food is not drugged." The three men look up warily at the comment. Satisfied with the whole statement, they go back to eating. "My king, husband, was recently killed. I do not have much of an appetite."

Jaml does not look away.

"You want to hear? It is not polite table conversation. I would not want to offend either one of you." Her eyes search but cannot find a negative reaction. "Very well then. About six months ago, reports were given that several men disappeared from their homes. My husband, the king, dispatched a squadron north to eliminate the problem. At this point, we all believed some wild cat or bear had ventured into the region and was wreaking havoc."

"The squadron did not return. Another squadron was sent out. FIve days later a lone soldier returned with stories of female demons preying on the wants of men and killing them. We questioned why he was not killed."

"And why was that?" Jaml asked the obvious question.

"The soldier admitted that he likes young boys so their charm did not work." The queen pauses for a breath

"Is there any way we can talk with him?" Kem asked, wanting to gather more information.

"He killed himself shortly after revealing his desires." The queen closes her eyes as if remembering the sight of the young man found in a room, his wrists slit wide open.

"Oh." Kem's eyes drop

"The next morning, a head was found on our doorstep. A missing soldier. The people panicked. I was scared. Then men throughout the kingdom begin to disappear, only to have their heads returned. The king ordered that anyone who wishes to take refuge inside castle walls at night will be accepted. At first, only a handful came but as the attacks became regular more and more citizens came in."

"So the attacks happen only at night?" Kem shares a glance with Jaml.

"Yes. Only at night. Only to men. So my husband led the third charge."

"And?"

"We have not heard from anyone in that war party. No heads, no nothing." The queen fights back tears, not wanting to show weakness to anyone, especially those in the hall. "But enough of me and my problems. Why have you graced us with your presence? Have you come to help us?"

Jaml takes a deep breath

"Had we known. Our destination lies on the south side of your kingdom. We travel from the kingdom of Colley where demons presently sit on the throne. We are on a quest to find and secure the Dagger of Fire, one of the weapons of the Apocalypse. It is imperative that we find this dagger lest final days fall upon us."

"Has God forsaken us?" The words are soft but the impact is great. Both Jaml and Kem are taken aback. Not once had this entered their mind but to hear another person's voice it shakes them to the core. Kem speaks up

"Of course not your Highness. God is still with us. Trials and tribulations are the work of Lucifer and he is strong at work. We must have the faith of Abraham and the strength of Samson if we are to emerge from this darkness. Remember God's children roamed the desert for 40 years and God never forsake them. No my queen, God has not forsaken us. He is still here and watching over us, seeing how much faith we have in Him. He will deliver us from evil, trust that."

"Thank you for the kind words." A smile creeps over her face. "You have passage through my lands. But I must warn you. Once you have entered into the southern mountains, your faith will be indeed tested."

"How so." Jaml sits up.

"Inside the mountains is an abomination of God. A man over eight lengths in height with the head of a bull. Legends call it a Minotaur. Lucifer has truly outdone himself with this one. Spears do not break his skin. The horns on top of his head have tasted multitudes of soldiers' blood. Rumor has the minotaur being indestructible."

"Lucifer cannot make anything God cannot kill, believe that." For a moment Jaml's face becomes hard. "Thank you your highness for this great meal and wonderful hospitality. We would like to get our evening prayers at the church and rest for our journey tomorrow."

"Of course Jaml. I am sure Father Nom will show you the way to our church. Afterwards we will find suitable quarters for you. For the night of course." The queen's voice is soft and warm. Sincere in her message.

"I will not hear of it, your Highness." Father Nom sits up in his chair. "These children of God will have the best room in the church!"

"Of course Father Nom." A giggle follows her comment

"It is settled then. After we finish, I will take you two to the church and show you where you will lay your head for the night."

A collective laughter fills the room.

It isn't long afterwards that Father Nom is leading the two travelers through the streets to the church at the end of the road. They find themselves watching kids playing in the streets, not having a care in the world. What causes Jaml and Kem to lock eyes is the lack of men. Outside the soldiers, they are hard pressed to find any men walking around the tent city. It is too much for Jaml.

"Father Nom, where are the men? Outside of soldiers, where are the men?"

Father Nom takes a deep breath. "Scared. Simply put, very scared. What the Queen failed to say is the monsters have been plucking men from the streets recently. No male is safe. We have very few men left that are not soldiers or clergy. The ones that remain hide underground at night."

"Still no attacks during the daytime?" Kem walks between the two men.

"Not yet." The priest takes a heavy sigh. "But it is only a matter of time, we feel, before the demons begin attacking during the day."

The trio continue their stroll through the streets towards the church. The two warriors remain silent as they watch the women hurry about their business, heads ducked or constantly looking towards the sky. One mother quickly grabs the collar of a little boy to pull him roughly to safety. The little boy gets pulled yelling and screaming.

Priest Nom shows them to their separate rooms where the duo spend the next hour praying to God for guidance, strength, humility and direction. Jaml emerges from his room to find Kem already standing there. She looks at Jaml, her gaze is returned. They look at each other for several minutes, emotions and feelings being shared without words.

"Then it is settled." Kem nods at his statement. They turn around and head back into their rooms. A necessary detour has been agreed to.

With the rise of the sun, Jaml finds a plate of fruit, nuts, and grains waiting for him outside his door. He takes the plate inside to enjoy his meal. He reads the scriptures and prays his morning prayers after the meal. He finishes up with his hand to hand combat moves. He does not push himself like usual, he needs to talk to the Queen as soon as possible and taking time to bathe does not seem the best idea.

A soft knock on the door brings Jaml from meditation. He jumps to a squat position from the ground, where he sat with his legs underneath him. He opens the door to find Priest Nom standing there with Kem behind him.

"God's morning to you." Priest Nom's happy disposition raises an eyebrow to Kem.

The duo allows themselves to be led back to the castle to speak to the Queen. Jaml allows a little distance to gather from the priest before leaning over to his partner.

"Did you tell him of our decision?"

"No. He says he is always like this. Something about God's gift of day and how we should rejoice in it."

A short time later, they arrive at the palace which, to Jaml's opinion, looks very different from last night. Jaml does not remember seeing the flower garden to the right. Every imaginable flower and color is in full display. He counts twenty maidens either pouring water or grooming the flowers. To the left is a multitude of

223

statues commemorating the past heroes of Sagin. The water fountain in front of the statues is an angel with her hands to the heavens, asking for divine intervention or just praising God, he cannot tell.

The trio walk right by the guards with no interference. As a matter of fact, Jaml notices none of the soldiers give them any notice, so different from the scrutiny they were under the night before. There seems to be a hint of hopefulness in their eyes, hope this kingdom sorely needs.

Large wooden doors are opened for the group, allowing them entry into the throne room. They can see Queen Lanea sitting at the other end of the hall on her throne. She continues to wear a black dress to commemorate the death of her husband. On top of her long brown hair rests a throne of diamonds and gold. Jaml can only imagine the weight of that throne in present times.

All three kneel in front of the throne, their heads bowed. Jaml speaks.

"Thank you, Queen Lanea, for taking time to see us today."

"I wish you well on your journey, Reaper" Her voice is once again burdened with sadness.

"Our journey has taken an unexpected turn. We have prayed and the Lord has shown us a different path. One that involves purging these demons from your land and restoring faith to your people." Jaml keeps his eyes down.

"What are you saying Reaper?"

"We will continue on our journey for the Dagger of Fire but only after we rid your land of its curse. We will need any directions and information you might have."

"Our Lord has truly blessed us today." Queen Lanea looks over to her general. "We will give you anything that you need. Anything. Our hearts have been lifted."

"Your Highness, please allow us to kill these demons first." Kem softly says

"Of course Kem. General, please make sure you have given them anything they need and all the information that we have gathered."

"Of course your Highness." General Fen, the monster of a man, acknowledges her orders.

"It is settled then." Queen Lanea continues. "I insist you stay one more night so you can properly prepare yourselves for the upcoming battle."

"Of course your Highness."

◆

The bright rays of sunshine cresting over the horizon finds two figures readying for their journey. They pull and tug at the ropes, securing the supplies to the horses. They both look up at the warm sun, giving thanks for another beautiful day. Jaml slides his bedroll into place when Kem gives him a nod to his rear. Jaml turns to find Priest Nom approaching, a huge smile across his face.

"Good morning children of God." He holds his arms wide open as if looking for a huge hug.

"Good morning father." Jaml bows slightly "I want to thank you once again for your hospitality and information. Everything you have given us will be essential for our success."

"No worries."

"Good." Jaml's continues. "Is there something you have remembered? Some more information that will aid us in this fight against demons."

"No Reaper. I wish that I had more information." Nom's cheer takes a momentary dip but rebounds nicely. "Queen Lanea sent me to make sure that you have no other needs before you take off this morning."

"Just one question, priest." Jaml looks over at Kem who simply smiles. "How does a priest and leader of God's children not wear a cross?"

Nom quickly places his hand over his chest, surprised to find no cross there or that anyone would notice. After a moment of surprise, the smile returns.

"Oh my. Thank you, Reaper. I must have forgotten to put it on this morning. I assure you that the cross means everything to me. In my haste to do my Queen's bidding, I must have forgotten to put it on."

"Of course. I look forward to seeing it around your neck next when I return."

The two men nod before Nom hurries back towards the castle. Kem watches the man disappear before she turns to Jaml.

"You shouldn't have let him get away like that."

"Kem." He chuckles. "I need to know how many heretics there are in this kingdom so when we return, we can squash the entire group out of existence."

The two share a smile before mounting their fresh new steeds. They take a last look at Sagin before heading towards the nest of demons

✦

The rest of the day is uneventful, along with the night. The duo moves along the trail peacefully, leaving plenty of time for conversation and reflection. The next morning they pack up their supplies before eating a breakfast of dried fruit and oats, washing it down with a fruit juice that neither can place.

They pick up the pace the second day, knowing they could reach the nest after midday. Rolling plains with sparse trees are the landscape at the moment. There are clear paths that they ride along. They clear a small hill and notice a small group of men riding in the distance in front of them. As far as they can see, there are five men in the group and appear to be heading in the same direction. Of the five, three appear to be dressed for war. The sun reflects off the chainmail armor the three men wear. Each one has a broadsword at their side and a spear attached to the side of their horse. The other two men appear to be farmers, wearing a simple brown shirt and trousers. These two wear no armor but are armed with a longsword and throwing axe.

"Do you think they are going to the same place as we are?" Kem looks over to Jaml.

"No doubt. Do you think we should join up? Help each other? Bigger group to challenge the demons."

"Only if you want to die." She smiles. "They are emotion filled. Simply means when the fighting starts they will break formation and leave our backs exposed. We follow and see what happens,"

With the decision made, they pull back slightly so the group ahead does not see them.

As the sun passes its zenith and the heat increases, the group ahead enters a small forest at the base of a mountain. They do not stop but plunge headlong into the forest. Jaml and Kem pull their horses up and dismount.

"Told you. No plan, just rush in and die."

Jaml acknowledges her statement with a shaking of his head. They dismount and tie up their steeds. They pull their weapons free, take time to have a quick snack of dried meat and berries before heading into the wooded area. The trees are not particularly close together so they are able to drudge through the forest. Eyes continue to scan the tree canopy overhead as well as the surrounding areas, looking for any sign of demons. They take their time, not wanting to rush into a situation they cannot win. Just ahead the wooded area ends with a small mountain.

They slow down and proceed with caution as they approach the edge of the woods. A cave opening is located about twenty feet up the cliff face but a path has been carved up the side of the mountain to the entrance. Jaml's foot hits metal. Both look down to find a sea of skeletons and armor scattered around the ground under the opening. They look at each other, Kem speaks first.

"These bones have been cleaned."

"Keep awake. Over there are the horses from the other men. They have already gone up but I don't hear anything." Jaml motions over to the horses tied up on a tree some paces away, near where the walk up platform starts.

Reaper makes sure the protective medallion is around his neck before he pulls the twin blades from their scabbards on his back, blades glistening black. The twin blades are in fact the Sword of Darkness, one of the four weapons of the Apocalypse, reshaping itself into twin blades for its wielder. The medallion he wears around his neck protects him from the evil that resides within the blade. Without it, Reaper would be battling to keep his sanity each time he draws the weapon.

The blades, as with all weapons of the Apocalypse, were forged by Lucifer as angel killers, the only weapons made specifically for killing angels, fallen or otherwise. During the Great War of Hosts, Lucifer forged the weapons and gave them to his most powerful generals, the Four Horsemen of the Apocalypse. These fallen angels were experts at war and enjoyed killing for nothing more than the act. When God cast down Lucifer, he showed mercy on the Horsemen and instead of killing them God imprisoned their souls inside their weapons, proclaiming that if they enjoyed killing so much, they would kill for eternity by another's hand. Only when the four weapons are brought together and the incantation recited, will the Horseman be set free from their weapons to once again wreak havoc amongst the heavens, as proclaimed in the Book of Revelations.

Reaper leads the way up the walkway and into the cave. What they thought as pitch black darkness is only the front of the cave, which turns sharply downhill once inside. The path is lit by a series of torches that align the walls all the way down. A closer look reveals each torch is being held up by a skeleton hand that is attached to the arms bones which stick out of the wall.

The duo turn the next corner to find the end of the tunnel, a lighted room can be seen at the end. They walk their way down the hall. Light music hits their ears and a heavy perfume invades their nose.

They get to the end of the hallway and pause for a second, their backs pressed against the wall. Reaper motions to Kem to be ready to move. He wants her to move to the right while he takes the left. He gets halfway through a three second count when suddenly.

"Don't be shy Reaper and monk. Come into the light so we can get a look at you."

Reaper and Kem lock eyes. Both shrug their shoulders and stroll into the light.

What they see is astounding.

The room feels like a hot bath. Steam appears to be rising from the rocks themselves, giving a cloudy haze to the room. There are no torches or openings here but it is as bright as a mid-summer day. There is no furniture in the room, simply barren rock. Sitting in the room are three succubus, female demons that prefer the taste of male blood over the female blood. Succubus take the form of beautiful, irresistible women clad in nothing more than a silk covering. In their demon form, they are extremely pale with a mouthful of elongated fangs, fingers and toes turn into claws and leather wings extend from their back enabling them to fly.

Usually the sight of a succubus in demon form is enough to scare any person, unless they are under some sort of spell. The five men that preceded them were definitely caught up in their spell. All five men are lounging around the clawed feet of a succubus like a lapdog waiting for a treat, instead of the revenge bound men that stormed the cave.

"What do we have here? A Reaper and a monk, interesting. Have you consummate the union? How does it feel to take the flower of a monk? Oh, to taste the juices of a deflowered monk."

Kem steps forward, both hands on the staff, ready to battle. Jaml's arm raises up, holding her in place, he feels the anger rising in his friend. He takes a quick glance, giving her a wink.

"That is good demon. Have you ever felt love? Or just created to serve as whores?"

The other two succubus perk up, turning their heads to gaze at the threat level that speaks. They both turn their bodies, ready for the inevitable battle.

"A Reaper with a mouth, something I haven't heard before. But then again, I sense an evil surrounding you Reaper. An ancient evil that I have not felt since…." Her eyes lock onto the twin blades in Reaper's hands. "Of course. My master."

"Your imprisoned master, if you have forgotten."

"Not for long with you holding the blades. I never knew my master could transform himself to other weapons. I know you battle everyday Reaper and you will lose this battle. My master's will is much stronger than yours. You are a fool to think you could wield and control a Horsemen of the Apocalypse. It is only a matter of time for you to fall and he will be set free." She waves her arms outward, signifying her master's freedom.

"Not on my watch demon, simply meaning you will not be around if he ever gets free." Hands grip the hilts even harder, ready for the battle.

"Is it true Reaper that you will not kill another human? Let's find out. Bring me their heads my pets." She strokes the hair of the man sitting at her feet. As on command, the men rise to their feet and grab their weapons. Jaml can see the pupils are dilated, meaning they are under complete control of their masters and will do anything the succubus says.

"What now Reaper?" Kem's voice is higher than usual, her anxiety level skyrockets. Her decree forbids her killing humans unless it has been determined they are evil. The fact these men are under the spell of a demon does not make them evil, it makes them victims, the thing monks have pledged to do. Protect the innocent.

"Either they fall or we fall." His voice is calm as a lioness waiting on her prey.

"Our oath."

"You can either knock them out or hope they don't get up or we kill five men and ask God for his forgiveness. What do you think?"

They begin to pray aloud, in unison.

"Dear Heavenly Father, forgive me for my sins. The ones I have committed and the ones I am about to perform. I pray you understand our situation and forgive us for what we are about to do."

Both end her prayer with "Amen."

Four men attack, two centered on each of them. Two men, dressed in armor, attack the Reaper while the two farmers attack the monk. Reaper steps into the attack, brushing aside the clumsy downward swing of the first warrior before crossing his blades above his head to catch the second attack. The first warrior stumbles forward, trying to catch his balance. Before the second warrior can disengage, Reaper fronts kicks the soldier in the midsection, which sends the warrior stumbling back crashing into the stone wall. Instead of killing the man when he is down, Reaper turns around to face the first warrior who has regained his composure and advances fast.

The first farmer swings his axe wildly, not really knowing what he is aiming for, just swinging. Kem takes a step back, allowing the axe to swing harmlessly by. Kem sweeps the man's feet from under him, forcing the grunt and wind to escape from his lungs once he hits the ground. The man rolls to his side, clutching the back of his head, feeling the trickle of blood coat the inside of his fingers. He is out of the fight for a few minutes. She turns to the other farmer who looks a little more competent with his sword. He stabs at the monk, who is expecting the attack. Using her staff, she blocks the strike to counter by twirling her weapon, catching the sword in the move, knocking the blade from his grasp.

The spin kick catches him in his midsection, driving all the air out from his lungs. He bends over and quickly regrets it. She grabs the back of his head, pulls it downward to meet the upward strike from her knee. She feels the familiar breaking of bone against her knee. The man stumbles back before falling on his butt. His nose is completely smashed against his face, blood flows from the wound in a steady stream. He turns to spit his two front teeth out of his mouth.

Reaper catches the side chop against his black blades, stopping it instantly. He reverses his body, crashing his elbow into the warrior's face, sending the man backwards. Instinct tells the man to raise his sword in a defensive position for the incoming strike. He screams in pain and rage, the strike not coming from overhead. He feels the deep bite of the black blade across his stomach. A second cut comes instantaneously across his neck. The warrior staggers back, confused on which to hold in place, his intestines threatening to pour out or the flow of blood from his neck. Not quite deciding which is more important, he falls to his knees before dying.

The second warrior regains his feet and watches his comrade fall in battle. He screams his battle cry and wholeheartedly and recklessly dives into battle. He swings widely from side to side, trying to cut his friend's killer in two. Reaper takes two steps back, each step to avoid another wild swing. After the second swing, Reaper steps forward and plunges his blade into the man's neck. The warrior drops his sword with a bewildered look on his face. Suddenly fear covers his face as he realizes that he is all but dead. He begins to mouth the twenty third Psalm but collapses before he finishes the first verse.

Kem twirls her staff with such skill and speed that the man on his butt cannot see it, just the blur of the spin. Her skill is such that he simply sits there, dumbfounded. Suddenly the spinning stops and the staff comes crashing on top of his head. It takes a moment but he soon feels the blood running down his face. He opens his mouth to say something, only to have a mouthful of blood coming spewing from his face. A sucking sound invades his ears as Kem pulls her staff from his caved in skull. He topples over dead.

Kem looks over to her second adversary and notices he is not moving. Completely passed out.

She walks over to stand beside Reaper, weapons ready. The last man finds himself standing in a very peculiar position. In front of him are two monks he watch slaughter, as there is no better word, his comrades and behind him are three sexy women that he feels compelled to follow, or felt compelled. It is like a fog cloud is lifting from his head and in front of him is a brand new world. He looks over his shoulder and screams!

Three demons are behind him. They appear as pale as maidens with most of the features of said maidens. Their hair color remains what he remembers from before so he can tell which one is which. That is about the only thing that distinguishes them from each other. Their hands and feet have become elongated to form claws.

231

Sprouting from their backs are wings that are the same size as they are. The wings are folded back but that does not mean he does not know what they are. Their faces are similar from before except their mouths which now reveal long razor thin fangs throughout.

The man turns back to face the humans, a look of distress and fear washes over his face. Before one word can escape, a mouth clamps down on his neck, fangs sink into his soft flesh as a succubus enjoys a quick snack. Kem takes a step forward, prepared to fly into action once again. The arm of the Reaper holds her still.

"Not yet. Too much magic to combat. Patience." Despite talking to Kem, his eyes never leave the scene in front of him. The man twitches uncontrollably in the demon's grip, she drinks his life force, sucking on every drop.

Once he stops moving, the demon drops her victim.

"Tis a shame. Now you two have prematurely killed our dinner. For that we cannot let you leave. Better yet, you will become our next meal" All three demons shriek in glee.

"Now" Kem whispers.

"Not yet."

Kem wonders what is holding Reaper's hand. As she watches, the smoke is getting thinner, clearer. Kem smiles. She doesn't know that the smoke is but whatever it is, Reaper is waiting for it to clear. The succubus begins to inch forward, crawling on the walls cautiously, expecting the two humans to launch into battle.

"Now." The word is spoken softly with the only person to hear it being Kem.

In unison, the two monks launch their attack. Reaper takes on the brown hair while Kem launches at the redhead. To her surprise, the blonde immediately retreats to the top corner of the room, undoubtedly using her attack to assist one of her sisters.

The brunette takes several swipes with her claws at the Reaper who simply moves out of the way, his swords never engaged. Her wings unfold, pulling her into the air to gain the advantage. Reaper remains in the ready. She dives towards him, her clawed hands reaching for his neck, wanting to tear his throat out. Reaper waits patiently until ready. He twists his body, giving his back to the succubus.

Instead of finishing her dive, the creature quickly reverses direction. She holds up her arms to reveal nothing more than bloody

232

stumps. She looks down to find her hands lying on the ground. She screams a loud high pitched yell of anger and pain.

The redhead succubus hovers near Kem, trying to scratch or catch the monk in her fierce grip. Kem keeps her at bay with a series of jabs and counter attacks with her staff. One of her jabs is a bit slow and the demon pounces on it. She grabs hold of the staff and pulls, trying to throw the monk off balance.

Kem pulls back on the staff causing the creature to laugh. Both know a human is no match for a demon strength for strength. Kem leans back, pulling with all her might as the demon continues to laugh. The succubus begins to pull harder, giving the monk the choice of letting go or being pulled to her death. Either way, the demon licks her lips in anticipation of the taste of blood, warm heart pumping blood.

Suddenly Kem catapults up the staff, completely catching the demon off guard. Before the demon realizes what is happening, Kem has pulled herself up the length of the staff being held by the succubus. The demon releases the staff but it is too late. Kem has grabbed the back of the demon's neck for support. She throws her legs around the demon's torso and releases a barrage of punches at the demon.

The first two punches connect with the nose, bursting it into a spray of blood. The next set of punches connect with the eye/temple area of the face. By the third strike there, the demon has lost her orientation and focus. The two combatants plummet towards the ground, all the while Kem delivers blow after blow to the head of her opponent. At the last moment, Kem places her forearm against the neck of the demon.

Both crash into the ground with a satisfying thud. Kem is slow to rise, her body aches. Even though the demon broke her fall, she still feels the pain of the hard ground. She opens her eyes to find the face of the succubus, her eyes wide open, unmoving. She notices a stream of blood flowing from the corner of the mouth.

Kem rolls off the dead body of the succubus, only to fight the blinding lights of nausea. She rolls to her knees but cannot move further. She looks up to find the third succubus staring at her. Wings open right before the demon launches itself at Kem. As much as Kem wants to fight, she knows she cannot. Her body aches from the fall, she still feels nauseated and her right hand, her dominant one, is aching so much that she cannot pick up anything. She watches in disbelief at the demon coming for her.

She gently closes her eyes to begin praying that God will accept her into his kingdom. A scream brings the monk to open her eyes. The demon is mere paces away but is screaming and clawing at itself. Looking closer and Kem can see one of the black blades embedded in the demon's side. The succubus crashes into the ground, still trying to pull the blade from its side. With each passing moment, the demon appears to grow old, its skin becoming the color of ash, the blonde hair turning gray.

Moments later the succubus does not move. All its hair is gray and the skin an ash color. Reaper calmly walks over and snatches the blade from the corpse on his way to Kem. When he arrives, he looks down with a smile

"You look bad."

They both laugh. Jaml gently pulls Kem to her feet and hands her the staff. She accepts it with a nod and decides to use it as a walking cane. The duo walks over to each succubus and make sure of death by removing each head. They find enough kindling to may a pyre and burn all the bodies. Satisfied all is done, the two walk out of the cave, Kem still using her staff as a cane.

They decide to stay in the woods for the night, not wanting to break a horse's leg or get attacked while they are blind by the darkness of night. Jaml ensures Kem did not break any bones, especially her shoulder. He gives her some balm which she rubs into the sore spots and almost instantly they begin to feel better. They share some dried meat and berries from their supplies and decide to get some rest. Jaml takes first watch and ends up staying awake all night so Kem can rest and heal.

The next morning the two say their prayers and go through their combat drills before packing up the camp site and leaving. They push their animals hard and by midday they are well away from the carnage in the cave. This also eliminates any conversation as the focus is getting to the pass leading to the south mountain. According to all the intelligence they have, the entry to the Minotaur's lair is on the east side of the south mountain. Their hope is to get to the pass by nightfall and leave with the Dagger of Fire the very next day.

The mountain range they head towards is not really a range. For some unknown reason, in the middle of flatlands sit four mountains, all close together. Folklore tells of a horrific battle in which a band of fallen angels made a last stand against a battalion of the heavenly host. The leader of the fallen, Minotaur, was a fierce warrior but a selfish one. He was also known to overindulge in carnal desires. It is said he would take twenty girls to his bed nightly in order to satisfy him. Women begged and pleaded to be part of his nightly orgy. As the battle on the plains raged on and the outcome was inevitable, Minotaur did the improbable. He sacrificed his final four Fallen to save himself. He transformed them into mountains so the heavenly host was unable to get to him.

After the war, Lucifer sat in his domain licking his wounds and deciding his next move. He knew that he had lost the Four Horseman, they had been transformed and taken away. As he received reports back from his different lieutenants, he heard about what Minotaur did to save his own life. He called for Minotaur to answer for his actions, which the fallen one refused. The punishment for his sacrifice was a transformation by Lucifer himself. He placed Minotaur back inside the mountains and cast a spell that bound him to the mountains. If he was to ever travel more than one mile from the mountains, he would surely die. Also, to make sure he would not enjoy the desires of women, he was transformed into a beast, part human and part bull. His desire for women was turned into a desire to taste flesh.

Beautiful red and orange rays fill the sky when the duo reach the mountains, which look more like a fortress than mountains. The mountains are definitely not natural, they sit eerily close to one another with the base actually growing together. A person would have to climb the height of a castle wall to get to the division of the mountains from one another. There appears to be no way in or out from the center but Jaml was given a secret passageway into the center and to Minotaur himself.

Neither can find a suitable campsite that provides good or even adequate cover. The four mountains sit in the middle of rolling plains as far as the eye can see. There are no animal sounds, wild or otherwise. Then again, as Jaml points out, there are no birds overhead. Not even a vulture. They cannot hear any wildlife coming from the mountains. It is as if the entire area is dead of any forms of animals.

They decide to camp a quarter mile from the base of the mountains. That way no one should be able to launch a surprise attack. More dried meat and berries provide the meal along with watered down wine. The two eat, indulging in light conversation, mostly about their childhoods. They share several moments of laughter and giggles. After the meal, they practice their skills for a time before indulging in their nightly prayers. Kem volunteers to take the first watch so Jaml can catch up on his sleep he missed the previous night. Jaml accepts but both find they cannot sleep, facing the dangers tomorrow as well as getting hold of one more weapon of the Apocalypse. So they spend much of the night planning what to do once they get back to Colley, looking forward to meeting with the angel Allie and placing the dagger in her care.

Morning sunshine comes over the horizon, bringing light and a warmth to the area. Jaml's eye opens at the light before he leans back for a great yawn. Apparently the two of them fell asleep sometime last night as Kem still rests. He takes a swig of water to rinse his mouth out before saying his morning prayers. By the time he finishes, Kem awakens and goes through her prayers. Once finished, they share breakfast while checking their weapons. Kem finds no cracks in her staff and Jaml cannot find any nicks in his black blades. He checks the medallion around his neck that keeps the demon in the blade at bay.

Satisfied that everything is in order, the two decide to leave the horses there so the horse wouldn't be killed in the upcoming battle, or if they need to make a quick getaway. Jaml spots the crack in the rock where the opening is found, without a word, the two warriors head straight to the crack, death awaiting them inside. They reach the crack and Jaml pushes on it to find the rock moving inward. Jaml places two hands on the rock and pushes, the rock sliding to reveal an opening. He is about to go into the opening when Kem touches his arm, getting his attention.

"If the Minotaur is truly a fallen one, only your black blades will be able to harm or kill it. Correct?"

Jaml thinks about it before answering. "I guess you are right. This changes things. Tell you what, I will distract and occupy the beast while you get the dagger. If he is too strong, after you get the dagger, we get out of there fast. I have never fought a fallen one and don't know if I am skilled enough to kill it. If I am to meet my Savior today, make sure you get the dagger back to Allie."

"Of course."

They step inside to find nothing short of horror. The ground is dirt, no grass or shrubs are found. Yet it is hard to see the dirt as it is covered with bones, human bones. The whole area, the size of the small kingdom, is lit by some sort of magic as the opening at the top is covered in black clouds that don't seem to move. The lighting has an eerie red tint to it as if the room is washed in blood. As the center of the space is a stone throne, just as dark and evil as the rest of the room. Sitting next to the throne is a pillar, a piece of gray stone extending up from the ground. Floating in the air above the pillar is a dagger. The hilt is as long as the blade with a skull at the base of it. The blade is black, identical in color to the short swords in Reaper's hands.

Sitting on the throne is a hulk of a being. From the distance the creature was holding his chin in his hand while resting on his knee. As the two walk forward, he looks up. One of the punishments for the Fallen is the huge horns on their forehead while they are in their natural form. These horns extended four feet from his head, curving upward. The creature's eyes are bloodshot red. His skin is jet black which gives his eyes that much more of an evil presence. He smiles at his visitors, sharp fangs extend from his mouth.

"Ah, I am glad you have finally arrived." His deep voice echoes throughout the space

"Minotaur, we have come for the dagger and only the dagger. I have no desire to kill you today, demon. You are imprisoned here and that is good with me." Jaml's answer fills the room with just as much authority.

Minotaur bursts into laughter. "Do you think little human that you have the skills or ability to kill a Fallen?"

"Former Fallen. Now you are nothing more than a cursed beast." Reaper's words bite deep, eliciting the response he is hoping for.

Anger.

Minotaur's right hand grips the arm of his throne in anger but he continues

"The war has been handed down to humans and demons but that doesn't give you the ability to kill a Fallen. I am willing to show mercy little one only because you came with a purpose. Leave now little ones before you incur my wrath and I taste your blood. Besides, I cannot give you the dagger, I am compelled to guard it with my life."

Reaper reaches behind his back to pull out two short swords, the blades completely black. He holds the blades down at his side while he walks forward. Kem stands back, allowing Reaper to engage the Fallen completely before she makes a move for the dagger. She watches intently as Reaper walks forward, almost stalking the monster in front of him.

Minotaur raises his eyebrow at the weapons. "My informants did not make me aware of this."

"You mean the nest of succubae? They will not be informing you of anything any longer. They have been judged through the power of Jesus." Reaper continues to move forward.

"The power of Jesus? Do not mistake your killing as the will of God." The creature stands to his full height, a full eight feet. He steps down from his throne. "Killing is part of life, if you remember anything else before you die today, remember that."

The two adversaries stop within twenty feet of each other, looking for any openings that can be exploited. Minotaur licks his lips with a smile, any normal human would shy away in utter fear. But this is Reaper Jaml, the best of the bunch armed with one of the angel killers. He does not shy away but rather blows the Fallen a kiss.

Minotaur leaps into the attack, his claws swiping at the man, meaning to cut him open and watch all his entrails fall out. Reaper takes several steps back, analyzing the attack but much more than that, he realizes he has irritated the monster who attacks in anger. On the third swipe of the huge weaponized claw, Reaper strikes at the hand, making a shallow cut across his arm. Minotaur cries out in pain, for the first time in ages the creature feels pain.

Minotaur turns and faces Reaper, sheer anger colors his face. He looks down at the cut across his arm and waves his hand over it, closing the wound instantly. But Reaper notices the scar that remains. So the wound is closed and healed, or is it healed? Reaper readies himself for the next wave of attacks. This time Minotaur closes more cautiously, fully aware this human can harm if not kill him.

The second wave is more calculated. The swipes and stabs with his claws keep Reaper at bay, sounds of metal grating against bone are heard throughout the space as two fighters battle for the upper hand. Minotaur brings both hands over his head, bringing them down onto his enemy. Reaper raises his blades for the defensive move when suddenly he finds himself flying through the air, the breath taken out of his lungs. He slides through the sea of skulls. The growing mountain of dead bones stops him. He takes a deep breath only to find pain. Broken rib, the creature is stronger than he could have imagined. He gets to his feet, brushing the dirt from his clothes.

Minotaur is laughing again. "What's the matter boy? Did a little kick cause you some discomfort? Maybe a broken rib or two?" His laughter borders on hysterical.

Kem watches Jaml struggle to rise from the ground. He gets to his hands and knees before resting. She fights the urge to get involved. Jaml is very clearly in the plan. He is going to distract, if not sacrifice himself to allow her to get to the dagger. If he is going to fall, his dying breath is to destroy the blades by using one against the other. She is to take the dagger back to the angel Allie for safe keeping.

She shakes her head to clear it of her instincts and begins to move forward. She slides around the insides of the mountains, attempting to hide in the shadows, becoming one with the darkness so the evil Minotaur will keep his attention on Jaml, allowing her to steal the dagger.

Jaml rises to his feet, stands erect and takes a deep breath, ignoring the pain in his side. He reverses his grip on his weapons and walks back towards Minotaur. After recovering the space he lost due to the kick, he stands ready for the next round. The laughter slowly dies as the Reaper gets nearer and nearer until finally the space is once again silent.

"That was pretty good. Hurt a little as well." Jaml takes another deep breath to show Minotaur the injury is not as serious as it actually is.

"I will hand it to you Reaper, you are worthy to bear the cross on your back. But the inevitable will happen. You will die today Reaper and I will like the marrow from your bones." The words are matter of fact, no malice, no emotion.

Reaper drops into a battle stance, one blade held high while the other held at waist level. Minotaur appears to reach for something in the air. His hand disappears only to reappear carrying a mace. The handle of the weapon is a bright red as if made of blood. The mace head is black, not as shiny as his blades but nevertheless black. An angel killer.

Minotaur inspects the weapon before looking up at his adversary. He nods his approval, licks his lips in anticipation of tasting blood and stalks towards the monk. He begins to twirl the mace causing the wind to whistle. Without warning, the monster launches forward, mace raised high for the strike.

Reaper waits patiently for the strike and at the last moment, he rotates his body to allow the mace to harmlessly fly by. He completes his rotation, slicing across the back of the Minotaur who howls with a mixture of pain and anger. The monster lands in a crouch position before looking back over his shoulder at the man who caused the pain. A growl escapes the fang filled lips along with a stream of spittle

Reaper returns to a fighting stance, looking at the monster in front of him. The creature continues to stare in disgust but does not move. Reaper knows Minotaur is waiting for the cut to heal but he chooses not to attack and possibly walk into a trap. Minotaur's smile returns and Reaper knows the wound has closed. How do you beat a creature who can heal himself in seconds?

His time to ponder runs out, Minotaur returns to the attack. Wielding his mace with little effort but maximum effect, his blows move Reaper back, causing the human to concentrate on living, not killing. Minotaur comes with an overhead smash which Reaper uses his blades to divert the strike to the ground. Jaml kicks at the knee, wobbling the Fallen just a bit, enough so Reaper can move behind the giant. Reaper plunges his blades repeatedly into the back and plexus of the creature. Stab after stab produces a new flow of blood dripping from a fresh wound. With each stab, the monster arches his back even more, writhing in pain. Reaper never lets up, he continues to stab Minotaur.

Reaper notices the slight movement in the Minotaur. He looks up from the carnage he caused, several open wounds dripping blood while other holes close, to find the creature's arm flying towards him. He lets go of his blades, which are still embedded in Minotaur's back, and braces for the blow. The impact is what he thought it would be, thanks God for warning him in time. Reaper finds himself once again flying through the air to crash into the sea of skulls.

He is better prepared this time and was able to jump slightly into the air as the huge arm of Minotaur crashes into him. This allows him to absorb the blow and worry about being stuck by a bone in the ground, which didn't happen. He comes to a complete stop to find Minotaur fighting desperately to grab hold of the blades stuck in his back. Everytime he attempts to wrap his finger around the hilt, he draws his hand back as if in pain. In the corner of Reaper's eye he finds Kem ready to grab hold of the dagger. He takes all this in and comes to a plan of action.

"What is the matter beast?" He rises to his feet and brushes the dirt and dust from himself. "Do my blades hurt? Can you feel the sting? I have noticed that wounds in your back cannot heal with my blades still stuck in them, which means you are bleeding out. How much Fallen blood must fall before you die yourself?"

"You worm infested cretin!" Minotaur glares at Reaper with such contempt. "I will slowly kill you and drain your body of its life juices. Then I will have my way with your little friend."

Both males look over and freeze. At that precise moment, Kem's fingers wrap around the hilt of the dagger. She looks up, sensing something is wrong, to find two sets of eyes locked in on her actions. One has fear for her and the other loathing. Either way the situation does not look good for her at that moment. Out of pure reaction, she snatches the blade from its magic stand and shoves it into her satchel.

"You whore!" The monster turns and begins to lumber towards her, obviously still in pain from the blades but also from the loss of blood. Reaper reacts slightly faster and reaches Minotaur just as he gains speed.

Reaper leaps on Minotaur's back and realizes there is not much he can do. If he takes the blades out, the wounds will close and he will recover. Yet if he does nothing, this behemoth will simply carry him over to Kem and kill them both. Reaper says a little prayer and looks down. Perfect!

Reaper drops from the monster's back and quickly yanks the blade from the back. Minotaur yells but keeps moving towards Kem, desperately making her way towards the opening. She knows she will not make it. Reaper runs even with the monster before swinging his blade like a woodsman intent on chopping down the largest oak in the forest. Instead of chopping at a tree, Reaper buries his blade in the ankle of the monster, handicapping him.

Minotaur collapses to the ground, his left leg completely useless, his Achilles tendon severed. The monster lets out a roar that shakes the entire place, frustration, fear and anger fuel that rage. He reaches for the blade but like before, fingers are met with a searing heat that burns the Fallen to his bones. He struggles to focus his eyes and appears to somewhat rock back and forth in confusion and pain. He finally sits down with a heavy sigh. He looks over at the fleeing figure of Kem nearing her destination, the secret opening. He slowly realizes he cannot get to her before she leaves due to the blade that sliced through his Achilles tendon and renders him useless.

He looks over his other shoulder to find Reaper walking towards him, dragging his mace in tow. He continues to watch as the monk reaches where he is sitting. He begins to giggle at the irony of it all. How he betrayed Lucifer and escaped his wrath only to fall to God's wrath, the one being he joined in the insurrection. After all this time, he is going to fall to the thing that insurrection was about, man. His laughter gets louder, filling up the room, causing Kem to stop her escape to find out what is going to happen. Reaper stops in front of Minotaur.

"Ah, the victor goes the spoils. Take good care of it for me, it has served me well."

"I am not taking it." Cold and direct.

Minotaur raises his eyebrows.

"I see. You are the first human to kill a Fallen, quite an accomplishment if you ask me. Will you take up the mantle of Fallen killer?" He chuckles even though he cannot find humor in his death. "I always thought it would be one of the Cardinal Sins but I guess I am wrong. Of all the Fallens, I will be known for dying first at the hands of a human."

"No you won't"

Minotaur looks up to watch his own mace flying towards his head. He closes his eyes in anticipation of the contact. The instant the pain of the mace erupts is the last thing Minotaur knows.

"Is he?"

"No. He is beaten and no longer a threat to us. I know I am Reaper but I will only kill when completely necessary. His death is not necessary."

"Good. Let's get out of here."

"You got the dagger?"

"Yes, completely necessary."

They both laugh. It has been a long day and wounds need to be taken care of.

Chapter 13

"We must get the dagger back to the angel Allie. That is of the utmost importance!"

"You will not make it that far. We are going to have to stop in the Kingdom of Sagin. You need a healer, unless of course you want to die in the first battle we come across?" Kem places her hands on her hips to make her point.

"Fine." Jaml winces in pain.

The two left the south mountains after securing the Dagger of Fire, leaving Minotuar behind. Before Jaml pulls his blades from the Fallen, he has real apprehensions. He knows the wounds will heal but will that lead to another battle, one Jaml does not feel comfortable he would survive. He instructs Kem to stand next to the entrance, ready to run through if things go bad. Satisfied that she is safe, Jaml looks at the unconscious monster. He considers taking the mace with him but decides against it. He remembers Minotaur pulling the weapon out of thin air and wonders if he has the mace, will Minotaur be able to pull himself out of prison through the mace.

Jaml pulls his blades free and unsheathes them. He watches the wounds on Minotaur close and immediately the Fallen begins to stir. With all his injuries, Jaml knows he would not be able to outrun a healed Minotaur, let alone defeat him. Thoughts of tying him up brings out a painful laugh. He finally decides his best alternative. He picks up the mace and drags it over to the semi-conscious being. He notes the bottom of the mace does not have spikes protruding so it should not kill. Quietly he lifts the mace up and allows the weight of the weapon to do the work, he simply guides it. A hollow gong sound signifies the consciousness of the Fallen leaving him.

Once satisfied Minotaur is not rising anytime soon, Jaml turns and makes the long journey to where Kem is waiting.

The next morning, they wrap up Jaml's ribs tightly knowing the ride across the plain and down the hill where the succubae nest was, is going to be painful. Healing medicine is applied to the numerous skin scrapes and cuts all over his body. They share a breakfast of nuts and fruit before heading back.

Not many words are spoken. Kem watches Jaml struggle with staying on his horse and stay conscious. She knows his injuries are very serious if he refuses to admit it. If they do not get the correct healing balm on him soon, he may not make it. She pulls her horse next to his to make sure he does not fall off his horse and potentially cause more damage or death. She notices the fever setting in and knows she is running out of time. What she needs to do is rest him but every moment away from real help is a moment he may end up dying, so she trudges on, praying for him the entire ride to Sagin.

They stop for the night and set up camp in the woods. Kem allows Jaml to sleep while she keeps watch over the camp. She spends the night praying and guarding, not sleeping. By the dawn of the next morning, she feels exhausted. She breaks camp and places Jaml back into the saddle before heading out.

It is not long before the duo break through the wood line and spot the kingdom about half a day's ride away. Kem resists the urge to break in a gallop to get there faster. She looks over to her friend, who sits in the saddle, head resting against the mane of the horse. His fever broke which is a good thing, he is on his way to recovery. The pace remains the same, progress slow but steady.

Well past the sun reaching the zenith, Kem leads Jaml's horse and the two pack horses to the gate of the city. She watches with apprehension as the gates swing open. Even though they left on their quest in good standing, royalty are weird and fickle, one day you are the hero and the next your head rests on a spike. What raises her suspicion even more is the leader of the procession is none other than General Fen.

"Pay attention Jaml. I hope you have enough just in case we have to make a quick escape."

"Told you." The response is shallow.

The general leads a group of twenty soldiers to meet them. The war party stops just in front of the two travelers.

"Mission?" His voice is one of command, not feeling.

"Completed. The nest has been destroyed." Kem tilts her head to get a feel of what might happen next.

"Dagger?"

"Not in my possession." Kem lied. She does not feel comfortable enough to tell them she has two of the four Weapons of the Apocalypse. Fen looks at the slumping Jaml.

"Seems he has seen better days. We better get him to the healer." He turns to bark orders at the soldiers. "Welcoming Party, attention! About face! Forward march!"

The company of soldiers obey each command and soon Kem finds herself leading only Jaml as they ride through the gates and merchant row on their way to the castle. Once they pass through merchant row, they make a sharp left. A smile appears on Kem's face as she recognizes the churches that appear. They make their way to the large building on the right. Monks come scurrying out from the building like rats on a ship. One monk helps Kem off her steed while four others ease Jaml down from his. They lay him on a board and begin moving back inside. Kem makes a move towards the church and her friend then stops to look back at General Fen. Sensing her predicament, he makes the decision for her.

"Go and tend to him. I will let the Queen know of your success. She will be patient and looks forward to your report once your friend here is out of the woods."

"Thank you General. May God bless you." She hurries inside, not wanting to miss anything.

It has been a week since Kem and Jaml came back from the southern mountains. The monks have worked around the clock to bring Jaml back from the near dead. He stayed silent for the first four days. On the fifth day, his eyes open and he proclaims how hungry he is. Soon after, the healing process has continued and Jaml gains his strength back day after day.

On the seventh day, Kem finds Jaml standing at the window. He is dressed in monks garb standing with his hands behind his back, eyes locked in on the morning sun. She approaches him from behind, trying to not startle him. Instead, it is he who scares her.

"Do you have the dagger?"

"Of course." She takes a deep breath. "Hidden."

"Who knows?"

"What?" Irritation seeps into her voice. She doesn't appreciate the interrogation. " No one."

"Good." Jaml turns to face Kem. "I am sorry for the words but we have to be careful."

"I am not a child."

"Never meant to insinuate you are. I nearly lost my life for that dagger. No one needs to know about it. No one around here needs to know about my blades. I do not get a good feel about this castle. Something is off. My gut keeps pointing at the Queen." He looks directly at her.

"I agree. There is something off. Something evil. The Queen? I think not. If she wanted us dead, we would be dead. There is something off here though. Whoever it is cannot kill us outright because of the work we did for the queen. Let us bid farewell as soon as possible from this place. Else we are going to get involved with a war." Her eyes never leave his.

"I agree. Tell me everything you have shared with these people so I will not say the wrong things."

Kem obliges and recounts all the information she has shared with the people of Sagin. The two work together to fill any questions that might arise. Their story does not include any mention of the dagger but does tell the stories of the five men seduced by the succubae as well as the battle with Minotaur. Through one of the monks, they send a message to the Queen that Jaml is awake.

The rest of the day is spent resting. The monk returns a short time later to inform them there will be a feast that night to celebrate Reaper's return, the death of the monsters and finding closure for the many men that have died in the demons' grasp. Rumors fly that the Queen will not wear black to the feast, something she has not done since her beloved was killed.

Jaml lounges in his quarters when he is interrupted by a knocking at his door. Instincts have him reach for a blade. He catches himself and decides to answer without the thoughts of battle clouding his mind. He slides the blade back into the sheath and walks over to open the door. Standing there are twelve young ladies. Each is dressed in a bright yellow dress, fitted to their particular body figure. The front of the dress is lace covering silk. The dresses flow to the ground. Each of the maidens carry a suit fit for a prince. The first maiden bows slightly.

"For you. Our Queen insists you feel like royalty tonight for tonight you are our royal guests! Where should we start?"

247

The maidens flow into the room, finding a place along one of the walls. Once all inside, a guard closes the door, allowing privacy. It doesn't take long before Jaml finds the outfit for him. A simple light purple long sleeve shirt over black pants. Over the large is draped a deep purple waist cape, which would enable him to attend with his weapons. Thoughts of Kem came to mind. Wonder if they were able to persuade Kem out of her monk garb.

Once his attire for the evening is picked, the maidens leave the room without comment. The door is closed momentarily before someone else knocks. Jaml shakes his head as he opens the door. Standing there is Kem, still dressed in her monk garb. She walks in, allowing him to close the door behind her. She casually walks to the center of the room before turning around, a look of exasperation on her face. Jaml knows the source but waits for Kem to speak on it.

"I am a monk, not some trollop they can put on clothes to parade around the room. They never asked, just assumed I would be fine dressing up. Well I'm not. I will be attending this feast in my monk's attire and if they do not like it, they can kiss my…"

"Whoa there milady! I very much doubt they meant any disrespect when they sent those maidens to your room. I am sure they had the best of intentions. Besides this is supposed to be a feast in celebration of you."

"I never mentioned anything about maidens. How did you know?"

"Because I will be wearing a purple shirt under a matching cape." He gives her a wink.

"So you knew all along?" Her frustration threatens to come at him.

"I figured. It was either that or you had to kill some demon while everyone watched or since I didn't hear anything breaking, I assumed it was your garb for the evening."

The two share a smile before he shows her his outfit for the feast. Afterwards they go over once again their stories about the events of their quest. Not to lie but to omit any mention of the dagger. Neither feels comfortable sharing that piece of news. Also the weapon Jaml uses was one found on the ground in the southern mountains, not the angel killers that rest on his back. They lounge around eating on the tray of fruit in his room until the maidens' return, this time to bathe and dress them.

Jaml feels like the prince he portrays in Colley, dressed in silk after a fresh bath. His wounds are wrapped tightly to ensure no bleeding during the feast. He continues to walk gingerly around the room while getting dressed and definitely on the way to the hall. He has to stop twice on his way to the hall, to catch himself and allow the nausea to subside. A maiden accompanies him and gently wipes sweat from his brow.

They finally make it to the hall where the feast is already in full swing. The doors are open and Jaml is taken aback from the invasion of his senses. The hall is huge in itself but tonight is crammed to the doors with people. The feast table normally seats one hundred warriors but tonight it is used as a food holder only. All benches are removed so no one can use seat preference to start a war.

On top of the table is more food than Jaml has ever seen. From meats at the far end to the different types of potato preparation in the middle to the bevy of fruits and breads at the opposite end, there are enough different tastes to satisfy any palate. Serving girls walk throughout the hall, taking food from the table to every corner of the hall. Ale girls walk around carrying large pitchers of ale, refilling tankards whenever they get low. Serving girls are dressed in pink while the ale girls are dressed in white dresses.

At the far end of the hall is the royal and distinguished guest table which is placed perpendicular to the hall table, allowing anyone sitting at the royal table to have a clear view of the rest of the hall. This table has its own array of food, some different from the food at the general table. At the center of this table is Queen Lanea and true to the rumors, she is wearing a purple dress, the same shade as Jaml's shirt. Small flowers line the crown on top of her head.

To her right is General Fen, dressed in a flowing red shirt. Next to him are the two advisors Kark and Wayv, both men dressed in white. On the other side of the Queen is Kem, dressed in her monk's garb. Like any warrior of God, her eyes continually scan over the crowd, looking for threats or Lucifer's minions.

Next to her is an empty seat, obviously for him and ending the table arrangement is Father Nom, also dressed in traditional monk garb. Jaml follows the maiden around the edge of the wall towards the front of the hall. Once there, the maiden disappears and Jaml is left climbing the small stairs to the platform by himself. He manages well and is greeted by Queen Lanea herself. He bows respectfully before taking his spot at the table.

The feast continues well into the evening. Jaml and Kem eat sparingly, just in case their skills are called into battle, and mingle with the guests at the table. Jaml does notice that Queen Lanea and Kem seem to be getting along well, their conversation does not include anyone else, they being the only women at the royal table or for some other reason, Jaml is not sure. Either way, he is happy that Kem has found someone she can talk to, especially since his "wife" Canda turned out to be an agent for evil.

Queen Lanea nods at the head trumpeter and the room is suddenly filled with the loud bellowing from the group, silencing the crowd. The Queen stands and addresses the crowd.

"Tonight my people, our history comes to an end. An end of needless death and destruction. An end to countless fear from our men and their mothers, sisters, daughters. Our Lord and Savior Jesus Christ himself sent to us a weapon of his wrath. He blesses us with the company of his chosen warriors. Tonight we celebrate the life that is to come!"

The entire hall erupts. Whistles, tankards banging on wood, and stomping can be heard throughout the kingdom and felt inside the hall. Lanea waits patiently for calm again.

"The demons that haunted us are no more. I have sent a patrol of warriors up there and tonight we will hang the heads of the demons on pikes for every living person to see. Say your prayers tonight my people, but say them with grace and thankfulness. We have been delivered by the hands of God, known to us as Kem and Reaper!"

The hall once again erupts for several minutes. Queen Lanea patiently waits again.

"A new dawn is upon us and we have you to thank for it." She motions to Kem and Jaml. "You are welcome in this kingdom for all time. I beg you to stay for another week at least. Your injuries have not yet healed and I insist that you give yourself time to heal. What say you?"

Again the hall is filled with shouts of joy. As it quiets once again, Kem and Jaml share a look. Kem stands and bows to the queen.

"Your hospitality has been great and we are grateful. We accept your further hospitality."

250

For what seems like forever, Jaml finds himself shaking hands with everyone, accepting well wishes and hugs. Next to him, Kem watches intently, noticing his winces and beads of sweat on his forehead. Once his stance begins to slouch, she leans over to the Queen to let her know it is time for Jaml to rest. The Queen gives her blessing and Kem immediately guides Jaml out of the hall.

Once outside, Jaml thanks Kem for her help and allows Kem to lead him across the court towards the church region and their quarters. The two have to stop several times to allow Jaml to catch his breath and rest for a second. As they walk, their conversation is light, often ending up in laughter causing another break, Jaml laughing and moaning at the same time.

Over the next two weeks, Jaml's recovery is accelerated, he wonders how much the medallion plays a role in it. He suffers some discomfort when training but is able to walk and exercise daily. Kem involves herself in the church, giving to the needy and leading prayer. When she is not leading these activities, she spends time with the Queen, offering spiritual guidance through the King's death as well as simply being a woman and the Queen having someone to talk to.

In the evenings, the duo attempt to uncover what is going on in the kingdom.

✦

A gentle breeze goes across the soft skin of Queen Lanea. She stands out on her balcony that oversees the entire kingdom. She can remember when she would stand out here in the arms of her husband but that was two seasons ago before he went off to protect his kingdom and perished at the hands of the succubae.

She inhales the cool air, savoring the gentle hint of rose and mint from the royal garden below. She smiles at the weight that has been lifted. She watches as the streets are still full even though the moon is at its zenith. It feels good to see her kingdom once again being vibrant and alive. Since the celebration the kingdom has settled back into a routine. Traders have begun making the trip to sell their wares in her marketplace. Coin flows freely, reminiscent of days long ago. Hopefully, soon every aspect of their lives can return to normal. Men remain weary for their safety and often still cower in the shadows and alleys if a shadow flies overhead, even as simple as a bird.

With one last breath the Queen turns and walks back through the window walkway to her room. The room is completely dark and with the gentle breeze, it is no wonder the room is dark as the candles have obviously been blown out. The pale moonlight offers her some soft lift she uses to find the flint. Most royalty would simply call the soldiers to do the mundane things like lighting a candle but Queen Lanea is not raised that way. She is fiercely independent and often refuses the assistance from her advisors or soldiers. A couple strikes with the flint and a candle comes to life. She picks up the candle and turns to light the remaining ones.

"What a lovely night. Wouldn't you say so Queen Lanea?"

The words are raspy, almost as if the source was fighting off a summer cold. Lanea swings her candle in the direction of the voice to find its source. To her astonishment, the source is a red creature standing as tall as most men. She holds the light a little higher to shine a little brighter in that direction. She gasps at the full sight of the creature. Besides the red color, the creature has a mouth full of razor sharp teeth surrounding two sets of fangs. Wings protrude from the creature's back, folded into place at the present moment. A set of horns stick out from the creature's forehead, revealing without a question the creature is a demon.

She spans the room with the candle to reveal three more demons, two of which carry a net between them. She reaches and grabs the dagger on the desk beside her.

"Now now Queen Lanea, is this necessary? You cannot stop us if you want to and your little friends are at the monastery, so you are all alone here. Your little guard friend tasted good but if you want to call him, go right ahead."

Queen Lanea feels the urge to cry but her pride keeps her in check. Her mind races to a solution but none come. She is trapped in person and in mind, with no recourse that will lead to success.

"Do not worry my Queen. We are not here to kill you. Our master would like to meet you."

"Why does he want to meet me? I didn't kill Minotaur, Reaper did." Her confidence begins to return.

"Precisely."

"You motherless cur." She lunges and is quickly wrapped up in a net. Every time she struggles, the net entangles her even more. A short period of time later, Queen Lanea finds herself completely wrapped up in the net. Two of the demons casually walk over and pick her up. They walk over to the outer ledge, climb on the parapet, and leap off with her in tow. Their wings unravel and soon Queen Lanea finds herself flying over her kingdom, wrapped in the arms of a demon.

✦

"Father Reaper! Father Reaper!"

Words that invade sleep followed by hands shaking brings about only one thing. Instincts. The young monk does not know or comprehend what happened next, only the end result. In one fluid motion Jaml uses the monk's weight against him by grabbing the wrist and flinging him over the bed. The monk's back slams against the unforgiving wall, driving all the air from his lungs and causing lights to flash before his eyes. Fingers wrap around his neck and squeezes, not allowing any air to replenish what the wall drove out. Once the lights cease to flash, he finds himself staring at a jet black blade inches from his face.

"The Queen has been taken." Is all the monk could muster and even then the volume is so low he thinks Reaper might not hear it and kill him.

Jaml releases the man's neck while he apologizes for the pain. He grabs his belt, which holds the other blade, and sprints out of the small room, leaving the monk to try and regain his composure. Dressed in sleep pants and night shirt, Jaml flies through the monastery.

"Hey!"

He looks over his shoulder to find Kem giving chase. She too is dressed in a nightshirt with night pants, her staff in her hand. He pauses for a second to let her catch up. Seconds later, they are both sprinting across the market towards the palace. The guards standing guard quickly move aside to allow the two warriors by, Normally they would salute but shame at failure causes the soldiers to do nothing more than look down in shame.

The two race through the halls and climb the stairs with little effort, they hit the top floor running, no evidence of fatigue. They find General Fen, Wayv, and Kark standing at the entrance to the Queen's chamber, their faces full of fear and bewilderment. Jaml and Kem arrive at the same time, stopping at the three men in front of the chamber's door.

"She has been taken." Kark mumbles in the direction of the warriors.

"How could this happen?" Wayv's response is emotion filled, almost to the verge of tears.

General Fen leads the two warrior monks into the room where they find blood smeared all over the walls spelling out the words 'Sacrifices must be made'

"Is this her blood?" The general's quiver in his voice reveals his deep concern.

"No. She is alive." Jaml turns from the scene on the wall to the general. "This is not her blood. This is a message. If you follow the trail of blood after the letter 'e', it goes over to that dark corner where you can barely see a pool of blood and a male hand."

The general follows the instructions and barely sees the remains of a soldier, the head a few feet from the body.

Jaml lowers his voice. "There is something wrong here general. I and Kem have felt it since we got here. Thought it was the nest of succubae but that was dealt with."

"I cannot lie. Queen Lanea has felt it too. As have I. Usually there is a squadron of soldiers outside her door. We assumed as you did that it was the succubae but now. My foolishness may have caused my Queen's life."

"No worries. I will go get her and bring her back to safety."

"We!" Kem steps next to Jaml, her face a stern glass stature.

"No Kem. Have you not read the message? This is a trap. They want my head and if it is my time to go, I do not want your death on me when I stand before the Angel Gabriel." He does not look over at her. "I need you to stay and protect the good folk here. When the queen returns, she will need comforting, especially if I do not return with her."

"Sounds like someone wants to die. You are not completely healed, this is a trap, you don't know how many there are and regardless, you are going to be outmanned."

"Thanks for the vote of confidence."

"Shut up. The only reason I am allowing this is I know what is important and the mission must be completed."

"Thanks for your understanding." Jaml turns and begins to walk away.

Wayv walks over to Kem. "Are you really going to let him go alone? Is it going to be dangerous?"

Kark leans in behind him. "He may need backup. Is it wise for him to go alone?"

"You talk to him. He has spoken and so have I. If you want to send a battalion after him, be my guest." She dismisses the two men with a wave of her hand. She continues down the stairs ignoring the continued pleas from the advisors.

Jaml walks back over to General Fen who shares a nod with him.

"Where has she been taken?"

Within the hour Jaml is riding out of the Sagin heading east. Once he clears the gate, he pushes his horse to a gallop, every moment is precious. Even though they want him, he is not sure if she will be killed for sport. General Fen gave him detailed directions, guiding him through the northern forests to where he thinks the queen is being held captive. It is the only logical place close by that is remote and idea for a trap. Easily defended from massive attacks yet deserted enough for this occasion.

The day is uneventful as he encounters nothing but simple forest animals going about their everyday life of survival. Most scurry away at the sight of him with a couple watching intently from a safe distance. The forest itself is not overly dense, allowing him to maneuver himself and his horse without incident.

Yet there is something wrong. Jaml can sense another presence close by. Either by the rustling of the leaves or a shadow not in the right place, Jaml knows he is being followed. He told Kem she is not to follow him, without question. Yet he knows someone has been following him for about two hours. He catches a glimpse of the figure moving parallel from his position. Originally, thoughts of a big cat came to mind or a bear but the figure is moving too coordinated for either of those. The logical explanation is man.

He comes to a dip in the land and takes the plunge with his horse down the hill. He quickly jumps off the horse and clambers back up the hill where he waits. The figure rushes over the edge, expecting Jaml's move as an attempt to get away. Instead, hands grab his oversized coat and flings him through the air to land at the bottom minus the air that is forced from his chest. The figure rolls around on the ground, trying to escape the Reaper. The figure finally stops rolling to find a jet black blade inches from his neck. Caught with no chance to escape, the figure pulls the hood down to reveal an elderly man coming out of middle age. His white beard extends past his neck, his skin tanned a dark brown much like leather. Yet his green eyes reveal intelligence, vast amounts of intelligence.

"I mean you no harm Reaper." The voice is deep and powerful, almost too powerful

"I will judge that. What is your name?" His voice is forceful.

"Are names important? More important than information?" Puzzles, always puzzles

"Only if you want to live. I am sure the information you possess I will find out soon enough but is your life worth the puzzles?"

"Such violence from a Reaper. You are a monk."

"A monk trained to kill the enemy of God. Right now, you appear to be a threat. Following me without permission and refusing to tell me who you are. Sounds like you might be the enemy. Three, two."

"But I am not the only one following you. How about…"

"Me?" Kem walks into the clearing, holding her staff loosely in her hand. "He knows about me, old man. You, on the other hand. Well, let's just say he is very nervous these days. One slip up and squirt, squirt goes your blood. Just saying."

Jaml takes a quick look up and wink at his partner.

"Alright. Can I sit up first?"

"No" The blade slides further, this time touching the old man's neck.

"Stop! My name is Bray. I live in these parts and would like to share supper with you. I have information that would be useful I think."

Jaml's blade instantly disappears and is replaced by a hand. Bray grasps the hand and is pulled to his feet. He dusts himself off before saying.

"Let us relax over there in the clearing and break bread."

"Lead the way." Jaml motions with his hand for Bray to lead the way. The two monks follow the hermit into a small clearing where they quickly set up a perimeter and sit down to break bread. Jaml pulls out dried meat, cheese, a loaf of bread and fruit for the camp to share. To the monks' surprise, the hermit named Bray says prayers. The three of them sit and eat in silence, the monks' eyes never stray far from the hermit.

When all is finished, Bray leans back against a tree stump and pulls out a thin piece of wood to pick the extra food from his teeth. When he finally finishes, Bray looks over at the two monks.

"I think it is time I came clean."

"Please do Paladin." Jaml responds immediately.

"Well done Reaper of the black blades." Bray chuckles at the quickness of Jaml. "How did you know?"

"Your eyes are the first clue. They are not clouded with age. The second clue is how easily you move amongst nature despite your age. It is as nature itself is helping you. Lastly, the trees seem to bend out of your way. You never once had to move your head or brush aside the branches as you ran. As a matter of fact, the leaves seem to reach up and catch you when I flipped you. Add it all together and you get a paladin. Now, what information do you want to share with us this evening? Also, why did you refer to me as the Reaper of the black blades? Besides the obvious."

"Stories of how the Reaper with the black blades killed a nest full of succubae. Very impressive." Bray pauses for a second before continuing. "As for myself, I have lived in these woods for many years. I commune with animals and nature on a regular basis. They tell me many things. You are walking into a trap."

"I know. What I don't know is whose trap it is. Demons are never that bright to hatch something like this, at least the lower level demons anyway."

"Do you still have the medallion?"

"How do you know about the medallion?" Jaml inadvertently reaches up to touch his chest where the medallion is housed.

"As great as you are Reaper, there is no way you would have been able to withstand the urges of one of the horsemen. The weapons you seek and possess are not just the weapons of the Apocalypse, they are the Horseman of the Apocalypse. God placed their souls inside the weapon and they yearn to be free. The medallion you hold protects you and the righteous, but they are still able to talk with their minions."

"Are you telling me that as long as I possess this sword that is two, it will call on demons to attack me?" Disbelief fills his head.

"That is correct. I would venture to say it is not the sword behind this, it is the knife. The knife is of this region and the demons would recognize it and therefore do its bidding. The sword is from another region and demons would question the source of the words."

"That would mean there are demons in Sagin. Who?"

"It is not the Queen rest assured. She is of pure Godly intentions. As for their identity, I cannot say for certain. What I will tell you is beware of those close to the Queen, for it is they the dagger talks to."

"Thank you for your wise words and warning." Kem gives the paladin a slight bow. "You are more than welcome to stay here with us for the night. But I warn you, I have never seen a paladin in real life and I will want to ask questions." She gives the man a slight smile. Jaml follows that with a slight bow.

"I would be honored to stay. But I warn you monk, I love to talk. And if you get me started, I cannot promise I will not talk all night."

"Then it is settled." Jaml's words breaks in. "I am going to sleep and you two can talk all night long. I will be gone when you rise but that has been the plan all along. Thank you again Bray for your insight and knowledge. I promise to heed your warnings and listen to your advice. Pray that we are enough for this. I do have one request."

"Yes Reaper." No hesitation

"If we do not return, I ask you to leave the comfort of your forest and complete the mission to save the Queen as well as seek revenge on my killers."

"It is done." The two men clasp forearms. "But I do fully expect you to pass by this way and share another meal with me. Agreed?"

"Agreed."

The rest of the evening went as agreed to. Reaper volunteered to take the first watch in order to get a longer rest. Bray informs both of them that there is no need for a sentry as nature would alert him if danger approached so Jaml said his prayers and laid down to rest. He is soon asleep. Kem and Bray stay up well into the moon high talking about a multitude of subjects to include what a paladin is and their duties under God.

The bright morning sun rays strikes Kem on her face, rousing her from a well-deserved sleep. Hands rub any sleep remaining in the body away before she rolls over. Bray continues to sleep soundly. She looks beyond Bray to where Jaml slept to find nothing. She rolls to her feet, searching the area to find Jaml. Her search finally falls towards the compound direction to watch her friend, Jaml, disappear into the woods.

She clambers to her feet and reaches for her cloak when Bray stirs not far away.

"He has gone?"

"Yes. And it is time for me to leave as well. Thank you for the company and the conversation. I have learned a lot today."

"It is not time to say goodbye."

Kem immediately tenses. She has heard of men forcing themselves on women, taking them sexually.

"What do you mean?" Her entire body tenses, ready to strike down this man who claims to be godly.

"Oh, I am so sorry." Bray takes a step back, holding his hands up as he realizes what his words must have sounded like. "I am going with you. I have prayed for years for guidance. What is my mission in life? What has God asked of me? And my prayers were answered last night. It is time for me to get into this war. I have lived a life of peace with very little danger. I convinced myself that I was not responsible and should not get involved. Our talk last night opened my eyes. The Lord spoke to me through you. It is time for this paladin to stand and be accounted for. We must hurry, Jaml is going to need us. Of that I am sure."

✦

The forest suddenly gives way to a large plain. The grass is very sparse on the plain, the majority is simply dirt. At the far end is a small outpost, small enough to house no more than one hundred soldiers. This outpost has obviously been unoccupied for several years as moss and vines have invaded and overtaken the outside of the wall. Parts of the wall itself have crumbled over with age, exposing into view large portions of the inner outpost. Even from a distance, Jaml sees there is no one there. Not soldiers, wives, families, or prostitutes. Simply abandoned.

Jaml urges his steed forward towards the outpost. His eyes scan continuously for any signs of life or demons. He does notice the forest life does not venture out of the woods. No birds are chirping from the outpost nor are there dogs barking. This outpost reminds him of the succubae lair that he encountered a few short weeks ago. The lack of forest wildlife confirms the whereabouts for Jaml. He has come to the right place, the demons are here. The smell of death is absent, good. The Queen is alive, for now.

Jaml dismounts and ties his horse to a nearby tree, loose enough so if there needs to be a quick retreat, his horse is prepared. He reaches behind to draw his two blades, instantly hearing the soft voice in the back of his mind, not loud enough to understand the words. Most would believe the sound was the blade sliding against leather but Jaml knows it is the Fallen Horseman trying to influence him. The medallion on his neck keeps the Fallen at bay. He holds the blades down as he walks forward. The gates are ajar enough for him to step through.

He does so cautiously.

Inside the gate, the compound is barren. Houses have crumbled over time, many covered with the same moss and vines that grow on the outside and just like outside, and there are no other plants or animals here as well. He listens intently and hears nothing. Then a cry for help.

The Queen!

He sprints through the compound to the other side. He stops in his tracks at the sight in front of him. Strung up in a wooden cage is Queen Lanea. Other than a dirty nightgown with a few tears and some new bruises, she does not look bad. There doesn't appear to be any grave injuries or extensive bruising or blood. Below the cage sits a demon in a makeshift throne. The throne is made of wood and vines holding it together. The back of the throne extends higher than the demon's head, giving him a resting spot for his head.

The demon on the throne is larger than most demons he has encountered but not as large as a Fallen One. This demon is a head taller than Jaml and has the usual red hue for his skin color. His face is grotesque to say the least, absence of a nose, just two holes where the nose should be. The enlarged mouth is filled with fangs and an oversized green tongue that flicks out every couple of seconds. This demon does not have wings. Jaml does not know if any size wings would support that huge body. Large curved claws rest at the end of his fingers, more for tearing flesh from bone than holding fine morsels of food.

"Welcome Reaper. You are in my house." As with most demons, words are slurred and many times hard to understand due to the lisp and elongated tongue.

"I would say hand over the Queen and I will let you live but I would be lying. Hand over the Queen now and I will make your death quick and merciful."

The demon erupts in laughter.

"You dare come into my house and threaten me? What makes it even more hilarious is you come alone to challenge me and all my friends."

The demon holds his arms wide and instantly large numbers of demons appear. They appear in the trees and abandoned houses. They crawl out from the ground as well as fly in through the sky. Some are armed with swords, spears, and axes while others simply rely on their claws and teeth. When they all emerge, around ten are flying while double that number emerge from the houses and ground, fully armed. Most demons carry a sword or spear. Jaml is happy that none use bow and arrows.

"What is the matter human, cat bite your tongue?" The demon laughs at his own comment.

"No demon. I just feel pity on these poor creatures. Just because you are bigger and stronger, they will die defending you, something they do not believe in. They will die trying to please you. They don't quite understand you are no better than they are. They don't understand they are about to die, not for a cause, but because you don't have the courage to face me first."

The demon looks more irritated than before, he talks with his teeth bared.

"You are correct but die for me they will. Don't worry, I will leave them some scraps from your carcass to munch on. After all, I am not that evil." Again he breaks out in laughter.

"But you are that ugly!" Jaml's comment silences the demon.

The demon looks past Jaml's shoulder to see who else dares to challenge him. He finds himself looking at the local paladin and by his side is a monk. The paladin is dressed in battle armor, complete with a green shield and broadsword. The monk standing next to him is in her monk's robe, carrying a staff. Both stand ready for battle. A puzzled look shows across Jaml's face as he turns to look over his shoulder. Kem, he expected, she is part of the plan. Bray on the other hand is a complete surprise. What is the paladin doing here? This is not his fight.

"Well, well. If it isn't the scared paladin of the woods. Have you recently found some courage to come face me? Or have you come because of your woman's backup? Is she good in bed?" The demon's attempt to goad the paladin into action does not seem to work. A simple smile across the face of the paladin makes it clear that the demon's words are having no effect.

The two warriors nod at each other, a show of respect and acceptance of the help. Reaper turns around slowly to face the demon once again. He grips the twin blades and rolls his neck.

"Time to dance."

Reaper walks towards the horde of demons who respond with snarls and growls towards the humans. His walk turns into a jog once Kem and Bray catch up. He winks at Kem before bursting into a full run. The demons waste no time in attack as well. The two forces meet with a crash as the battle begins.

It doesn't take long for Reaper to inflict serious damage to the ranks of the demons. His blades sing their death song, cutting off limbs that seek to stab him. More than once did an arm drop to the ground still holding a sword. Slashes across the eyes of a demon renders it useless and soon dies under the backswing of the blades. A demon is successful in burying his claws into Reaper's shoulder and regrets it. Reaper reverses his grip and swing upward, separating the arm from the demon. The second blade buries itself into the soft midsection of the demon before being ripped violently out, leaving the demon to bleed out all over the floor.

Fighting valiantly next to Reaper is Kem, the warrior monk. Even though she has vowed to never use a sharpened weapon, her Bo staff does damage quite adequately. She whirls her staff with precision, striking with deadly impact. More than a few skulls are crushed like ripe watermelons under her staff. She whirls it, striking a demon in the midsection, breaking whatever bones are located there. She follows up with a sweeping motion, discarding the demon elsewhere. The range of the staff keeps her opponents at bay, unless she wants them to come closer. The demons she does allow to come closer soon feel the crack of the staff, crippling the demon altogether.

Even though his precision is not as deadly as the other two, Bray holds his own in the battle. He swings his broadsword, cutting down demons in his path. Slicing limbs from bodies and slicing into skulls along the way. He feels teeth sink into his shoulder. Instead of tearing the flesh away to cause more damage, the demon latches on, satisfied to drain the paladin of his life. Bray grabs hold of the demon's neck and squeezes. The strain forces the demon to let go and Bray shoves his blade into the open maw of the demon. He snatches the blade backward, tearing away the lower half of the mouth.

After a few minutes of battle, the three humans find themselves standing in the midst of dead demons. Bodies are cut open or smashed in. The only thing they all had in common is they are dead. The three warriors look at each other with care, inspecting their wounds, measuring how much more than can do this. Satisfied with each other, they look over to find the large demon standing there.

The demon stands up, his height is impressive, standing a full head taller than Jaml. He looks at the three victors and slowly begins to clap his hands. The claps quicken and soon he is giving a full applause for the work done before him. Abruptly he stops.

"Impressive. Now it's time for the main course."

More demons begin to appear. The attacking force is much larger than the force the warriors just destroyed. These demons looked enraged at the sight of their brothers dead on the battlefield. Wherein the first group looked like hunting dogs sitting, waiting for the command to attack, this group looks and feels like rabid dogs pulling at their chains, ready to kill and maim.

Jaml looks to his right then to his left, gauging his two friends. Both breath heavily, exhausted from the recent battle. Their bodies are caked in blood and gore, most of which are not their own. All three have scratches, nicks, and bruises but nothing life threatening. He knows Kem will be able to handle herself and fight to the end, but it will be the end. The paladin is another matter altogether. The man is bleeding from his shoulder where a demon bit him, which means venom is running through his veins as they speak. If Kem cannot get the ointment on that bite soon, the battle will not matter as Bray will simply die of poison.

"Get behind me."

His stern voice cuts through the air. Both Kem and Bray move to take up positions behind Reaper. Jaml turns to face his friends.

"Promise me you will have my back when this is all over."

"You know I will." Kem's tone shows no fear or hesitation. She will die protecting him, of that he is sure. He is at peace. He turns to address Bray who stands in place bewildered. "Follow her directives, do as she says without question. Just know that if you do not, she will probably kill you right there and then."

"I understand." Despite the words he spoke, Bray does not know what is going on.

Reaper walks forward. He holds his twin ebony blades at his side. The demons are in an uproar, barking and growls fill his ears. He can see demons licking their lips in anticipation of a meal. He watches the lead demon laughing, all other thoughts leave Jaml's head.

"What is he doing?" Bray leans over, whispering in Kem's ear. "Shouldn't we be at his side? Otherwise he is going to die out there."

"He will not die. You must not know why they call them Reapers."

"I don't. Can you enlighten me?" Worry invades every word Bray speaks.

"Ok." Kem neither loses her eyesight of Jaml nor her concentration. "Reaper was an Angel of God in the Great War of Hosts. One of the mightiest warriors to lead the angels into battle. When the time came for the war to be taken up by man, Reaper knew man would need assistance as Lucifer's demons would be a formidable opponent. Reaper sacrificed himself to be that assistance. His essence is used at the end of a monk's training to infuse that monk with angelic power. The receiving monks were known as Reapers. In times of desperate need, when all seems lost, a Reaper can call on the power of the Angel Reaper to save them. Monks pay a heavy price for this gift. The power to harness and use the angelic power saps power from the monk. As long as there is evil in the area, the monk fights on but the longer he uses the power, the longer his recovery."

"Are you telling me he has the power of God? Like Jesus?" A bewildered look crosses his face

"No paladin." Her head shakes at his comments. "It is of God but not through God. The essence of the angel Reaper flows through his body but his body cannot sustain for long periods of time the heavenly power that will course through him. The catch is as long as there is evil in the area, the essence will continue to control him. If he is unable to kill the evil in a short time, the essence will kill him."

Bray looks over at Kem with fear in his soul. He then looks at the man about to sacrifice himself for their safety.

Reaper stops within ten paces from the horde of demons. His face is a mask of calm, determination and generally at peace with himself. He looks up towards the heavens before reciting the prayer.

"Through the Power of God, I charge thee Reaper. Deliver the Lord's vengeance upon evil" His eyes go completely black in color and everyone looking would swear he glowed.

The demons cannot wait any longer and charge forward, eager to taste the warm blood of Jaml in their mouth, his screams filling their ears. They pay no attention to the fact there is something different about the man. Besides his eyes going completely dark and a slight glow around his body, his stature is different, taller. And then they realize their mistake.

Reaper explodes in motion. His arms become a whirlwind of blur as he rushes into battle. The demons react the only way they know how, attack. The twin ebony blades rip through the host of demons as a warm knife through butter, hacking off arms, legs and heads. Limbs fly through the air as a flock of birds running from the hunt. Even when a demon is able to raise his weapon in defense, the ebony blades go through the weapon to end the life of the creature holding it. The carnage is immense as demon after demon falls under the blades of the Reaper.

Reaper twirls away from a slash to return the movement, his blades ripping through the face of the attacker. He lands to shatter a sword with a backhand and a stab to the face of another opponent. His first blade cleaves a demon in two followed by a decapitation from his second blade. He finds it hard to move with so many dead creatures at his feet and so much blood making the footing difficult, the ground not being able to absorb any more blood, leaving numerous puddles of slick essence of life all over the battlefield. Reaper knows he has to move the battle lest he slips and loses his footing. He knows a fall here would probably mean his death as the demons would instantly swarm over his body. So move the battle he does by walking as he kills, pressing forward, his attacks creating a path of destruction, leading him to a cleaner patch some distance away.

With his feet once again on dry ground, Reaper continues his assault on the demons. One demon lunges at his fate and is met with a swipe of his blade across the creature's neck, opening another fountain. Before Reaper can react, a demon has flown down and dug his claws into Reaper's back. Before the creature is able to bite, Reaper places his blade between the pain of the claws and slices upward, cutting the creature in two.

After several minutes and several minor cuts later, Reaper stands in the midst of fallen demons. His clothes are drenched in blood, demon blood. His weapons drip the same blood, his face is covered with the same blood and gore. Yet Reaper stands there, glaring at the last demon, the lead demon in front of him. He wastes no time in stalking forward, ready to do battle one last time. HIs eyes remain completely black and the soft glow remains. The remaining creature has a look of bewilderment on his face, he has never seen a human move and kill like that. He has heard stories about angels doing it but had never seen a human capable of it.

"What are you?" Fear mixed in with loathing drips from the question.

"I am God's instrument. And with this instrument God has destroyed all the vile creatures of Lucifer here. All save one but that will be corrected shortly."

The demon reaches behind the chair and pulls out a two handed double blade axe. The axe handle is as thick as Reaper's leg and also as long as well. The blade on each side of the axe is over four feet in length which makes the weapon impressive. When the demon holds the hilt, each blade extends halfway up his arm.

Without hesitation Reaper moves forward, his strides so smooth that Kem thinks him floating. He does not pause but walks into his attack. His blade comes forward towards the creature's chest. The sword meets the axe in a thunderous clang. The adversaries stare momentarily at each other before Reaper brings his other sword into play. The creature sees the blade swinging his way and immediately disengages and leaps backward. Reaper's second blade slices across the demon's chest, causing a howl of pain. The creature rolls to his feet and brings his axe to bear.

He has no time to recover as Reaper moves forward without hesitation. The demon brings his blade to the side in order to block the Reaper's strike. For the next moments, the demon finds himself slowly retreating as Reaper presses forward, strike after strike, driving the demon to the wall. The demon has no opportunity to counterattack, Reaper keeps him at bay with strike after strike, coming in all directions.

A single kick changes everything. The kick buckles the demon's leg, throwing him off balance. In doing so, the demon has to let go of the axe with his right hand in order to catch himself. He reaches out to the wall, keeping himself upright, a mistake he will never be able to fix. With the axe in his non-dominant hand, the demon cannot fend off the relentless attack by the Reaper. Reaper changes tactics at this time. Instead of using skill and finesse in his combat, he reverts to brutal overhead strikes at the demon. The demon holds up his axe as blow after blow reigns down on him. The speed of the attacks keeps the demon in the same position. If he lets go of the wall to use both hands on the axe, the human will surely cut him down before he recovers his balance. His only option is to take the pounding and hope his arm holds out until his knee stops hurting.

Suddenly one of the blades hooks underneath the axe head and pulls up. The second blade cleanly goes through the forearm of the demon. He screams in pain as he watches his arm hit the ground, still grasping the axe. The demon leans back against the wall, the stub of his arm dangling at his side, the river of blood drenching the ground underneath. He looks up at his killer and smiles.

"Who sent you?" Reaper walks over to the demon, glaring him in the eyes.

"What does it matter? You have killed me already so why should I give you any information?" He coughs up blood.

"You are right, you are going to die. You will bleed out in great pain for a while or I can give you your axe and let you die in battle. Your choice." Reaper takes a step back to give the creature some room.

"Give me my axe." The demon growls for the last time

In the distance, Kem and Bray watch as the demon tries one last attack. He screams Lucifer's name and lunges at Reaper who casually steps aside, swinging his blade as he does. The demon's head hits the ground rolling, his body frozen in place for a moment before collapsing into a heap.

Jaml turns and starts to walk towards them. He smiles, winks at Kem and collapses.

"How long is he going to be out?" The female voice seems so long away, yet very familiar

"I do not know." Another female voice

"We have been here four days." Her voice is louder, almost irritated.

"We could be dead." The words are calculated.

"I am sorry. Please forgive me Kem, I have misspoken. I only worry about my people in my absence. I know without him we would not be alive." Concern fills her voice.

Jaml slightly opens his eyes to find himself looking at the night sky, trees tower over him, partially covering the sky. He turns his head slightly towards where he heard the voices and feels heat. Directly to his side is a small fire providing the heat. To the near side of the fire sit two women, the darker skinned woman is Queen Lanea and the other is Kem.

"I won't be alive much longer if I don't get some water."

Both women jump up and quickly move to him. Kem produces a flask of water, holds his head up and gently brings the flask to his lips. She drips the water into his mouth, knowing too much will do nothing but make him sick. He forces himself to take the drips with patience despite his urge to start gulping the water.

After a few minutes of sipping water, Jaml regains strength enough to sit up. Kem gives him the flask, allowing him to take control of his recovery. Lanea offers him a bit of bread which he takes. After eating the bread and continuing to sip on water, he leans back against a tree.

"How long have I been out?"

"Four days." Kem's expression is one of worry. "I was beginning to worry whether or not you would ever wake."

"It was mostly my fault." The young queen admits. "I have been restless these past two days not knowing how long you would sleep and how long I would have to be away from my people. They must be worried about me. I just hope Kark and Wayv will be able to keep things going in my absence."

"I am sure General Fen is keeping everything in order." Jaml's remark brings laughter from the group.

After dinner, Kem leads the group in prayer followed by conversation. The women tell him Bray returned to the woods but not before giving them the protection of the forest. This meant they would not have to sit watch at night, the trees would protect them and alert them if trouble came. For that Jaml was thankful. Next, they talked about his experience with the Reaper essence inside. The best way to explain it to them was a divine feeling overtaking his body. It didn't hurt, just peaceful. He doesn't remember the fighting, just a sense that God had it in his hands and everything would be alright. Minutes later, Jaml is fast asleep, leaving the two women to talk about what they heard.

Two days later the trio packs up and heads back to Sagin. The mood is light as they share stories and experiences they encountered in their travels. Despite the lighthearted conversation, Jaml has not told either one of the women what the demon said before he was killed. Both women can sense his uneasiness but they do not inquire. He will tell them when the time is right.

The trip is a day and a half and when they emerge from the woods, Lanea's face lights up with happiness. In the distance they can see the tall wall and towers of Sagin on top of the small mountain. Immediately Lanea spurs her horse onward, eager to return to her palace and the comfort of home. Neither of her companions know the feeling but are sympathetic to her feelings.

As a child, Kem was given to the monastery as a nun but her talents were soon recognized. Her feisty behavior and constant fights with the other nuns in training brought ire from the nuns to her behind or knuckles. She was labeled incorrigible and was marked for expulsion when a monk noticed her. He loved her abilities and her fierce independence so he took her under his wing and began training a monk. After fifteen winters, she was ordained a monk, given a staff, and told her mission to spread the word of God while defeating the minions of Lucifer. She has never known her parents, they gave her to the nunnery after five winters. The nuns beat her and her monk did nothing but train her. She considers herself blessed despite the hardships she endured as a child.

Jaml started out stealing food and drink for his parents. If he came home with not enough, he was beaten. After nine winters of constant beatings and fights, Jaml ran away and struck out on his own. His life didn't change much, he continued to steal and fight but never had to endure another beating again.

A couple winters later, he stole bread from a bakery and in his attempt to escape he ran into a monk. Instead of beating him or turning him over to the city guard, the monk paid for the food and asked Jaml if he would like to sleep in a bed that night. Reluctantly Jaml said yes. After a couple of weeks of feeding, he began to teach Jaml about the word of God. Jaml listened only because better, tastier food was provided after each lesson. Berries, jams, sweet bread all came after a lesson. It wasn't long before Jaml became his apprentice. That didn't last long as Jaml quickly mastered the fighting techniques. The monk took him to the high eastern mountains where he dropped young Jaml off. Jaml was quickly learning new techniques as well as weapons. For a six winter program, Jaml finished in three. He was chosen to become a Reaper and has wandered ever since.

Three horses gallop through the countryside, making their way to the castle. Many on the road recognize the Reaper and monk but very few saw the beauty of the queen under all the filth and dirt that she has endured. The ones that see her despite the dirt immediately fall to their knees, giving homage and thanks for her safe return.

The group approaches the gate. Jaml quickly takes the lead citing they do not know who or what is in charge. Both women look at him weirdly but only Kem knows Jaml is holding back something. Some information he obviously thinks will put the Queen's life in jeopardy. He motions for the party to stop just out of arrow range. Looking over his shoulder, he winks at Kem, letting her know to get away if it goes bad. She returns a slight nod back. As Jaml walks his steed towards the gate, Kem turns to look at a confused Lanea.

"What is going on? This is my home. Why are you keeping me here, away from my home?" Her voice begins to rise.

"Queen Lanea," Kem's voice is soothing as she attempts to calm the young queen down. "The demon said something to Jaml. I don't know what but he is afraid for our safety."

"Kem, it is a demon. They all lie."

"That they do. But let's look at the facts. You are taken in the middle of the night. The demons knew exactly where you were and they did not harm you. Their intentions were to draw Jaml into an ambush and kill him, me and you. This all happens right after we are able to kill the succubae nest and help you restore order to your kingdom."

The totality of the past few weeks finally hits Queen Lanea like a ton of bricks. Her shoulders droop under the weight of the truth she just heard. Her greatest fears have finally come to be true, as much as she hopes it was her being paranoid, the truth is as she fears.

"My God. I have demons in my court. Don't I?" She looks over at Kem.

"Either demons or demon servants." Kem's eyes never leave Jaml, his safety paramount.

"Then we will find and kill....."

"We will wait!" Kem's sudden glare catches Lanea off guard, startling the woman. "Jaml has a plan and the fact he hasn't said anything tells me he is not completely certain who the enemy is. We will wait for his plan."

"Does he think I am a demon then?"

"No. We have talked about that possibility and find your heart is pure." Kem goes back to looking at Jaml.

Jaml pulls his horse to a halt. He waits patiently for his death or the gates to open. To his relief, it is the latter. Three horses come thundering out, their riders dressed in full armor. The lead rider has the Queen's colors on his cape. Despite the helmet on his head, Jaml easily recognizes General Fen. The riders pull up in front of Jaml, General Fen quickly pulls his helmet off his head, worry etched in his face.

"Is the Queen?"

"Safe and unharmed."

"Thank God." The worry washed from his face. "Where?"

"On the horizon, just out of arrow's reach. We wanted to make sure all is safe for her return. It is good to see you general. The kingdom has been in good hands." The two men clasp forearms.

Minutes later the general's mood becomes even happier when his eyes lay on the Queen. He immediately drops to his knee, followed by the other two soldiers with their heads bowed.

"Get up General Fen." She demands. He rises to his feet and is immediately caught in an embrace. Her slender arms are locked around his burly midsection and immediately he feels her body sobbing. He closes his arms around her back, allowing her to vent all the emotions she has been hiding for so long, realizing her mortality and how close she came to dying. The emotion is enough to send the strongest person into tears, and General Fen has always said Queen Lanea is one of the strongest people he knows.

After a few minutes, Lanea takes several deep breaths and pulls away from her general, her royalty back intact. She straightens her dress, turns and remounts her horse.

"My people are waiting to see their Queen. I will not have them wait any longer."

"My Queen. Your people can wait for a couple more hours. We need to get you presentable. What would your people and your enemies think if you went parading around looking like this? The people are fully aware you were taken." Fen's eyes quickly avert from her.

"How did that happen?" Her voice is agitated."

"I do not know my Queen. All I can tell you is they know."

"The same nest of demons that have infiltrated your kingdom. They want to show you as weak and fragile, just in case you did get rescued. I believe the general is right. We need to get you presentable once again." Kem looks at the Queen in a discerning way. "May I suggest to Milady that you have a slender sword when you are presented. It tells the people you are strong and nothing will deter you. It also lets your enemy know that you have won, you have conquered the demons and are ready to rule once more."

"Wise observation." Jaml gives a low bow from his horse to Kem who rolls her eyes in response.

Kem dismounts and goes over to Lanea. She quickly covers the Queen's body in her monk's cloak, pulling the attached hood over the Queen's head, covering her face. While the cloak is being put in place, General Fen sends one of the soldiers ahead to clear the back entrance to the palace. Once her look is complete, General Fen officially bids them farewell for everyone to see. He and the remaining soldier turn back into the castle as if the visitors are nothing but common merchants.

After the general leaves, Jaml leads the group into the castle, turning left immediately to avoid the marketplace and large crowds. What they didn't want is for anyone to recognize the Queen and the alarm sounded. They want to put her back on the throne and in power before anyone knows she is here. Demons are present in the kingdom and a public challenge so early in her return could cause unnecessary conflict. Better to get her to the throne before anyone is aware of their return.

Jaml and General Fen decided to take her to the general's house. This way the Queen can take a much needed bath away from anyone that might do her harm. Fen also released all his servants, save the two who are going to do the bathing. His wife watches from the upstairs to make sure no one comes during this transformation. Three travelers come upon the general's house and are quickly ushered inside. Jaml and Kem remain in the front room, just in case intruders arrive. The two servants quickly lead the queen to the bathing room where they undress her and get her into soapy water.

Fen arrives and fetches one of his wife's riding outfits. He adds one of his own capes, so the Queen is draped in her royal colors. The soldier who accompanied the general arrives with a rapier, just the right size for the Queen. After bathing the Queen, the servants dress her in her new outfit. Satisfied that she looks like a warrior queen, the group covers her in a clean cloak to lead her through the back side of the palace.

Jaml leads the small group of Kem, the Queen and General Fen's wife through the back halls. The daily call to arms followed by the Queen listening and ruling on affairs of the state will occur within the hour. Fen and Kark handled the issues up to now in the absence of the Queen. They all know the hall is emptied before the call to arms to give the ruler an opportunity to relax and get their minds right before the barrage of issues that are sure to come. The plan is to have the doors open and Queen Lanea sitting on her throne.

They arrive at the back door to the hall and are met by General Fen, dressed in his full military uniform. He bows at the queen and ushers her into the room, getting her positioned on her throne. He nods his approval at the rapier hanging at her side. She gives the burly general a wink followed by a hug with his wife. Jaml and Kem remain in the back hall, just in case they are needed to protect the Queen. With everything in order, there is nothing to do but wait for the call to arms.

"Jaml, is there something we need to talk about?" Kem talks low enough so only they can hear each other.

"What Bray told me?" Jaml looks over to Kem.

"And the demon."

"Ok. You need to know. Bray said there are two demons in the kingdom. These demons gave information to the succubae nest and to the Queen's captors. They work to undermine the kingdom for an eventual takeover. He could not identify the traitors so there was not much he could do."

"And the demon."

"Before he let out his last breath, he informed me there was only one demon. The other is a demon worshiper, those that expect Lucifer to triumph and rule this world in sin. The demon is Wayv."

"And the demon demon worshiper?"

"Nom."

A look of astonishment and disbelief fills Kem's eyes. How can a man of God, an ordained monk, believer of Jesus turn his back on his religion to worship Lucifer? The hypocrisy of the entire situation is too much.

"Are you sure? Could the demon be lying?"

"I get it Kem. I feel the same way yet there is no other explanation. I don't think Wayv could have done all this by himself. I am going to confront them and see what they say. I expect Wayv to reveal himself but like you, I hope I am wrong about Nom."

She nods at Jaml returning her attention to the hall where Queen Lanea has taken her place on the throne to wait for the hall doors to open. She takes a deep breath before looking over at them, concern and relief on her face. With her hair pulled back and tied, her look has changed from a beautiful young Queen to a fierce warrior. Somehow the whole experience has changed her, she has lost some of her naivety, substituted with a dose of determination and fire.

Finally the doors are pulled open, allowing only the advisors and dukes to enter. The crowd whimsically enters the hall, just another day without direction. Then someone notices who is sitting on the throne and slowly the crowd begins to pay attention to what's in front of them. Queen Lanea, a different version, is alive and well. She sits on the throne as a Monarch, not someone's widow Queen, her jaw locked tight as her eyes roam over the spectacle in front of her.

Kem and Jaml watch the crowd recognize the Queen and immediately drop to one knee to her rule. She remains motionless as the hall falls quiet. Once everyone is in proper protocol for her status, General Fen steps up from her side to address the crowd.

"The business day of the Sagin court is now in session. Our Queen is presiding over today's business." Formalities, just formalities but the formalities give instant credibility to her station. If anyone is to question her rule, this would be the time. There is an eerie silence in the room that is until

"Rise my loyal people of Sagin. It is true, I have returned. Without assistance from the monk and Reaper, it might not be so. We have vanquished yet another nest of demons in our kingdom and I vow to you to continue this fight. Our people will no longer live in fear! Let Lucifer be put on notice that the kingdom of Sagin is a God fearing one and we will not bow to his evil minions. We will continue to fight and destroy until our kingdom is cleansed."

A huge cheer arises from the crowds. Many clank their weapons and bang their cups on the tables. Queen Lanea of Sagin has just proclaimed her throne a throne for and of God. In the back, Jaml finds Wayv quietly moving out one of the side doors. The man looks around to make sure no one is watching. His eyes instantly lock in on the eyes of the black man in the back corridor. Jaml gives him a slight nod which Wayv returns. Wayv goes through the side door while Jaml fades back into the hallway.

Wayv walks confidently and quickly down the hall. He doesn't bother looking behind himself, he knows Reaper is on his way and knows who he is. He needs to get to the little church quickly and leave before Jaml finds him to end his life.

The little church is not a church at all, simply a room used for services for the royal family, especially if one is sick or wounded. It has also been used by former kings in times of invasion. Behind the altar is a fake wall which can be moved out to access a tunnel leading to a special set of horses outside the wall. If the kingdom is to ever be overrun, the royal family would be able to escape to gather reinforcements and retake the castle.

Wayv turns the corner to the final hallway that leads to the little church to find Nom standing there with six soldiers at attention. Wayv closes the distance to his faithful companion and servant, embracing the man standing before him.

"It is good to see you Nom. The Queen has returned. I do not know what happened with the ambush but Reaper is back as well.

We must get out of here before he finds us as he will surely execute both of us."

A look of utter horror fills Nom's face.

"Does he know about us?"

"Yes I do." The voice is loud and fills the hall. Both men turn their heads to the long hall Wayv just came down to find Reaper standing there. "It is amazing that you two would think one of your brethren, the demon, would keep your secret when he has been given the type of death he wanted. And before you ask Wayv, I know you are a demon and your pudgy friend here is a demon lover. I can understand you Wayv, you cannot help it. You are a miserable creation from the Fallen and do not know anything else. You don't have free will, you are merely a pawn to be thrown away at a whim. Now you, Nom, how can you turn your back on the Lord God, your savior? He died for you and this is how you repay that debt? Sleeping with a demon? I normally have pity on my non demon foes because they do not know any other path. Today I will not have pity on your soul because you know God and have chosen to turn away from him."

Wayv begins to laugh while Nom becomes furious. Wayv speaks first.

"Me? Pawn? Please! I am no more a pawn than you. The really sad thing is you actually believe you have free will. Let me enlighten you Reaper, you are nothing more than a puppet, a talking puppet. Have you seen this God? Has he spoken to you? No on both counts. You cling to faith as a baby to his blanket. And like a baby, if the blanket is taken, all you can do is cry and whine. Open your eyes Reaper. Join us, listen to the blades and we can find favor with Lucifer. You would become his champion. Better a champion than a dead piece of meat."

"You are blind!" The words stammer out of Nom's mouth. "I have seen the great promises Lucifer is promising. The alternative? Live poorly for a God I don't know? I would rather enjoy myself."

"Then you are nothing more than another Eve to fall under Lucifer's empty promises. I no longer have pity on your soul but I will send your soul to hell." Jaml slowly pulls his blades from their scabbards.

Nom loses his courage and quickly hides behind Wayv who simply smiles at Reaper.

"Just like a soldier, draw and kill. That is all you know how to do. So let me help you." Wayv raises his hands to point at the six soldiers standing at attention. It occurs to Jaml that the men have neither moved nor spoken during this entire time. He looks closer to find each soldier has enlarged brown pupils. lycan!

Almost on cue, the six men begin their transformation into the lycan men fear. Tremendous amounts of fur appear all over the exposed skin, hands stretch into makeshift paws capped with claws, sharpened for the kill. Jaml knows to let their transformation complete would mean a huge fight leading to the demon escaping. He attacks! His blade flies across the neck of the nearest lycan, resulting in a blood fountain spewing life force from the creature. A paw reaches for its neck but too late, he is dead. Jaml completes a full spin, lowering his blades to chest level, his chest. The blades bite deep across the midsection of the next lycan. The creature steps back, his entrails flopping out of his body and onto the floor.

"Come."

Nom snaps out of his trance at the command from Wayv. In all his years Nom has never seen such a spectacle. Watching Jaml in combat is like watching an eloquent dance perform for royalty, nothing wasted, the form flows like water. Nom clears his throat, regaining his composure and quickly follows Wayv into the altar and freedom.

Yet the question sits in the back of Nom's mind, did he choose wrong?

Reaper thrusts his blades upward, through the creature's midsection and into the lungs. The lycan immediately attempts to scream but his punctured lungs have already filled with blood, leaving the scream to sound more like a sick gurgle. Reaper twists his blades before ripping them out of the creature's hide. Reaper looks at the altar close behind the demon and its slave. He knows he has no time to waste, he needs to dispatch these creatures before his quarry gets away.

He suddenly leans back, avoiding the clawed paw whose intent is to rip him in two. The creature regrets the attack as his arm is still fully extended when a blade separates the arm from the lycan at the forearm. The lifeless arm plops to the ground, the lycan holding his arm in rage, moving towards an attack when the second blade plunges into the side of the lycan's head. Reaper does not break stride, intent on getting to the altar and his prey. He violently jerks his arm, tearing the blade from the front of the lycan's head. Blood and brain matter splatter all over him, the creature's face being completely ripped off.

The final two lycans look at each other, hoping the other would have a suggestion except dying. Neither one finds the answer he is looking for so they both look forward to the man who has killed four of their brethren in a matter of minutes. A loud roar fills the room, shaking some of the paintings off the wall, Reaper merely smiles.

Reaper explodes in a sprint towards the lycans. He hurls a blade. The creature on the right roars in agony as the blade finds and penetrates his fur covered hide, burying itself in the lycan's midsection, causing the creature to stumble backwards. The second lycan makes the ultimate war mistake. He gets distracted, concerned about his battle buddy. The lycan looks over at his buddy and does not see the man close with incredible speed. The lycan turns his eyes to his opponent just in time to see the other ebony blade plunge into his face.

Jaml shoves the blade into the creature's face to the hilt. The stab is so violent and so quick the creature has no time to make a noise before he dies. A thud is heard as the body of the lycan hits the floor, dead. Reaper does not slow, in one fluid motion while running, he steps on the creature's chest, reaches down and pulls the blade free without breaking stride towards the altar door. He passes the gravely injured lycan with the blade in his gut, reaches down and pulls the blade free without breaking his stride.

He reaches the door and pulls it open, not concerned with traps, only with catching the traitors. He doesn't realize he breaks a thin string that is tied across the hall. He continues to run until movement catches his eye. He looks over to find a metal ball swinging towards him. He can do nothing but raise a hand. The ball crashes into his forearm, throwing him like a rag doll against the wall, sending him into darkness.

Queen Lanea lounges in her chamber. The day's event was more taxing on her than she thought. Sitting on the throne for hours talking about the most mundane topics is not her idea of work but it is something that must be done. Topics ranging from moving troops to the south border in retaliation for the other country to determining which farmer had access to a nearby creek and everything in between. At the end of the day, she is back in command, no question on her fitness to rule.

As she lounges in a simple gown, her thoughts are elsewhere. After one of her sessions, Kem whispers into her ear about Reaper going after someone. After the second session, Kem whispers Reaper has not returned and Kem is going after Reaper. That was hours ago and Lanea sits in her chambers, her heart heavy without knowing what happened to her friend. Soon after the meetings wrapped up, Lanea dispatches a detachment of soldiers led by General Fen to find her two friends. They returned a short time later with no luck. Not being one who accepts defeat, General Fen obtained the Queen's blessing to head back out and look for Jaml.

Lanea takes a sip of wine from her glass goblet, worry drains her emotions faster than she drains her goblet. She shifts on her couch, hoping maybe something magical will happen. She has prayed and prayed again for the safe return of her friends, and grows ever frustrated at the results or no results that have occurred. Suddenly there is a knock at the door. Lanea leaps from her couch and opens the door. The sight before her leaves her breathless. She takes a step back in disbelief.

General Fen and Kem stand before her. In between them is the unconscious form of Jaml, a steady stream of blood running from the side of his face.

"Come in. Come in." Lanea's voice is full of worry.

They drag Jaml's body into the chamber and lay him down on the couch. Kem runs over to grab a cloth and some water. She immediately begins to wipe the blood from his face which seems to bring him back from the darkness. His head begins to turn from side to side moments before his hand brushes the wet rag away.

"Thank you. Thank you all but can you please get that rag away from me?" He opens an eye to stare at the monk Kem. Despite the room being poorly lit by design, the amount of light is still a lot for Jaml who squints at his friends.

"Fine." She removes the rag and sits him up,

Jaml gives her a smile before looking over at the Queen. Before he begins, the Queen regains her stern command voice.

"Who is it? Who has betrayed me and my people?"

"I love your straight to the point, my Queen but can I have a moment?" Jaml takes a cup of water from Kem and sips on it. The sips soon turn into gulps as Jaml only now realizes how thirsty he is. After downing the contents of the cup, Jaml attempts to open his eyes fully but again reverts back to squinting.

"Your moment has passed." Her determined expression does not go unnoticed by Jaml. He looks up and straight into her eyes.

"Wayv is a demon."

"Are you sure? Oh my God." She cannot help but to look away in astonishment. Memories she has with him and the intimate conversations she shared with him over the years come storming back. Decisions where she followed his advice without question all of a sudden must be questioned. She has courted his advice long before the King's death.

"He has a human worshiper. Someone who believes Lucifer will rise again and lead his army to victory. Someone who believes the demon Wayv will lead him to salvation. Nom."

"No!" Queen Lanea looks horrified at the news. Jaml cannot tell if it is more about Wayv or Nom. What he does know is her outburst caused great pain in his head. He fights the nausea even as he watches the Queen battle her demons, ones he knows all too well.

General Fen quickly finds himself catching a falling Queen and gently sitting her on her couch. Kem gets her some water which she downs immediately. She looks up at General Fen, tears swell in her eyes, pain rushing through her body.

"He told my husband the people would honor him as the greatest king if he went to kill the demons himself. He talked my husband into marching into a battle.... Wayv knew he was going to die. He sent my husband to his death!"

Everyone can see the rage building in her, from the body tension to the clenched fist to the hard jaw. She looks back at Jaml, fighting back tears of hate.

"Did you kill him?"

"No I did not. My carelessness entering into the not only allowed the demon to escape but has put me in my present situation. I apologize for my failure." His words trail off.

Her demeanor lights slightly as she looks around the room at her trusted friends standing there.

"No need to apologize. Your actions are noble and greatly appreciated. Without you, I would never have known about the treachery in my own house. I would be sitting with my husband in heaven wondering what happened. You have my gratitude for your efforts."

"Thank you, milady."

"I know you and Sister Kem will be leaving soon to return to your quest. I am just thankful for your help in my kingdom. Know this, as long as I am Queen, you are welcome into my kingdom at any time. You two are truly my friends and I thank God for you. With all that said, I almost feel wrong for what I am about to ask."

Kem cuts her off. "No words needed milady. If we encounter either Wayv or Nom, we will give them the judgment of God. After we have finished with our quest, we will hunt down those dogs, both the demon and the betrayer of man."

A simple nod between the ladies is all that needs to be done. The oath has been given.

"No!" Jaml's proclamation both stuns and surprises everyone in the room, especially the two women who have just entered into a pack. Queen Lanea's eyes stay wide in astonishment while Kem's eyes narrow at her companion. Never has Jaml ever gone against Kem but now she feels betrayed.

"Forgive me, milady. Kem has misspoken. What she meant to say is we are not and will not leave until these two are being judged in heaven or sitting in your jail." His statement brings smiles to all in the room. "But first I must rest, all of you talking is giving me such a headache."

No one laughs but all smile. The Queen allows Jaml to use her couch to rest. She places four soldiers outside the door and three bowmen on the parapet. The two ladies go enjoy girl talk.

Chapter 14

Two figures crouch on top of the bakery shop. The night air is warm with the smell of impending rain. Clouds have created a blanket of darkness over the city, eliminating both the starlight and moonlight from the city. Perfect for the two figures who watch and wait, their position hidden from the casual person walking by.

The streets of the city below are well lit by the street torches that burn brightly throughout. Lit by the night guard, these torches light up most public ways throughout the city as well as most alleyways. Originally put in to ward off the succubae and give the archers time to shoot down the demons, the Queen chose to keep the torches as a means of deterrent from night crime.

Both figures on the roof are dressed in black outfits, complete with masks that cover their entire face save their eyes. Reaper is dressed in his familiar black pants and tight shirt. His black cape gently sways in the breeze. His blades sit crossed against his lower back. Kneeling next to him is his partner dressed in a matching outfit, despite her objections. The black pants shirt combination is form fitting, not only ideal for stealth but also reveals her femininity which she does not like. Her staff is strapped to her back, her only comfort in this entire situation.

The duo watches the house across from their position. They have been trying to locate Wayv and Nom since their escape. Every time they get close to capturing their quarry, the two men seem to find a way to escape. General Fen suggested the two men have sympathizers amongst the population. Kem could not believe any man would turn his back on the Lord, her anger boils at the spineless men in this kingdom. Reminds her of Colley and the issues they will be returning to shortly.

Earlier that evening, the two had a conversation with General Fen. One that was uncomfortable but needed to be had.

"Please don't judge them too harshly. Many of the men in ranking positions do not think it is proper for a woman to rule without a male. They have brought that up repeatedly and Lanea will not hear of it. Not sure if the courting is for her sake or potential for one of them to become king. She refuses to marry if it is not for love. I am sure the conspirators are doing it to push Lanea into marrying. They are God fearing men but simply misguided." General Fen explains the situation as he sees it.

Since then, the two have not included anyone on their excursions or investigations. They have closed the net around the whereabouts and now have the exact location. Due to Jaml's previous encounters with lycans, the two have waited for the proper moment. Jaml knows that Kem's staff is not blessed and would have little impact on the beasts. Kem reminds him of their previous encounter with lycans. Reluctantly he gives in and now they wait for the moment to attack.

They watch as servants load up chests onto the wagon, a good indication the two of them are planning a night get away. Neither man has emerged from the building but Jaml feels it will be soon. He indicates no lycans. Kem nudges him and points to the north where there are four soldiers waiting. Jaml shakes his head before hunching his shoulders at his partner.

They watch as two men quickly exit the building and climb into the carriage. A servant closes the door before climbing into the top of the carriage. He grabs his reins and nudges the horses forward. The carriage moves quietly through the city, as not to disturb anyone. Disturbance will lead to questions, ones they rather not have to answer.

Jaml turns to Kem.

"You ready?" Her response is a slight nod. "Leave the marks so I can follow and catch up. I hope to be at your side by dawn. If not, take down the demon and the traitor and bring Queen Lanea their heads."

Kem flies across the rooftops unseen. She is able to keep up with the carriage with no problem, remaining undetected against the night sky and simply because no one bothered to look up for danger. She makes her way to her horse that is tethered just inside the city wall.

As Kem scurries across the rooftops to keep up with the carriage and their victims, Jaml waits quietly for the demon's entourage to pass by. He waits patiently for the four horsemen to ride past his position. He watches intently as they move closer, no weapons drawn or any sense of heightened security. They are too secure in their position with Advisor Wayv, probably thinking this convoy is completely unnecessary. That is going to change.

Out of nowhere, a figure drops in their midst, causing the horses to spook, rearing up on their hind legs, crying out danger in their midst. Before the four soldiers are able to get their horses under control, the figure is already in action. The figure jumps onto the horse of the highest ranking soldier, plunging his blades into the man's sides, pushing the blades all the way in, piercing the lungs. The soldier struggles some, his lungs filling with blood quickly, the pain of being stabbed causing orientation and confusion. His arms flail wildly, reaching for a weapon until Reaper rips the blades from his sides. The instant wave of severe pain overcomes the soldier who becomes limp prior to dying.

Reaper flips off the back of the horse before somersaulting onto the next horse. This soldier is somewhat prepared. He has his dagger drawn and waits for the assassin to land. Reaper lands on his feet and instantly jumps. As he vaults over the soldier and avoids the stab, he turns his body and launches one of his blades. He watches the blade bury itself deep in the back of the soldier. Reaper lands on his feet, the element of surprise over with two soldiers left.

Both soldiers have dismounted and are presently changing. Limbs crack into place as the human side disappears to reveal the lycans inside. Fingers and toes elongate into claws. Their jawlines snap and reshape itself into a muzzle, covered in fur. Once fully formed, the two remaining lycans roar at the figure standing in front of them.

Reaper wastes no time in attacking. He closes the gap between him and the lycans almost immediately. His blade comes alive in his hand. The first lycan takes a swipe at the man only to watch his hand fall to the ground. The lycan rears his head and roars only to have it cut off before he finishes it. A swift backhand from Reaper opens the throat of the lycan. Blood spurts out as a broken dam in a river. The lycan attempts to cover the slash and keep his life force inside. He quickly loses the battle as blood continues to gush from the open wound in his neck. The lycan slowly drops to his knees before falling flat on his face.

The last lycan savagely attacks, jumping into the air, claws and fangs bare, eager to taste human blood. Reaper waits patiently for the attack to arrive. The lycan lands inches from Reaper and immediately bears down, ready for the kill. Reaper steps in closer making it near impossible for the creature to stab him with his claws. Reaper slams his blade upward, through the underneath of the mouth, through the head and into the brain, killing the creature instantly.

Reaper rips his blade free from the lycan, allowing the creature to collapse to the ground. Reaper walks over to the second lycan and retrieves his other blade. After sheathing his blades, Jaml leaves the scene, letting the soldiers clean up the mess when they find the carnage in the morning.

Kem hears rustling behind her. She shifts slightly, just in case it is not Jaml, her fingers wrap around her staff, the grip tightening as she prepares for an attack that she really does not think is coming. Early in her travels, she realizes being prepared is a must, she has lost fellow warriors because they were not ready for battle.

"How is everything here?"

The familiar tone of Jaml's voice brings relaxation to the moment. She doesn't pull her eyes from the scene in front of her, neither does she turn her head to speak.

"Sitting here for a while. Apparently waiting for someone before leaving. Other than that, nothing."

"Hope they are not waiting for their military escort. It is not coming."

Kem turns her head to find a smiling Jaml standing there. No apparent cuts visible through his uniform. All appears to be well.

"Are you ready to do this or do you need time to rest your bones?" The sarcasm is lighthearted and appreciated by both.

"Only if you promise not to talk them to death." Kem cuts her eyes over to Jaml on that remark before smiling.

The two warriors back out of their hiding perch to make their way over to the coach in the clearing. Resting in the camp is Wayv, Nom, the driver and a soldier. With only three adversaries, Nom didn't count, the duo decide a frontal attack is in order. The warriors get to the edge of the camp before Kem puts up a question.

"Which do you want, the lycans or Wayv?" Kem's question breaks the silence

"I prefer Wayv unless you have an itching to scratch." Neither look at each other, their focus is solely on the battle that is to come.

"No itch here. You take the demon while I handle the Lycans." Her fingers wrap tightly around the staff as she eyes her two opponents.

"Sounds good to me." Jaml exhales slowly.

Reaper draws his blades as the two walk into the clearing. All four men look up in complete surprise. Wayv is the first one to recover his composure.

"Well, if it isn't the bane of my existence. I can assume my little entourage is not going to make it?"

"Let's just say they are looking for their heads." As he speaks, Jaml watches the two soldiers begin to climb down off the carriage.

"Pity that. I guess there is no way to persuade you into letting us go?

"No. You are going to have to pay for your crimes and you need to be exposed for what you really are." Kem's words are filled with anger. Her demeanor reflects the anger in her voice, every muscle tensed and ready for action.

"Oh yes, the little monk with the attitude. Are you still protecting the whore queen you hang out with?"

Kem feels a hand on her arm, steadying her. She looks over to find Jaml looking at her.

"Don't let him get to you. He knows the only way he wins is if one of us is not focused. So don't give him the opportunity. He has already been exposed."

She winks an eye at Jaml before addressing Wayv.

"So close, demon. Unfortunately for you, this is simply business. Not personal."

Both warriors watch as the transformation begins. The two soldiers begin to burst out of their armor, fur and muscles begin to bulge through. Wayv's skin begins to turn red while he grows into the grotesque demon that he is. Claws extend from his fingers. Fangs replace teeth. Wings extend from his back. Within seconds, Wayv has completed his transformation from human form to full demon. In his hand he wields a broadsword like a dagger. The two lycans stand ready on two hind legs, each grasping a sword.

"Playtime human"

Carried by the wings on his back, Wayv swiftly closes the gap with Reaper. His sword strike is met with a loud clang by the twin ebony blades of Reaper who throws the large sword to the side, opening up the demon. He quickly steps inside the demon's guard, reversing his grip, looking to plunge his blades into the demon's side. Again the wings flap and this time carries the demon to safety.

"Nice trick demon. Why don't you come over here so we can see who is the better fighter." Reaper steps forward, ready to engage once again.

"I will have to be a little more prudent than that Reaper. I have heard of your skills and I recognize those blades."

"Are you telling me that I am not dealing with another stupid demon?"

The two engage once again.

Not far from the two combatants, another battle wages. Kem battles the two lycans. Her staff whistles through the air, blocking a series of lycan strikes before delivering her own. In lycan form, the two soldiers are clumsy in their attacks, hanging on to their humanity while denying their new normal. The result is Kem easily thwarting off their attacks easily while punishing them with precise strikes of her own.

The first lycan, longer hair than the other one, swings his blade high, attempting to decapitate the monk. She holds her staff firm, blocking the attack while allowing her to spin inward. She punches the lycan with little effect. The response is what she wants, a lycan's unfazed and unfocused, trying to boast on a strike that did not affect him. The lycan throws his head back to laugh at such an attack when he feels the true one. The staff is slammed against the knee, buckling the lycan. She twirls her staff overhead before crashing it against the shoulder, crushing it.

Lycans are impervious to external damage, hence swords are useless. A soldier can cut, slice, and even cut off limbs only to find regeneration occurs. What most don't know is damage under the skin remains, as long as the skin is not broken. The regeneration factor occurs only when the skin is broken so the damage inflicted by the monk is taking its toll.

The lycan screams in pain at the impact and breaking of bones. He stumbles back, swinging his blade wildly in an attempt to keep the monk away. Her sights have moved on. She spins to face the second lycan who sustained injury from their previous encounter. The lycan struggles to keep its balance due to the damage to its knee. What makes this lycan more dangerous is the lycan has discarded its sword and now attacks solely with its claws and jaw, both more formidable than a sword in a lycan's hand.

Due partially to its injury, this lycan attacks more like an animal than a human. Kem moves to engage this lycan immediately. It swings claws at her, trying to rip open the woman's intestine. Kem easily side steps the attacks and moves forward. Her staff moves faster than an eye can follow. The result is a strike to the ribs, breaking one, followed by several strikes to the legs and body of the lycan, causing instantly bruising.

She twirls her staff overhead before moving in for the kill, her body is a whirl of motion. A strike to each leg roots the creature in place, followed by a strike to the creature's lower back, causing pain enough to keep the lycan reaching for the pain. She follows this by jumping high in the air, staff twirling. The descent of the body coupled with her slamming the staff down is all that is needed. The staff, gaining incredible speed, crashes into the skull of the lycan. Bones collapse and splinter under the force of the staff. Kem watches her staff crush the lycan's skull, the staff stopping just above the creature's eyes. A little blood flows from the lycan's eyes, nose and mouth before it topples over dead.

Wayv hovers just out of Reaper's reach. The demon glares down at its adversary, the Reaper Jaml stands confidently ready. Wayv knew beforehand he could not beat this demon killer but never knew to what extent this Reaper's skills. Wayv looks down at his leg, mangled beyond repair. In human or demon form, he will never be able to walk without assistance, thanks to those damn swords of his.

The demon hovers above with a decision to make. Flee with a cripple leg and possible wrath coming from Lucifer or engage one final time and die in battle but his dreams of rule would never happen. His greed is too much.

Wayv spins in the air, wings flapping frantically, hoping to escape before Reaper can get to him. Reaper watches the demon turn his back to flee and smiles. He takes one blade and launches it. The short sword sinks through one of the wings and into his back. The demon arches in agony but determination carries him away.

For a second, Jaml thinks he will have to hunt the injured demon down to retrieve his sword. Instinctively he holds up his hand towards the fleeing demon. The blade is ripped out of the back of the demon to return to Jaml's hand. The excruciating pain is almost too much for Wayv to bear. His good wing flutters momentarily before regaining its composure. The demon is able to fly away using only one wing.

Jaml turns to find Kem standing there, staff in hand, dead Lycans at her feet.

"Trust a man to botch up the job and let a demon escape."

They both laugh.

"Let's get the traitor and get out of here." His words take some of the luster from the moment but seeing a monk cowering in dread underneath the carriage is more than enough to lighten the mood once more. "Come here boy before I send the monk in after you."

Kem gives Jaml a harsh look, how dare he use her as the bad guy but to his defense, Wayv had used words to work up her emotions almost to success. Knowing his life hangs in the balance, Nom looks out from beneath the carriage with the warmest look that he can muster.

"Hi there. There is a logical explanation as to why I am traveling with such a despicable monster. You see, he threatened me, that's right. He threatened me with my life if I didn't help him. I am so glad that you two came and rescued me."

"Shut up traitor." Kem's words came out as harsh as she had hoped. Both Nom and Jaml are taken aback at the tone of her words. The expression on Nom's face indicates the man may have soiled his pants. "We are not here to judge you. Our task is to bring her back to Queen Lanea so she can pass judgment in the land of man and you may hear your judgment in front of God."

The reference to being judged by God sent slivers to fear running through his body. For a person to be judged by God, he must be dead. The thought of him dying scares Nom to his core. He agreed to throw his lot in with Wayv because he, like so many others, believed a woman cannot rule and since she refused suitors, she needed to be removed from the throne so a man, the rightful ruler, could ascend the throne and rule.

Now Nom finds himself groveling like a homeless dog in front of a female monk and one of God's killers, fully exposed, weaponless, non-skilled in war, begging for his life. How times have changed, a week before he was sitting in luxury, plotting to overthrow the Queen. He was all on board, eager for the day a man would once again sit on the throne. Now how foolish he feels.

"Please monk, don't kill me."

"I will not kill you. That is not by place. But if you don't get here in a hurry, I may forget my place."

A fire crackles in the middle of the clearing. The dead Lycans have been prepared for burning in the morning. Jaml went hunting and returned with two rabbits and soon they were being slowly cooked over the open flame. Sitting next to him is Kem waiting patiently for the small game to finish cooking, she is famished.

Sitting against the carriage is a tied up Nom. His wrists are bound behind him with thick ropes. His legs are likewise bound despite Kem's objections. She preferred his legs unbound, daring him to run away through the woods. Jaml quickly recognizes her intentions to hunt the man down. After a quick harsh discussion, that Nom could hear every word, Kem relinquished her wishes and Nom lives for another night.

Jaml removes the rabbit from the flame. He pulls one from the stick and hands it to Kem. They say their prayers and begin eating the hot bland meat. Despite the lack of spices, the two tear at the flesh as if it was seasoned by the best chefs in the land. After eating, Jaml pulls a slab of jerky from his pack and stuffs it into Nom's mouth. The monk chokes on the tough jerky, causing him to cough a couple of times. He struggles and finally is able to moisten the dried meat enough to eat. He chokes down a couple more pieces before settling back against the tree for a long but restless night. Jaml takes the first shift, sitting across from the monk, staring at the man with hatred. Kem lies on her bedroll to get some sleep, Nom knows the death stares will only intensify once Kem's shift begins.

The next morning, Nom is tied and secured to the horse's saddle. Once he is secured, the duo cleans the campsite to include spreading the ashes as well as burning the lycans animals. Next they set fire to the carriage. They watch casually as the carriage burns to the ground. They want to make sure they leave no evidence of them being there.

Satisfied that all evidence of the battle from the previous day is eradicated, they climb on their horses and head back to Sagin and Queen Lanea where they will turn this traitor over to face charges against the kingdom. They take one more look over to make sure they have left nothing before heading back.

The ride back to Sagin is a bit longer, due to no imminent chase or escape occurring. The conversation between Kem and Jaml is lighthearted, more about the countryside than the captor on the horse next to them. Their captor, Nom, rides quietly, his thoughts around the torture and death that will obviously occur when they get back to the castle. He realizes his life is in forfeit unless he can convince these two to set him free.

"I know where Wayv is heading. I can show you. All I ask is that you release me and I swear I will never set foot in Sagin for as long as I live."

"Let me get this straight." Jaml turns in his saddle to face the monk in ropes. "You expect two warriors of God to believe a heretic who has turned his back on his church, the word, and God himself. You have a better chance crying to Queen Lanea for killing her husband. Be thankful you are making the trip back without loss of limb or blood."

"Keep quiet lover of Lucifer, lest I forget my word to Jaml and crush your skull right here." Kem's words drip of hatred and desire for blood.

Nom shrinks in his saddle knowing any chance of survival rests on the Queen's mercy. These two want his blood. He doesn't want to give them the opportunity so he does not speak again on the journey. He spends his time trying to decide if God hates him as well and if he should even attempt to pray. He pictures a bolt of lightning striking him down immediately when he says those frightful words, Dear Heavenly Father

Rays of sunlight break through the blankets hanging over the windows. Jaml thinks about rolling over, thoughts of heading back to Colley is all he needs to pull his eyes open. He rolls to a seated position at the edge of the bed. He rubs his eyes and gets up, time to depart the kingdom of Sagin.

After morning prayers, Jaml heads down the corridor to the Great Hall, where he intends to find General Fen and others still feasting and drinking. He opens the side door and does not believe what he is seeing. There is no one in the hall and the hall is completely clean. He has never seen such a thing, a clean hall the morning after a feast, especially since he expected to find drunk soldiers sleeping amidst half naked bar girls.

"Not what you expect?"

The booming voice of General Fen is heard from the other end of the hall. A smile creeps across Jaml's face as he turns to face the man who he would consider a friend. Friends outside of other Reapers are very rare for a Reaper. They are used to and embrace the solitude that is the life of one. More often than not, a friend turns into a liability, exploited by whichever demon finds out. What begins as a friendship often ends up a mercy killing. Jaml knows Fen can definitely handle himself but why put him in that danger?

"I would agree General, not what I expected at all." Jaml turns to face the burly man.

"After you left, Queen Lanea shut down bars and taverns after the moon's zenith. The thought of her husband dying at Wayv's hands took its toll on her."

"And the people?"

"After the horrors of the succubae, people were not too anxious to get out and about. They have obeyed without incidence and many have embraced it as the new normal."

"Anything new from Nom?"

"First bit of pain and he sang like a canary. Gave us a list of males who were following Wayv. We are in the midst of rounding them up. They will be tried and prosecuted. Several have tried to leave through the gate this morning. Rounding them up on the streets and at the gates makes it a whole lot easier than going to their houses and doing it that way. Now it's my turn. Are you really leaving?"

Jaml takes a deep breath

"I am afraid so. We have to get back to Colley and get this demon blade and demon dagger into the hands of someone who knows and can handle the power."

"You would need an angel to get that done." Fen begins to laugh at his remark then realizes Jaml is not laughing. He stops and Jaml winks at him. "I don't even want to know. If you ever find yourself

292

in a bind, send word and I swear I will battle Lucifer himself at your side."

"Your loyalty is much appreciated and reciprocated."

The two men clasp forearms before heading to the Queen's chambers.

It takes the majority of the morning for Kem and Jaml to give and receive reports from the Queen and other dignitaries. Most of the conspirators have been rounded up, stored in the dungeons under the castle to await their trials. Queen Lanea's mood is one of happiness lined with sorrow for her two friends that are leaving. Her mood remains the same unless someone mentions the conspirators, at which time anger quickly fills her heart, her temper flares at the mention of them. Jaml asked once about the fate of Nom and never asked again.

The sun is past its zenith when Kem and Jaml climb into the saddle. Both the Queen and the general are in attendance, along with several others, to see the Reaper and the monk off. Jaml grabs the reins of the two pack horses.

"Thank you once again Queen Lanea. Your generosity is greatly appreciated and will never be forgotten. May God shine his light on you and bless you and your people daily." He bows his head slightly along with Kem.

"I am sorry that this is all I can do for you. If you ever need anything, the kingdom of Sagin will welcome you." She waves her hand in farewell.

The two warriors urge their steeds forward but not before taking one last look at the friends they are leaving behind. They guide their horses through the marketplace towards the main gate.

"As much as I would like to stay here, we have got to get these weapons back to Allie." Kem looks over at Jaml, who slowly returns her gaze.

"You can stay. You and the Queen have created a bond, of that there is no doubt. Be her personal bodyguard and advisor, General Fen would welcome the help. I may be reckless but I think I can handle getting back to Colley all by myself."

"Not from where I sit. Or do you remember how we met? Seems to me you are a bad judge of character." The remark elicits laughter from both of them. "But your words ring true. God's path for me lies here but I will not leave you without cause. After we finish cleansing Colley, I will return here to take up my position as personal guard and counsel."

"Guess I am late on this. What will your official title be?"

"Mother Kem."

Jaml nods his approval. The duo ride through the gate.

Chapter 15

Kem and Jaml ride nonstop to get to Colley. As they enter the outer reaches of the kingdom, they decide to stop for a rest. The day is long and the sun weighs heavy in the west when the two spy a farm just off the main road. A good spot as ever to rest and get some information from the locals about the recent activity in the kingdom.

As they near the farmhouse they saw in the distance, a child takes off from the field towards the house. From the distance the child looked no more than fourteen summers old, old enough to work the land but not old enough to claim his own land. Like so many farmers in this region, the boys follow in the footsteps of their fathers while the daughters find suitable husbands to raise a family. A simple life, both agree, meant for hard working people, God's people.

The boy returns with his father, both men armed. The father wields an old sword in his hand, rust begins to show along the base of the blade next to the hand guard. The leather wrapping on the hilt has begun to tear away, exposing the metal underneath. He wears no armor, simply brown trousers with a white shirt so stained that most would agree is also brown. The boy is wearing almost identical clothing, not so many stains. In his hands, he holds a large pitchfork, the three forks are long enough to skewer a man completely through.

The bearded man steps forward. "What can we do for you?"

Jaml leans forward in his saddle. "Rest. We mean you no harm and want nothing that you would not offer. Our horses are tired and we are thirsty. We can drink from the spring over there."

"How can I be sure? You are obviously armed. I do not want any trouble. How can I be sure you are not a demon from the castle?" The farmer stares at the two travelers. "Besides, I don't trust anyone that covers their face. It tells me you have something to hide."

The two travelers pull back their hoods, revealing their faces. The father stares at the two travelers while the boy behind him immediately drops to his knees.

"Father, she is the one. I will never forget that face. Remember the bear? She is the one."

The farmer turns to see his son on his knee before turning back around to drop to a knee.

"Forgive me priest. Times are deadly and I did not know you are the one that saved my son two seasons ago. Please forgive me. Whatever you need, just ask. All we have is yours."

Kem dismounts. She walks over to the farmer, gently getting him to his feet by his arm. She does the same to the boy before returning to face the farmer.

"Please do not kneel before me. I am a simple instrument of God. I do recognize you, it is Junior, is it not? You have grown quite a bit of hair on that chin since the last time I saw you."

The farmer answers as the boy is too busy blushing. "We are humble that you remember his name. It is Junior and I am Martiz. My wife, Lisa, is in the house."

"How can I forget such a brave young man? You have raised him well Martiz. We do not want to intrude on your family so if we can rest in the barn. We will leave under the moon and once again thank you."

"We will have no such thing!" Martiz's voice came across harsher than he wanted but the message is clear. "You two are our honored guests and will dine with us. You are to rest in our room until you need to go. I will hear nothing else on the matter."

"Then it is settled." Kem's response and tone lightens the mood. Jaml dismounts and grabs the reins of the horses, allowing Kem the time to visit with Martiz and Junior.

Dinner got delayed as Lisa had to add to the stew. As the meal cooks, the five of them sit at the table to talk. The conversation begins with a recounting of the rescue as told by Kem. She recounts traveling to a small community over the mountain when she hears the roar of a bear. She quickly flies over the hill to find Junior standing his ground with the bear, who was after the sheep he was guarding. Junior is armed with the same pitch fork he bravely stood his ground hours before. The bear suddenly rears up on its hind legs. Before Junior could readjust, the bear takes a swipe and connects on the side of the boy's head. Junior flies through the air to land on his back, semi-conscious. The bear stalks closer. Junior rises on wobbly legs, determined to fight off the bear and save the flock.

Determination rages in his eyes, despite the blood that pours freely from his temple.

The bear senses the boy's declining health so moves in for the kill. It rears up, ready to deliver the killing stroke when a staff strikes the wrist of the bear, eliciting a howl of pain from the animal. The monk does not wait. The bear is subjected to a series of blows to its head and torso. The bear retreats in order to confront its newest enemy. It finds a monk draped in brown cloaks standing in front of it. In her hand is the Bo staff. The bear rears up, ready to attack. Kem ducks the swing, striking the bear with a series of blows and jabs to cause the maximum amount of damage possible. Realizing there is an easier meal somewhere else, the bear turns and runs off. She makes sure the young man is not in any danger of dying before leaving him.

Martiz picks up the story recounting finding his son walking towards the house, his shirt pressed against his head. Martiz meets the boy halfway to escort him to the house where Lisa tends to his head wound. They remember him telling them about the monk infused with God like speed who came and saved his life. It is Kem's turn to blush.

After dinner, Martiz sits with the two guests as Lisa cleans up the dinner and Junior does his night chores. The sun has all but set. Jaml cannot help but bring up questions about Colley.

"Martiz, you mentioned earlier about demons from Colley. Is the kingdom overrun with demons?"

"After you left Reaper." A look of surprise crosses Jaml's face. "I recognized you when my son recognized Kem. Everyone knows the black Reaper. Anyway, after you left the kingdom went crazy. In retribution for the death of their kids, the king and queen have put the entire kingdom in martial law. Most, if not all, churches have been burned to the ground. People are sacrificed on the regular now, for any infraction against the crown. Every night the kingdom looks like it is on fire. Our taxes have tripled. I am glad you have returned. Our people need you right now, they need a sign from God."

"I apologize for the pain that my absence has caused. I am back now."

"Are you going to finish what you started?"

"I will not leave you all until every last demon is either dead or has run away." Jaml looks over the table, catching each person's eye. "I will finish this. One way or another."

A collective sigh fills the room. Martiz leans back against his chair, satisfied with the response. An excited yes escapes from Junior's lips. Kem smiles at Jaml, knowing he is willing to lay down his life for these people, just like in Colley. Oh, how she misses Colley, and the companion of the Queen. She is anxious to end this and return to her calling.

The two warriors leave under the blanket of night, both eager to return to the church and purge this kingdom of its demons. Not surprising, Martiz is correct, the kingdom does look like its burning in the night sky. As they get closer, they can make out flames burning in the night sky. Soldiers are positioned on the terrace, armed with crossbows. Patrols of soldiers are patrolling around the walls of the kingdom.

The two warriors of God hide in some bushes near the east wall, gathering intelligence before making their move. They make note that there are four patrols that overlap on paths. Two moving clockwise while the other two move counter clockwise. They are able to count to nearly two hundred before the next patrol comes into view. The issue are the soldiers on the terrace with constant view of the wall.

Concern fills Kem's expression but Jaml cracks a smile.

"Are you going to share your grand scheme because I don't see a way into the kingdom? That smirk on your face tells me you have something up."

"Over against the wall is an opening. The only reason I know of it is from Sister Karva. She showed me as a history lesson about the kingdom. Who would have thought it would come in handy?"

After timing the rotation of the guards to perfection, Jaml and Kem find themselves walking in the dark alleys inside the walls. They are constantly ducking into shadows as patrols of soldiers roam the area... The soldiers are not actively searching but rather making their presence known. Occasionally a beggar appears on the road and is swiftly dealt with, usually a physical pounding from one or more of the soldiers. Both Kem and Jaml find themselves with clenched fists and tight jaws at the beating the defenseless beggars have to endure.

The two of them make their way through the alleys of the kingdom until they come upon his villa. The outside of the villa seems intact with minimal damage. The doors are intact and his paid guards are in position. Not knowing the situation inside the villa, they decide to have a word with one of his guards.

They encircle the villa to find the rest station, a small clearing with a table that Jaml had put in place for soldiers on their break where they are able to sit and relax a bit. Sitting in the rest area is a soldier named Fil. This soldier is very young but eager to show his loyalty and bravery. Jaml only hopes his loyalty is still intact with him.

Jaml silently walks up behind the soldier and quickly covers his mouth to eliminate the sound. A dagger is pressed against the soldier's neck. Knowing he is beat, the soldier holds his hands up in surrender.

"You do know this is Duke Jaml's place. Your best bet is to leave while you still walk. When Jaml finds you have violated his villa, he will have your neck on a spike."

Jaml smiles at the comment. No one knows he has been gone for the past months. Good, then the men will remain loyal and the work silent. His head housekeeper has done a fantastic job. He carefully loosens his hold on the soldier.

"If you call out, I will be forced to hurt you." The soldier nodded his understanding of the situation.

He turns the soldier around to reveal his face. The soldier immediately sighs in relief.

"Fil, I need you to tell me the situation in my villa."

"Yes sire." The soldier looks confused by the request. He does not know that Jaml has been absent for some time now but complies with the strange request. Jaml learns the king has moved some of his soldiers into each villa in the kingdom but assures Jaml his soldiers remain loyal only to him. His friends remain in the villa under his protection. Jaml thanks the man before taking his absence. He thinks about telling the soldier everything but determines why put him in that situation. Instead, he thanks the soldier and tells him to continue his patrol as well as commending him on his bravery in the face of adversity.

He returns to the alley and fills Kem in with the situation. They decide not to return to his villa yet but go and find out the fate of his friends. They methodically move through the shadows and alleys towards the church, avoiding all patrols and citizens alike. The less people see them at night the better.

They make the final turn and realize the source of the red haze from afar. The church, along with several other buildings, are burning. The closest the heat allows them to get is the other end of the street. Kem covers her eyes by placing her hand against her forehead in order to get a closer look.

"Oil."

"What?

"They keep the buildings lit up at night with oil. A constant reminder to the people that Christianity will not be tolerated here. They have turned this into a prison. Soldiers have become guards. But to what end?"

"Us. More specifically the weapons. They know we will not abandon these people, it is not our way. They wait for us to reveal ourselves. Let's get back to my villa and come up with a plan."

Kem needs no other instruction and follows Jaml back through the streets.

Once back to the villa, Jaml leads them through the servant's entrances. All the servants knew Jaml had taken a leave and according to the soldier, were loyal to his name and covered for him. When they saw their Duke walking through their quarters, their faces lit up with happiness and pride to know their Duke was back where he belongs.

Not surprising, word of their return spread quietly like wildfire. By the time Jaml greets all they encounter and makes their way to his main quarters, they are greeted by a trio of their friends, Indi, Tyra and Blait. Jaml notes Blait has recovered from her ordeal nicely. Bouncing back from the kidnapping and torturing at the hand of Princess Jala is enough to permanently damage any person. But here Blait stood, life back in her eyes and a smile on her face.

Hugs and shakes are quickly gone through before the group quickly moves to the study, a room reinforced with thick brick making it sound proof. Jaml usually used this as his prayer room, a place where noise would not disturb him.

The room itself is nothing elaborate, furnished with a desk and chair. Jaml is surprised to see a table and five chairs added to the opposite end of the room. Obviously his guests have been using this room for more than meditation.

"We didn't know when you were coming back and needed to meet and plan."

Jaml turns to look at Indi.

"Thank you for keeping the faith and moving forward. Tyra, if you don't mind, can you please gather all of my house staff and personal guard. Please do this quietly so the king's soldiers remain unaware."

Tyra nods and leaves the room. A look of bewilderment is left on the faces of Indi and Blait. Kem walks over to Jaml with her back to the others.

"Do you think this is a good idea?"

"They have sacrificed over these past weeks and deserve to know why they suffer. If that means one of them turns us in, so be it. Their lives have been ruined already and they deserve to know. Do you have objections?"

"Yea. About time."

The two share a smile.

Within an hour, every member of the house staff and the leaders of his guard are quietly standing in the room. Many came in and hugged Jaml, welcoming him back. Some share concerns but all are happy to see him. Praise to God is said often, bringing joy to Jaml knowing their faith is unwavered. Once everyone is inside, Jaml hops up onto a table. He looks over the small crowd, enjoying the moment but to look into their eyes. He does not detect any evil or ill will towards him.

"Brothers and sisters in Christ, thank you for welcoming me with open arms. I know many have wondered why I left in your moment of need and I am sure some of you hold resentment." Murmurs fill the room as people look around. "It is ok, I cannot blame you if you do. I am back now and have no desire to leave you again. What I do know is I owe you an explanation."

"No sire. You do not. You have treated us well and taken care of us. We hold steadfast in faith and stand behind you. We know you cannot tell us everything. We trust in your judgment and actions." Captain of the guard speaks loudly and is met with cheers and support.

Jaml takes a deep breath.

"I am thankful for this. But it is time for me to come completely truthful to you. After I am finished, if any of you desire to leave, then I hold no ill will towards you. What I am about to say will put you in grave danger and if you are not willing, I will release you of your obligations and will say goodbye with a smile and hug." All eyes are on him. "I am Reaper. I am the one who has been fighting and killing demons for the past months. All of this has been because of me. The martial law and executions are to draw me out. I have been away searching and obtaining the weapons of the Apocalypse and keeping them safe. Now it is time for me to defeat Lucifer's servants and free this land."

A cheer erupts from everyone in the room. Hope has returned.

"All I ask of you is to keep this secret. If the demon king finds out before we are ready, I fear for your lives."

Nods give Jaml his answer.

Kem leans to his ear.

"It is good for you to get this weight off your shoulders."

"Is it? My fear is not everyone is honest and there are some traitors in this group. Puts everyone's life and family at risk. Hope I am doing the right thing by these people, only time will tell."

Despite Kem's reassuring smile and hug, Jaml cannot help but feel the weight of his house on his shoulders. He realizes there is no way to know if all are on his side so he prays for their safety. He has business to take care of so after giving hugs to his staff, he jumps back on top of the table.

"Please go about your day as if nothing has changed. If the soldiers think there is a change, your lives are in danger. No go and go about your chores. I will join you tomorrow."

The crowd files out of the room. Jaml stands by the door, thanking each one for their faith but also taking note of anyone who seems squeamish or unsure. The signs of either a traitor or someone who is conflicted about tonight's events. Once everyone leaves, Jaml informs CPT Heme, the captain of his guard, of the ones who may betray them. He tells the captain to keep an eye on each of them but do not move without his authority. Under no circumstance will harm come to any of them without his knowledge and consent. The grizzly soldier gives him his thanks and quickly dispatches his men.

When Jaml stands in the room along with Kem, Indi, Tyra and Blait, he motions for everyone to sit. Kem sits beside Jaml, Tyra sits arms locked with Indi with Blait on the other side. Jaml silently says a prayer for guidance.

"What happened?" His question is very direct.

Indi speaks up.

"There were several proclamations made from the king regarding uprisings that were occurring throughout the kingdom."

"Uprisings?" Jaml looks confused

"Sorry Reaper. There…"

"Jaml. Please. I consider you a friend." He gives a smile to Indi

"Thank you Jaml. As do I. The night Reaper, you, saved Blait, many saw the demon princess fall from the tower. They also recognized the clothing and put it together. The king and queen could not deny it so they claimed a demon must have kidnapped and murdered their daughter. They had no clue and the queen publically cried. The king swore vengeance. Many accepted this explanation and felt for the royal family. Some did not. Demonstrations began to spring up and occasionally became violent. Many were arrested and some executed for conspiring with Lucifer. The royal family realized they needed a fall guy so Jesus became Lucifer. Christianity became the worship of Lucifer. This did not go well with the faithful but some joined in the mob hunt. The churches are kept burning to demonstrate their point. Priests were rounded up and jailed and the king said they had destroyed Lucifer's place of worship. Supposedly hell has broken out in those places. People live in fear that Lucifer will rise from hell soon. Some have caught the soldiers setting fires and have been jailed as heretics. All priests and heretics will be burned in two days."

"That will not happen."

"Thank you Jaml. I should tell you that one to get burned is Karva."

Kem interrupts. "We will prepare tomorrow."

Jaml looks at the warrior beside him.

"Rest up. I go out tonight. Alone."

✦

The door at the Boar opens emitting a lone figure. Despite the warmth of the night, the small man wraps his heavy cloak around his body, the hood covering his head. He looks in both directions before moving forward down the main street. A slight smile covers his face, the dice were in his favor tonight. He doubled his purse tonight, a visit to his favorite whore is inevitable. He dreams of the hard sex he will have followed by her cooing and stroking his hair, allowing him to lose himself in her embrace. Nothing would make him happier right now.

Since this whole sword business came about, he has lost half his customers with the remaining becoming squeamish. Thoughts of lost business fill his head with anger, but not to overshadow the pleasure he is destined to have. He often wishes he had never decided to handle the job. His biggest benefactor, Duke Indi, has disappeared. Nothing since that demon fell off the kingdom. Hell, since then, he has only handled illegal products like the lotus from the east. No more artifacts.

Vair turns left at the corner and notices a figure standing at the end of the road. The figure gets his attention due to no one else on the street able to stand erect. At this hour, no one is out besides drunks and lotus smokers, wallowing in their drug of choice. He squints his eyes to see if he can make out who it is. The hood draped over the face on the figure hides his features, Vair loosens his blade. He has never walked away from a fight and he will not start now.

He approaches the figure, his hand resting on the hilt of his long dagger that is tucked into his sash. The figure does not move, makes no menacing movements towards him. Vair initially assumes one of Bala's assassins but knows that the guild has been destroyed. He stops ten paces from the figure, his identity still concealed behind the lowered hood. Vair tries once again in vain to look through the lowered hood to see who the person is.

"Evening stranger, what can I do for you? But first, I am at a loss. You obviously know me but I don't know who I am talking with."

"Reaper."

"I heard you left and left us with this crap. Crazy king who many suspect is a demon. Soldiers are ransacking their own people without fear of prosecution. Many say you woke a sleeping monster and then left."

"I did but I am back now. But enough about me. Tell me what you know about Karva."

"Why?"

"Because you want to leave here unmarked and not in pain."

"Sounds like a good option." Vair removes his fingers from his weapon. He knows he would lose against this man so why even try.

"She is to be executed in two days. Christianity has been deemed as the work of Lucifer. The king has convinced people that Lucifer is the leader of Christianity and that is why he never noticed that his daughter was a demon. People believe him and her death has become a sign for a new age."

"Are people that blind?"

"Blind? No. Desperate for answers, yes. When you were here last, you exposed a lot of evil in this city. You single handedly destroyed my lucrative business. The evil that has lain beneath this city for years was all of a sudden exposed, then you left. The leaving part was not the worse part. You see, when you left, you left the church exposed and without a champion to fight for it. Did you really expect Karva to be able to fight the demons in the castle? She is going to pay for your actions with her life in two days, something she does not deserve."

"Then you are saying this is all my fault?"

"I will probably die tonight but yes. I am saying Karva's death and so many more will be on your head!" Vair cannot believe what he is doing. His voice has risen and he finds he is almost yelling at Reaper but at this moment, he needs to vent. To let out his anger that has been building, from losing his contacts to watching innocent people die for no reason. As he finishes and stands there, he feels hot tears streaming down his face.

Through all that, the man in front of him has not flinched, has not exhibited any emotions. Reaper just stands there. For a moment, Vair wonders if the killer of demons is a demon himself. Any normal man would say something if not step forward and kill him. But the man in front of him does not.

"Say something damn you! Kill me! Show me that this all means something to you."

"I am sorry."

The words are simple and unexpected. Vair stands there as Reaper turns and walks away. He wants to yell curses at the man but he cannot. In those three words Vair felt all the weight Reaper has on his shoulders. He understands the pain and guilt that comes with being a Reaper. While many, including himself, thought Reapers were these magical warriors sent by God to defeat Lucifer, Vair sees the anguish that comes with the position. He knows Reaper is going to save Karva and the church even if it costs him his life.

Vair watches as the man disappears in the shadows. Thoughts of his prostitute and the pleasures there are no more. He knows there will be a reckoning coming. A shiver runs through his spine, a warning of death and carnage that is about to occur in the streets of Colley. He knows the only chance he has to live is to leave tonight.

He likes his life.

Jaml meets Kem in the dining room early in the morning. She looks up from her plate of fruits and pastries to acknowledge the man coming in. He is dressed in a simple white shirt with black trousers. Without asking, she knows his blades are strapped to his lower back. His head and face are freshly shaven.

"Morning Kem. Thank you for doing as I asked." Jaml urged Kem to go with more traditional clothing so they would not attract any attention. He trusts his house personnel to keep his identity and whereabouts secret. For their safety, Kem has forsaken her traditional monk garb and cover to dress in more womanly attire, a simple brown dress that falls to her ankles, a deep brown sash around her waist along with a simple head covering.

He sits in an empty chair across from Kem where a plate of fruit and pastries sit. A goblet of water sits there as well. Jaml eats the food in silence, each enjoying the fresh meal, so much different from the dried meat and fruits they have been eating on the road.

After the meal is over, they both put on travel capes to further blend into the crowd before leaving the villa. By the time they leave, the streets are teeming with daily activity. The street vendors have long ago set up for their daily business. Women, with small children in tow, move from vendor to vendor, buying daily supplies and household goods.

The streets are perfect for the two, packed with people. Soldiers and assassins are going to have a hard time recognizing them among the crowd. They move through the people at a slow pace, satisfied not to cause a commotion amongst the people. They keep their heads down as soldiers on the upper parapets scan for anyone suspicious. Stopping at an occasional vendor to buy a piece of fruit or trinket keeps eyes off their movements.

The two make their way towards the city square to find soldiers putting together gallows for the execution. Soldiers stand guard while others do the manual labor. They approach the nearest soldier, one standing off to the side, more concerned with the two females in the alley than watching for construction. He leans on his spear, casual and unobservant to his surroundings.

The duo casually walk up to the soldier, allowing him to see their hands to show they mean no harm. The soldier regards the two with annoyance as it takes them away from the females in the alley.

"What do you want?" The annoyance drips from every word from his lips.

"We are humbly in debt to you sir." Jaml keeps his eyes averted, playing the role of a common man who is not familiar with the ways of the kingdom. It also keeps the soldier from getting a good look at their faces, putting their lives in danger.

"Go on then. What do you want? You are disturbing me."

"Forgive us please sir. We just arrived at the kingdom and our first sight is this gallows. Who is it for and when can we see it being used? We don't have this kind of thing where we are from."

"Well, welcome to Colley where we hang all heretics of God. We are a God fearing people who will not stand for anything Lucifer. We know this Christianity is nothing but a ploy from Lucifer to fool us. It didn't work, we know what this Christianity truly is, and will not tolerate it. The Satan worshiper Karva will be executed tomorrow night for all to see. We will become the light of the world in our fight to defeat Lucifer. Come on back out tomorrow night to see us carry out God's plan."

"Thank you sir." Jaml bows slightly, furthering the soldier's apparent dominance. "We will make sure to stay to witness God's work."

"Good. Begone now, you have wasted enough of my time." The soldier refocuses on the two ladies in the alley, both of whom are openly flirting with him through smiles, winks, and waves.

Jaml and Kem quietly leave the soldier. They walk around the square, making notes of attack points, choke points and avenues of escape if needed. Once they have enough for a preliminary plan of action.

The two make their way around the outer walls of the kingdom, making note of all guard shacks and choke points. They also make note of where the archers are located. All these things must be taken into consideration if they stand any chance of pulling this off. They

307

make their way to the front gate and shake their heads at the sight there.

Over a hundred spikes are sticking out of the ground, each spike well over twenty feet high. On top of each spike is a human head impaled at the top. Kem is the first to notice the heads and nudges Jaml who casually looks up. What he sees turns his stomach. He recognizes some of the dukes and high officials, people loyal to the crown but are dead because of it. His eyes continue to scan over the field of heads, looking and praying for those he recognizes and for the ones he doesn't, he simply prays for their souls.

Anger fills him. Countless dead people, to what end? To find him? To make a point? To show dominance? The king and queen must pay and pay they will. The deaths of so many innocents must be avenged.

Chapter 16

Two lanterns emit a low level light throughout the room. Sitting at the table inside the room is Kem and Jaml, solemnly finishing up their prayers. Both know the stakes and danger of the mission tonight yet neither have balked nor questioned the plan. In spite of all they have been through over the past months, they both know tonight might be the end. They have dictated the battles and battleground in all their previous adventures. They knew the odds and understood how to overcome them.

Both are dressed in all black, from their trousers to their form fitting tops. Their boots are also black. Jaml has his blades strapped to his lower back, hilts point out for fast and easy draw. Around his waist are a series of throwing daggers, one of his many skills. Contrary to his countless sharp weapons, Kem is keeping it simple. She brings nothing but her staff and hand to hand combat skills. Due to her vows against sharp weapons, she is allowed to carry only blunt weapons. Many of her brethren like to carry a spike less mace to club their adversaries. Kem prefers her staff and nothing else, which she is able to shrink the staff through mechanisms to a walking staff length.

This situation is different. The stage is a public arena where hundreds of people will be gathered to witness the death of their friends. Numerous demons will be on hand, knowing these two will attempt a rescue. Both king and queen will be present and may join the battle at any moment. The crowd reaction may be against them as they know not how intense the Christ is Lucifer belief.

Yet their plan is simple. Make their way through the crowd, keeping as low a profile as possible. At the appropriate time, Jaml is going to leap on the stage and grab Karva. Kem is going to collapse the stage immediately afterward. Staying on the ground is inviting death so getting to the rooftops is imperative. Once there, they must make their way to the south wall to escape. Once over the wall, they should be able to reenter through secret passageways to his villa.

From there, they keep their friends safe and hidden while the army scours the countryside looking for them. Once the search loses intensity, they will smuggle the entire group away to safety.

"And if a Fallen shows up?" Kem's question invades his thoughts, breaking his concentration. He looks up at the lady with a sour look on his face.

"Thanks for that bit of information. Not that we are already against insurmountable odds, you want to throw that one in."

"Sorry Jaml. But it needs to be addressed."

"Then we die gloriously."

Her slight nod tells him all he needs to know. She, too, is fully prepared to die for Karva. He knows there will be no hesitation, he is satisfied.

"It is about time to do this." He does not look at her, his words his only sight.

"All glory to God."

"All glory to God."

The lanterns go out, plunging the room in complete darkness.

Despite being hours after sundown, the market square is as full as it would be at midday. More people fill the square now than during the hot trading period. Ale and wine is sold by the goblet along with a bevy of delicacies. Little wooden gallows are also for sale, commemorating the evening's events. There is an air of carnival to be found despite the main attraction being the death of a human being. Jaml has a hard time grasping how man can celebrate with such vigor the death of one of their own.

The sight of people celebrating the death of one of their own only validates how far man has to go. A true child of God would never celebrate a person's death, even if the sin was against him. The sight sickens him but also inspires. He knows his work is not close to being completed. The death of Christ will not be in vain, he pledges his life to it.

Both he and Kem wear long cloaks with hoods drawn over their heads to hide their features and blend in more readily with the crowd around him. They arrive early enough that the soldiers are not out in force yet. Only a few mingle around the fringes of the square, lazily patrolling the crowds. Jaml knows a more forceful presence will arrive soon as they prepare for the purpose of the evening. The duo approach the stage in the center of the square. A wooden square stage with a single pole in the center. Hanging from the pole is a noose.

The sight of the noose sickens Jamal. The woman they wish to die is no more a demon than he is. On the contrary, she is a true warrior as well as a child of God. He cannot pull his eyes from the rope hanging from the wooden piece. Anger fills his every fiber.

"She will not die. We will not allow it, you have my word." The soothing words from Kem bring a calmness over him.

"Thank you Kem."

"I have to leave now in order to get into position. Are you well?"

"I am refocused, it is time to finish this."

Kem turns and disappears back into the crowd, leaving the Reaper to stand and deal with his thoughts.

It isn't long before the square fills with observers and travelers alike. Word of hanging a heretic travels fast in a kingdom that has suffered so much. Many cling to the hope of faith, to watch a heretic hang will go a long way in restoring that faith. War and hunger brings doubt in any man's mind. The hanging brings so much to so many, a welcomed diversion to their miserable lives, reassurance that God has not forsaken them and hope that tomorrow will be better.

The sun quickly dips below the west wall, casting a deep shadow over the square. Jaml has seen the military presence increase tenfold. Soldiers are now positioned around the stage to keep the crowd back. They are not equipped with deadly weapons, only staff to keep the crowd in check. Soldiers killing civilians would have an undesirable effect and could lead to unnecessary death and carnage. They are not equipped to deal with death. Killing a few will take the desire to fight out of them. The initial battle will not be as deadly. He might have a chance to escape before reinforcements arrive.

A smirk appears in the shadowy depths of his hood.

After the night torches are all lit, the true party begins. Merchants fill the square selling their wares, several stands open selling their wares, ale, beer and wine. Even the women of the night are out in full force, offering nights of carnal passion after the killing.

The sights, smell and sounds of the evening continue to disgust Jaml. How can people take such joy in the killing of another man? Many have asked him the same question and his response is always

311

the same; "I take no pleasure in killing. The Lord has called me to do his will and there are times that killing is involved."

After a righteous killing, Reaper has always found time to pray for forgiveness and his soul.

Jaml has to refocus himself. These people are simply following who they trust in man instead of trusting in God. Unfortunately there will be a reckoning for their blind misguided faith.

Trumpets pull him from his thoughts, drowning out the conversations of the hundreds. A group of soldiers emerge from the castle, marching proudly as if in a parade, knees lift high in cadence to the sergeant's chant. A total of eight soldiers march in formation, three in front, three behind them with a soldier on each side to form a square.

As the group marches forward, making its way through the crowd, a chorus of boos, hisses and derogatory names erupt from the people closest to the formation. Jaml's heart sinks as he knows it is Karva inside that formation, probably scared and beaten, marching to her death.

Jaml waits impatiently as the soldiers march right up to the gallows. They stop in unison to the sergeant's command. Two men emerge from behind the formation carrying a step ladder which they position against the edge of the gallows in front of the formation.

Jaml makes his way through the crowd, focusing on the group in front of him. The soldiers are armed only with spears. He holds the advantage in close combat, meaning he needs to attack and keep his enemies close if he is going to have a chance at success. Close combat also shields himself from the archers above that is until Kem is able to dispatch them.

He patiently watches two soldiers come down from the platform to meet their human sport. To their dismay and despite their prodding, a beaten and bruised Karva walks up the planks with her head held high. Despite the yelling, cursing and getting hit with fruit, Karva reaches the top of the platform to take her place between her two captors. She neither says a word nor acknowledges anyone's presence, eyes fixated on the horizon while her lips silently prays for her soul as well as the souls of her killers.

If she hadn't been so engrossed in her present situation, she would have seen the flash of blackness whisk by her face, as it were, her eyes lower to the ground at the first sounds of screaming. Once she does not feel the noose drop around her neck, she looks up to find herself in the midst of chaos, soldiers running to the opposite side of the stage, only to join in on the screams. She turns her head frantically, searching for whatever evil has overcome these people, expecting to find a demon bearing down on her.

Instead she finds the whirlwind of death known as the Reaper. In each hand he wields a black short sword, the ebony blades slicing through metal and skin with the ease of a knife through butter. The soldiers, armed with only a staff, are no match for the wielder of the black blades. He turns to face her, his handsome face covered in blood that is not his own.

"Come on."

She does not hesitate and quickly steps over dead bodies to stand next to Reaper. He looks up to find all the archers have disappeared. A smile creeps over his face, Kem is good. He knows his fortune has been good thus far and he doesn't want to push it.

"We have to go. Now!"

His hand grabs hers before they leap off the stage. He looks over at her.

"We have to get to the rooftops now."

He leads her through the panicked crowd, pushing people aside so he can get to a ladder that suddenly appears draped off the side of the building. Karva grabs hold of the rope ladder desperately working her way up. She can feel Reaper right behind her giving her a sense of both safety and urgency.

She reaches the top and climbs onto the roof. Reaper joins her on the roof. He turns around and with one swing severs the rope ladder. They both watch the ladder fall to the ground.

"Keep moving. More archers are on the way and I do not wish to become a pin cushion."

The two race across the flat ceiling, thankful the ceiling is firm and stable.

"The space between rooftops is not far in distance. Do not slow and do not look down. When I say jump, do not hesitate. If you do, we both will crash below and be quickly overcome by soldiers."

He does not have time to wait for an answer.

"Jump!"

They both fly through the air to come crashing down on the next rooftop. Reaper had released her hand, not wanting to get tangled and inadvertently cause her injury. He rolls to his feet and quickly turns around to find Karva getting to her hands and knees. He grabs her waist to hoist her to her feet.

"Move."

She doesn't have time to probably thank him but makes a mental note if they survive. They race across the next rooftop to once again launch themselves off one building and crash down onto the next. Reaper looks over his shoulder to find archers positioning themselves. Luckily, soldiers with swords are racing over the rooftops, inhibiting the shot of the archers. Obviously no one with rank has arrived yet.

Reaper grabs hold of her hand before making a run at the next roof. After the landing, Karva's breathing is labored as she struggles to catch her breath. She looks up at Reaper but says nothing. He is risking his life to save hers and she is not going to complain about anything. He senses her desperation and fatigue.

"The next one is lower so it will be an easier jump. Ready?"

"Yes. Let's do it."

He gives her a small smile before grabbing her hand once again. They run, Reaper dragging more than she is running, before leaping once again into the air. Karva is relieved that Reaper is telling the truth. The next ceiling is indeed lower than the previous ones. As before, he rolls to his feet and picks her up. She attempts to catch her breath.

"Don't worry. This way."

Reaper leads her to the back edge of the ceiling where there is another rope ladder hanging. A big smile appears on her face as she turns around, lies on her belly and begins to descend down the rope ladder. Reaper watches her go down the ladder, eyes darting from her descending to the soldiers steadily making their way towards him. About halfway down, an arm extends out of a window and pulls Karva inside the building. Reaper waits for the hand to reappear before cutting the rope ladder the hand quickly pulls the ladder in.

The ebony blade slides back into its home as Reaper once again takes off running. With Karva safely gone, Reaper is no longer cumbersome with the lady he rescued. He takes a quick look over his shoulder and takes off running in the opposite direction. Above all, they must chase him in order for Karva to get away successfully.

He makes the jump from the roof, launching himself forward through the air. He lands in a forward roll to his feet, never breaking his stride, once again at top speed. Two roofs later he glances back to find the soldiers still chasing but losing ground. None appeared to stop and at the building where he dropped Karva at. Satisfied no soldier witnessed her escape, Reaper focuses on his own safety. He clears three more roofs before he sees an opportunity to disappear in the crowded streets below.

"Going somewhere?"

Reaper stops to look to the right. Standing confidently on the edge is Prince Manda in full battle gear. On his upper torso is the breastplate bearing the house emblem. Arms are bare save the metal bands around his biceps. Draped on his shoulders is the cape of royal color. He holds twin blades of the Roman Empire, one in each hand. Pants and boots complete Manda's look.

Reaper turns to face the last and youngest demon child of King Taras.

"What do we have here? The baby of the bunch. Decided to get off your mom's breast?" Reaper can see the anger in the demon's eyes. "Or are you that eager to see your brother and sister in hell?!" Reaper almost laughs at the demon losing his self-control.

"We will see who sees their family in hell." The words spill out Manda's mouth along with spittle, the anger building very quickly in the warrior.

This time Reaper laughs aloud. "Listen, go get your mommy and daddy. I'll wait. Maybe after killing them you might stand a slim chance. As it stands, you are not even a warm up for me. Run along junior so the adults can fight."

Manda explodes in such fury that Reaper looks surprised. The prince runs directly at Reaper at full speed, his blades twirling, searching for blood. Reaper reaches behind his back and draws his twin ebony blades out. Instead of waiting for the attack, Reaper charges to meet the prince in the middle. They meet in the middle and immediately their blades begin their songs of death. The prince opens with a series of slashes and cuts to Reaper's midsection, aiming to end the battle early. Reaper stands his ground, his blades twirling, deflecting the prince's attack.

Despite being on the defensive, Reaper begins to move forward. He recognizes Manda is borderline out of control and is fighting as if

315

he needs to prove his worth. Reaper's comments did its job creating an out of control killer where a calculating tactician is needed. He watches Manda begin to panic, he cannot understand why he is backing up while on the attack. Manda begins to panic, his attack patterns begin to deteriorate to wild slashes and chops.

Exactly what Reaper wants, an out of control fighter. He waits for his opportunity to present itself. He doesn't wait long when Manda over extends his slash with the intent of slashing Reaper across the chest. Instead, Reaper side steps the clumsy attack and brings his left blade across the midsection, cutting below the chest plate, drawing first blood. Manda backs away quickly, the sting of his wound catching him off guard. He looks down to see the damage, blood trickling from a cut across his midsection, not fatal but deep enough to weaken him if this battle goes on.

The clock is now ticking on Manda. He has to find a weakness in Reaper and kill him before his wound begins to affect him. Manda has turned from a wild warrior out for revenge to a wounded warrior who needs to end this battle quickly. Either way Reaper holds the upper hand in this battle.

With a battle cry, Manda charges forward. His twin blades held low, primed for attack. Reaper waits patiently, his blades ready to end this battle. The ebony blades meet Manda's overhead chop high in the air. With all four hands in the air, Reaper steps through with a front kick to Manda's midsection, sending the prince stumbling back.

Reaper watches Manda's eyes turn red, a sign the demon is about to come out.

"Don't want to expose the family secret, do you?"

Manda looks around to see soldiers all around, watching their prince battle the demon killer. They all see the wound but no one moves forward to assist the prince. Manda does not know if the soldiers hate him that much or are afraid to fall in the wrath of Reaper. Either way, these soldiers will die due to their decision not to get involved.

I don't need these imbeciles anyway. Manda collects himself, weighs the blades in his hands and smiles.

The smile alerts Reaper, but too late. He spins quickly but feels the sting of a dagger sink into the back of his shoulder. He completes the spin to find Canda, the woman who masqueraded as his wife and

316

ultimately betrayed him. With this action, the betrayal is complete. He almost gets caught up in facing her once again which would have ended his life. He dives forward into a roll and back to his feet, away from the attack on his back, the dagger still sticking out of his shoulder.

He spins to face the prince and Canda. The pair begins to move apart with the intent of encircling him. They count on Reaper not attacking Canda, which they are correct. Reaper realizes he must kill Manda before Canda can get to him. He has now become as desperate as his prey Prince Manda. Not wanting to wait for the attack, Reaper lunges forward at Manda. He attacks ferociously, putting the prince immediately in retreat mode.

Manda backs away even as he deflects blow after blow, his skill is nowhere near that of the Reaper. Out of the corner of his eye, he can see the lady Canda moving quickly towards the back of Reaper. Joy fills Manda's demon heart at the sight of the female moving in to plunge her dagger into his oppressor's back. He attempts to stand his ground and give Canda the time she needs.

Canda raises her dagger over her head, prepared to plunge the blade into Reaper's back for the glory of Lucifer. She has played her role very well, allowing Reaper to help a poor wretch. Cloth her, feed her, play the role of wife so his deception is believable. She walked around town and attended parties as his wife. Her betrayal will be complete when he dies at her hand. She cannot wait any longer. The deed must be done and the betrayal complete. Lucifer will be so proud.

She slams the blade downward, anticipating the feel of his muscle collapsing as the blade buries itself deep in his shoulder. But that feeling never comes, even as the blade descends, it is stopped by a staff in mid attack. She feels sharp pain in her wrists, sharp enough to jolt the blade from her hand.

She looks to the side and finds the gaze of Kem, ripping a hole in her soul. Kem's deep green eyes burrow into Canda's soul, letting the lady know she has failed and will never get another chance. The staff quickly slaps her hands down before striking her across her chest. All happening before Canda is able to take a breath. The painful gasp she is able to take due to the staff strike burns. Her chest is struck three more times immediately, the last sends the lady flying across the ceiling.

The desperate look on Manda's face lets Reaper know Kem has his back, both literally and figuratively. Knowing his back is protected, Reaper presses forward. The goal is for Manda to either die as a human or transform into his true form to try and escape. Either way, Reaper will successfully dispose of another demon in the kingdom. His strikes are fluid, deadly, making Manda have to retreat to stay alive.

Manda knows he cannot keep up with his opponent, at least not in human form. But if he takes on his true form, everyone in the kingdom will know what he is and what has transpired over the last months. But if he stays true to his human form, he will die in a matter of moments. Reaper's swordplay is not becoming desperate as many warriors do when they increase the speed of their technique, no, Reaper has not only remained in control but his accuracy has become deadlier.

Another cut is opened on his face, right above his head. Manda struggles to maintain not only his composure but also his technique. Blood from the cut drips into his eye, momentarily blinding him. He shakes it off but knows with every passing second, more blood will drip and he will not be able to shake it from his eyes. Eventually he is going to have to wipe and when that happens, his defenses will be down and Reaper will surely kill him. The next problem he has is space or lack thereof. He has retreated almost to the edge of the building where he is not in a flight or fight mode.

Manda lets out one final battle cry before launching himself at his enemy. He charges with both blades pointing directly at Reaper's chest. He awaits the demon in human form, arms dangling at his side, an ebony blade resting in each hand. He shows no emotion, just a stare that tears through the soul. The statue does not move until Manda gets close enough to stab at him. Faster than the eye can see, Reaper sidesteps the suicidal charge and brings his blade downward, slicing through the man's wrists. Manda's forward momentum carries him past where Reaper stands triumphantly.

Manda hears it before he witnesses his hands fall onto the hard ceiling ground. He stares in bewilderment as the stumps that moments before carried his weapons. Blood squirts from the stumps, soaking into the roofing material. He lifts his stumps to eye level before he begins to scream. Pain begins to settle into his arms, drawing out long ear shattering screams.

Reaper quickly grows tired of the noise, drawing attention to the scene. He kicks out, the boot connecting with the prince's chest, sending him over the edge of the building. A few seconds later, the screams stop when the thud of a body strikes the ground.

"Reaper has killed the prince!" The yells reverberate throughout the square.

Reaper looks around to find soldiers running into the square, with the intent to trap the warrior here and capture him for the king. Soldiers' intent on apprehending him in the name of God without the knowledge they are not serving God but Lucifer unknowingly. These men are putting their lives on the line for a cause they do not understand or comprehend. Reaper cannot be mad at them for they do not understand what they are doing. Here they come with the intent of capturing him, bringing him to the king and judgment passed on crimes that were never committed. God, please forgive them.

Reaper has other ideas.

Reaper launches himself over the side of the building, tucks into a forward roll before landing in a crouched position on top of Manda's corpse. The impact destroys both the demon form inside and the human form outside. The result, if anyone was to pay attention, was an enormous amount of blood streaming like open rivers from multiple orifices, more blood than a natural human to have.

Reaper takes a full sprint to the nearest small group of soldiers heading his way. He lowers his shoulder and bowls into him. The front two soldiers are knocked over, the back three are able to move out of the way of the two bodies tumbling in front of them. Reaper finds himself right where he needs to be, in their midst.

His blades appear in his hands as he swings them around. Both blades bite fatally into the midsection of the soldier to the right. He continues to spin, reversing his grip to slam the blades into the neck of the second guy. He kicks the knee of the middle guy, dropping him to his remaining knee.

Reaper can feel the other two soldiers getting to their feet and gathering up for an attack. He slashes down, the blade splitting the face of the soldier in front of him. He spins on his heel, launching one of the ebony blades. The soldier gasps aloud, looks down to stare at the blade protruding from his stomach.

Reaper does not wait and attacks the remaining soldier. The ebony blade meets the blade of iron. The soldier stares in amazement as his blade explodes on contact, like a melon dropped from a rooftop. The Reaper swings his blade, slicing through the soldier's neck. Reaper casually walks over to retrieve his other blade from the soldier on his knees. He pulls his blade from the carcass in front of him while behind him, a head slides off a soldier's neck.

Reaper does not wait, he takes off on a run. This time he finds an opening in the circle of soldiers fast closing around him. He turns slightly right as if to charge another group of soldiers in the streets. The soldiers immediately form the traditional phalanx formation, front shields down to the ground, spears pointing through, and a staple of the Roman Empire. Reaper almost bursts out in laughter at the predictability of the soldiers and how easily they can be manipulated. The sight of five of their brothers falling in battle to him is enough to unnerve most men, soldiers including even the battle tested ones.

Reaper maintains full speed, the soldiers brace for impact. Instead of burrowing through the formation, Reaper runs up the formation of shields before launching himself upwards to the nearest rooftop. In one smooth motion, he is able to catch the edge of the building, places his feet firmly against the side of the building and catapults himself onto the top of the two story building.

Once Reaper had jumped down to the ground after the fight with Manda, soldiers had quickly made their way to the ground to help corner the man. So intent on surrounding Reaper, none remained on the rooftop. Reaper smiles at the vacancy of people on the rooftops. As he runs from building to building, he of times looks down at the soldiers muscling their way through the crowds, trying to keep up with the running warrior on the rooftops.

It isn't long before Reaper finds the soldiers falling further and further behind, the crowds in the streets becoming too much for them to navigate. Reaper recognizes the opportunity to lose himself in the crowd below. Without pause, Reaper drops to the ground, pulls his hood over his head, sheathes his clothes and blends in well with the populace. Minutes later, soldiers push their way by him, trying to find the man who just killed Manda. Reapers allows himself to be pushed and shoved aside as soldiers search frantically for him.

Satisfied that he is no longer in danger, Reaper casually makes his way through town square to the preordained meeting spot, Two Cross. Despite the religious name, the establishment is nothing more than an oversized bar with tables and benches throughout, not the accustomed four chair tables that are found in most bars in town. When the doors open, it is Duke Jaml who walks in, dressed in black trousers and a yellow shirt and that is visible under the cape that he has thrown over his shoulder. A smile gleams from his face, instantly bringing the mood of the room up. He hugs a couple of patrons before buying them a round of ale.

His ears are filled with the escapades of Reaper, tearing through the soldiers, saving the nun Karva before killing Manda. Word has it the King is offering ten thousand gold pieces for his head. Yet many of the patrons in the Two Cross are the best trackers and bounty hunters in the whole region and none are actively searching. One hunter said it best.

"Hunt down the Reaper? I'd rather hunt down Lucifer. Better chance of success."

Despite the roar of laughter that followed, Jaml cannot help but have some pride in his reputation. Either that or these men can see through the king and his family and knows who the true demons are. Jaml buys everyone another round before settling in his chair in the corner, his back against the wall. An hour later, a woman walks into the bar, wearing a full length robe complete with the hood over her head and a staff in her hand.

The female walks casually over to the table where Jaml is sitting. He looks up with a smile when he sees the eyes of Kem. He stands, giving her a nod which she reciprocates. The duo sits down, and a barmaid appears to drop off a mug. Kem looks up at the lady with a smile.

"Water please."

"Of course milady."

The barmaid disappears, leaving the duo alone.

"How is she?"

"Beat up pretty well. She has a broken bone, rib, but that is the worst of it. Multiple bruising and she is having problems with breathing and walking."

"And if we need to exit this city tonight?"

"She will not make it."

"Then let us go so you can begin fixing on her."

"What do you think I have been doing?" A bit of irritation creeps in her voice.

"Doing the best anyone can. Forgive me Kem if I sound ungrateful. Believe me, I am forever grateful. I meant to say let us get back so you can work your magic on her."

"I know what you meant. I am tired, as you are. We both need to rest so let's get out of here." The two rise just as the barmaid returns with the mug of water. Jaml pays her as for four mugs and sends her on her way with a pat on her back. She looks over disappointed as she was wanting that smack to be on her rear. Jaml smiles and shakes his head at the lady who sticks her lip out in a pouting face.

"Oh." Kem interrupts them.

"What is it?" Concern creeps once again in his voice.

"I am sorry for killing your wife." A smile creeps across her face before she begins to start giggling. "Now you are free to pursue as many barmaids as you want."

"Shut up." They both erupt into laughter. Two tired companions in desperate need of rest.

Chapter 17

The heavy curtains over the windows keep the room in darkness, allowing for the occupants to sleep much later than normal. This is the case for Jaml, who is lost in his heavy sleep, dreaming about the events of the past months. Despite the deepness of his sleep, his body continues to twitch and jerk to the contents of his dreams. His heavy blanket has long been kicked to the ground, a casualty of troubled sleep.

A shadowy figure glides across the room, careful not to make any noise and be efficient in every movement. Even in pitch blackness, the figure navigates the pitfalls of the room to find success at the window. The curtain is flung open, bright streams of daylight invade the room, bringing the sleepy warrior to consciousness.

Jaml rolls over to place his back to the open window, his feeble attempt to block the sun out once again. While lying there waking up, he begins to move and flex his arms and legs, the aches and pains from the previous day's battle are felt. New bruises and cuts have grown sore causing the man known as Reaper to moan.

Jaml slowly opens his eyes to Flo's bright smile greeting him. One of the saddest parts of returning for Jaml was to find out his friend and longtime employee, Anna, passed away. According to many, her heart broke when Jaml left and she could not stand hearing the news of his battles and escapades. She finally succumbed to a heart attack and passed away. Guilt and responsibility for her death still sits on his shoulders. Constant prayers have been said for her soul.

He was also so relieved to find out Flo stepped up immediately and took over Anna's duties without question.

"Morning sire. You have slept most of the day away. Not like you." After the revelation of who Jaml really is, most of the staff remains. Flo was one of the first people to stand up afterwards and pledge her commitment to him and God. Most of the other housekeepers remained solely on her dedication to Jaml. He knows he owes a tremendous amount to Flo and the other people who stood up early. More importantly, her smile is contagious.

"Morning Flo. Have I really slept that long? I was thinking it was midmorning at best." He winks at the lady standing next to his bed.

"You know goodness well it is well past midmorning, the sun tells you so." She places his trousers on the edge of the foot of the bed. She quickly retrieves a suitable shirt for him to don. "The sun is almost at its zenith. You and Lady Kem arrived late last night with that priestess Karva in tow. She seems pretty beat up and Kem has been working on her most of the morning."

The mention of Kem quickly wakes Jaml fully up, on reflex, he sits up, the covers falling to his waist, revealing his muscled upper body. Along with the muscles comes multiple bruises and cuts causing Flo to gasp. She is a widow from a soldier and thought she had seen everything but to see the new bruises and cuts along with the scars that crisscross his body takes her to a new level.

"Is everything ok?" The soft question is all that is needed to snap Flo out of her trance. She blinks her eyes multiple times to shake the canvas of battles from her mind. She nods feverishly to let Jaml know all is well. "Where are they?"

"Very good Sir Jaml. But first you must dress and eat. Afterwards I will take you to them."

"Flo. I need to go now."

"What you need is to eat and get dressed!"

Jaml thinks about responding but knows Flo is right and only looking out for him. He can feel his stomach cramping and growling for food so he gives in. Flo leaves the room to allow Jaml the privacy to get dressed. He quickly puts on his trousers and shirt just as Flo returns with a plate of fruit and dried meat,

He sits at the small desk table, says his prayers, prompting him to start eating. Flo watches over him as if he was her son, making sure he eats properly.

After eating, Flo motions for Jaml to follow her out of the door. He wonders how time has lapsed but more importantly, how Karva is handling things.

He jumps out of his chair as Flo moves to grab hold of the handle to the door. She opens the door, allowing the man instant access to the hall but Jaml has to control himself as he does not know where to go, instead he steps out of the door, into the hallway and waits for his friend as she casually closes the door and walks next door.

Jaml wants to get angry at the deception but cannot.

"How come you did not tell me Kem and Karva are simply next door."

"Would you have dressed and ate?"

Jaml simply laughs at her logic.

She opens the second door and peeks inside. A few seconds later, she looks back at Jaml.

"Everyone is dressed appropriately for you. Go on in, what are you waiting for?"

Flor has to laugh at the expression on Jaml's face, astonishment mixed in with humor. He shakes his head while entering the room. Once inside, the feeling of death overcomes him. There are only two candles providing light, purposefully keeping the light down. Sitting in front of him is Kem, her back to him, her head lowered to the patient lying on the bed. He slowly looks over her shoulder to find Karva lying there, asleep. The rise and fall of her chest suggests shallow breathing.

Kem senses him and looks over her shoulder. She gestures towards the door with her head. Jaml backs out the door, his eyes never leaving Karva. Kem dabs Karva's head one more time with the cool wet cloth before joining Jaml in the hall. She closes the door behind her.

"Is she going to make it? When I grabbed her, I didn't know."

"She will make it. Her faith and body has been tested greatly."

"Did they violate her?" Anger quickly rises in his voice. If they touched her like that, God's mercy would not be enough. Lucifer will not be able to protect them.

"There is no bruising along her inner legs so I don't believe she was violated. She has broken ribs, a couple broken fingers and extensive bruising around the upper torso."

"How did I miss that?"

"Don't be hard on yourself. She had clothes on and you would not have been able to see it. Her body was running on adrenaline which allowed her to run and jump. When she realized she was safe, she collapsed and has been in that state since. She will be physically scarred. I hope they were not able to break her spirit."

"For their sake, I hope so." Hatred seeps with his words, igniting a cautionary look from Kem.

"Stay focused. The one thing we need to do is keep our emotions out of it."

"Agreed." Jaml takes a deep breath. "Keep her comfortable. I am going to figure out our next move. This has to end soon."

"Good." Kem smiles at the warrior before stepping back into the dark room to stay vigilant with Karva's rehabilitation, leaving Jaml standing alone in the hallway with his thoughts and emotions battling for control.

✦

Death.

Over the past year, death has come calling to the house of King Taras. With the murder of his youngest son, Manda, he has officially lost his legacy. Despite being the creation of the Fallen, demons still hold many of the same emotions as humans, Lucifer made sure of that. Lucifer created demons to be the replacement for humans, to win the war and be the primary inhabitants of God's earth. To enslave God's creation, man. To provide the ultimate humiliation to the Almighty.

Now King Taras broods. Contemplates his next move. Ever since that Reaper arrived, nothing but death and failure has followed. For that the Reaper must pay. He will witness the death of everyone he knows and when the Reaper has been stripped of everyone, only then will Taras end his life, slowly. He has never tasted Reaper blood but vows to savor and enjoy every strip he takes from Reaper's bloody body.

Revenge started with the abduction and torture of that nun Karva. It would have been perfect if she would have dangled from a rope yesterday but Lucifer did not see fit for that to happen. Instead he witnessed the death of his last heir. For him to lose everything must be essential. It will keep King Taras focused on what must be done. Essential for the destruction of Reaper and the beginning of the end for man.

King Taras sits back on his throne, a knock on the throne room bringing him back to the present. A smirk comes across his face as a plan begins to formulate in his mind.

326

"Enter my servant." King Taras sent a soldier to find General Wyr, the leader of his human army.

The door opens, allowing the general to enter. His braided grizzled beard dangles down to his chest, almost the same length as the ponytail dangling from his head. Dressed in full battle gear, to include a broadsword at his hip, the general approaches the throne.

He kneels in front of his king, head bowed low.

"Rise my faithful servant." The king's voice holds no inflection, just authority,

"Yes milord." Wyr rises to his feet to stand confidently in front of his king. His hand rests on the hilt of his blade, the other balled in a fist to slam across his chest, a salute.

"The heretics have not left our city. We must crush the devil lovers and extinguish our land of their deception." Taras carefully uses words. He must feed his deception, his web of lies that fills most people in the kingdom. The church is presently viewed as a cesspool of Lucifer worshippers, one that needs to be eradicated from the kingdom. When the time is right, Taras will reveal his true identity and intentions to enslave humans. He lives for that day but until then, he must continue to carry out the deception and destroy the young Christians from within.

"Your will is my command."

"My will is for you to attack the church tonight and squash what is left of the devil worshippers. Do it quickly and mercilessly. Then go to Duke Jaml's estate and eliminate everyone, for they are surely devil worshippers. Come back to me once this is done."

"As you wish milord." Wyr bows low before spinning around on his heels to stride out of the throne room.

Queen Sera appears from behind the throne to take her place at Tara's side. Her long white gown has a deep plunge in front, showing the inner slopes of her ample breasts. The slits on the side of the dress extend upward to her hips, exposing her long legs with each step. The king looks over at his queen, a look of satisfaction on his face.

"It is almost over. Soon we will have these cretins back in our command. We will rebuild better. We will bring in more of our brothers and sisters and soon we will enslave these cretins forever. Lucifer will rain praise and power on us. We will be the point of attack against God. We will be the spearhead of the Apocalypse."

"Yes darling, of course. But first we have to make these animals suffer for our loss. Their incompetence has cost us dearly. We will rule without our babies and for that they will suffer."

King Taras looks at his bride, her quest for revenge to be paid in blood. He loves it.

"I want that Reaper's head on a spear, but not before I suck every bit of his brains out. Make him suffer, yes, then let me have my revenge. I want him to die slowly, watching me eat his flesh from his bones. Promise me my love. Promise me that I will have this." Her eyes are locked with his, waiting for the answer that she wants to hear badly.

"Of course my dear." His words bring a smile to her face. "You will have your revenge and anything else that you desire. He will be yours. I will find joy in your carnage."

"Thank you King Taras. Thank you my love" She leans forward, kissing him deep with satisfaction. Soon she will have her revenge and nothing is going to stop it.

✦

"They're surrounding the church. No easy escape." Kem pulls back from the window, letting go of the curtain. She turns to look at Jaml, who sits on a stool finding his calm.

"Who leads them?"

"General Wyr himself. I am counting right at fifty, taking into account what the other nuns are telling me. No telling how many demons in human form out there. Worse yet, are there Lycans?" Worry begins to creep in Kem's words despite her confident stance and deliberate movement.

"Depends on how desperate the king is. With this many people, I doubt any demons are among them. He feels these humans are enough to take us out. I would have been worried if the group was only ten, then demons would have been expected. We need to move. How is Karva?"

"Not going to be much help, more of a burden. I could possibly wake her and move her but she will have to be helped. I am going to be honest, if it was just the two of us, my money is on us. With these innocents, I am not so sure."

"Don't lose faith. God will provide. We will just have to make it just the two of us. Move the innocents to the cellar and instruct them to bolt the door. Do not open it until we tell them."

"They will be trapped if we don't win." Concern is in her voice.

"If you two die, we will be hunted and killed as well." They both turn to look at Flor. "Get us down there and don't worry about us. If you die, we die. Either here or in our homes, we will be hunted and killed. If you are truly worried about us, don't die."

Jaml and Kem look at each other, a smile on their face.

"Let's get to it." Kem's voice is once again booming in confidence. "Flor, get two of your people to move Karva to the wine cellar. Then get you and your people down there. Once inside, we will cover the door and try to disguise it for you. There is enough food down there for at least a week. Do not open the cellar until we come for you. If we don't come for you and they do not find you, remain down there and use the supplies. Wait the full week before coming out. Hopefully they would have moved on at that point, searching for an escape door and trying to find you. Make your way out of the city to never return. You will be able to find refuge in the kingdom of Sagin. Just tell the Queen or general your story and I sent you."

"I would do that. But I would much rather you take me there yourself." A slight smile from Flor.

"I will do everything I can to make that request happen."

The two ladies hug before Flor walks away, her high pitch voice is heard barking commands. Kem turns to face Jaml who stands silently with a smile on his face.

"She will make us proud. Now let's make sure you walk her to Sagin." Reaper sighs heavily.

"Time to end this." Determination is heard in her voice.

The two of them follow the small group of innocents to the cellar door, located on the floor of the sanctuary. By the time the two warriors arrived at the opening, Flor successfully placed all the innocents of the church inside. She is standing at the entrance when they arrive.

"All is ready." Her voice cracks as the finality of the situation hits her. She may never see these two again. She may never see the light of day again. Tears swell in her eyes.

"Now stop that." Kem gives Flor a big squeeze of a hug. She holds the lady at arm's length. "We will be back before you know it. Everything will work out as God sees fit."

"Stop preaching." The two women chuckle at the remark. "Just make sure you two take care of each other and come back to us. Everyone down there is proud to have met and known each of you."

Jaml steps up and hugs the lady. She pulls away but not before kissing him on the cheek.

"Now go do what you do." She walks down the steps into the candle lit room below. Jaml closes the door as soon as she clears the opening. He hears the wooden bolt slide into place. The two warriors slide the pew back into place, over the entrance way. The work is so good, the wood slides into place perfectly, almost invisible to the naked eye.

"Let's go." Jaml leads the way down the hall towards the back door. Kem's recon has revealed a thinner force out of the back. Maybe they can fight their way through this small force before the main force gets to them. The only chance they have is to disappear into the night, drawing the soldiers after them. It will give Flor and the group precious time. The soldiers will burn the church down after they leave, hopefully before the trap door is discovered. The door is lined with steel so those inside will not burn. The bulk of the army will be concerned with them so the group should be able to get away with minimal casualties.

They look at each other, the feeling of dread but determination is in their eyes. Kem grips her staff and takes a deep breath. Reaper draws his twin blades and says a small prayer, thanking God for the will and skill for the battle and to have Kem at his side. After the prayer, he looks back at Kem.

"I am going to use the incantation. Use the opportunity to get away. Meet up with Flor and if you wish, bring back an army to exact your revenge. Cleanse this land of evil. Promise me."

"Promise."

"Have you lost your mind? I thought I taught you better than this Kem? Rushing into insurmountable odds with nothing but a pick stick and a muscle head!" The voice startles both Kem and Reaper.

Reaper and Kem both turn simultaneously to find a group of bald monks standing there, an oriental monk at the helm. Kem's face lights up as if she has opened up the most valuable gift of all.

"You made it! I was afraid my message had not reached you." She turns to Reaper, a look of confusion on his face. "Reaper, this is Seve. My master monk. These are my brothers in Christ."

Reaper follows Kem over to the group of men. He clasps forearms with the monk Seve and instantly feels the raw power in that grip. Jaml remembers the trials to get the Axe and promptly lost it. Nevertheless, Jaml knows Seve is a formidable opponent and definitely an honor to go into battle at his side. Truly a blessing runs through his head.

"I am honored Seve and grateful that you would join us in battle." He turns to Kem. "How? When?"

"When you slept the last time you used the incantation. The Lord revealed to me that we were walking into a battle we could not win without help. So I sent word through the birds back to the monastery but did not know if it worked."

"You couldn't tell me?" Reaper raises an eyebrow.

"Well, you know." She winks at him before turning to Seve. "How long have you been here? Why didn't you reveal yourself earlier?"

"Didn't know if you needed us. No need for twenty battle monks to just walk into town, brings unwanted attention. We arrived here the day before the rescue. We were prepared to assist but you seem to have it in hand. Plus it was a pleasure watching a Reaper at work. Impressive training, I must say." A slight bow from the battle monk to show his respect.

"Respect." Reaper slightly bows back. "We were just about to break out the back door and make a run for it. Care to join?"

"Why run." A smile creeps over Reaper's face at Seve's remark.

"Front door then?" Reaper reverses his direction.

"Front door then." Twenty one battle monks follow the Reaper.

The group arrives at the front door. Reaper turns to the group.

"When I open this door, fan out. These are not battle tested troops so the initial shock might be enough. Make your way to the south gate. If you cannot make it with the main force, meet up at the river where it pools into a lake. Careful, there may be some demons and Lycans in the group so watch your back at all times. Good?"

A simple nod is enough for him. He draws his blades, the ebony blades catch the monks' eyes and some whispers are heard.

"So it is true. You are in possession of a demon's weapon. How are you able to control it?"

"With this." Reaper pulls the medallion out from under his top. "Controls the calling from the Sword of Darkness. The angel Allie has blessed this curse onto me. Fear not, I control it not the other way around."

We are in the midst of a legend." Seve cannot see the darkness in Reaper's eyes so he knows the warrior speaks the truth.

"Let's keep it as a legend and not as a martyr." He turns to the door. "May your will be done O'Lord and may the blood of your son forgive the blood that I must shed cause in your name. Amen" Reaper kicks open the door to find himself looking at half a garrison of soldiers in front of him. This is going to get bloody. "Through the Power of God, I charge thee Reaper. Deliver the Lord's vengeance upon evil"

Reaper charges towards the soldiers in his way. As he closes the distance, he can see red eyes in the back of the troops, battle lycans. He will leave the human troops to the monks; he must take out the battle lycans.

Two soldiers approach him, swords drawn. The soldier on the left slashes down at Reaper's shoulder who simply side steps the slash before bringing his blade up, the tip penetrating under the soldier's chin. Reaper's blocks a stab by the other soldier while yanking his blade from the dead soldier's chin. A river of blood erupts from the open wound. Reaper does not pause but slashes across the other's back, his blade biting through the back plate, chainmail and the soft flesh underneath.

Reaper easily goes through four more soldiers before he finds himself standing in front of six battle lycans, all still dressed in human form in human armor. The human mouth of the lead lycan sneers in disgust at the man in front of him.

"You realize you don't stand a chance in human form. You better transform while you have the chance." The lycans do not fall for the ploy. They know if they transform, the rest of the soldiers will know instantly that the king is a demon and his plans will instantly fall apart. Instead the lycans draw their blades but pause when they see the ebony blades in Reaper's hands. Doubt covers their face. Like the monks, everyone has heard the stories of the ebony blades.

Rumors say the blades are from the Four Horsemen but nevertheless, it is confirmed that the blades are the very least lycan killers.

The moment of doubt and hesitation proves fatal for them. Reaper is quickly in their midst, slicing and cutting with both blades, putting the lycans immediately in defensive mode, Reaper takes full advantage of his upper hand, and two fall immediately in the first wave. The remaining four retreat, trying to regain some composure in the battle.

Reaper is relentless, pushing forward, both blades efficiently singing their death song. A lycan jumps in front of the blades, sacrificing himself so his brothers have the opportunity to recover. The sacrifice works as the lycan is quickly cut down and Reaper finds himself facing the remaining lycans, who begin to fan out.

Reaper laughs aloud at the notion these lycans have a chance because one of their numbers got in the way of his blade. He is under the power of the angel Reaper and no amount of planning is going to save these creatures.

He attacks with such ferocity; it proves too much for the lycans. Despite having outflanked their opponent, the lycans found themselves on the defensive. Reaper moves with enhanced angelic speed and abilities, too much for even enhance lycans can handle. Servants of the dark have never seen such speed and skill, many were not created during the actual Heavenly Wars. These three will die witnessing the speed and skill of an angel. Or a human enhanced with angel like abilities.

Two quickly die in a mass of blood and guts, leaving the remaining standing alone, looking for a way to escape. The lycan thinks about turning but even if he wins, he will be executed as an agent of Lucifer. With one last battle cry, the lycan attacks. His sword with precision, his attack very calculated, meant to use the other's speed against them. He will lure the Reaper into his trap before killing him.

A great plan except the lycan miscalculates the Reaper's speed. He presses forward only to find the Reaper's blade attacking everywhere. The lycan feels the pain of a cut in his side followed by a cut across his chest. A third cut appears on his thigh. The lycan soon feels the blood flow from each cut. Two moves later, the head of the lycan flies harmlessly through the air to bounce several times on the ground.

Reaper turns to look over the battleground. The battle monks are handling themselves with precision and effectiveness. He can only spot two monks amongst a sea of dead soldiers. Such a waste of human life. These soldiers are dying because they refuse to acknowledge who the king really is. These soldiers would rather hang onto the notion that the king is real and everything they have done in his name is based on justified actions through the king's sermons.

His scan turns back to the church, which begins to burn, lit by soldiers simply following orders. He notices a small group of soldiers walking into the church. His initial thought is the innocents are safe, they are not going to be able to find them. Why would they be going into a burning church they just lit on fire unless they know exactly where the innocents are. Reaper breaks into an angel enhanced run towards the church. Along the way, his blades continue to sing the song of death, chopping down soldiers who stand in the way.

He reaches the door and pauses, not wanting to walk into a trap that ends all this. He listens carefully for the voices of the soldiers which he picks up almost immediately. His breath slows as his eyes close to concentrate on the voices inside.

"It is somewhere in the sanctuary. The door is under one of the pews. Once we find it, no one survives, no one."

Just as he thought. Someone has betrayed him and given the location of the cellar to the king. Who the traitor is will be found out later, for now some soldiers are going to have to pay unnecessarily.

"You got one thing right. None of you will survive." The tone is firm.

The group of four soldiers turn to find themselves looking at Reaper. The man is dressed in all black save for the droplets of blood sprinkled on his clothes, none of which is his. His ebony skin almost glows in the torchlight of the church. In each hand he carries a short blade, blood drips from each blade. The soldiers have heard stories that Reaper killed a Fallen. No man has ever killed a Fallen but what if the stories are true. A look of terror covers their faces.

Reaper charges the group, blades twirling in the air, searching for human blood,

The lead soldier falls with the first taste of blood, a quick slash across his neck, opening a flood of blood. The second soldier fares no better when Reaper completes his turn and sinks both blades into the soldier's chest like a warm knife into soft butter. The third soldier releases his battle cry and charges, his axe held high. Reaper is patient in allowing the attacker to get close. He sidesteps the downward chop to sink his blade into the man's neck. The blade enters and exits, leaving the wound to spill the man's life force. The move is so fast the soldier is dead and doesn't know it. He stumbles forward before looking bewildered, the feel of liquid running down his neck. He considers if it is sweat but the pain reveals to him his fate. With one last grasp, he falls over dead.

The last remaining soldier stands there weighing his options. He just watched three of his comrades die within a minute and Reaper did not break a sweat. He looks to find the door behind Reaper and wonders if he can make it. Will Reaper let him make it? On either side of the church are windows, open windows large enough for him to fit through. With a yell the last soldier breaks in a run towards the nearest window, thoughts of his family spur him on, driving him to the window.

He can smell the blood and sweat from the battle outside. Thoughts of volunteering for this special assignment runs through his head. Right now regret fills his head. This whole day has been filled with nothing but death and now he finds himself running for his life from a man he can never hope to defeat. The battle rages outside but at this point he cares not who is winning, only escaping the killing machine in the church.

A sharp pain engulfs his right thigh and he finds himself tumbling to the ground. He crashes into a pew, destroying the wooden bench under his weight. Rolling onto his shoulder turns into both a blessing and a curse. The action prevents him from landing face first into a pew and breaking facial bones, possibly causing death. For that he is thankful. Unfortunately the roll separates his shoulder. He screams in pain while scrambling to get to his feet. He takes a glance at his wounded leg to find an ebony blade protruding from both sides of his leg.

The soldier once again attempts to get up and once again he crashes forward into another pew. He looks over his shoulder to find Reaper stalking towards him, like the angel of death himself. He

335

turns, clawing at the ground in an attempt to escape. Tears and sobs pour from the soldier, he knows he is going to die, that is inevitable.

He looks behind him once again to find Reaper standing over him. "Have mercy, please!"

"Like you were going to show the innocents in the cellar? Tell me soldier, why shouldn't I just kill you where you lie?" Disgust drips from Reaper's words.

"I was just following orders!" The man bellows loudly as if in great pain.

The orders excuse is one of the things Reaper cannot stand. He would rather hear a soldier say he enjoys killing innocents than blame his sins on another person. Saying someone told him to kill somehow exonerates him. Instead of killing him, Reaper yanks the blade from the soldier's leg, pain is too much to bear. The soldier passes out.

Reaper considers his options. He can leave the group in the cellar where they are defenseless. This was the original plan but things change. Their exact location is known and what is to say more soldiers don't come calling. Especially when this group does not come back. By that time he will be out of the city and unable to help them. The other option is to pull them out of the cellar and lead them to safety himself. But that will mean putting them in jeopardy immediately and possibly losing some along the way.

"What are you waiting for? Let's go!"

Reaper looks back at the door to find Kem standing there with six monks at her side. He quickly finds the blood on her clothes but does not see any injuries. Good, not her blood. He also notices her staff is gone, replaced by Aikido sticks, short fighting sticks favored by monks and warriors from the East. The edges of the stick are caked in blood.

"Been busy?" Even in dire situations, the two are still able to banter back and forth

"Not all of us are able to sit around contemplating life. Once you figure it out, we need to leave."

The decision was made, one he knew the answer to but needed confirmation from a friend. He walks over to the designated pew and kicks it over. The wooden seat topples over to reveal a door in the ground. Reaper knows the door is closed from the inside and no one in there is going to open the door, per his instructions. He pulls a blade, reverses grip and slams it in the hair line opening. He hears the clank of the lock falling to the ground and thanks God for his aim.

Reaper throws open the door to find himself looking at scared faces, ones expecting soldiers to invade their room, killing anyone alive down below. Once they recognize the man standing in the doorway, a collective sigh comes from the room. Flo pushes her way to the entrance, bringing a smile to Reaper.

"What are you doing here?" A motherly tone is used.

"You can spank me later. Your position is compromised so you are going to have to trust us to get you to safety. Staying here will only result in your death."

Reaper watches as horror fills the room below. Realizing that someone they trusted had compromised their position and soldiers had come to end their lives. Sobering news for anyone to take, but even more so when the threat on their lives is so close. Flo speaks up.

"Well you heard the man. If we stay, we die and for one, I have no desire to see my heavenly Father today. Move along now." Despite her firm voice and take charge attitude, Flo is screaming inside. She has never been in battle, never had someone sent to kill her and here she is.

Vulnerable and weak, relying on a man, until recently, she thought was nothing more than another pampered royal from another country. Now she knows his true identity and cause, he is one of the elite killers for God. She had never met one in real life but heard stories of specially trained fighters who travel around killing Lucifer's demons. For years she heard the stories of such warriors but dismissed them as children's stories. Then again, she also dismissed the stories of demons and the Fallen.

In the past months, she has seen demons transform out of humans, Lycans as well. Then this, a man skilled enough to kill both creatures of evil. She has watched him and continues to watch him put his life in peril's way for people who do not know him and definitely don't look like him. All for the glory of God. His faith and strength is unmatched. And here he is again, caring for those who cannot care for themselves.

With the group standing on the floor of the church, two monks move into the cellar to retrieve Karva, the wounded nun. They move her up the ladder through a series of handoffs before placing her on a makeshift stretcher, a rug secured on either side by two long poles. They secure her limbs so that she will not fall off during the transport.

"You two keep close to me. We travel fast and without mercy. Any stoppage will be our death. Unfortunately, strike to kill not to wound. Move to the east side where we will be able to leave the city. Everyone, stay close but do not get in the way of the monks."

The crowd nods their understanding of the Reaper, who nods back before winking at Kem.

"They have taken great losses in the initial battle. If we wait any longer, they will be able to gather more soldiers. So stop talking Reaper and let's go!" Kem kicks open the front doors of the church to find a dozen soldiers there, armed for battle but mentally wishing the monks were somewhere else.

Reaper does not give the soldiers time to recuperate nor organize. Immediately he is in the midst of the soldiers, cutting his way through the carnage towards safety. He does not look back to see what is happening, his complete focus is carving a path through these men and assume his group is in close proximity.

Battle cries ringing in his ears informs him of everything he needs to know, so he presses forward. He shows no mercy, which will only get him killed. He pauses to look towards his left, his ears picked up on something. Additional soldiers are running to his position. The monks are tired, the people scared. He grabs hold of Kem's cloak at the shoulder.

"Get these people out of here. I will cover your back." A command, not a request.

"Good luck. Make sure we share the sunrise together."

"Deal. Now get them out of here." Without hesitation or a response, Reaper moves to the side of the group. He listens for the clamper of his retreating group as he stares at the cluster of soldiers heading his way. Fingers grip the hilts of his blades, songs from the God's words on his mind.

"Ready?" The word startles Reaper who instantly looks towards the voice. Standing there is a monk, his bloody staff held at the ready.

"Yep." Reaper turns to find another monk standing there, aikido sticks held firmly

"What are you two doing?" Irritation fills his voice but gratitude swells in his heart. "You don't have to do this. You don't have to die here." He came to grips that this is where he was going to fall, by sheer numbers alone. He wasn't sure if the power of the Reaper would come back. He had never used the power so close together and is not sure if his body is going to be able to handle it. The angelic power might be enough to kill him. Now having two comrades by his side, especially two as skilled as these, he finds himself having hope in keeping his promise to Kem.

"Don't start crying Reaper. This is our choice. Besides, we cannot let you have all the fun, can we? Are you going to use your angelic powers?"

"Don't know if it will work. I just finished using it and don't know if calling on it so soon will kill me or even work."

"Then we best get to fighting."

The two men exchange smiles. Reaper says another short prayer before leading the charge against the reinforcements. The three warriors plow into the group of soldiers, disorganizing them. Now they are inside the group of soldiers, the three warriors begin to wreak havoc from the inside. The soldiers have never seen three humans move so fast and in coordination like this. Where one has an opening and in danger of being struck down, another cuts it off. Soldiers fall under the ebony knives and monk weapons like summer wheat at harvest.

All three men have shallow cuts across their bodies but nothing that is life threatening or even major. The soldiers have not been able to impede or even slow down the advancement of the warriors. Reaper notices the crowded field is thinning, meaning they are close to their objective, the east gate. Once they fight their way through there, they will easily get lost in the forest.

A sharp pain explodes in his shoulder. He looks over to find a shaft protruding from it.

"Archers!"

His warning comes too late for one of the monks, his body riddled with six arrows. The body hits the ground, the soul already on its journey to heaven. Reaper looks to the other side to find that monk in a dive roll back to his feet, only one arrow finding its mark. The positive is the archers killed most of the remaining soldiers opposing their escape, Reaper and his comrade take advantage of the situation and take a full sprint towards the gate.

The unexpected spurt catches the archers off guard, many of whom find themselves fumbling with their arrows, scrambling as their targets approach. Many know if those two get close enough to the wall, their arrows will become useless. None want to stand in front of General Wyr as a failure. Yet in their haste, they quickly become failures.

Despite the arrow sticking out of his shoulder, Reaper's speed does not diminish. He makes up the distance to the wall quickly, fast enough that very few arrows are released in time. The monk makes it to the wall almost simultaneously. They glance at each other before the nod of approval. Reaper breaks the shaft of the arrow before pushing the arrow through. The monk imitates the procedure to the arrow sticking out of his forearm. Free from projectiles, the two men know they have very little time before they are once again in grave danger.

Reaper points at his eyes followed by pointing at the gate, there are three soldiers standing there, the look of fear across their faces. They grasp their swords, arms shaking, hoping the killers go somewhere else. Unfortunately they are wrong.

Reaper and the monk spring into action, their weapons moving in intricate patterns meant to confuse and disrupt the enemy. This is not needed here, all three soldiers, upon seeing the two warriors, drop their weapons and flee immediately, wanting no part of the carnage they witness.

When the two arrive, the gate is unprotected. The monk leans his staff against the wall and grabs the wheel to the lever that opens the gate. Reaper turns around to face that enemy that has not arrived. He watches as they gather at a safe distance, one that keeps them away from the ebony blades.

A few grunts later, Reaper feels a finger tapping him on the shoulder. He looks back to find the monk standing there, obviously tired and worn out but successful in opening the gate, a chore for three men. A smile brings the monk back to life. Both men sprint out of the gate to be lost in the wooded area in front of them.

Chapter 18

A week has passed since the destruction of the church and the subsequent escape. The group traveled for two days until they came across the town of Oluf which took the refugees in without question. Many in the village heard about the purge of Christianity in the city and their escape. To have the refugees in real life, telling of their tales and experiences, is absolutely amazing. The elders of the village are lost in meditation and prayer, how to bring these people peace in their time of need.

Reaper had arrived hours after the main group and met with the leaders the next day. He assures them he is taking full responsibility for any actions of the refugees. In the days that followed, everyone has been on their best behavior, working hard for the village.

Karva's condition improves despite the hastily attempted escape. In three days, she is up and walking around, albeit gingerly. Jaml attributes her recovery to her prayers and stubbornness.

From the first day at the village, Jaml begins making plans to reenter the village to withdraw any others that need to get away. Thoughts enter his mind on Indi and his wife, along with Blait. They're welfare and safety comes to the forefront of his mind. He knows he will have to risk all once again to be successful.

So he rests during this week.

On the evening of the seventh day, Jaml approaches the council. With all the eyes of the elders upon him, he enters the circle to talk. His black leather armor hides most of his healing injuries, giving the impression of perfect health which is far from the truth. Bandages still cover a multitude of injuries suffered last week. The long cape is draped over his shoulders, the hood drawn over his head, giving him a fierce powerful look.

"Good evening good sirs of the village." He receives many nods of approval from the council before moving on. "First and foremost, it is truly God's blessing for us to be standing here. By the grace of

God we were able to survive and escape the evil clutches found in Colley. I came here to ask for another favor."

Masks of concern cover many of their faces as talks of war crept into the conversation. Jaml had heard of such conversation and knew he needed to stop any further festering.

"I am not asking for you to fight our battle. I would never ask you to place your people in danger. You have been nothing but warm and inviting. What I ask of the council tonight is that you continue to watch over these people. I have some unfinished business to take care of as well as rescue another friend of mine along with his wife."

More whispers.

"I promise I will not bring this war to your doorstep. If my mission is not complete, you will never see me again."

"We cannot combat the armies of Colley, they are far too large and advanced. Do you swear on your life?"

"Yes."

More whispers. Just as Jaml begins to worry, too much whispers are never good. After several minutes of continued whispering, the Chief finally breaks away from the group to address the man standing there.

"As the Chief, I urge you to reconsider your position and just stay with us here. As a friend, be careful and the best of luck on your mission, the Lord is with you."

Jaml bends at the waist towards the Chief, giving him the respect he deserves. The Chief returns the gesture. They grasp forearms to complete the salutation.

Jaml leaves the circle with a look of determination written across his face. His features seem to bloom in excitement and determination. With determination, he strides back to his camps, eager to get back on the mission.

Later, under the guise of night, two horses with their riders leave the village heading south. Despite knowing Colley lies to the north, the duo decides to travel south for safety reasons. Satisfied they are not being followed, the duo turn west and begin their big circle back to Colley.

The next day, their travels are easy and without incident. Few people are on the road and even fewer are willing to carry on a conversation. Most people instantly look down at the ground, hoping no one notices them. Obviously these people have gone through tremendous pain and suffering at the hands of the demon king and now search in vain for a place to relocate. One where the hand of the demon king cannot reach. Jaml weeps for these people, caught in the middle of a war they knew nothing about. Family and friends dying by the hands of creatures they have only read of in the Bible and stories told by the old women of the village at bedtime. Truly the horrors they have endured over the past months are far more than any normal man or woman in their lifetime.

Later that evening the two of them can see Colley in the distance. Instead of a joyous smile ending their travels, the only reaction either one gives is a heavy sigh. No orange glint presides over the city which means the fires have all either burnt themselves out or have been put out. Either way, the city has returned to calm.

Kem points out a flash to their left which elicits a nod from Jaml. They continue to watch. It doesn't not take long to notice and track a few more flashes. The two look at each other before Kem speaks.

"Lycan patrols, seems like the king is not going to trust his humans after all. He sent the big dogs."

"Do we go in fighting or wait till nightfall?"

"Nightfall."

"Agreed."

Two warriors dismount and relax against a nearby tree. They share some dried jerky before laying their head back and resting. Several minutes later, Jaml looks over to find Kem asleep, her chest gently rising and falling in rhythm. He smiles before laying back, contemplating on the events since he arrived, from being a simple Duke from the kingdoms in the south, going out at night to accomplish his goal of killing demons. He finally realized where the weapons of the Apocalypse were hidden and from there his life has been one battle after another. He has even used the power of the Reaper and actually killed a Fallen.

"Your turn."

Jaml looks over to find Kem staring at him.

"Looks as if you need it. Take a few, you will need it very soon."

Jaml nods his approval before tucking his chin against this chest and enters into a light but restful sleep. One without dreams or distraction.

He opens his eyes to find a darkness that envelopes the land. The sun has retreated for another day, leaving the open sky and bright half-moon to give adequate light for any who are trained. His eyes quickly adjust and finds Kem right where she was when he went to sleep. She looks up to find his eyes open and alert.

"Welcome back. Are you ready?"

"Give me a moment and we can go."

Jaml disappears into the woods to return a moment later, his full alertness back upon him. His eyes dart back and forth, searching for any unnatural movements or something that is out of place. Kem smiles inside, good to have him back.

"What's the plan?" Her attention is locked fully in.

"We have to find a way in. Once inside, we can assess the dangers but need to locate Duke Indi and the girls. Once we find a way to get them to safety, we can begin to plan an attack to end this."

"Sounds great but how are we going to get in? More importantly, how are we going to get by the Lycans patrols?"

"We will find a way in, have faith. As for the Lycans, we do not engage unless completely necessary. Agreed?"

"Agreed. Let's go back to the last village and take a look around. Hopefully we can find another way in." Jaml likes her suggestion and nods his approval.

Kem and Jaml stake out the inn, listening for anyone who is heading into Colley. It takes a couple of hours but they hear from a large merchant who announces his intention to enter Colley and become filthy rich from his fur rugs, the best quality for thousands of miles around. The merchant challenges anyone to find better quality fur anywhere in the known world. Satisfied that no one would or could stand up to his challenge, he drains his mug one last time before heading out of the tavern.

Right before he reaches the door, Jaml firmly grasps his upper arm.

"Excuse me sir, can I have a word?"

"Get your filthy hands off of me, you dark hued devil before I begin to scream you are robbing me." Disgust fills the words and actions of the man. Partially from the large amounts of alcohol in his system but partially due to the fact he doesn't like black people.

"Just one word." Their eyes meet and the merchant instantly realizes this man is no one to mess with. "I need your help."

"I cannot help you." His tone changes tremendously, more humble but his message is still the same. "Please sir, let me go. I cannot help you."

Not wanting to make a situation out of this, Jaml slowly lets go of the merchant's arm. The merchant slowly walks out of the door, their eyes never parting until the merchant is out of the door and the door swings shut.

"Well, that went well." Kem appears next to Jaml, her frustration very evident.

"It went perfectly." A slight smile

"How so? Please enlighten me. As far as I can see, you were rejected faster than a whore in church."

"That's good." Jaml allows himself to laugh at the comment. "What we need to do is get to our horses and follow along. He will be needing us soon enough."

Kem looks sideways as Jaml turns and continues. "He has my scent. I am sure the king has given my scent to all his pets. Once they pick up the scent, his little guards will be overwhelmed. That is where we come in."

"Save the day. Clever, very clever." Kem jabs Jaml in the side. "I am going to have to keep an eye on you."

They leave the tavern and immediately head to the stables.

It has been a weird night. After proclaiming his superior goods, the merchant was stopped by a strange, powerful black man from the south kingdoms. The man wanted to talk with him but he does not converse with the savages from the south. He never has and never will. Their skin has to be diseased somehow to be that dark.

They left the village two hours ago and he has felt followed ever since. The merchant sits inside his personal carriage, no luxury left out. Fur rug sits on the floor of the carriage, walls ordained with fur.

He moves to the center of the carriage, away from either window, making him a smaller target. He, nor his hired soldiers, have been able to shake the feeling nor have they been able to find the source. Only that they all feel eyes on them. The soldiers ride with their swords in their laps, their eyes constantly scanning the wood line for the attack that is coming. They can feel it.

Suddenly the most chilling howls erupt from all around them. So chilling were the howls that the horses became spooked, many rearing to their hind legs. The howls continue, further disorientating the soldiers and horses. Suddenly a flash appears on the right side, only to disappear to the left, leaving a soldier sitting on his horse, both hands grasping at his neck. Blood pours from the gaping wound on his neck, quickly covering his hand and the front of his armor. The horse rears once more to successfully dislodge the soldier from his saddle.

"What demon is that?" The young soldier screams, fear enveloping him.

"Shut it soldier. Remember your training. Whatever it is, it will die by our swords." The leader is a burly man of many campaigns. The biggest of the soldiers, the leader hoists a large mace hammer instead of a broadsword. His beard extends down to mid-chest, resting against a much used and dented breastplate. He sits atop an oversized black warhorse, fully armored.

The men quickly respond, drawing their swords, circling their steeds around the carriage for protection. The merchant pays more than most and supplies them with anything and everything they need. He has bought their lives, figuratively and actual. They will and have laid their lives down for him.

The leader takes his place at the front of the carriage horses before moving the carriage forward. Nerves are tweaked, silence becomes the norm. Yet, what is more unnerving is suddenly the forest is just as silent. Nor birds tweet or insects hum, just utter silence.

The silence is broken by the yell of another victim. The soldiers watch as what appears to be a wolf drags another of their brethren into the forest screaming.

"Lycans." The leader utters the word before raising his voice to give his commands. "Close ranks. Sit in twos, side by side. They attack from the sides. Halberds out. Let's move boys!"

Minutes later, the soldiers are riding side by side, their halberds sticking out, as commanded. The group moves forward cautiously, preparing for another attack. The leader sees three men standing in the middle of the road. All three are dressed in simple tunics and pants. They wield no weapons but show no fear from the soldiers approaching them.

The leader holds his fist up, universal signal for halt. Everything behind him comes to a halt. He leans forward in his saddle, getting a good look at the three standing there.

"Morning neighbor. If you don't mind moving aside, we will be on our way."

"We cannot do that." The man in the center takes a step forward, taking the leadership role.

"May I ask why not?" Most would have laughed at the comment but he knows who these three really are. Their chances of living through this is slim unless he can give these three what they want.

"Reaper's head."

"I do not know whom you speak of. We are the eight soldiers and the merchant inside whom we protect."

"We can smell Reaper inside. Give him to us and you have my word, you can walk away with your lives."

"There is no one inside but the merchant. He is no Reaper, I can assure you. Whoever told you we accompany Reaper that is a lie. Loss of life need not happen here. There is no need for that. Let us pass. What you are looking for cannot be found here."

Suddenly the door to the carriage bursts open. Merchant steps in plain view of all on the road, his arms raised up as if he was nailed to a cross.

"There has been a mistake here. As you can see, I am indeed no Reaper. A simple misunderstanding." Suddenly the encounter with the black man comes to mind. Some say Reaper is black. Could it be? "Sir, what you are sensing is indeed Reaper. I ran into him at the tavern back there. An uncivilized man, if you ask me. He tried to talk to me, rubbed up against me when I said no. I gave no thought to it but that must be what you are smelling."

The leader rolls his eyes back. One thing he cannot stand is a pompous merchant who doesn't know how to shut his mouth. And this one is about to get them all killed. He knows he must act fast if anyone is going to be able to walk out of here alive.

"Listen sir. The merchant is telling the truth. We do not know the Reaper and definitely not hiding him. Let us be on our way."

"Yes, let us pass. I will compensate you with furs, the best furs this land could buy. My furs will keep you warm at night, either alone or in the presence of a woman."

The mention of furs seems to infuriate the three men.

"Kill them before they transform. That is the only chance we got."
Leader screams his command before kicking his horse into action.

The three men begin to transform. Their jawlines crack into place
as their hands and feet elongate. Their overall height grows
tremendously, reaching eight feet. The lead lycan launches himself,
fangs and claws extend outward. The warrior and the beast collide in
midair. The lycan sinks its claws into the man's shoulder, springing
blood from fresh wounds. The soldier rams his blade into the
midsection of the beast, pushing the blade into the beast. The beast's
momentum is greater than the soldier's, sending both to the ground,
the lycan on top. Immediately fangs sink into the soft neck flesh of
the soldier. The soldier twitches violently as the lycan tears the neck
out.

The rest of the soldiers are frozen in fear. The sight of a man
turning into a wolf is intense, one that most men cannot fathom.
These soldiers are no different. Despite the command from their
leader, none of the soldiers moved, they were cemented to the
ground in fear. Then they watched their best die in such a gruesome
death, it is too much to bear. They turn their horses around and kick
them in full retreat. The other two lycans spring into action, their
paws catapulting them in chase.

The remaining lycan stands up from his victim, mouth covered in
blood. He slowly strolls towards the merchant, a large tongue
appears to remove the blood from its muzzle. The merchant thinks
about running but the sickening sounds of men dying tells him all he
needs to know, he cannot outrun this thing.

The lycan stands over the merchant, his claw like fingers
wrapping around the man's neck. He effortlessly picks the man up,
feet dangling in midair.

"Now what lies did you tell me? I can smell the strong scent of
Reaper nearby, not some weak scent from a brush by."

"I swear to you. I only speak the truth. I am not Reaper and the
only man I have been in contact with must be your man. It has to
be."

Suddenly a booming voice

"One thing is for certain. He is not Reaper. Doesn't have the balls
for it. Pees too much."

The merchant and the lycan look down to find a puddle of pee
beneath the merchant's legs. The lycan and the merchant look at

348

each other, look down, and look up again before the lycan begins to laugh. The voice continues.

"I offer you the same choice you gave my friend here. No more killing, you simply walk away and you live. Otherwise I will have to kill you myself."

Two large objects fly through the air towards the lycan and merchant. The objects hit the ground with a thud. The beast instantly recognizes the heads of his two companions. He looks up to find a figure walking towards them. The figure is dressed in a tight black top and pants. A hood covers his head and extends down past his knees. The figure casually strolls out of the woods onto the road, then stops. He pulls back his hood to reveal a handsome black man with no hair. The lycan recognizes him as Reaper while the merchant recognizes him as the black scum who wanted to talk to him in the tavern.

"Well, what's it going to be, beast of Lucifer?" Reaper reaches behind him to pull his twin ebony blades free from their scabbards.

"King Taras is going to reward me greatly when I bring in your head."

"Your choice. Your funeral."

The lycan tosses the merchant aside like a child who is tired of his doll before charging at Reaper with his battle cry. The man known as Reaper does not make a cry, nor any other noise while meeting the charge of the lycan with his own.

The warrior and the beast come together and instantly the battle is over. The lycan takes a swing with one of his huge paws, eight-inch claws ready to rip the flesh from the human. Reaper twists his body towards the creature, at the same time bringing his sword up. The blade goes through the hairy arm with no resistance to send the severed limb flying through the air. The lycan screams in pain while watching the lower half of his arm spin away from his body.

Reaper wastes no time in ending the fight. He reverses his grip on the hilt of his blades before plunging them into the chest of the beast. The blades sink into the flesh of the beast with little opposition. The creature stumbles back, its eyes locked on the twin blades draining its life force. It falls onto its back and takes its final breath before dying.

The merchant crawled to the base of his carriage and remained there throughout the battle. Now he feels a shadow settle over him.

He knows he is going to die here on an empty road, with no chance to sell his furs and live the great life. He takes a deep breath to wait for his death.

"I'd have words with you merchant."

The man looks up to find Reaper and a female monk standing over him.

The north gate into Colley usually is crammed full of merchants coming to sell their wares. But since the burning, there are more people leaving than arriving. The gate is heavily armed with six soldiers in the group checking people in and twice that number above, armed with bows. Soldiers go about their business with the same drudgery that has befallen the kingdom. No sense of urgency, just going through the motions.

This is the situation that the merchant's wagon comes to. The driver of the carriage, the lone soldier who survived the attack on the road, brings the carriage to a halt. When asked where the merchant is, the soldier is told he sits inside the carriage with his new wife. Another soldier walks around the carriage to the covered bay and opens it to find furs stacked up. There are white, brown and black furs along with a couple of red furs. The soldier closes the bay and nods his approval to the soldier in front of the carriage.

The soldier walks down to the carriage door and opens it. Inside he finds the merchant and his wife sitting across from each other. The merchant has changed his clothes and is wearing a stylish green tunic over brown pants. His wife is dressed modestly in a simple emerald dress that extends from her neck to the floor. A simple necklace adorns her neck.

"Can I help you?" The words bite with disgust at the soldier.

"No merchant. Checking to make sure you are not harboring fugitives. King's orders, you understand."

"Or course. The trails are alive with bandits and such."

"Of course." The soldier is about to close the door when he pauses. "Where is your protection?"

"Cleaning up some bandits. They will be along shortly. I am sure they will not have any trouble getting in." The merchant reaches inside his tunic and drops two gold pieces in the soldier's palm.

"No issues at all."

The carriage proceeds through the gate and makes its way through the marketplace, trying to find the perfect spot to set up shop to attract customers. The merchant instructs the soldier to maneuver towards the east side of the marketplace, alongside other merchants with expensive wares. The rich side of the marketplace.

Once in place, Kem removes the dress that covers her monk's attire. She throws on her cape and draws the hood over her face. Once dressed and feeling like herself again, she kicks the side of the carriage. A figure lowers himself from the underbelly of the carriage. Jaml dons his cape and hood before addressing the merchant and his driver.

"Forget what you did here today and you will never have to see or deal with me again. Otherwise, I will hunt you down." The tone, almost menacing, puts the merchant on edge.

Both men nod feverishly. Satisfied the message is delivered and understood, Jaml and Kem disappear into the crowd.

They blend in effortlessly for hours, picking up information as they go. Eavesdropping into conversations and learning the fate of the city after the burning. One thing they listen for but no one talks about are his friends, Indi and his wife. They continue walking around, searching for any information that would help them find out what has happened to their friends.

The duo makes it to the west gate when Jaml suddenly goes weak in his knees. Kem immediately catches him by his arm, holding him steady.

"What is the matter Jaml?"

"No, no, no." More despair fills each word.

Kem turns her head to find what buckles one of the strongest warriors she knows. To the right of where they stand are the pikes of damnation. This is where the king places all the enemies of the state's heads. This is where Bala's head was placed what seems like an eternity ago. Kem scans the nearest heads until she finds what he fears. To the right center is Indi's head on a pike.

Just then a middle aged woman dressed in a servant's dress passes by. The two would not have noticed save for two things, actions and words. The lady purposely bumps into both of them, gaining their attention. Jaml's hands instantly reach for his weapons underneath his cape. Kem lifts her staff slightly, ready to strike. Without looking, the lady whispers.

"No need for that. I know who you are. Put your weapons away, follow me before someone else recognizes you weeping over a friend."

"Where are the women?" Kem asks

"Not here. Not yet. Stop talking and come."

The lady walks away, followed by Kem and Jaml.

The duo follow the lady through the marketplace, stopping occasionally to look at some carts and making sure they are not followed. They leave the marketplace to enter into the tavern section of town. They walk by three tavern before she turns to walk into the Heaven's Gate.

This particular tavern has four chair tables spread through the main hall. Despite the hour, the tavern is half filled with patrons getting a head start on drowning their sorrows and pity into a small goblet.

As they walk into the tavern, very few heads look up to see who entered the tavern and all simply go back to their drink once their curiosity is sated. The lady leads the duo through the tavern to the door behind the bar. The bartender simply looks up and nods at the lady who acknowledges the greeting with a nod of her own. The one barmaid on duty looks over and simply goes back to wiping down the table she is at.

The lady opens the small door and ushers them into the well lit room. Jaml leads the way, his right hand resting on the hilt of one of his blades. Inside, there are barrels stacked four high of lager and beer lined against three of the four walls. The last wall has flasks hanging from hooks on the wall, each flask being the equivalent of one fourth of a barrel. The flasks are filled with imported wine from the home of the church. In the center of the room is a wooden table, basic rectangular design found in most large taverns.

"Please sit, we don't have much time." The lady pulls out the chair for Kem before urging Jaml to take a seat as well. "Flo is my sister."

The tension level drops along with the rising of trust.

"What happened?" Kem leans back in her chair while Jaml sits at attention. The lady continues.

"They know who you are now so you cannot go back to your villa. They came the day after the burning. Anyone still in the villa was put to the sword. Your friend was dragged across the courtyard by a horse before losing his head."

"And what of Lady Tyra and Lady Blait?"

"You haven't heard?" The lady's head hangs low, ashamed of what is about to come out of her mouth. "They are to be publicly beaten and things.

"What things?" Kem speaks before Jaml could. She can see the anger building up in Reaper but knows whatever is about to be spoken, he must keep his thoughts together if they are to have any amount of success.

"Milady." The lady looks up at Kem, her eyes begging for a way to escape the situation. Kem sees the reluctance but knows it must be said.

"Go ahead."

"They are to be taken by whomever wants a piece." Her voice trails off.

"WHAT!"

"Jaml, you are scaring her."

Kem's soft voice is sufficient to bring him back. He takes a heavy sigh, lets out a breath, and says a quick prayer.

"When?"

"The beatings start at nightfall. They will be beaten into submission all night. By morning they will be ripe for any man willing to pay the price for her."

"This isn't the first time the king has done this. Is it?"

"No. Some of the ladies from the villa were given the same treatment."

"My villa?!" The anger is still laced in his words but now is controlled.

"Yours and some others. The burning was not just about the church. It was the burning of decency in this kingdom. After that, most have left."

"And why not you?" Suspicion is heard in his voice.

"A young girl named Allie revealed herself to me and told me to wait."

"So you stayed." A question more than a statement.

"If an Angel tells you to stay, you stay." The lady makes the statement firmly

353

Jaml and Kem look at each other, smiles on their faces. Jaml turns to the woman.

"I guess I would stay as well."

Later that afternoon the three are joined by a fourth in the backroom. Seve stands by the door, taking in all the information he just heard. Disbelief is the only expression on his face. He shakes his head slightly at the entire situation. Jaml and Kem sit at the small table in the center of the room, thinking about options to save the two women, Blait and Tyra. All four agree that the entire situation is a trap meant to either capture or kill Reaper. Jaml accepts the probability of his survival is very slim but these ladies do not deserve what is about to happen to them. Jaml looks across the table at the others there

"Are we all good with the mission?"

"I don't like it." Kem speaks boldly. "You are going to be exposed to both archers and soldiers alike. This plan is centered on the ladies, which is good, but what about you?"

"I will be alright. We will finish this tonight." Jaml looks out the window. "One way or another, this ends tonight."

After a few moments of awkward silence, Seve speaks out. "With that being said, I don't see anything wrong with the plan. My only concern is the execution. You have to give us time to disperse in the crowd or you and your friends will die. Wait for my signal before you make your proclamation."

"What do you suggest?"

"Look for a fire."

"Fire?"

"Fire."

The sun begins to touch the west wall when the crowd begins to make their way into the town's square. They come to witness another degradation of a female sinner, two harlots deserving of what they will receive. Some come heavy with coin, hoping to purchase a moment to teach the harlot's repentance for their sinful ways. People begin to position themselves for the best views. Rooftops are soon crowded as many want to see every angle of punishment they will receive. Soldiers begin to light the torches around the square to ensure enough light for the evening's festivities.

So enthralled with the upcoming spectacle, none seem to notice a single figure emerge from the shadows to quickly blend in with the crowd. The hooded figure moves with the crowd, blending in perfectly. He eventually makes his way to the front of the stage and readies himself for the upcoming battle. He silently prays for the strength for the upcoming battle and the courage to see it through to the end.

He glances around to make sure no one has identified him. No soldiers are making their way over so either no one recognizes him or people no longer care. Either way, he is safe for now. He takes up a position where he will be able to get to the stage in seconds, the lives of his friends are at stake on ability to move fast.

The sun has disappeared behind the walls of the city which is now being lit by torches. Jaml watches as archers take their place on the parapets. No doubt about it, this is a trap. Military reinforcements move into position by the gates. They are ensuring all avenues of escape are closed. Which begs the question, do they know I am here? And just biding their time for him to make the first move and reveal himself. He scans again and does not notice any additional soldiers in the crowd. They are waiting for him.

Soldiers emerge carrying a large flat board. The board is eight feet high and eight feet wide. In all four corners dangle leather restraint straps. Four more restraints dangle in the middle, two up top and two down below, the whipping board. The board has four brackets on the back to stand and support the board which the soldiers fasten to the stage. Two additional soldiers bring out cheap sheep skin rugs, obviously for the raping that is supposed to occur. Once everything is set up properly, the soldiers walk off the stage.

Minutes later a procession appears. Twenty soldiers riding five abreast ride proudly in front of the royal carriage. Their ceremonial armor shines brightly, having never been a part of a battle. The soldiers do not look around but ride as statues, their steeds marching in unison. The carriage is golden with oversized wheels and an outside canopy made of white silk and gold lace trim. The carriage is drawn by a team of six horses, trained to prance and attack alike. Following the carriage is another patrol of soldiers riding proudly.

Anger swells as Jaml watches the carriage stop at the outdoor pavilion, set up specifically for this occasion. The demons in human form exit the carriage and walk up the portable stairs to take their place on the pavilion. Soldiers position themselves on either side of the king and queen to discourage and protect the two. Jaml's hands clenched into fists as he fights the urge to attack now. He looks around and does not see any fire.

HIs patience is waning, his anger grows. His eyes are fixed on the two demons perpetrating as royalty, impersonating God's creatures in a most grotesque way. He realizes his fingers are wrapped around the hilt of an ebony blade of the Fallen. He forces himself to relax, takes his hand away from the hilt and takes a deep breath. He looks around and finds what he has been looking for, a small plume of smoke appears behind the stage to the north end.

Even though flames cannot be seen from the square, Jaml knows the monks are ready when he starts. Things are beginning to come together when suddenly a resounding gong is heard across the square. Eyes turn to the base of the castle where a door opens. Instantly the crowd erupts into a chorus of screams and grunt noises as the latest victims will arrive shortly. Three guards walk in front of the captives with three behind. The square is complete as a soldier walks on either side of the prisoners. The square of soldiers completely obscures the view of the prisoners from the crowd.

The front three soldiers lead the two females up the steps to the platform. The remainder of the soldiers make a semi circle around the steps, ensuring no one can get to the platform without permission. The two women walk frailly up the stairs, their heads hanging low. Both are dressed in a thin white dress stained with blood from previous beating. They are bound by the wrist and loose by ankles that they are able to walk with little trouble.

With the third soldier standing guard, the other two strap the ladies in one at a time, their front side pressed against the board, their arms and legs outstretched and secured by the ropes attached to the board. Once secured, the soldiers walk back down the stairs and fall in line with the other soldiers. They march to their posts where they take up position in front of the stage, along with the rest of the detail.

A burly man appears on the stage, dressed in a brown vest with matching brown pants. His hairy arms are bulging with muscles in a constant state of flexing. He wears a black hood covering his whole head. The only visible parts are his eyes, nose and mouth which are seen through sewn holes. In his hand is a bull whip. The end of the whip extends out to seven cords meant to maximize the pain inflicted in its victim. He carries the whip downward, the end dragging along the wood.

Jaml looks once again over the nearest buildings and sees what he needs to see. Fire.

Flames extend high into the air from a building, reaching up towards the sky, reaching for the nearest clouds.

Jaml peels his eyes from the flames back to his friends, strapped to a board like a dead animal. The masked man raises a hand into the hand, bringing the crowd to a frenzy. The people in the crowd are screaming and yelling for the women's blood. They want the festivities to begin, to watch two women beat and raped for their pleasure. The man pumps his fist in the air while turning around in a circle. The crowd responds with even more noise.

Suddenly the man on the stage stops moving and stares at his chest. Imbedded in the middle of his chest is a dagger, buried to the hilt in his chest. The crowd immediately goes silent as their source of entertainment is standing still staring at the dagger sticking in his chest. The man falls to his knees, the King and Queen on their feet behind him.

"Who dares interrupt?" The King's voice booms over the marketplace.

"I dare." Comes an equally loud and commanding voice.

The masked figure of the Reaper steps forward to stand directly in front of the soldiers at the stairs. Reaper stalks to the stage where the soldiers move aside like Moses parting the Red Sea. Without pausing, Reaper walks onto the stage just as the man with the whip falls forward dead. Reaper walks over the dead body to stand in the center of the stage.

"I dare demon spawn. You are going to release these two women as your day of reckoning has arrived."

"How dare you!" The King rises to his feet, anger filling him fast. "How dare you come here, defy my authority and dare call me a demon. The only demon here is you, follower of Lucifer."

Reaper laughs. "Me? Follower of Lucifer?" Reaper pulls a blade from the sheath behind his back. He exposes his arm and cuts himself, letting the red blood ooze from the wound. "Everyone can see my humanity. Cut yourself King so we can all see your humanity." They both know if the King cuts himself, it will not bleed red and his farce will finally fail.

Infuriated with the situation, Taras rises from his makeshift throne. "I grow weary of your interventions, I think it is time for you to die."

Taras begins to transform. First his fingers begin to elongate, forming long claws meant for tearing flesh from bone. The next transformation is the forming of the demon wings, two large red wings extending from his back. At full extension, the wings extend more than ten feet in diameter.

Reaper tilts his head to the side.

"What is the matter human? A male demon with flight? That's right. Lucifer has granted his most loyal servants with flight. It's time to tear every last strip of skin from your carcass."

Reaper laughs aloud, infuriating Taras even more. "Or has he made you even more weak and female-like?" The insinuation of weakness is all Reaper needs. Taras is losing his ability to think and becoming more beast-like with each passing moment.

Taras has completed his transformation into a full demon. His face no longer resembles that of the king, just a grotesque shape with large sharp fangs to tear flesh away from bones. His skin has taken a dark red hue. Arms have grown unnaturally long while legs have expanded in girth to form tree trunks. A tail has also appeared, with a pointed end.

Reaper pulls his twin black blades from their scabbards, holding them low awaiting the attack. It does not escape him that Queen Sera has also transformed into her natural form, a succubus. The crowd reacts to the sight of their king and queen turning into Lucifer's demons, screaming and yelling as they run for safety. Their thirst for female blood is no longer a priority or even a desire. People are trampled as the masses attempt to run and hide. For fear of dying but more embarrassment.

The demon that was Taras launches from the pavilion, landing in the middle of the stage. Reaper takes a battle stance causing Taras to erupt in laughter.

"Impressive. I see you are wielding the Sword of Darkness. Thank you for bringing me my prize. Your just rewards will be a quick death. But first, you have taken many of my brethren from me. As your God is so fond of saying, "Eye for an eye". Without warning,

Taras swings his arm backwards. To Reaper's horror, the demon extends his fingers. The claws protracting from his fingers rip through the soft flesh of Tyra's neck. Large amounts of blood explode from the wound, spraying the stage floor. Her head sags to the side. Reaper knows she is dead but grateful for the quick death and the fact Tyra never saw it coming.

Reaper explodes into action, closing the gap to the demon in one bound, and his blades coming to instant life. Taras finds himself retreating as the Reaper onslaught comes to life. His blades move faster than the eye can see. The only thing saving Taras is his demon induced speed and giving of ground.

Satisfied that he has pushed Taras back far enough, Reaper quickly turns his attention to Blait, who hangs on the board sobbing with the expectation of death coming for her next. Reaper takes up position when suddenly two monks appear on the stage and quickly cut her near lifeless body down from the board. Using extreme caution, they carefully lower her to another two monks two quickly whisk her away.

"Clever but unnecessary." Taras laughs at the rescue. "The only death I want to see now is yours."

"Then come kill me if you can." A sneer comes across his face, baiting the demon into action.

Reaper's hounding is all it takes for Taras to attack. The demon springs forward, his wings at full extension helping him cover the necessary ground quicker. The demon flies by but not before taking a swipe at the human with his massive claws. Reaper simply spins with the swipe, avoiding it completely. As he completes his full spin, his blade lashes out narrowly missing the leg of Taras.

Taras turns around, his massive wings keeping him aloft in the air. The two males glare at each other. Reaper whips the blade in his right hand, sending the ebony blade spinning in through the air at Taras. The demon almost laughs as he moves to the side, the blade twirling by. Taras, seeing the man down to one blade, immediately dives forward, aiming to Reaper's exposed defenseless right side. He rears his clawed hand back, poised to strike the deadly blow when suddenly Reaper's blade appears in his hand. Taras attempts to roll to the side to avoid the slash but he cannot avoid the strike. The blade slices through his demon skin, opening up a deep cut.

People in the crowd gasp at the sight of demon blood. If watching the king turn into a demon was not enough, now they see the dark demon blood pour from the wound in his side. Taras hovers overhead, placing a hand on the open wound.

This is Reaper's mistake. Eager to finish the battle, he forgot about the queen. Immediately after launching himself at Taras, excruciating pain explodes from his back. He tumbles back to the earth and into a roll. He turns to see the succubus licking his blood from her claws. Then he feels his begin to stiffen.

"What is wrong ole mighty Reaper?" Queen Sera, the succubus, laughs. "Did I forget to tell you my claws are dripping with poison. What's the matter Reaper? Feeling a little stiff?"

Taras lands in front of him and attacks. The demon's claws swipe and lash out at Reaper. Taras sensing the moment of his victory.

"Not yet my love. Give it a few more seconds and his head will be yours to feast on." She begs her king to stop but to no avail

"No poison is going to take this moment from me. I want to kill Reaper, not a stiff corpse!"

Because her claws bit into his upper back, the poison attacks his arms first. Reaper realizes he cannot move his arms fast enough to stand and fight so he finds himself backpedaling, avoiding his death by the hands of Taras.

In his eagerness to kill Reaper, Taras overextends his stride. Reaper sees the opportunity and attacks. His training as a monk turned his entire body into a weapon, not just his arms and weapons. His side kick strikes true at the demon's knee, sending the demon wobbling on an unsure leg. Reaper quickly spins kick, connecting in the demon's midsection, driving him to the ground.

Reaper immediately stands firm. "Through the Power of God, I charge thee Reaper. Deliver the Lord's vengeance upon evil"

Instantaneously Reaper feels the poison disappear. The power of the Reaper Angel courses through his body, not only healing but energizing every cell. Jaml welcomes the angel's power coursing through his body, powering his mind, body and soul. He looks at the two demons flying over him.

"May your will be done O'Lord and may the blood of your son forgive the blood I must shed to rid your earth of evil. In your name. Amen" The simple phrase uttered from his lips clears Jaml's mind, focusing him on what must be done.

Taras throws all caution to the wind, completely blinded by his desire to kill this man, to rip him apart. So he attacks. He lands in front of Reaper, his arms instantly swiping at the human. Reaper ducks under the first blow before attacking the second blow. The ebony blades cut through demon flesh and bone, severing the lower arm midway up.

Taras howls in pain but remains blinded by rage. He presses forward with only one good arm determined to kill this human. He swipes downward, his claws missing their target. Reaper steps back to let the swipe fly harmlessly by before stepping back in close. His left blade opens the demon's midsection with one cut. Taras grabs at the open wound exposing himself. Reaper takes advantage and rams his blade through the bottom of his jaw, the blade piercing the demon's brain, killing it.

Reaper yanks his blade free, allowing the corpse to fall to the ground one last time. He turns to face Queen Sera. The two stare at each other, waiting for the other to move. Sera just witnessed Taras die at the hands of the man who took her daughter and sons away from her. For the first time, she knows how it is to be alone, and she blames the man in front of her for that. But reason tells her that she cannot win this battle. The human is with Angelic power and she cannot stand against that. Being more prudent than her late husband, Sera turns to flee. Instead, she finds herself staring at her master.

Quel stands nearly ten feet tall, his wings nearly fifteen feet fully extended. His face is beautiful but his skin is red. Most forget that the Fallen were once God's Angels. The War of Hosts pitted brother against brother as the angels who followed Lucifer, once higher than Gabriel, second only to God himself. The followers of Lucifer were defeated and were cast out of Heaven. Through this Casting, the defeated angels were no longer Angels of God but simply known as the Fallen.

Quel wears nothing more than a loincloth, his muscles exposed for all to marvel at. He holds in his right hand an axe, just as black as the Reaper's own blades. Reaper recognizes the Axe of Damnation.

"Master, you have come to witness my revenge on the human who has taken all from me." Sera turns to face Reaper.

"What I believe I was witnessing was my servant running from God's servant in battle. Warriors of Lucifer never run. We would die for the cause, sacrifice ourselves for the chance to smite God. What I see here is a coward."

Sera turns to face her master, fear is painted on her face as an artist creates a masterpiece.

"Please master."

"You bore me." Quel waves his hand. Sera explodes into a thousand small pieces.

Chapter 19

66"I mpressive."

Quel turns his attention to the man standing below him.

"I have heard so much about you Reaper. You have piqued my interest by catapulting yourself over the rest of Reapers. And I see you have one of my brethren trapped in a weapon."

"These things." Reaper looks at the ebony blades as if they were nothing more than trinkets. "As far as your interest, I do what I can."

"Don't mock me." Quel lowers himself to the ground. "A simple spell like you just saw and you will be nothing more than blood."

"Not while I am infused with Reaper power." Jaml tilts his head. "Was I not supposed to know that? Sorry."

"Guess I will have the pleasure of taking your head myself." Quel moves forward.

"I guess so." Jaml walks forward.

Once the two get into range, they explode into action. Quel using his axe and Jaml fighting with his short swords, the battle begins. The speed at which the two fight is remarkable, the human eye cannot follow nor the brain comprehend the speed.

The two stand toe to toe, their fighting skill unparalleled, Jaml finds himself fighting possessed, his actions no longer his own but of the power coursing through his body. The attack, counter attack becomes a true display of God's power.

Jaml takes a step forward, his blades engaged fully. He places his foot down and instantly catapults through the air. He tucks into a backflip to land in a crouched position. He looks up to find Quel walking casually towards him

"I heard you killed one of my brothers. I see in your soul that this is true. I also see my brother was already broken. You didn't kill him, you simply rushed him home to Lucifer. I am not broken Reaper. I will not fall to a simple human. You don't have what it takes to kill me. Simply surrender and I promise a quick death."

"You're killing me with your rambling. Please shut up and let's get this on." Jaml does not wait for an answer. His enhanced movements are like lightning and the two are once again dancing with death.

Both fight for leverage and the upper hand in the battle. Yet both are so skilled that neither is able to gain any ground let alone any kind of leverage. In the back of his mind, Jaml wonders how long he can go like this before the power runs out or he simply falls due to extreme exhaustion. It is in that moment that first blood is drawn. Quel's fist connects with Reaper's jaw, sending him flying through the air to crash into the ground.

Reaper quickly gets up, spitting blood from his mouth. He stalks forward, his face a mask of determination. The two once again engage in battle. Neither gives ground, nor surrender. Quel moves to the right attempting to flank Reaper but Jaml is already moving to intercept. Reaper takes a second step, this time on a rock, uneven ground. Quel makes him pay. The edge of the axe slices through Reaper's body armor like it is not there, leaving a long open gash across Reaper's chest. Blood flows from the cut.

Quel laughs at the little man staggering backwards. He extends his hand, white lightning shoots from his fingertips, engulfing Reaper. Jaml clenches his teeth, fighting back the urge to scream in agony. He drops to one knee.

"Help me Heavenly Father."

"Then trust me." God's words ring through his head. Jaml closes his eyes.

"Thou I walk through the valley of the shadow of death, I fear no evil. Thy rod and thy staff, they comfort me." As he recites God's scriptures, he extends the blades in front of him. The lightning explodes inches from the blades.

Quel lowers his hand, seeing the attack has been rendered useless. He watches Reaper slowly rise to his feet, smoke emitting from his body. Jaml takes a deep breath before looking up at his adversary.

"Is that all you got?"

Quel attacks, the axe swinging back and forth, to most it seems like random movement but Reaper knows better. Right before he engages with Reaper, Quel's speed increases tenfold. Reaper finds himself once again locked in battle at speeds he never knew existed. The two do not move, their legs locked in place, their arms moving in intricate motions, probing, attacking, and trying to find a weak point in each other.

This time Reaper draws blood. He follows a block with a midsection swing. Instead of blocking the blow, Quel opts to take a half step out of the way. Reaper quickly reverses his grip with the backswing coming at the Fallen's neck. Quel is able to move enough to prevent a fatal blow but not fast enough to prevent injury. Quel steps back, raising his fingers to his neck to find a cut across the side of his neck, a small trickle of blood dripping.

No words are exchanged. Both realize only one will survive, at the most. Quel's handsome face cracks a smile, his confidence high despite the wound on his neck. His eyes look towards the ground which begins to shake. Reaper squats lower, steadying his fighting posture, waiting for the attack.

The ground begins to buck under them, fissures appearing in the ground. Quel continues to smile at the struggles of his human enemy, sensing the victory close at hand.

Without any warning, Reaper breaks into a sprint towards Quel. The Fallen is not expecting such brashness from a human and struggles to break the concentration needed to hold the spell. Finally the spell breaks just in time. Quel has to retreat to try and thwart off Reaper's attack. The human is relentless, his blades twirling and striking, no longer trying to find an opening but create one.

Quel can do nothing but stay on the defensive. He moves his axe back and forth, up and down, defending himself from the relentless attack. The fallen angel yells in pain when a blade opens a wound across his midsection but the attacks continue.

Quel spins in a complete circle to slow Reaper down enough to mount a counterattack. The move cost him another open wound, this one across his lower back. A small price to pay for the force punch. The spell launches Reaper twenty feet through the air to come crashing back to the earth.

Reaper rolls over to his knees before rising back to his feet. He feels the three broken ribs on his side. Exhaustion racks his body but surrender is not an option. He has been tasked to rid the world of evil and nothing will stop his mission save his death. He looks over at Quel and forces a smile.

Quel stands on unsteady legs. Three wounds bleed freely, meaning if he doesn't end this quickly, he may bleed to death. The wounds being caused by heavenly weapons means he cannot heal them without spells and time. He has to see this through.

For the first time Jaml feels the power of the Reaper Angel beginning to wane, so there are limits to a power he once thought limitless. In his mind he knows he has to kill Quel before the power escapes him because he is no match for Quel without it. Enough power for one maybe two engagements, then he is on his own.

"God, thank you for this moment of my life. If I am to die, I pray I have done enough to enter into the kingdom of God. This life is good and I hope I made you proud. Amen."

Reaper launches his attack, his ebony blades eager to taste more angel blood. The two beings locked in battle, sheer will is all either has left. The desire to survive and live another day has long been the goal. Blades clank, sparks fly and grunts can be heard as the two attempt to gain the upper hand and win this war.

As if on cue, Jaml's foot slips just as Quel attempts to pierce the man with his axe. The slip takes Jaml to a knee, the blade of the axe whipping just over his head, extending Quel's stance. Jaml launches upward, his blades extended in his hands. Both blades pierce the angelic skin, biting deep into Quel. The fallen angel takes several steps back, the look of disbelief masks his face.

Jaml does not waste the opportunity. He runs and jumps at the being, his hands grabbing hold of the blades protruding from the chest and shoves the blades until nothing but the hilts are visible. Quel takes three more steps back before falling to his knees. Jaml grabs the Axe of Damnation and raises it over his head. Quel looks up at the last moment before the axe is buried halfway through his skull.

The cast out angel topples over, dead.

Jaml turns to find himself looking at soldiers all around him. He grabs hold of the hilts and yanks the blades free from the angel's chest. He turns to face the soldiers for one last battle. He staggers slightly before falling face first on the ground.

◆

It's time

Eyes crack slightly open, welcomed by soft light. Eyes shut before once again peeking from under protective lids. Nothing changes the second time so the lids retract fully, welcoming the eyes completely.

Jaml turns his head to find the source of the light, a single candle half burnt down on a small wooden table to his right. *Am I dead? I must be dead, there is no way I could have survived those soldiers.* The last thing Jaml remembers is being completely surrounded by soldiers after killing Quel, the Fallen. After that the world goes blank. *At least I was able to rid the earth of two Fallen but wish it could have been more.*

He turns his head from side to side, taking in the entire situation he finds himself. Besides the simple bed he is currently laying on and the table to his right with the candle, there appears to be no other furniture besides two wooden chairs near the foot of the bed. The walls are bare and appear to be made of simple wood and mud. *Please don't let this be heaven.*

He sits up and rubs his hands over his face, waking himself even further. He finds hair on his face and on top of his head. He hasn't allowed his hair to grow since entering the monastery, those many seasons ago.

He attempts to stand and instantly finds himself crashing to the floor. He tries to catch himself but only succeeds in knocking over the table and the candle on top of it. He reaches down to snuff out the wick before anything catches fire when a door he didn't see opens. The flood of outside light interrupts the soft darkness of the room, causing Jaml to cover his eyes with his forearm.

"Oh my word, what have you done? Let's get you back in bed, sire, you have not recovered fully yet." He recognizes Flo's soft voice in his ears. He smiles.

He feels her hands grab one arm as another set of hands grab the other. He reluctantly cracks open an eye to find Karva pulling at his arm. *It is good to see her up and about again.* He does not fight the women as they hoist him back onto the bed, lay him down and cover his legs once more. One of the ladies closes the door while the candle is relit. He opens his eyes to find Flo and Karva standing there.

"Welcome back to the living Jaml." Karva's familiar voice brings another smile to his face.

"How long have I been out?"

"About two weeks sire." Worry creeps into her voice. "We prayed but thought you for dead. Kem assured us that you are too stubborn to just die and told us to be patient."

"Where is Kem?"

"She left three days ago." It is Karva's turn. "She received some message and said it was time for her to assume her new role. Whatever that means."

Jaml knows what it means. She has gone to the kingdom of Sagin to take her place as Lanea's personal guard and confidant. Something dire must have come up for her to just leave. He says a short prayer for her success. He is going to have to go visit when he is able. He owes her that much.

"Now rest, sire. You have killed Lucifer's servants and brought God back to this land. Rest, you deserve it." Flo tucks the blanket under Jaml's armpits before tucking in the sides. Jaml tries to recount what all happened but soon finds himself once again asleep.

✦

Three months after the Battle of Quel, as many of the people have come to call it, Jaml is once again on his feet. He is able to walk and train. He spends many hours in prayer, letting God heal his physical and mental wounds.

The people have asked Karva to assume the throne until a rightful heir is found, so her days are filled with decisions for the people, which she continuously prays for guidance. Jaml politely turns down Karva's invitation to stay on as her commander as his calling is elsewhere.

All the Lycans have either escaped or fallen in battle. The city of Colley works hard to resurrect the churches and places of worship. Karva regularly gives sermons and leads prayers for whomever needs to hear the word of God.

His time has come.

As he pulls himself up onto his horse, Jaml cannot help but feel a sense of accomplishment. He takes in a deep breath before urging his horse towards the East gate. Time to visit an old friend before continuing his travels.

He carries the Sword of Darkness, which remains as twin ebony blades. The monks took the remaining weapons of the Apocalypse, vowing to separate and hide the weapons in monasteries far from each other. Each weapon under the protection of a different monastery, never to be joined again. As for the ebony blades, Jaml knows God has a plan.

God's plan.

About the Author

My name is J.R. Lightfoot Jr. I am a high school Social Studies teacher and coach in Fort Worth Tx. I coach football, track and soccer. I am married to the love of my life, Kim. Together we raised a blended family of five kids, four of which are grown and out of the house. We also have 3 dogs. I still get out and play soccer in the adult leagues. I started writing as a stress relief and fell in love with telling stories.